Thin
ICE

Also by Meg O'Brien:
The Keeper
Eagles Die Too
Hare Today, Gone Tomorrow
Salmon in the Soup
The Daphne Decisions

Thin
ICE

Meg O'Brien

A Perfect Crime Book
D O U B L E D A Y
New York London
Toronto Sydney Auckland

A Perfect Crime Book
PUBLISHED BY DOUBLEDAY
a division of Bantam Doubleday Dell Publishing Group, Inc.
1540 Broadway, New York, New York 10036

DOUBLEDAY is a trademark of Doubleday, a division
of Bantam Doubleday Dell Publishing Group, Inc.

All of the characters in this book are fictitious, and
any resemblance to actual persons, living or dead,
is purely coincidental.

Designed by Bonni Leon

Library of Congress Cataloging-in-Publication Data

O'Brien, Meg.
   Thin ice / Meg O'Brien. — 1st ed.
       p.   cm.
   "Perfect crime."
   "A Perfect crime book."
   1. Women—United States—Crimes against—Fiction.   2. Sisters—
United States—Fiction.   I. Title.
PS3565.B718T45   1993
813'.54—dc20   93-8460
                                                                    CIP

ISBN 0-385-42572-4
Copyright © 1993 by Meg O'Brien
All Rights Reserved
Printed in the United States of America
November 1993
First Edition
10 9 8 7 6 5 4 3 2 1

ACKNOWLEDGMENTS

I would like to extend my belated thanks to many of the people who through their love and support have given this book and others life and direction.

First, to my children and their families, who have listened to my woes as well as my triumphs with patient ears: Amy and Peggy Koenig, Robin and Darrell Weiland, Tiffany and Joshua Weiland, Katherine O'Brien Ketner and Scott Ketner, Kevin and Becky O'Brien, and Greg and Constance Koenig.

To just a few of the best writing friends anyone could hope to have: Michael Mesrobian, Lia Matera, Lee Hsu Callaham, Jane Tiemann, Robert J. Bowman, and Gloria White. Thanks for loving advice and laughter, and for being there.

To the girls from Bonita Street, for helping through the early days: Dimity Nyhus, Candace Craig, and Nancy Mahl.

To Mona Horwitz and Maylon Hamilton, the greatest "landlords" a struggling author could ever have. And to Mona again, for being, from the early days, a good and loving friend.

To Marjorie Bowman, Kathy Johnson and Paul Schindler, and Doug Lunsford. And to Pindéy Shahi, Barbara Stone, and everyone at the South Bay Spine Center in Torrance, California.

For technical advice: Special thanks to Don Wortman (Master Don) of the Kuk Ki Do school of martial arts in Redondo Beach, California. To the crew of the *L.B. Long Beach* and the Connolly Pacific Company, who provided technical support and inspiration. To Russell Perreault in Doubleday publicity, for all his energy and hard work on previous books. And special thanks to Linda Gross, my editor, who brought to this book valuable assistance in the field of medical research, as well as a clear editorial eye.

Last but certainly not least, I would like once again to thank my agent on this and other books, Dominick Abel, for his constant encouragement and support.

Many of the legends in this book are from *Myths and Legends of All Nations*, Littlefield, Adams & Co., 1981. I would like to thank the authors, Herbert Spencer Robinson and Knox Wilson.

The Kill

Chapter 1

It was past midnight in Georgetown. A light rain had begun to fall. It tapped on the windows of gated town houses, the cloistered shelters of the rich. Now and then a car would pass, and the young woman would shrink back into shadows on the cobbled street. She had to force herself not to run, not to call attention. Her teeth chattered, and a thin silver cross moved against her throat. The red dress the woman wore was tight, and drenched in sequins. It gave little protection against the November cold. The style was at odds with the silver cross, and too sophisticated for a slender twenty-eight-year-old woman with the wide, darting eyes of a frightened child.

A phone booth on the corner beckoned. One call, she thought. I can make one call. They'll never know. *But even as the thought came, a long gray car screeched to a halt at the curb.*

She backed up against a wrought-iron fence, feeling it bite into her spine. God, let me be invisible, *she prayed.* Hide me. Protect me. Keep me safe in the shelter of Your love.

But he had seen her. He stepped from the car.

"You left without a coat, Mary Clare. I was worried." His voice was smooth as butter melting in an August sun. Smooth and practiced, an actor's voice, caressing one moment, reassuring the next. She could almost believe . . .

"Yes." She tried to laugh, to pretend she had come out only for a walk. Knowing the charade was hopeless. "I guess I forgot."

He put the fur around her shoulders. Its silky lining was cold, colder than the early winter air. His fingers touched her neck and lingered too long.

I will die, *the woman thought.* I will die rather than go back there.

"Get into the car. I'll take you home." The man gripped her arm, his fingers biting into muscle. Mary Clare began to obey, then stopped. "I . . ."

His voice became angry. "Do it."

She broke away, sobbing, and went running down the sidewalk, then out onto the street. The clatter of her heels was like a spur, urging her on—steel bullets skittering over wet asphalt. She could hear him behind her, and she ran faster, her breath coming in short, hard gasps. A fiery pain began in her side. There was a light ahead— some kind of bar, a Pinocchio face for a sign. Gepetto's. She ran toward it. She heard the car follow, voices calling. "Stop her!"

She burst through the door of the bar and halted, clutching at her side. The bartender, gray-haired and weary, glanced up curiously. His expression turned to shock, then was quickly masked. Several patrons looked and turned away. Mary Clare raised a hand to her face, felt the trickle of blood that had caked there. It had happened, she remembered, back at the house. . . .

She smoothed her long auburn hair, gripped the fur coat tighter, and moved slowly, painfully, to one of the cheap plastic stools.

"What'll you have?"

She raised her eyes. They were green and filled with pain.

"Ya gotta order," the bartender said. Behind him the hands of a clock pointed to the hour, one thirty-five. The face on the clock was that of Nixon, with a long Pinocchio nose.

Mary Clare touched the cross at her throat, gripping it for strength. Did she even have money? Had she dropped the tiny, impractical purse somewhere?

No, it was right here, its shoulder strap firmly in place around her neck. When had she thought to do that?

"Ya gotta order," the bartender said more insistently. "This ain't no hotel lobby."

"Wine, then," she answered quickly. "A glass of wine." Her voice was whispery but cracked—dry leaves blowing over a grassy hill.

"White?"

"Yes. Anything." She wanted only to sit, to catch her breath, be safe for just a little while.

The bartender poured something from a green bottle with a foreign label. Mary Clare took it, but didn't drink. Her hand shook. Drops of wine scattered on the scarred wood of the bar.

"Do you . . . do you have something I can write on? And a pen?"

The bartender shoved a cocktail napkin at her, followed by a pen from behind the bar. She took it gratefully and began to write with a hurried scrawl. "Nikki, I'm in terrible danger. . . ."

She managed only a few more words before a rush of cold air told her that the door behind her had opened.

She stiffened, but didn't turn. Staring straight ahead, she looked into the mirror over the bar. A tall man with an angular face and thick brown hair stood inside the door. The hair was damp with rain, the expression a mask of anger.

"You want something, mister?" The bartender folded his arms.

The man didn't answer. His gray eyes were glacial as they fixed on Mary Clare.

"Look," said the bartender, "no trouble here, okay?"

"Mary . . ."

She closed her eyes. Quickly, by feel, she scribbled something in the bottom corner of the napkin. Her fingers were white with tension as she moved slowly, carefully, to drop the pen. Then she picked up the napkin and, hardly seeming to move, stuck it inside the low neck of the red dress.

The man walked closer. He stood behind her. "Come home with me now."

"That isn't my home," she whispered.

"Come with me!"

"No!"

A man a few seats down turned their way. He was huge—dressed in leathers, with a silver skull buckle hanging below a paunch. Every inch of exposed skin was covered with tattoos.

"Hey," he said to the man with Mary Clare. "Hey, you. Asshole." Without taking his eyes from the man, he reached into a jar of pickled eggs on the bar. Pulling one out, he sucked the whole egg in, like a python swallowing a rat. Then he chomped down once. A sickening POP could be heard. Little bits of boiled egg yolk slipped out between his lips.

"Stop bothering the lady," he said.

The tall man stiffened. "Stay out of this."

The mass of tattoos stood, creaking leather. "You want me to do something about this guy, lady? You want me to peel his ass?"

The green eyes turned to the newcomer. An angel in bizarre disguise, she thought.

The kind of man who would appoint himself ombudsman of his

neighborhood, the kind who always had to settle things, to be in charge.

Thank you, God.

"Yes . . . please," she murmured gratefully. "I just want to get out of here. Alone."

The man picked up his beer and took a pull. Pieces of egg yolk slid down his chin. He wiped them away with a thumb.

"Go ahead. I'll make sure asshole doesn't follow." He planted himself between Mary Clare and her pursuer—a rock-hard wall.

Mary Clare nodded. Her hand jerked as she took a few bills from the purse and laid them on the bar. Then she slid from the stool, dizzy for a moment. She turned, white-faced and unsteady, to the door.

"I'll find you," the tall man said grimly. "Count on it."

She gave a small cry and ran into the street. The gray car was out there, motor running, its beams like searchlights in the mist. But half a block away, nearly invisible through the heavy white shroud, stood a yellow-and-black-checkered cab. Mary Clare ran toward it. She heard the gray car jam into reverse and, daring a glance back, saw it come over the curb, the door open like a scoop to grab her up.

She was within eight feet of the cab when its off-duty sign lit up and it began to pull away.

"No! Stop!" She ran faster, trying desperately to grab the passenger door. Her fingers locked on the handle, then slipped, nails screeching on metal as the cab sped up. Her palm caught and tore on loose chrome. She let out a cry and grabbed her hand as taillights disappeared into mist. Pounding footsteps closed in behind her.

"Mary, wait!"

She whirled to the left, toward a building with tattered shades at broken windows, no lights. Some kind of warehouse. There were iron stairs along the side, in an alley, and at the top a catwalk over to the next building—Leo's Printing, according to the sign, with huge rolls of paper showing through its windows.

Within seconds she was at the foot of the stairs, then tearing up them, her bloody hand over the blossoming agony in her side. Her chest constricted, the lungs so tight they felt as if they were collapsing.

Tough old cobwebs broke across her face. Something black

skimmed before her eyes, something large, with legs. It landed in her hair. She screamed, grabbing at it, fingers closing on its fat, soft body. She screamed again—at the spider, at him, at everyone who wanted to control, to invade—

She flung the spider into space, and tore on.

At the top of the stairs she fell against a metal door. Her fingers searched desperately, but there was no knob, no way to get it open. Across the metal catwalk was another door. She ran along the catwalk, her high red heels catching in its grid. She tripped, fell, righted herself. At the door she yanked at a rusted handle. It squealed, protested. She yanked again and again. "Let me in! Let me in!" She pounded on the door, breathing the words, then shouting them over and over. "Someone, please—let me in!"

The door opened suddenly on blackness. Mary Clare tumbled through it. A massive object rammed the side of her face. She reeled. Her vision faded; her arms involuntarily closed around her attacker for balance.

She froze.

The thing she clung to wasn't human. It was something large and long, something hanging—

Sight returned. In the darkness she saw the white shape. Her shaking fingers told the rest. Canvas—a punching bag. No man.

A cry of relief escaped her throat.

Someone had hung a punching bag there—some employee, probably, who worked out by the open door during lunch hours, and he'd gone home and forgotten to lock the door for the night.

The saints were with her, then. Even the ones she no longer believed in.

No others doors up here. Nowhere to go but down. Mary Clare lurched down a flight of service stairs. Somewhere along the way she dropped the burdensome fur coat. At the first landing she heard the footsteps again behind her. Plummeting down two stairs at a time, then three, she twisted an ankle and lost her balance, falling at the next landing. She gripped the cold rail to pull herself to her feet, then staggered the rest of the way. Bursting into a narrow, dank hall at the bottom, she saw an Exit sign and bolted through it.

The alley again. Rain came now, in thick opaque sheets. But she could see the gray car at the far end, blocking her escape. She ran *the opposite way, deeper into the alley, despairing that it might dead-end. But no—an offshoot opened to the right, loaded with trash cans. There were missing slats in a battered wooden fence. She pushed through, the red dress catching on nails, the flimsy material ripping.*

A weedy yard. She raced through it, ignoring the sore ankle, the throbbing ache in her side. Wet, icy strands of grass clung to her legs, grabbing her ankles like dead, frozen fingers. She ran on and on, to a driveway of broken cement and out into another street. Liquor stores, bars, pawnshops, a small grocery.

She ran past them, the dress wet and clammy, her lungs burning, close to collapse. She rounded a corner and nearly rammed into a cab idling at the curb, its "Available" light on. She tore open its door and tumbled into the backseat.

"Sa—Sacre Coeur Convent," she stammered. "On Wisconsin. Hurry!"

The driver nodded; the cab began to roll. Mary Clare looked out the rear window. There was no one standing in the street where she had been. No gray sedan—none that she could see.

She leaned back, fighting for breath and wiping rain from her face. Her hand shook. The palm was bloody. She stared at it, forgetting where she had injured it. Again she glanced behind.

Cars—all alike in the gloom. No one speeding, no one chasing— only headlights and rain. Seeming peace.

Except that here, nothing was as it seemed. The Lincoln Memorial . . . the Washington Monument . . . the White House . . .

A city of illusion.

Mary Clare felt the wound on her temple. Tears welled, and she brushed them away. She had wanted to do so much, had believed in so much.

An overwhelming depression smothered her fear. I wish I'd listened to you, Nikki, she thought. Big sister, so much smarter than me.

She leaned her head back, relaxing in the moment of relative safety. Remembering.

She had followed Nikki here from Boston ten years ago, getting off the plane with a bucket of tropical fish: two guppies, three angels, and a beta.

"A major step forward," Nikki had teased. "Remember how you always had sticks and caterpillars in your pockets, growing up?"

She remembered that. And a night a year later. "I'm getting my own place, Nikki. I can't live with you anymore."

Their mother had just died of cancer. Mary had attended the funeral alone. Coming back to Georgetown, heavy with grief, she'd begun to pack. She was moving onto campus. Into a dorm.

"How could you be so cold, Nikki? She was only forty-five."

"I'm sorry. I just couldn't be there." Nicole had stood in the bedroom they'd shared for a year, tears in her eyes. Pleading with her sister to understand.

Mary remembered that as a teenager her older sister was always angry, always rebelling. Their mother had favored Mary, the "good" child. But Nikki had never blamed Mary for being the chosen one, had never involved her little sister in her mortal struggle with their mother.

Families. Not always as they seem, either. Smaller but no less isolated cities of illusion.

And now? Dear God, what would happen, now? Was there anyone left she could turn to?

Only Paula. It wouldn't be easy. But Sister Paula would help.

The cab lurched through dark, tree-lined streets and skidded to a stop across from the Cathedral of the Sacred Heart, with its vast hospital complex looming behind. Mary Clare pulled money from the small purse and thrust it at the driver. She sprang from the cab. Running across the wet street, she barely glanced at the church, its gray spires dripping with rain, its stained-glass windows brightly illuminated from within. She tore through the grounds to the convent behind the church—Sacre Coeur—huddled in the shadow of the seven-story Sacred Heart Hospital.

Where it all began, she thought with a sob. And nothing there the way it was supposed to be.

Her heels caught on the flagstone path, her sore ankle twisted. A dull ache began in her head. She slipped on the wet concrete steps, then righted herself and banged on the arched wooden door, wrenching at the knob.

It was locked. And he had taken away her keys.

"Sister Paula! Sister Paula, let me in!"

Endless moments passed. Had no one heard her? Mary Clare leaned wearily against the door, her eyes closed. Suddenly it opened and she pitched forward. Strong arms enfolded her. "Sister Paula— thank God! I need your help."

There was no answer. Mary clung to the woman she had come to think of as a friend, her cheek pressed against the damp fabric of Sister Paul's habit.

"You're all wet," Mary said shakily, gaining strength. "Have you been out in the rain?"

She opened her eyes. The fabric against her cheek was black, not the hospital white of Sacre Coeur. And the height was all wrong, the arms too strong—

She looked up and grew faint with horror.

"Mary Clare, Mary Clare . . . you were always so predictable."

The man she thought she had escaped from shook his head, as if saddened, almost, to find he was right.

"We knew you'd come here."

OBITUARY NOTICE
The Washington Post, November 11

Mary Clare Ryan, twenty-eight, died early this morning when her car plunged into the Potomac River just south of Georgetown. Ryan received her doctorate in biochemistry from Georgetown University and was employed as a research biologist at Sacred Heart Hospital in Georgetown. She is survived by a sister, Nicole Ryan, an associate professor of mythology and comparative religion at Georgetown University.

Services will be held at Sacred Heart Cathedral on Wisconsin Avenue on Friday, November 13, at 10:00 A.M. Donations to the Parkhurst Foundation for Cancer Research, in lieu of flowers.

Chapter 2

The century-old pipe organ thundered, its well-cared-for reeds mellow and pliant, the power and range of its chords hammering at Nicole's spine. The voices of a choir of nuns, all dressed in white to celebrate this Old World funeral mass, were raised in uplifting song. They praised God for having brought their young friend to this time and place, this moment that made up for all of life's woes, this carrying over of the soul into eternal bliss.

On the long, dark journey that is life, there comes, once in a while, great bliss.

Not words from the nuns' hymn, but something Nicole had written years ago, during a week-long seminar on mythology. She had believed the words then. She didn't know if she believed them now. There had been too many losses this year—and nothing resembling bliss in any one of her thirty-four years.

With painful effort her green eyes fixed on the priest who stood solemn-faced at the altar. Then the white coffin, a blanket of white roses on its satin cover. Her sister lay in that coffin. Her little sister, full of life one day, and then . . .

You just never know. Never think something like this will happen to you. And all of a sudden it's too late to make up. There's no one left to hear the words. No one left to forgive.

Tell her now, a voice hammered inside Nicole's head. It played counterpoint to the massive organ. *Tell her. Tell her now.*

Tell her what? That I'm sorry? That I regret not having understood more, not listening, not being a better sister?

Tell her that I thought we had all the time in the world?

She fought back tears. It wouldn't do to cry in front of all these nuns, their faces alight with the fervor of their faith, singing hymns of joy because one they had loved was going to God.

But when someone dies after a long illness, you at least have time to prepare. What do you do when, suddenly, they're just gone?

Gone all those years ago, really. From the day of our mother's death. That's when the rift began.

Mary had been so passionate during her freshman year at Georgetown. Night after night they'd had discussions in Nicole's apartment

—discussions that escalated into friendly, yet vigorous, debates. Mary Clare at eighteen, Nicole soon discovered, could pose a hypothesis more cleverly than she at twenty-five.

Nicole could still see her little sister—straight-A student, honors grad—striding around the apartment in plaid skirt and knee socks, munching on pizza, waving her arms excitedly.

"Think, Nikki! It's not red meat and Twinkies that's killing us. It's something on the planet, something that's destroying the immune system and allowing damage. The same sort of thing, scientists now believe, that destroyed the Roman Empire, the Mayans—all the world's great cultures. It's something that returns at regular intervals and weakens the system, allowing in the viruses that hide through the years. Cancer, AIDS, leukemia, even the lesser infections like viral pneumonia, they've all been around for centuries, just waiting for a chance to attack. Have you any idea how many people get viral pneumonia these days? How many miscarriages there are, and damaged fetuses? Even cats are getting leukemia, for heaven's sake! And it could all be stopped, if science would only get to the root of things before it's too late!"

Mary's interest in biology, only a seed in high school, had blossomed at Georgetown. Excitement turned to passion. A hunger for research took over.

"Nikki, scientists are only inventors at heart. The great inventors —Edison, Bell—they opened their minds to the messages, just like Abraham and Moses. Remember the biblical stories about Moses being taught by angels to prevent epidemics, like typhoid and cholera? To have the people bury their excrement outside their camps? And antisepsis! Long before Semmelweiss, Moses was being taught about the cleansing of skin and clothes after handling the infected or dead. *Angels* brought these messages to him, Nikki. Because he was open to it."

Playing devil's advocate, Nicole had argued that it made just as much, if not more, sense to attribute biblical visitations to beings from advanced planets—not angels.

"Well, then." Mary had shrugged. "Maybe we're talking about the same thing. We just perceive it differently." She would laugh in those days, her sense of humor still intact. "How about this: angels with two hats."

The two hats was a teasing reference to a myth that Nicole had once paraphrased from a book by Joseph Campbell, *The Hero with a Thousand Faces.*

Once there was a man who walked down a road wearing a hat. The hat was red on one side, black on the other. The people on either side of the road thought they were seeing two different men, but he was one and the same. They only perceived him differently.

Nicole had tried to convince her sister that religion was that way, too. "There are parallels to every Bible story in all cultures. The Jesus and Buddha stories—the saviors who came to bring light to the world—all tell of the same miracle, happening over and over to different cultures at different times, with the hero simply given different names."

Mary Clare, always open if not agreeing, loved the story of the man with the two-sided hat. She had even turned it back on Nicole the night of their worst argument—the night in her sophomore year at Georgetown, when she'd announced her intention to move out.

They were in the kitchen, in Nicole's town house in Georgetown. Nicole was still working on her doctorate, exhausted after a long day in the library. Mary had returned earlier that day from their mother's funeral in Boston. With snow piling into high drifts outside, the tension in the tiny kitchen was as thick as the ice that glazed the mullioned windowpanes.

"I'm moving out, Nikki. I've already arranged it."

Nicole paused in pouring the coffee. Hot steam drifted upward, enveloping her face and bringing welcome warmth to a sudden cold invading her bones. "I wish you wouldn't."

"It's time. Time to grow up, go out on my own."

"That's not why you're doing it. You're still angry with me. Mary, don't leave in anger."

"Dammit, Nikki! I know you never got along with her. But to not even see her buried, not even say goodbye—"

Sinking heavily into a chair, Nicole felt more tired than she ever had in her life. "I said goodbye long ago, Mary. I wish you could understand."

"Well, I don't. I never will."

Nicole had looked at her sister, so young, so noble and upright.

Her heart turned over. "I love you, Mary. I'll always look after you. Isn't that enough?"

"I don't know if I believe that. Will you leave me, too, someday?"

There was no possible answer, no way to explain. Mary had moved out. And from that day forward, she had changed. On entering college the year before, Mary had pulled away from the Church a bit. While not denying her faith, she had discovered, and romanced, her intellect. Attendance at Mass gave way to class. Practices such as weekly confession, which Nicole had always scorned as outdated and absurd, were discarded for an evening out, a movie with a friend. Nicole never said a word—but she had been relieved. Her rift with their mother had involved a rejection of her fanatically held faith. It was good to see Mary grow and begin to explore new avenues of belief.

But after that fight, after their mother died, Mary had gone back to the old ways. Mass every day, novenas each week. She had even made friends with several of the nuns on campus, those from the Order of the Sacre Coeur. Some were in Mary's classes at Georgetown, studying to be research assistants, nurses, practitioners. And while it seemed natural enough that they became friends, it also seemed to Nicole that Mary was becoming too ingrown.

"It's as if our mother is pointing a finger at you from the grave," she said, dropping into the dorm one day. "You don't have to let her control your life now."

"I'm doing what I want to do," Mary argued.

"I miss you. I don't see you enough. Mary, except for church, it seems like all you do is study. And your only friends are those nuns."

"If the fact that I have nuns for friends is all you can find to worry about, Nikki, I'd say you need to get a life."

"But God, Mary! They're so backward."

Sacre Coeur, an order that ran hospitals and placed nursing sisters throughout the world, hadn't yet moved into the twentieth century—at least not by American standards. With roots in Old World France, it still required its nuns to relinquish their individuality and live within a rigid structure.

And now Mary—whom Nicole had hoped would spread her wings

in college and fly—was becoming absorbed into their common and, as she saw it, stifling womb. The ensuing argument over this issue had lasted through the night, and the man with the two-sided hat had been part of it.

"The people on either side of the road," her sister had reminded her reasonably, "thought they were seeing a different man—because his hat, on each side, was a different color. But they were seeing the same man, Nikki, the same thing. Just as you and I are seeing the same thing now. We only perceive it differently. You're the one who taught me that."

I should have kept my mouth shut, Nicole thought now as the priest raised his arms and murmured ancient words. "Lord have mercy on us. . . . Christ have mercy on us. . . ." *I shouldn't have criticized her life, her decisions.*

Mary had gone on to get her degree, then her doctorate, and then to work in research at Sacred Heart Hospital. Closer than ever to her faith, and to the nuns, she lived in a small cottage near the convent and hospital. She worked eighteen-hour days, became isolated, almost obsessive about her work.

Until a year or so ago, when things had begun to change. The sisters' infrequent telephone calls became lengthier, warmer; they found a common thread in their ostensibly dissimilar fields.

Mary was studying the Brazilian rain forests and became fascinated by the shamans there, who were teaching research scientists about the healing properties of herbs. It happened that the South American shamans were one of Nicole's favorite topics for discussion in her classes in mythology.

Mary began dropping in on Nicole in the evenings. Nicole openly admitted to seducing her sister with an old favorite—thick slices of crispy-crust pizza, loaded down with extra cheese and pepperoni. They would sit on the floor in front of the fireplace, in jeans and sweaters, munching and talking—almost like the early days.

"The shamans have a holistic approach to healing," Nicole said one night. "They see the total, universal picture, and they immerse themselves in nature. They intuit truths that we as a culture are blind to, because with all our technology, we've become too removed from our origins."

"You're absolutely right." Mary's pacing was perhaps less erratic than when she was eighteen, but her focus was no less intense. "Too much of science is *closing* minds today. Most researchers are so intent on working within the paradigm, with following prescribed procedure, they don't allow room for the flashes of brilliance—for divine inspiration. They actually think they can uncover truth without uncovering God!"

She marched over to a limp philodendron in Nicole's living room. "And you know what they consider healing? This!" Breaking off a diseased tendril, she held it high. "Cutting away the offending limb. I want to begin with the root. The limb should never have the chance to become diseased."

Staring at the hapless vine, she had made a face. "Nikki, you sure don't take care of your plants very well."

Tossing aside the dying vine, she knelt before Nicole, grabbing her hands. "Do you know that with genetic engineering, it's now possible to plant corn so that disease is stopped before it begins? What if we could do that with human beings? And there are tomatoes that stay ripe longer. The gene is turned off that makes them soften as they age. Think what that same kind of biotechnology could do for aging in people!"

"I know, I know." Nicole pushed her sister's auburn hair gently back behind an ear, a habit from childhood that she'd missed when Mary was gone. "And they're trying to grow coffee beans without caffeine, and tobacco without nicotine." She had heard it all before. "But, Mary, there's an argument against genetic engineering, too. Once you begin altering bacteria, the balance of the ecosystem could be destroyed."

"There will be safeguards against that. And Nikki, genetic engineering is only an updated version of what Luther Burbank did when he crossed roses, and fruit trees. There was a furor then, but look at what we've got now—Santa Rosa plums! What could be safer than a Santa Rosa plum?"

Nicole had smiled at her earnestness. She had to admit that her sister's tunnel vision about work, and her almost cultlike alliance with the backward nuns of Sacre Coeur, hadn't dimmed her enthusiasm. In fact, Mary Clare was regarded as somewhat of a wunderkind, now, by the scientific community. So much brilliance at such an early age . . .

Nicole swallowed the lump in her throat and brought her attention back to the church, to the incense and flowers, the crescendo of a jubilant hymn. "With choirs of angels preparing her way . . ."

The hymn ended. "May she rest in peace," the priest intoned.

In full charismatic bloom, now, the chorus of nuns bleated, "Amen!"

The priest tented his hands. "Oh, Lord, hear my prayer."

"And let my cry come unto thee!"

There was a bustle behind Nicole as four nuns and two lay people —associates of Mary's—rose from front pews and stood beside the white coffin, three on either side. Slowly, they began to propel the coffin, on its gurneylike stand, toward the rear of the church.

As the precious burden passed within mere feet of her left hand, Nicole wanted to reach out and grab it back, to cry, "Oh, God, Mary, this is all a horrible dream, isn't it? You can't be gone. You can't!"

Instead, she felt her mouth begin to shake, and then to move with words half-forgotten since youth and St. Monica's grade school. "The Lord be with you," she whispered along with the priest's final blessing. *And with your spirit.*

The soft weeping of several nuns could now be heard. The organ pealed. From the choir loft an alleluia chorus began. The entire congregation linked hands.

Nicole took the fragile, parched hand of the sister to her right and joined in this final, personal farewell. "Rest in peace, Mary Clare."

The sound of her sister's name trembled on every lip, resounding from corner to corner of the ancient church. The tears Nicole had fought so hard to hold back overflowed.

A damned Hollywood set, Nicole thought bitterly. Rain dripped from trees, streaming in torrents over ivy-covered tombstones. The requisite line of somber cars waited along a distant drive.

"Your sister was so beautiful," an elderly nun said. "We all loved her, you know."

The burial ceremony was over, the white coffin resting beneath a black canopy, waiting to be lowered into its grave. The sisters had covered their white habits with black raincoats. Most held black umbrellas. Off to the side, as if they knew the nuns took precedence in Mary's death as well as her life, stood lay mourners—technicians Mary had worked with, other scientists.

Nicole wanted nothing more than to get away, to run home and sit in the dark alone. The wind picked up, whipping at the scalloped edges of the canopy over her head. She drew her heavy winter coat around her, lifting the green velvet hood. Even so, a burst of rain pelted her face.

"A terrible accident," the nun said. "But she's with God now. You mustn't worry."

A woman who had introduced herself as Sister Perpetua spoke. "You look so much like her. The same lovely auburn hair—although yours is longer, and with a bit more red. And you have Mary Clare's green eyes. I always did say"—she turned to a tiny sister who stood bobbing her white-garbed head in happy agreement—"Mary Clare had such lovely, expressive eyes."

They were all around her, these chattering nuns with their glowing faces—so certain that everything was fine in death, when it seldom was in life.

"She was so looking forward to making that trip this week," Sister Perpetua said.

"Trip?"

The nun smiled understandingly at Nicole's confusion. "To Los Angeles, you know. The conference on immunology?" She patted Nicole's hand and murmured, "Well, of course you wouldn't be thinking of that, with all that's happened."

Nicole remembered, then, that Mary Clare had been scheduled to appear on a panel at a medical conference in Pasadena.

"That's why Mary was gone all week," Sister Perpetua told her friend, nodding wisely. "She was working on a paper."

"My sister was away?" Nicole was surprised. "She wasn't at work? Or the cottage?"

Sister Perpetua peered through her thick glasses and frowned. She opened her mouth to answer, but was cut short by a tall nun with dusky skin. "We have to leave now, sisters. The drivers are waiting." The woman's voice and intimidating expression moved the sea of black umbrellas along, creating a wave.

Nicole met the brown eyes of Sister Paula, the Superior of the convent of Sacre Coeur, as well as administrator of Sacred Heart

Hospital. She didn't much like her. The woman had a hard de-
meanor, a hostile attitude. Just recently, Nicole had asked Mary
Clare, "Why does that woman hate me?"

"It's not you," her sister had answered. "It's me."

"Why wouldn't she like you?"

Mary had shaken her head. "It's not important."

Sister Paula spoke politely, but without warmth. "There are some
personal items in Mary Clare's lab. I'm having them taken over to
her cottage. You'll be looking after her effects?"

It was the last thing Nicole wanted to do, so soon. But she nodded.
"Yes. I'll be there in the morning."

The nun turned away.

"Sister Paula? I . . . Sister Perpetua was saying that Mary Clare
was away somewhere this week."

There was no response.

"Sister Paula?"

The woman paused.

"I just wondered . . . do you know where Mary was?"

"I have no idea." The nun's coif hid her expression; her back was
rigid. Nicole wished she could see Sister Paula's face. Surely she
was lying. There was something in her voice.

"It's just that Mary always told me when she was going to be
away."

It was a contract, of sorts, they had made with each other—even
during the years they hadn't been close. In case anything happened,
and one of them needed the other, they'd always know where to
call.

"I thought—I know Mary reported directly to you at the hospital.
Wouldn't she have told you where she was going? I mean, an entire
week . . ."

Sister Paula's unfriendly eyes met hers then. "Your sister made
her own rules. If she had listened to me . . ."

With a grimace of distaste the nun walked away.

Nicole was alone, finally. Alone, and confused.

Mary, who loved structure so, had made her own rules?

Since when? And what had been going on in her sister's life to cause so much animosity on her supervisor's part?

The wind picked up, lifting the petals of white roses on the coffin. Their heavy scent mingled with that of fresh, upturned earth—the scent of the dead. It twisted around her heart.

Mary. . . . dead. In a stupid accident, a drowning.

Nicole had had a dream the night before. In the dream Mary Clare's face was no longer bright and eager with learning—but tight and pale, swirling beneath black waters.

She had heard Mary's voice in the dream, too. Even now she heard it, repeating over and over like an echo from the past. *Help me, Nikki. Help me.*

It was the plea she had heard so many times when they were children, and Mary Clare, six years younger, would get herself into one scrape or another. Once she had taken on a girl bully at school, because the girl had stolen a friend's lunch box. Mary did all right, too, nearly punching the kid out, until the kid's older brother came along. A monster. A teenage Schwarzenegger.

"Help, Nicole!" Mary yelled, her chubby legs rocketing across the playground, pigtails flapping.

She was grinning, though. Mary had loved that kind of trouble. And Nicole had warned her: "You'd just better watch out. Someday I won't be here to help."

Standing at Mary's grave, she clenched her fists inside the pockets of her coat. "I can't help you anymore, little sister," she whispered. "There's nothing I can do."

Her boots sank into sodden grass as she trudged heavily back to her car. Of the entire line of cars, only her own little green MG remained—although farther down the drive was a gray Mercedes with its motor running. Steam poured from its tailpipe, and the rear windows were fogged. An oversized antenna jutted out above its trunk.

She crawled into the MG, letting the heater defrost its windows. Her hands, even in leather gloves, were icy, her nose numb. *If this rain keeps up, it will probably turn to snow tonight. And it's not even Thanksgiving yet.*

She hated the dark winter months. Hated the cold.

Well, it suits the state of my soul. She cranked the MG's reluctant engine until finally, grudgingly, it turned over.

About twenty yards after she passed the Mercedes, she saw it pull out behind her. She was mildly curious. Who would be visiting a grave on a day like today?

Later, when turning the corner to her street, she was surprised and slightly uneasy to see the car on her tail. She recognized it because of the oversized antenna—certainly not from its color, gray, which was common enough in both Georgetown and D.C.

But the car continued on as she turned into her drive. Nicole laughed, feeling silly. *That's the thing about funerals. They make everything seem sinister.*

Chapter 3

Nicole awoke. Stretching, she yawned, listened to the sound of rain as it beat against leaded windows. It hadn't snowed overnight. She wouldn't have to shovel the walks. She began to smile.

Then it hit her—just the way it had hit her each morning since the telephone call three days ago: a dull, sickening thud in the pit of her stomach.

Mary's dead.

Would the shock of it ever wear off?

Moving abruptly, her feet struck a warm lump on top of the covers —Dylan, a neighbor's cat. Nicole had never much liked cats, but Dylan didn't care. He parked on her doorstep day and night until she let him in, then made himself at home as if there were no question of her love.

Like Dan, she thought, staring at the ceiling. *Before he went off to Los Angeles last summer.*

Dylan leapt to the floor, making noises of complaint as Nicole kicked the blankets in a rush of grief and anger. She sat up and reached for her white terry-cloth robe. Shrugging it on, she dragged herself from beneath the warm down comforter and pulled on socks. Then she used the bathroom and headed for the kitchen. Along the way she stopped in the hall, turning up the thermostat. The old furnace in the cellar came on with a familiar rumble.

The blue copper-hung kitchen was rain-dim, like everything else these past few days. By rote she shook the electric teapot, found it empty, ran tap water through its spout, and plugged the pot in. In the freezer were French-roast coffee beans in a plastic container. Still in a fog of grief, she drew them out, ground them, and folded the Melitta filter into its cone. Opening a can of tuna, she put it on a paper plate for the cat.

The necessities done, she sat wearily at a square blond-oak table to wait for the water to boil.

Her small apartment was on the ground floor of a converted town house, with lace-curtained French doors and a narrow garden on one side. She had been here since her student days at Georgetown, when rents were a good deal less. Even so, she had taken care of the gardens in summer for Clyde, the owner, as part of the rent. Clyde lived upstairs but traveled with his lover—an ambassador—more than half the year.

Mary had chipped in on expenses when she lived here, her first year at Georgetown. Then, when their mother died, there had been a small inheritance. Being careful, Nicole had managed to make it last. Now, liking the arrangement with Clyde well enough, she had stayed on even though her salary as an associate professor would have allowed her more space.

In her living room, reading by the fireplace on cold winter evenings, she barely noticed that the paint was becoming yellowed and the carpets worn. It had been a comfortable life—for a while.

She shivered despite the sweatpants and -shirt she had slept in, despite the thick terry-cloth robe. Reaching into her mental library of myths, she searched for a story to lift her mood. The ancient stories had always helped her to find balance—a place on the wheel of life.

For the moment mythology failed her. There was no balance now. With Mary Clare gone, all of life had turned mad.

Yesterday's newspaper was still on the table, weighted down by the wooden statue of Opochtli, Aztec god of fishing and bird catching. Mary, who had always loved fishing, had given her the statue for Christmas one year. Opochtli was said to have invented the harpoon, the fishing rod, and bird nests. He was nude, black, and had bird plumes and a rose-shaped crown on his head—altogether, a bizarre little guy.

She lifted Opochtli, studied him. Felt a tug at her heart. She set him gently on the counter.

Glancing at the paper, she noted that the news was typical as well. Washington politics and gossip. *Senator Garrick Hale announced today that if called upon, he will run . . .*

The water boiled. Dylan meowed and clawed at her sock to let her know.

Nicole remembered Mary telling her once that cats were the same age, intellectually, as an eighteen-month-old child. "Just what *I'd* want around the house for the next fifteen years," Nicole had grumbled. "An eighteen-month-old child."

Now she reached down to Dylan and stroked his back. "At least you know how to ask for what you want, don't you, old boy? 'Feed me, nurture me, love me . . .' Maybe I could learn from that."

She sighed, getting up to make the coffee—a one-cup, one-person Melitta. There had been a full pot every day when Dan was around.

"I always think a person should follow his bliss," Dan had said the night they were introduced by Mary Clare in a Washington restaurant. "Follow your bliss" was Nicole's favorite quote from Joseph Campbell. By the end of that evening, with Dan Rossi's eyes fixing on her throughout the entire dinner with intelligence and wit, Nicole knew she had met the one man for whom she had been waiting all these years. She and Dan Rossi were meant to be.

Be what? she repeatedly asked herself throughout the next year, when she and Dan had been more or less together. Dan, thirty-six, had come to Georgetown from Los Angeles to put together a series of documentary films. Having escaped the world of investment banking after several years, he was now making films that took stabs at politics and Big Business—exposing corruption, while exploring man's need for soul, rather than fiscal, development.

In general knowledge and talent, Dan Rossi was wise beyond his years; in relationships, a Peter Pan. Six feet tall, with curly, shoulder-length brown hair and a hard masculine jaw, he still ogled pretty waitresses in skimpy shorts, still slipped into sexist talk now and then without thinking. Dan's saving grace was that he'd call himself on it, with a shamefaced grin, before Nicole had the chance to.

It took her a while to realize that his interest in her was very much like his interest in those waitresses. She was someone to play with, to pass the time and joke with. A buddy. It took her a while, too, to know that this was a pattern—that Dan Rossi always kept his relationships light, that he really couldn't handle more.

An astrologer would have said there was a conflict in Dan's natal chart, she supposed. Robert Bly might have postulated that he had missed some important rite of male passage in his formative years. A psychologist almost certainly would have pointed out that like almost everyone today, he'd come from a dysfunctional home, and because of that, was afraid to commit.

She and Dan had explored life together for a full year, and gotten to know each other in a way most people never do. They had exposed each other's strong points and flaws, and come out of it liking and trusting each other—loving each other, even.

Yet in that entire year, they had never slept together, seldom even touched.

It was Dan who held back. Nicole told herself he had things to work through—past hurts, insecurities—but that his love, for all that, was equal to hers. If he didn't see that yet, wasn't aware of it or was afraid to look at it, she convinced herself this was because he still thought of love as that painful, crazy, infatuation stage called "romance"—offering not only excitement, but danger.

"Don't you see?" she had wanted to ask, time and time again. "We've bypassed all that. We've separated the wheat from the chaff without even thinking about it. And what we have is better than either of us will find with anyone else."

But before she could muster up the courage to say it to his face, Dan had dropped the bomb. They were out walking one day when he said, "I'm moving back to Los Angeles, Nikki. Next month."

It was July. And Nicole, who had actually thought they were getting closer in recent months, had nearly stumbled over a sidewalk crack.

"I don't understand. Why?"

"I've pretty much wrapped up my work here—and L.A. is where it all happens. I've got to be there. I've got to keep moving ahead."

"But you've built up so many connections here—you've put together a great crew. . . ."

She heard her voice rising. Tears brewing. And it wasn't what she wanted to say. She wanted to say, *What about me?* The words, and the tears, stuck in her throat. She felt like a fool.

By August, Dan was gone. Working in L.A., building a name for himself, she had heard. The retrospective on Joseph Campbell that they had researched together—the reason Mary had introduced them in the first place—was history.

Dan was history, too.

According to the books (Nicole had read all the books she could find on breaking up), once you roust a hopeless love from your heart, you create a vacancy for someone new. Her half-hearted Vacancy sign—posted in a haze of pain and anger, on the advice of well-meaning friends—had in fact attracted a couple of would-be-overnight guests. To date, however, no one had made it any farther than the check-in desk.

The problem was, she hadn't the heart for anything new. She'd become a badger, caught in a bag. Open the bag and you just might get your finger bit.

Nicole, sitting at her kitchen table with no one left now, no one who truly cared, covered her eyes. Her shoulders shook. *Mary Clare.*

If the three months since Dan left had seemed like hell, they paled in comparison, now that the genuine abyss had arrived.

The scent of brewed coffee brought her back. A glimpse through lacy Austrian curtains reassured her that at least it hadn't snowed in the night. The magnolia tree in the side garden was heavy with rain, its few remaining leaves dark and glistening.

Nicole removed the funnel-shaped filter and set it on the table. Coffee dripped from grounds, staining the blond oak. She barely noticed. Cup in hand, she crossed to the phone on the wall and dialed the direct number for Ron Sanders, her department head at Georgetown. He answered almost immediately.

"It's Nicole. I was hoping you'd be in."

"Well, you know how it is. . . ." He sighed heavily and clicked his tongue. "With staff being cut, Saturdays are becoming regular workdays. Uh . . . how is everything?"

"The funeral was awful. But I need to talk to you about something else. Do you have a few minutes this morning?"

"For you? Of course. Will you be coming in soon?"

"In an hour or so."

"I'll see you then."

She showered and dressed, pulling on a rust-colored sweater and long tweed skirt with boots. She donned a khaki raincoat and wound her shoulder-length auburn hair onto her head, covering it with an all-weather hat.

In the hallway she turned down the thermostat and took a green scarf from a hook by the door. "Dylan?" she called. "You've got to go."

No answer. No patter of little cat feet. Nicole sighed and opened the door. She stepped out. Her toe struck something, and she frowned and looked down. On the stoop was an Express Mail envelope.

She picked it up, glancing up and down the street. No familiar red, white, and blue truck. How long had the envelope been here?

Once in a while a manuscript she had sent to a professional journal came back this way. The driver, in a hurry, would leave it at the door without ringing. Had she sent something out and forgotten?

She opened the flap and stuck her hand inside. Her fingers closed over a long rectangular folder. She drew it out.

An airline ticket.

She read the attached, computerized itinerary: Dulles to LAX. Leaving Sunday, November 15. Tomorrow.

But she hadn't booked a flight to Los Angeles. She studied the ticket and saw that it mistakenly bore her name. Damn! The travel agency, one she used often, had her in their computer from other trips. They had somehow screwed up.

Stepping back inside, she shut the door irritably. *One more detail to take care of.* She would have to call and straighten it out.

In the kitchen once more, she called the travel agent from the phone on the wall. The agent was new—young and inexperienced. It took a good five minutes on hold and off, to note the flight number and other pertinent information. Nicole sank heavily to a kitchen chair. For long moments she heard the sound of computer keys clicking. Impatiently, she watched rain beat against the windows.

She rubbed her nose. It was icy.

"We do show that someone booked a reservation for you," the young woman came back with at last. "But like, well, it was actually a ticket transfer."

"A transfer?"

"Uh-huh. From a Mary Clare Ryan to you."

Nicole stared at tiny blue flowers on the kitchen wallpaper, until they blurred. "I don't understand."

"Well, it's like I said. A Mary Clare Ryan had the ticket at first. She called yesterday and transferred it to you."

Nicole gripped the receiver. "That can't be. It's a mistake. My sister died a few days ago—she couldn't have called you."

The woman's apology came in a rush. "Oh, my God, I'm sorry."

There was a silence, then telephones began to jangle in the background. "Uh, look . . . I need to answer another line. What would you like to do?"

She closed her eyes and rubbed her forehead, fighting for control. Even so, her voice shook. "I don't want to *do anything.* Can't you just cancel the ticket?"

"But like I said, it's paid for. . . ."

By some superhuman effort Nicole managed to hold herself together. "Then I believe," she said slowly, her jaw so rigid the words barely came out, "that the correct procedure would be to have your accountant issue my sister's estate a refund."

"Well, I don't know. . . . I mean, I don't know if that's the way it works."

"Just *handle* it," Nicole blurted out. "For God's sake, isn't that your job?"

The agent's voice was soft and uncertain. "Like I said, I just don't know. . . . I've only been here a couple of weeks."

Nicole dropped the receiver to its cradle with an angry thud.

Chapter 4

She walked the short distance in the rain to the campus, needing to move, to think, to figure this out.

Why would anyone have transferred Mary Clare's reservation to her? It didn't make sense—she had no business in Los Angeles. The agent had to be wrong; it was nothing but a computer glitch.

Yet she had seemed so sure. *"She called yesterday and transferred it to you."*

Who had called? This was crazy. Insane.

So why do you feel so uneasy, Nicole? Ever since the funeral . . .

No. Ever since that dream the other night. *Help me, Nikki. Help me.*

But guilt had brought on that dream. Guilt does strange things when people die. It makes you think you can still do something, anything, to make up for your failures—as a sister, as a friend. And the truth—the one you have to face, finally, and live with—is that you can't. Mary was gone. Nothing would bring her back.

She would learn to live with that eventually, Nicole knew. What she didn't know was how. She wasn't good at letting go—at being strong. At forgetting. She had weeded Dan Rossi out of her life, but not her thoughts. Out of her space, but not her heart.

How would she ever get over losing Mary?

Sometime in the long, wakeful night, she had decided to ask Ron to give her more to do. Unlike her mythology classes, comparative religion had been offered only in summer. But enrollments last summer had been high enough to justify offering it throughout the year. The budget was a problem, of course. She knew that. But she had some ideas. She'd lay them before Ron, show him how it might be done. Sometimes it took only a willingness on the part of administration to be creative—to see they could do much more.

The important thing was to throw herself into work. The apartment was too quiet. Too empty. And there were all those reminders of Mary, of the past few months when they'd begun growing close again. The long midnight talks about life, medicine, mythology, religion. True, they hadn't talked about their relationship as sisters. But recently it had seemed that Mary wanted to say more. Nicole held back, not wanting to press her—to test this new, still fragile connection.

The small ivy-covered building that housed Nicole's classroom was nearly empty, as it generally was on Saturday. *Thank God.* She wouldn't have to face scores of bright, not always eager twenty-year-olds. She took the stairs, then followed the wide hallway, its floor newly buffed to a sheen and smelling of wax. She turned into her classroom, looking around.

Old Quetzalcoatl—Aztec god of wisdom, the arts, and peace—welcomed her from his position in a corner by the blackboard. A full six feet tall (as the original god surely was not), his wooden image was decked out in a white robe and held a long staff in the crook of his arm. She walked up to him, poked his nose in a hello, and remembered a better time—last year, before she'd begun to burn out.

She and her students had studied a legend of modern times: Will Rogers. Will was said to be the greatest trick-roper in the world, and they had brought ropes to class to test how difficult the feat really was. Pushing desks off to one side, they dragged the statue of Quetzalcoatl from his corner and used him for practice. One kid even got so good he could throw two ropes at once—snaring the Aztec god around the shoulders with one, and Nikki with the other.

Caught up in the spirit of the project, Nicole had developed a certain skill at the art of roping. She'd worked at it secretly, night after night, in the enclosed garden outside her apartment. The big old magnolia tree became her favorite target, offering heavy, low-lying branches. Finally, she had practiced on Dan—roping him around the shoulders, and even, on occasion, catching him midstride and trapping his feet. All of which he had borne with amiable humor and grace.

The hours of practice paid off. In a class demonstration she had lassoed Ricky Morehead—an antsy, up-and-down, head-scratching journalism major—and kept him tied to his seat for a good ten minutes.

"What if there's a fire on campus? What if I have to get there fast and cover it?" he had protested.

"*This* is the biggest story on campus today," a girl next to him teased. "We've got photographers on the way."

Throughout the rest of that semester, Nicole had seen a new light

of respect in her students' eyes. They were more eager to partici-
pate, to listen, to learn. She felt as if she'd won at least a minor
skirmish in the ongoing war to catch the imagination and spark her
students' minds.

A nearby carillon sounded the hour, breaking into her thoughts.
Tiredly, she slipped into a seat, staring straight ahead.

Nothing had changed in her four-day absence. Nothing had
changed here, most likely, in forty or fifty years. The yellowed maps
of biblical times, of Grecian shipping lanes, of ancient Indian cultures and states; the smell of chalk, and mustiness of old books—all
had been a mainstay in her life, in the same way Mary's chosen life
and work had supported her.

Beyond her desk the blackboard notes told of a Native American
legend. Written by another teacher, they were clear, concise, and
intelligent. Running an absent finger along the chalk shelf, Nicole
realized that the thought of someone else teaching her classes—
"her kids"—no longer bothered her. Lately there had been far too
little satisfaction in the molding of young minds.

And why did they even seem that young, when she herself was
only thirty-four? It was a question that had recurred with disturbing
frequency the past few months.

"Nicole! I thought I saw you come in here."

She wiped chalk dust from her fingers and turned to smile at the
fortyish blond man who stood at the door. Ron Sanders—a man
whose intellect was so often overemployed, it showed in his face: in
the downward lines of the forehead, the thin mouth, and the worried
voice.

"Hi, Ron. Looks like you did all right here while I was gone."

"You have Nancy Darnell to thank. She's been scheduled only one
day a week up till now, and she was happy to take over for you." He
consulted his watch. "I need to listen for a call. Come on over to my
office, will you? We can talk there."

Nicole took another look around, nodded, and walked with him
down the hall.

Sanders peered anxiously at her. "How are you feeling—really?"

She sighed. "Pretty awful. Still in a fog. But I've got to pull out of
it, Ron. That's why I wanted to see you this morning."

"Of course. Of course." His wing-tipped shoes made nervous little tap-tap sounds the rest of the way down the hall.

A few minutes later Nicole sat on the edge of the chair next to Sanders' desk. Her legs were crossed, and her booted foot swung with agitation, back and forth, back and forth. Pale winter light spilled through tall windows overlooking a courtyard.

"I need more work, Ron," she said. "I need another class."

Sanders blinked. He reached into a center drawer and came out with rimless glasses. Settling them on his nose, he gave her a measured look like a fifth-grade geography teacher, waiting for an answer that he knows won't come, because the student didn't study the night before.

Nicole recognized the ploy and almost smiled. Ron wanted her to forget they had dated once after Dan left, wanted to reduce her to that fifth-grade student so she'd see him as the boss he was. Their date hadn't turned out well.

"Nicole," he began firmly, "I disagree. In fact, I've been giving this a great deal of thought." His tone became solemn. "You've gone through a lot the past few months. I realize that. And now, with your sister . . . Well, nothing more need be said. But certainly, the last thing you need is more work."

"Ron, I—"

He steepled his fingers, tapping thumbnails against his teeth. "I've already worked it out with Nancy. We're nearing the end of semester anyway, and she'll be taking over your classes for the remaining few weeks. If you feel better in January, you could come back for spring semester . . . although quite honestly, I'd like to see you take longer." He glanced away, at the large oak clock softly ticking on a bookcase. "With pay, of course."

She grew cold. "I don't get it."

"Nicole, you've burned out. Even before all this—this business the past few months—even before all that, you were on edge far too much. And that incident last month, when you lost your temper in class—"

She rose to her feet and jammed her hands into her pockets, the fingernails cutting her palms as they formed tense, angry fists. "We talked about that. You said you understood. You agreed that teachers go through that sort of thing, after a time." She had a sudden thought. "Is this because of the recent trouble between us?" *Because I rejected you?* she wanted to say. *I never meant to. I told you I was sorry I used you to get over Dan, sorry I was thinking only of me, not of you.*

Sanders flushed, from his neck to the roots of his thin blond hair. "Of course not. This isn't about us, it's about you. And, of course, your students. My first obligation is to them."

"But I'm all right, Ron! I mean, I'll *be* all right, I just need a few days."

He was shaking his head, fiddling with a black pen. Then he sighed, leaning back in his chair. "It's settled, Nicole. I'm sorry."

"I don't believe this. You're taking my job away from me at a time when I've lost everything else?"

"It isn't like that. I'm giving you leave—with pay, which, believe me, I will have to fight for—and I hope that when you feel better, you'll see that I've made the right decision. For you, as well."

The paternalistic attitude was too much. She wouldn't be treated like a child.

Still, she felt like a child. Nicole's eyes blurred as she headed for the door.

"Nikki, wait."

She paused, her hand on the knob. Turning, she saw that he had removed the rimless glasses, his fragile line of defense. He set them carefully on his desk, crisscrossing the stems. "You look so tired," he said softly. "Is there anything I can do?"

"Haven't you done enough?" she answered, her voice breaking. "For God's sake, Ron, haven't you done enough?"

She barely heard his last words. "I . . . I'm sorry, Nikki. We'll miss you."

Nicole crossed the campus, her boots scuffing through wet leaves. A few flakes of snow had begun to fall. She drew the belt of her raincoat tighter, against the cold from within as well as without. Her mind refused to process any more. She was numb. She didn't know what to think, who to talk to, where to turn.

Twenty minutes later she had reached the glittering white high rise of Sacred Heart Hospital. A long driveway led up a hill that was brown with winter grass. Closer to the street, nestled into a wooded area between the hospital and the soaring Gothic structure of Sacred Heart Cathedral, was the convent of Sacre Coeur. Small and country French in design, it seemed purposely minimal, as if to make a statement about the minimal value of the nuns—the worker drones—while the lion's share of cash went to the Houses of God and Hippocrates.

On an adjoining lot—once part of the convent grounds, but parceled off years ago to a developer—was Mary Clare's cottage.

Mary had loved being close to work, loved being able to work into the late-night hours and walk the short distance home. There were old convent-built paths leading to the cottage, giving easy access through the gardens. She never even had to go out on the street.

And she seldom did. Mary Clare had lived like a nun. Aside from Mass every morning, she worked, ate, slept . . . worked, ate slept. A simple routine. And a norm for research scientists, Nicole had come to understand. Most were intense, ingrown, even antisocial. Many were celibate as Mary was—no less dedicated to science than religious were to their professions.

She gave a shiver, hardly believing that her sister was no longer here. *I'll never find her here again. Never talk to her, never see her face. . . .*

She couldn't face the cottage yet. She wondered if Terry was at work, in the lab where Mary had been stationed the past few months while her own was being rebuilt.

She entered the hospital building and took an elevator to the fifth floor—to the smallest of the biology labs. Walking in, she couldn't suppress a shiver. Test tubes, long black benches, glittering stainless steel . . . they weren't things Nicole felt comfortable with. She liked warmth, color, plants, trees. The formality of the lab that Mary had loved because of its all-important structure turned her cold.

A man of medium height with sandy hair falling over his forehead looked up from a microscope. He had been Mary's co-worker and friend. Nicole had always wondered if he'd felt something more.

Seeing Nicole, he put down the slide he was holding, wiped his hands on a paper towel, and approached her. His thin face was tired and strained.

"Nikki! God, how have you been? I tried calling. . . ." His voice trailed off as he put his arms about her awkwardly.

"I'm okay, Terry." She patted his back.

He gave her an intense once-over. "You don't look well."

"Thanks." She made a grimace.

"Sorry." He took her coat and hung it on a rack by the door. "Sit down, I'll get coffee."

She followed him to a gray steel desk in a corner of the room. Next to it was a low bookcase, overflowing with notebooks. On one lop-sided stack was a Mr. Coffee, sitting at a tilt, with a couple of inches of bitter-smelling remnants in its pot.

Terry set thick brown mugs on the desk and poured. "Cream? Sugar?"

Nicole shook her head. He slid the mug over to her and leaned back in his chair. "Do you want to talk about it?"

She lifted the mug and breathed in the acrid steam. "I didn't see you at the funeral, Terry."

He toyed with his cup. "I came late, sat in the back, left early. All those nuns—those radiant faces—and you know how I hate religion. I thought that Mass would never end."

She smiled. "I know."

"How could they—God—*rejoice* over something as tragic as that? Mary was so damned young!"

Her smile faded. "I know."

His intense face grew pink. "It's like those school-bus accidents. Why do they always take children?"

"You noticed that too? I used to think it only happened to Catholic kids, and I was scared to death to go on field trips. Now, they're even getting the Protestants and Jews."

"They *who?*" Terry half smiled.

"Whoever. You know that saying, 'Only the good die young'? It comes from mythology. It's always been that way."

"Gives a person pause, doesn't it?" Terry picked up a pencil with teeth marks in it and tapped the desk absently. "I've been wondering myself about the, uh, well . . . the circumstances."

"Circumstances?" Nicole gave him a questioning look.

"About Mary Clare's accident. About it being an accident."

Her hands tightened on the mug. "What are you talking about?"

"Oh, I don't know. . . ." Terry ran a hand through his already tousled hair. "I just keep thinking . . . Mary was such a good driver. But she didn't like driving at night. In fact, she didn't like being out late at all. If she wasn't here in the lab, she was at the cottage studying, reading—hell, sleeping, so she could get back to work again. Isn't that just about all she did?"

"Yes. I was just thinking about that."

"What I'm saying, Nikki, is that it just wasn't like her."

"No. It wasn't. But that doesn't mean . . . Terry, what are you saying? That somebody—but that's crazy!"

He laughed softly, passing a hand over his eyes. "You're right. Oh, hell, she probably had to run out to the store for something, or to see someone. . . ."

"And the weather was bad. Remember, that storm came up suddenly. The police said there were skid marks."

They both fell silent. One of the lab assistants stuck his head in the door, glanced at their tense faces, and backed out, leaving them alone. Nicole watched him through the connecting glass window, straightening up mounds of papers on the desk that Mary had shared with Terry.

Nicole looked away. "One of the nuns said that Mary wasn't here at work all week. Or at the cottage."

Terry glanced up sharply. "I knew she wasn't here. But I thought she was holed up at home, working on a talk for the immunology conference."

"Not according to this nun. And she'd probably know. The nuns were always dropping in to talk. Mary said once that the constant interruptions were getting to her, much as she loved the sisters as friends. I told her she should get one of those recordings that hollers out when someone knocks, 'Stand back! Stand back from the door!' "

Her eyes filled at the memory of Mary's laughter at that. But Mary, as much as she grumbled about it, was never able to turn the nuns away. Anyone else—but not the nuns. *They're so innocent, Nikki. That's what I love about them, that innocence. Heck, I can't even pretend not to be home. They'd know. And they'd be hurt.*

"I wanted to ask you something, Terry. What do you know about that conference? The one in L.A.?"

"Pasadena, to be exact. Mary was supposed to speak at the Ritz-Carlton on a panel about immunology. Why?"

"I just wondered. Did she pay for her own airline ticket? Or was it covered by the hospital?"

"Not the hospital per se, but Century Pharmaceuticals. They were picking up the tab for her expenses."

"Really? I know Century funds the hospital, but still—that's a pretty big perk for a postdoc."

"Well, she put in for it. The board of directors chose her out of several other applicants on the basis of a paper she'd written for a medical journal last summer." Terry sighed, dropped the pencil, and rubbed his face wearily. "Immunology—one of our *sexier* areas of research these days, you know. As in 'hot, new, fundable.' "

And Mary, already known as a wunderkind, had been high profile. She would have added a bit of glitz to the proceedings—young, dedicated, and brilliant.

"Christ, what a loss," Terry went on. "First Rose Arnault last summer, and now Mary."

"She took Professor Arnault's death very hard."

A scientist of some renown, Professor Arnault had taken Mary under her wing several years ago. She had sponsored Mary's dissertation research in immunology, and in many ways she had filled the emotional void left by their mother's death. After completing her doctorate, Mary had chosen to do her fellowship work in her mentor's lab.

"They never found out what caused the explosion, did they?"

"Not specifically. Some sort of chemical accident."

Nicole gave a shudder. Professor Arnault was in the lab alone when it exploded; her body was found in the debris. Mary, devastated by the loss, had moved into this lab with Terry while the old one was being rebuilt. She had stepped up the intensity of her work, yet Nicole remembered now that she had never again seemed quite as ebullient about it. It was more as if research had become some sort of penance.

And what was it Mary had told her just a short time ago? Something related to her work, some fear that Nicole had shrugged off at the time as exaggerated on Mary Clare's part.

"You're right," Mary had said, her smile not quite working. *"Forget it. And please, Nikki, don't tell anyone what I said."*

My God, what was it?

"Terry, what was my sister working on before she died?"

He shrugged. "Mary kept her postdoc studies pretty much to herself. Something to do with immunology, of course. That was always her focus. Why?"

She sighed. "I don't know." The mental fog was setting in again; she couldn't think clearly. "Could Mary . . . could she have been involved in something she wouldn't want anyone to know about?"

Terry looked around the small lab, his tone not quite hiding rancor. "We don't exactly do top-secret work here, Nikki. NIH, maybe, but Sacred Heart?" His laugh was bitter. "Not in this department."

Nicole remembered Mary saying, "Century Pharmaceuticals is our major funding source, and they have their own scientists in-house. The hospital labs get only a small piece of the financial pie."

"The kind of work I care about, I have to do on my own," Mary had said. Professor Arnault had helped her to bring in supplementary private funding.

Nicole looked around the lab, trying to picture her sister here. Her brow would be lined, her mouth puckered in concentration, the auburn hair falling haphazardly from a ponytail.

She swallowed a lump in her throat. "I saw Sister Paula at the cemetery."

"God, don't get me started on that woman." Terry rolled his eyes.

"She seemed strangely hostile to Mary. I thought they were getting a bit closer since Professor Arnault died."

"Well, Mary reported directly to Paula after Arnault's death. They had their heads together all the time because of that. But I doubt there was any love lost."

Terry seemed tired suddenly. His thin shoulders slumped. Nicole looked at him with sympathy. "You loved Mary, didn't you?"

Terry made a grimace. He didn't answer.

Why were the wrong people always loving each other? Or was that backward—why are we always loving the wrong people?

Nicole glanced around, still not finding her sister in these cold, barren surroundings. Not even a sign that she'd ever been here.

"Sister Paula said she was having Mary's personal belongings picked up and taken to the cottage."

"Yes. One of the younger nuns came by earlier."

She took her coat from the rack and shrugged into it. "I'm on my way over there."

Terry walked her to the door. "Are you all right?"

"No." She shivered. "No, I'm not. God, I hate this."

He gave her another light hug. "I really am sorry, Nikki. If there's anything I can do . . ." He smiled awkwardly. "Keep in touch?"

"Yes. I'll call."

Chapter 5

Mary's cottage was small and built in the same French-country style as the convent. At one time it had housed the woman who cooked for the priest, whose rectory was on the other side of the church. Before that it had been home to the first three nuns who'd arrived here from France.

Over the years little had been changed. The floors were well-worn oak, their finish mellow with age. An alcove just inside the front door still held a statue of Jesus with his heart bared and alit with flames —*Sacre Coeur,* the Sacred Heart. There was a small bouquet of dried marigolds at His feet; Mary's favorite flower. Above the statue a stained-glass window allowed in rosy shafts of light.

Nicole stood listening, crazily, for a sound—for anything that might say this all been a horrible nightmare, that Mary was alive and would come into the hall with a smile and a bright "Hi, Nikki. I'm glad you came!"

Nothing. Of course there was nothing. Did she really believe there might be?

Glancing into the living room, she saw Mary's small fish tank, now dry, the beta and angels removed by the nuns. She didn't linger; there was too much pain in the sight of that empty tank. She avoided the kitchen, too, where they had had some of their best talks in recent months. So many memories. . . .

Thank God, Mary had been renting. She wouldn't have to decide what to do with this place, just gather her sister's things together and put them in storage until she had the strength to go through them.

She wouldn't even have to hire anyone to clean. The nuns had done that the day after Mary died. They'd cleaned, found an appropriate dress, and taken it to the funeral home—all the things that families usually do, the everyday motions that help them through the mourning process. The nuns had taken over before Nicole had had a chance to.

They'd even had a get-together after the cemetery, complete with refreshments and friends. Nicole declined to attend—unable to face more of their rapturous delight at sending another soul to God.

She took the stairway to the second floor. At the top was Mary's bedroom, and at the opposite end of the hall, facing the street, her study. A glance into the bedroom showed a neatly made single-width bed, a white cotton spread, a crucifix on the wall.

More of a nun's cell than a bedroom, she thought.

The front study was small, but accommodated a desk with a black metal gooseneck lamp, and notebooks. There were stacks and stacks of notebooks, hundreds of them.

Nicole riffled through one, with its painstaking handwritten notes. Formulas . . . charts . . . phrases she didn't understand. Now and then there was a simple medical term she did understand: pneumonia, trachea, thymus.

With a heavy heart she replaced the book. Would all this dedication be wasted now? Or would someone carry on her sister's work?

She pulled off her coat and rolled up her sleeves. Some of the notebooks were already in boxes, as if Mary had planned to store them away. She would have to get more cartons, and then she would have to make several trips to get everything home. It could take hours—a couple of days.

One step at a time.

She began to carry the heavy boxes across the room, stacking them neatly beside the door. As she worked, she built up a sweat. Her mind went on automatic, a process of numbing out that would help her to cross the next hurdle—Mary's personal belongings, the stuff of memories.

When the last carton was by the door, she wiped her hands on her skirt and turned back to the desk.

So many small things, still. What could she put them in?

A suitcase. Put them in a suitcase.

She crossed to the one small closet, twisting the glass doorknob. As the door opened, a whiff of incense rose to her nostrils. Mary's clothes had absorbed it from attendance at daily Mass—the way cigarette smoke lingers after a night out.

Nicole forced herself to keep moving. Dragging Mary's suitcase from the closet—the same green-and-white-plaid one with wheels that she'd had when she first arrived in Georgetown—she set it on the desk. Then she began to pile things in. Pens, pencils, paper clips, a paperback dictionary, assorted scraps and notes. A prayer book.

In the prayer book was a folder with an invitation to a Century Pharmaceuticals dinner at the conference in Pasadena, and another to a Century party afterward. Nicole stuck the folder in the suitcase.

The desk completed, she took a green-plaid lap blanket off the closet shelf and stood on tiptoe, feeling for anything that might have been stuck behind it. In a far corner her fingertips brushed a box. She stretched, catching a corner, and dragged it out. It was white, the size of a shirt box. She set it on the bed, lifting the lid.

Mary Clare's short life—past and present—lay within. Her high-school class ring, a small opal rosary, a picture of their mother taken shortly before she died . . .

Oh, God. Don't think.

Beneath the personal items were several newspaper articles about scientific discoveries. Most were heralded as ". . . not a cure, but hope for the victims of cancer." More recent articles promised ". . . a new drug, possibly a cure for AIDS." All had been generated by research labs in universities and pharmaceutical companies around the world. And most finished with a version of the following: "It will be several years before (a,b,c wonder drug) can be approved. Meanwhile, scientists at (d,e,f lab) are working on . . ."

The usual media hype, Nicole knew, that keeps the funding going. At the slightest hint of a breakthrough the labs go to the papers, hoping to raise the hopes of the public—who will then, if all goes well, put pressure on the politicians who make the budget decisions. Whether a cure actually comes from a,c,b wonder drug isn't always the point. The point is to get the funding and keep everyone employed.

She knew that Mary Clare must have scorned these articles. Why did she keep them?

Beneath the clippings, at the very bottom of the pile, was another article—dated a year ago—about a French journalist who had been kidnapped in Paris. Nicole vaguely remembered the incident from the news; she didn't remember the outcome. Odd, she thought, that Mary would have kept this.

As she put the article back, her fingers reshuffled several objects.

A small photo of herself in a heart-shaped frame rose to the surface. Nicole picked it up, memories rushing back.

She was so insecure then—fifteen and homely, as teenagers sometimes are. Ignorant about how to do her makeup or hair. She remembered what she had written on the back of the photo: *From the ugly duckling to the rose.*

Smiling, she pulled the old snapshot out to see the words.

Her vision blurred. She began to shake. Passing a hand over her eyes, she stared at what lay beneath the photo of herself. The frame trembled in her hand.

Behind her own picture, another had been concealed—that of a man with a strong, masculine face, shoulder-length brown hair, intelligent gray eyes.

Eyes that Nicole had longed, for an entire year, to find looking at her the way they were looking at the woman in the photo.

Dan Rossi.

And with him, Mary Clare. The two of them smiling at her from a piece of celluloid, their cheeks close together, expressions on their faces that could only mean—

Love.

Nicole continued to stare at the picture in horror. Then she pried it out with her fingernail and turned it over. It bore a date on the back—April of this year.

Her memory grabbed at the date, filling her head with pain. In April they were all three in Los Angeles together. Mary had attended a conference, and Dan was there to discuss a movie deal. It was Nicole's spring break; she had gone along just for fun.

At whose suggestion, though? Dan's? Mary Clare's? Or had she been an unwanted fellow traveler—inviting herself?

Oh, God.

The already tottering foundation of her life shifted with frightening speed and intensity. She couldn't think, couldn't move. Grief turned to anger. She turned the anger on Dan and Mary Clare—then on herself. Finally, she turned it back to them again.

How could Mary have done this, how could Dan—

A small sound at the door made her jump. She spun around.

Sister Paula.

The nun was frowning at the boxes by the door. "What are Mary Clare's notebooks doing here?"

"I . . ." Barely thinking, Nicole slipped the photo of Dan and her sister into the suitcase. She swallowed, finding her voice. "They were already packed. I'll have to come back, though, there are too many—"

"That won't be necessary." Sister Paula's dark, African eyes met Nicole's. "Mary Clare's work is the property of Sacred Heart."

"But—"

"I thought you understood. All of the work Mary Clare did while she worked for the hospital is legally ours. Your sister signed papers to that effect when she was first employed."

"I don't—"

"You may take her personal belongings. You may *not* take anything else. Is that clear?"

Confused, numb, her mind still whirling, Nicole couldn't even argue. Fumbling, she began to snap the locks on the green-plaid suitcase—not even wanting it now, not wanting to touch it, yet unable to leave it behind. She had to see the photograph again. Had to find some explanation for the betrayal. Or better, to find that for some inexplicable, insane reason, she had conjured up the entire thing.

And that was when she remembered what Mary had asked her not to talk about, all those months ago. It was shortly after the explosion in Professor Arnault's lab, and Mary had given her a small blue notebook and said, "If anything ever happens to me, give this to Dan. It's research for one of his films."

Nicole had laughed. "Nothing's going to happen to you." All her life Mary had looked for shadows under the bed. Whenever anything happened to a friend—from chicken pox to appendicitis—she would begin to think it might happen to her.

"Aren't you being a bit melodramatic?" Nicole had teased.

Mary's return smile never quite made it to her lips. "Even so, give him the notebook. And listen, Nicole, don't tell anyone. Okay?"

Chapter 6

Nicole lay huddled on her bed, her knees drawn to her chest. The photograph in her hand. Her skin was icy. The old furnace in the cellar was silent; she'd forgotten to turn the thermostat up.

She stared at the photograph again . . . proof that her sister had betrayed her in the worst possible way.

And Dan. All the while she had believed they were close, out there in California last spring—had it all been a lie?

A man with two hats. He had walked down her road—come into her life—wearing two hats. And while she had perceived him as one man, he had proved to be another.

But that's not the way the story goes, she remembered. *In the legend it was one and the same man, wearing one and the same hat. With different colors on either side.*

The message of the legend was that people on either side of the road simply perceived him differently.

Nicole closed her eyes. She crumpled the photograph in her fist. *Too much. It's too much. I can't think, can't figure things out anymore.*

Tears slid down her face. Blind pain turned to anger. She welcomed it. Nursed it.

Anger felt better than pain.

She was nearly paralyzed with cold. She tried to lift her arm to cover herself, but couldn't. The hands of the clock beside her pointed to midnight. Had she slept?

There was a sound at the bedroom door. It opened, casting light in a narrow shaft over her face. Nicole shook with fear.

I've got to get up, she told herself. *I can't let him do this. Not again. Move!*

She opened her mouth to scream. No sound came out. Her lips stretched wide in horror. They stretched so hard, the skin cracked and began to bleed. The blood ran down the sides of her face and made a thick, ugly puddle on the bed.

Only then did she know she was dreaming.

Chapter 7

The time was 2:01 A.M. A nearly full moon had disappeared behind clouds. The man stood in a small garden, looking through French doors and lacy, inadequate curtains, into the woman's apartment. He had been there a long time, watching.

The woman had come home late in the afternoon, looking pale and defeated. According to the tapes, she slept. Some time after midnight she awakened and began to tear things apart. She was still at it, frantically rummaging through closets, through bureau drawers and cupboards. He watched her lift her mattress and find nothing there. She rolled her bed away from the wall and ripped through boxes beneath it. She was like someone possessed.

She stood in the middle of her bedroom, frustrated. Crying. Then she dragged out suitcases and began to pack. Her packing was random, as if she didn't care.

She only wants to get away, *he thought.*

The man understood. She would go to Los Angeles now. She had no choice.

He concentrated on the sound of rain on the broad leaves of a magnolia tree. A weak moon came momentarily into view, then faded into mist again. The man jammed his hands into deep overcoat pockets for warmth. His thick brown hair was matted from the ice-cold damp. He didn't think of the cold. He thought one thing only:

Mary Clare. Goddamn your soul, Mary Clare.

The
Betrayal

Chapter 8

Loss Angeles.

Her third visit here in three years—and her initial reaction hadn't changed. The city crushed down the minute she stepped off the plane. The air was heavy—humid and threatening—filling up the lungs. It was as if all the frenzied energies in this town—rich, poor, bad, good—had come crashing together to form a thick layer just beneath the smog.

Nicole felt she could easily get lost and die here. Given some twist of fate that she couldn't at the moment imagine, she might move into an Old Hollywood–type courtyard apartment on some street like Sepulveda that goes on and on, with fast-food restaurants and pawn-shops as decor instead of ponds and trees. She could end up here at eighty, never having lived at all. Her friends would be other white-haired women who sat on folding deck chairs in the sun, exchanging pictures of grandchildren they never saw. "Teddy says they can't come this year for Disneyland. He's just been promoted, and he's got to work extra hard. And Janey has that nice new job at Springfield High. Maybe next year . . ."

She'd sigh and pat her tan, leathery chest with a veined hand, while the other women nodded sympathetically. No one ever came to visit them, either. Someone would bring out a pitcher of martinis and a deck of playing cards. The sun would set, and they'd each go to their tiny kitchenettes, feed the cat, pour another drink, and begin again the next day in the courtyard—another desultory exchange.

Nicole shook herself. *Why in the name of God am I here?*

The idea, vague and formless, had come to her after the dream. Something about confronting Dan: *"What did you do to my sister? Why did she go driving off in the night that way? Did you hurt her the way you hurt me?"*

Even Terry had agreed that it wasn't like Mary—the hour so late, and in a storm. Something had to have happened, something per-sonal and perhaps even painful. *Something she couldn't talk to her own sister about.*

And Dan had been in Mary's life. They had been close.

A shuttle approached the traffic island. *L.A. Express.* Its sign read:

SANTA MONICA. Nicole stuck out her right hand. Waved it. The driver saw her, braked abruptly, and jumped out. Confirming her destination, he loaded her bags.

After a few miles the only other passenger, a grandmotherly woman in the seat behind her, spoke. "Do you live out here?"

Nicole turned reluctantly, not wanting to talk. "No. Just visiting."

"Is this your first time?"

"No, I've been here before."

"I'm on vacation," the woman said, gazing gloomily out her window. "First time in my life I've ever been out of Nashville. My son-in-law gave me a ticket. An early Christmas present."

Nicole sighed and turned back. "Nashville is nice."

"At least you can see the sky there," the woman said.

Nicole glanced out the window. Over the Hollywood hills, night was setting in. The only way you could tell was that the sky was now a darker brown.

She checked into the Ocean Palms Hotel in Santa Monica, where she had stayed a year and a half ago, when she'd come out to do research at the Aztec Museum. The hotel was small, Spanish in design, and relatively inexpensive. Her room was on the fourth and top floor, looking down on the 3rd Street Promenade—streets that had been turned into an open mall. The hotel also had the advantage of being connected to a small rental-car agency. There was a budget car waiting when Nicole arrived. She checked in and pocketed the car keys. Carrying her own suitcases, she walked past an ornate indoor fountain to the elevators, punching the up button.

In her room she ordered a chicken sandwich and a glass of chardonnay from room service. While she waited, she dragged the phone to a round table by the window. Taking a small brown address book from her purse, she looked up a number in Pasadena. Picking up the phone, she rang through to the hotel switchboard, rubbing a spot between her eyes where a dull ache had begun. She asked for a number and waited for her call to go through, remembering how she had met Professor Henry Dirstoff.

A medical historian, and still a part-time teacher in his early seventies, he had come to Georgetown to give a series of talks about ancient European trade and its effect upon medicine throughout the ages. Nicole had been introduced to him after a lecture by one of her former teachers.

"Nicole is teaching mythology and comparative religion for us," the woman had said. "She's one of our brightest young assistants. And she thinks like you."

Nicole was in her first year of teaching at the time, still working toward a doctorate and writing a paper on the effect of commerce upon culture and religion. How the Catholic Church, for instance, had grown because of its fingers in world trade—and how it continued to do so. Certain religions argued today that Christianity had become a major force because of divine approbation—God directing its growth in order to save the world. Over coffee Nicole had asked the professor what he thought of this.

"If true," he had answered, "then God certainly used worldly ways to accomplish his feat. For all its beneficent roots, Christianity has grown primarily through human greed. The purpose of the Great Crusades, for instance, was to grab land for the Church—and just to make sure the knights did their job right, the religious leaders of the day offered 'indulgences'—Brownie points that, when added up after death, supposedly could 'buy' a person's way out of purgatory."

The professor had lifted his bushy white brows and given her a shrewd smile. "Depending on your sins, you might need a thousand indulgences to purchase your passage out of that netherland between heaven and hell. By trotting off on a Crusade, lopping off heads, and winning land for the Church, you might get five hundred indulgences to put in your purgatorial kitty. And guess who decided how many you got—and for what?"

Nicole had smiled. "The Church leaders."

"Precisely. So it was greed, fear, and superstition that built the early faith. And—as I'm sure you know, Nikki—may I call you Nikki? —a study of religions ever since proves that not much has changed. One has only to look at the strength of the television evangelists and how easily they convince the elderly and ill—sitting rapt before their sets at home—that mailing in donations will save not only their bodies, but their souls."

His face became solemn. "Sometimes I wish it were true. To save one's soul with a chit . . . ? Ah, well."

It was amazing to Nicole, as she came to know Professor Dirstoff better, that the cynicism of his lectures hadn't become an integral part of his personality. Instead, he was one of the gentlest, kindest human beings she had ever known. Their common interest in history and religion had given them the basis for a friendship—while a similar interest in medicine had linked him, later on, with Mary Clare.

Nicole, in fact, had stayed with the professor on her last visit out here—in April.

Her eyes closed. *Steady girl. Don't think about April. Shut it out for now.*

A harried female voice at the other end of the line brought her back. "Hello? Who is it?"

"Is Professor Dirstoff there? This is Nicole Ryan."

"Just a minute."

She could hear words being exchanged in the background, and wondered who the woman was. The professor had lived alone since his wife, Eleanor, had died twelve years ago. After a few moments, he came on the line. "Nikki? My dear little Nikki, are you all right? I felt so helpless when we spoke the other night. One never knows what to do."

"I know, professor. I'm all right. I'm here, actually, in Santa Monica."

"Santa Monica! But I didn't know you were coming here."

"I didn't know, myself, until last night. Professor . . . can we get together? I'd like to talk to you about some things."

"But of course. In fact, I would invite you to stay with me, but my niece—well, Eleanor's, actually—has just arrived with her little boy. . . ."

"No, that's all right, I'm staying at the Ocean Palms. But I've been thinking. I have Mary Clare's invitation to a Century Pharmaceuticals dinner tomorrow night. Also one to a private party afterward. Would you like to go?"

"Tomorrow night? Well, yes, of course I'd like to go with you. But can you wait just a moment?" She heard him talking to someone in the background; then he returned. "Austen is taking Michael to Disneyland, so yes, that should work quite well. But, Nikki, I suspect you will find the dinner quite boring. Those things generally are."

"I know. But I thought . . . I thought I might see people there who knew Mary. And you might know some of them too. Would you introduce me?"

"Nikki, dear, I would be happy to introduce you to any of Mary's friends and colleagues out here whom I know. But is something wrong?"

"I . . . I just have questions. Some things have been happening."

"What things?" he asked sharply.

She couldn't explain, unsure herself what she hoped to discover. "I'll tell you about it when I see you."

They made plans for tea at his house before the dinner. After hanging up, Nicole opened her paisley suitcase and shook out the one dressy outfit she had brought—a two-piece white silk, with a flared skirt.

Not much of a mourning dress. But she didn't own anything black and couldn't bring herself to shop. She hung the dress in the closet, then picked out a clean pair of jeans and a soft white shirt to wear in the morning.

Her order came, and the waiter bustled about, snapping a starchy white cloth over the table by the window. Her sandwich was hearty —chunks of chicken breast, celery, and golden California raisins bursting from a croissant. It was served with a flurry of Spanish and an overkill of ceremony. When the waiter was gone, Nicole reached into a flap of her suitcase and took out a thin white envelope. She sat once more at the table, propping the envelope against a candle. Sipping the glass of cool white wine, she stared thoughtfully out the window for a long time, picking at the chicken sandwich but barely eating. Someone played a guitar on the sidewalk below. Couples walked hand in hand, wandering in and out of stores.

Finally, the sandwich still barely touched, Nicole reached over and picked up the envelope. Opening it, she drew out the crumpled photograph of Dan and Mary Clare.

She pulled the candle closer, holding the photo up to its light. Searching out details: Dan's hair, brown and slightly curly, just touching the collar. His intense, handsome face—marred only by a crooked nose, broken in a sandlot game one adolescent summer. Gray eyes—always alert.

And Mary Clare. Not in the usual drab grays or browns she'd fallen into the habit of wearing. *You know me, Nikki, I haven't time to shop.*

And I've never really liked to stick out. In the photo she wore a ruffled pink blouse, white shorts, and tennis shoes.

They were on a boat of some kind. You could see a corner of what appeared to be a wheelhouse, and painted on it, the last two letters of a name: *AH.* Dan's arms encircled Mary Clare from slightly behind. Their cheeks touched. They looked excited. Happy.

Nicole set down the candle. She lifted the glass of wine with a shaky hand and sipped, not taking her eyes from the photo. Sound rose upward from the Promenade, voices and laughter. The guitar played a mournful Spanish tune.

She didn't realize, at first, that the wine was gone and the candle had burned to a nub. Finally, she set the photo facedown on the table. Grabbing her purse and the car keys, she fled the room.

Chapter 9

Combat boots.

A person would need combat boots to live in this town.

Nicole stood in the dark, leaning against a waist-high wall at the Griffith Park Observatory. Beside her was the white dome of the huge telescope. Below stretched Los Angeles, thousands of acres of lights like a carpet, as far as the eye could see. They glittered and sizzled, from Hollywood to Santa Monica, from the slums of Hawthorne to the overly consuming mansions of Beverly Hills.

Nine P.M. now, and there were people all over the place. Tourists coming to see the lights, the show. In L.A. the show was everything.

Professor Dirstoff had brought her here last April. She'd been depressed—frustrated about Dan and the way things were going, or to be exact, not going. The professor, always an extraordinary teacher, had proved to be an insightful psychologist as well.

Pointing out across the city, he had said, "Los Angeles, Nikki, dear, for all its abundance and pretense at joy, is rife with pain. This is an excellent vantage point for gaining perspective. Up here one can look down and think how insignificant it all is—not just Los Angeles, but life. As if one were standing on the bank of the river, watching the flood go by."

This was during the trip they had made in April—she, Dan, and Mary Clare. Mary was at USC attending the conference; Dan supposedly up north, checking out locations for a film. With time on her hands Nicole had wandered along Melrose, poking into boutiques. Hungry, she stopped to look at a restaurant menu taped to a window. *California "Burger": tofu, sprouts, mushrooms, raddichio, tomatoes . . . $9.95.*

Her neck began to prickle. She rubbed it, thinking it was the unaccustomed heat. It had been a cold spring in Georgetown, with even a light snowfall the previous week.

But it wasn't heat. It was Dan—Dan, inside the restaurant at a table by the window. Looking out. At her.

She thought she was seeing things at first. He had told her the morning before that he'd be away from L.A. for a few days. Yet here he was, speaking to a person across from him—a man, she remembered later—and then he was getting up, disappearing behind a dessert counter, and coming through the restaurant's door. Standing beside her.

"Nicole! Hi!" That charming, heart-wrenching grin.

"I thought you were up north," she had said, still off balance at finding him here. Remembering his words: *We've only got ten days here. Why don't you do some shopping, go to the beach. Get some sun. I've got to drive up to Salinas and talk to farmers, check things out.*

"I just flew back a couple of hours ago," he answered. "Had to talk to a producer."

They had both laughed. *Imagine meeting you here like this. Small world, even in L.A.*

Dan had taken her arm. "Where's your car? I'll walk you to it."

"What about your friend? Is that the producer?" She had glanced back toward the restaurant.

He steered her away. "He's okay. We were just saying goodbye."

"I still can't believe you're here!" She shook her head, smiling—not asking too many questions back then. Just glad to see him.

"I was going to call you in a little while. Where are you parked?"

"At the end of the block. That blue Chevette down there."

"Give me a lift back to Malibu?" He was staying with a friend, at the beach.

"Sure. But where's your rental car?"

"I left it at the house. My lunch appointment picked me up."

They had laughed some more at the coincidence, and on the drive to Malibu had filled each other in on the past twenty-four hours. They'd had dinner together at a quietly elegant restaurant along the beach. Dudley Moore was there, off in a corner with someone Dan recognized as a top agent. Liza Minellia dropped by. After dinner Nicole and Dan sat on the deck at his friend's house in Malibu, overlooking the sea, and talked about the evening, the stars they'd seen, their work. They had grown closer that night—or so she had thought.

Now she remembered that she was never fully satisfied with Dan's explanation for being in L.A. that day. Something about it didn't feel right. She had brought the subject up again, once, and he'd been irritated with her.

When they returned to Georgetown the following week, a distance had grown between them. And no matter what she did, or how hard she tried to narrow the gulf, it widened. Three months later Dan had told her he was moving back to L.A.

Back in her hotel room again, she stood at the window. A breeze blew from the ocean, cooling her cheeks. The Promenade was quiet below. She began to straighten up the table—something to do. The chicken sandwich had hardened. She put it and the wineglass back on their tray and set them outside the door.

She had left the picture of Dan and Mary Clare in a small puddle of wine. She picked it up, blotting it on her skirt.

The visit to the observatory, remembering the professor's words there before, had helped her to regain her strength. It was time to call Dan.

But how would it feel, hearing his voice—and knowing, now, about him and Mary Clare? Would she be able to keep her own voice even? Would she be able to keep from blurting out how hurt and betrayed she felt?

Yet she had no reason to feel betrayed. He'd had every right to see someone else. Dan had never made promises; never claimed to be more than a friend. The idea that he felt more was all in her head.

As for Mary . . . if Dan and her sister had been so close, why had he left Georgetown? Did something happen? She wondered if she'd have the courage to ask. Now that she was here, did she really want to know?

She picked up her address book again and flipped through the tissue-thin pages for Dan's number. Punching it in, she waited nervously. She hadn't been able to reach him before the funeral; there had been no answer, and his machine was off. Would she have to break the news about Mary?

Three rings. Maybe he wouldn't answer.

"Hello."

She almost lost heart. Almost hung up. "Uh, hi. It's Nicole."

"Nikki! Oh, God, I just heard—I've been out of town. I've been trying to call you since noon."

At the sound of his voice, she couldn't help it, tears began. She brushed them away, embarrassed. "I'm not in Georgetown. I'm here."

A small silence. He would be standing now, beginning to pace with the phone cradled beneath one arm. She knew so many things about him.

"You're in Los Angeles?" he asked.

"Santa Monica."

In the following pause she could hear laughter from the Promenade. Footsteps passing in the hall.

"Where are you staying, Nikki?"

"At the Ocean Palms."

"The Palms . . . that's not too far from me."

"I know."

Mary Clare had told her, a month or so ago: *Dan's staying at the house in Malibu. His friend is working on a film in Spain, and Dan's subletting.*

"Would you like me to come over?" he said.

"No. No, not now. It's been a difficult week . . . and then the plane trip. I need some rest."

"Sure, I understand. Look, why don't we have breakfast? I'll pick you up."

She thought about being in the car alone with him, the knowledge of him and Mary Clare like a silent, unwelcome passenger in the seat between them. "I've got a rental. I'll meet you somewhere."

"Okay. Well, how about Gladstone's? It's on PCH—"

"I remember."

They had eaten there before.

Chapter 10

In the morning she dressed in the jeans and boots, tucking in the white shirt and dabbing on pale lipstick. The drive up Ocean Avenue and then Pacific Coast Highway took less than fifteen minutes.

She sat down at a table overlooking the water between Santa Monica and Malibu. Several minutes later she looked up from a cup of coffee and saw him standing by the door. A reflection of light from the water glanced over his hair. It was longer now, touching his shoulders in loose curls, and a lighter brown from the sun.

He walked with more authority, she thought. Shoulders back, an air of success despite the jeans and maroon sweater that was threadbare at the cuffs. He had always worn clothes until they were barely there anymore. "For the price of a new sweater I can get a can of film," he would say. "Or a new lens, or plane tickets for a location shoot."

She remembered the first time she had seen him in that restaurant in D.C. She had looked up and, without knowing who he was, had watched him edge his way past waiters and crowded tables. He was head and shoulders above the rest, his eyes scanning the room with a bravadolike blend of self-confidence and vulnerability. Her heart had done unfamiliar flip-flops. Then he was standing before her at the table, and Mary Clare was introducing him. She knew in that moment that she'd better watch out. This was the kind of man she could have too many feelings for. She could get sucked in, lose herself, forget her own life and what she had planned to do with it, for a man like this.

"I met Dan at Sacred Heart," Mary Clare had said. "He was doing research for a medical documentary."

"And your sister was an enormous help." He had leaned down to kiss Mary's cheek, then held Nicole's hand a moment, studying her face. His glance was warm; there was an immediate rapport.

He was coming toward her now in Gladstone's. Closer up, he looked tired. His eyes were rimmed with a transparent blue, the way they got when he'd been awake all night. She remembered how she had always wanted to soothe that tiredness away—how she had been unable to keep her own eyes off him, even when they were

shopping together as they sometimes did. She'd watch him, fool-
ishly, in supermarket checkout lanes—watch him tease the clerks,
carry on lively conversations—and sometimes she would ache, she
had wanted him so much.

She remembered, too, walking a path around the Tidal Basin together beneath late-blooming cherry blossoms. And side by side
later that night at a concert along the Potomac—the air hot and
humid, sliding like a blanket of warm butter over her bare arms and
legs. Her upper lip sweating, but not from the heat. From wanting to
turn and press her mouth against his neck and taste him.

Her mouth was now dry. She couldn't speak. He was leaning down
to kiss her cheek, sliding into the chair opposite. Searching her
eyes.

"Nikki, I'm so sorry." He reached over and took her cold hands.

She stared, trying to read something between the new fine lines in
his face. Asking silently, *How could you have been in love with my
sister, and how could I not have known?*

"I still can't believe it." Dan tightened his grip. There were tears in
his eyes. "I can't believe she's gone."

"How did you hear?"

"A friend—Michael Korb—heard about it on the news in D.C. I
don't think you knew him. He worked with us on a film last year."

"With you and Mary Clare?"

"Yes. She helped with some medical stats."

"I guess I didn't know that."

What else don't I know about you? she wondered. *And how could I
have known you so long, yet so unwell?* It was as if he'd had one life
when he was around her, and another when he wasn't. People she
never met, work she was never a part of . . .

And Mary Clare.

"When was the last time you saw her?" she asked.

He released her hands and sat back. "Mary Clare? August, I guess.
Before I moved back here."

An uneasy silence. When she didn't fill it, he signaled for the
waitress, a young woman with long blond hair to her waist. She wore
white shorts, her legs slender and tan beneath them. She smiled,
nodded, and brought a cup of coffee, setting it down.

"The usual?" She leaned her hip against the back of Dan's chair in a familiar gesture, brushing his shoulder.

He gave her a smile and nodded. "Nikki?"

"Just more coffee."

"Let's see . . . was that regular, or decaf?" the woman asked.

"Regular."

She looked up from her pad. "Toast? We've got homemade wheat with nuts and raisins, and a real nice rosemary from the LaBrea Bakery."

Nicole sighed. "Fine."

"The rosemary?"

She gritted her teeth. "Whatever."

"Rosemary." The woman wrote it down.

When she was gone, Dan said, "How did it happen? Michael didn't give me any details. An auto accident, he said."

"It was late. Her car went off a bridge." Nicole toyed with a fork, scratching at spots left behind by a dishwasher.

"I wish I had known," Dan said. "I'd have come for the funeral, Nikki."

"Would you?"

He made an impatient gesture, running a hand over his face. "Of course. I'd have been there for you. And for Mary."

She glanced away, out the window at gulls wheeling above the fishing boats. "It all happened so fast."

A busboy brought coffee. Dan added cream and sugar to his and seemed to hesitate. He set down his spoon. "Nikki, why are you out here?"

She gave a shrug. "I needed to get away."

"I didn't think you liked L.A."

Her voice was tired. "I don't, much. But it's cold in Georgetown. And I guess I needed to think some things out."

He studied her face. "I never did feel that Georgetown was the place for you. Remember when we were out here last spring? You seemed to come to life in L.A."

"I remember."

While Mary attended workshops at USC, they had done Universal City, the Huntington Gardens in Pasadena, the southern beach towns—Manhattan, Redondo, Hermosa. Between Dan's meetings, there were long, lazy days on the beach.

At first.

Then suddenly Dan was either occupied or preoccupied most of the time. In the remaining few days of their visit, Nicole had learned to tourist by herself, to eat alone, and to swim or lie on the sand for hours, feeling the sun drift over the naked parts of her skin. Trying to tell the time by its passage of heat: Where was he now, at two o'clock, three o'clock? Would there be a message on the machine when she got back to the professor's house? Would Dan's voice be on it? Would he ask her to join him for dinner?

When the warmth of the declining sun finally reached beneath her chin instead of flat out, straight on, she would give herself permission to pack up blanket, radio, suntan oil, and go. She'd brush sand from her feet, throw a towel on the seat, and climb into the fifties-era blue Thunderbird convertible she had borrowed from the professor. Melting into freeway traffic on the 10, top down, hair flying, she would spin the old radio dial until it brought in a station with fifties-era music. She could almost imagine herself back there—hearing the songs her mother had sung around the house as she was growing up: *Try a Little Tenderness; Faith Can Move Mountains; Goodnight, Sweetheart.* Her blunt fingernails with their clear polish would tap the wheel as traffic stalled, impatient to be tapping the answer button on the message machine and hear Dan's voice.

She was a madwoman, back then. In the throes of unrequited love —obsessed. Pulling into the professor's circular drive, in the big old Pasadena house he'd grown up in, her heart would quicken. She'd slam on the brakes by the front door, jump out, rush up the stairs, fumble with the key, shiver as the coolness of the dark house struck her skin. Skidding on the Oriental carpet in the hall, she would dash into the professor's study, to check for messages on the answer machine.

Most days there were several for the professor. Students calling about term papers. Young lecturers looking for advice. Friends asking about plans for lunch.

Often there was a message from the professor himself. "Nikki? I wondered if you were free this evening. If so, would you like to take a little walk along the 3rd Street Promenade? Perhaps we might have a tiny espresso?" He would then go on to say that he'd be home around seven and merely wanted her to think about it meanwhile.

Sometimes Mary would have called. "Hi, Nikki, it's me, Mary Clare."

Breezy. In a hurry. Nicole remembered that now.

"Just wanted to let you know I won't be around tonight. I'm staying over with a friend from USC. See ya tomorrow, okay?"

On a late afternoon when one version or another of the foregoing had occurred, with still no message from Dan, Nicole had crossed to a window in the professor's study and stood there staring out. She had pushed aside heavy green drapes, a loneliness like none she had ever known falling like a weight upon her shoulder. The ten-day visit seemed now to be lasting a hundred years.

She noted the once-lush rose garden, now woody and dry from the drought. A broad lawn stretched a hundred feet or so to the street. It was patchworked with spots of brown. Beyond lay the hills separating Pasadena from Hollywood. Dense brown smog overshadowed them like an omen. Cutting off oxygen and view, the hills and smog seemed to point to some sort of societal parallel: Don't expect to get through to anyone in this land of obscurity. Above all, don't expect to build a relationship in a land where all things are veiled, where people can hardly breathe let alone articulate their feelings about themselves or each other.

Wondering if she should simply pack and go home, Nicole would grab a sandwich for dinner, digging deep into the professor's old Westinghouse fridge. Whatever was handy from her trip to the Santa Monica farmer's market—lettuce, tomatoes, onion sprouts—would be slipped into a pocket of pita bread. She'd take the food and a glass of wine and nestle in the window seat overlooking the back garden. There was a *koi* pond with a tiny bridge over it, and a fountain—dry then because of the water shortage. Japanese plantings encircled a three-foot-high Buddha, while Hindu temple bells tinkled.

An eclectic mix. "My parents were great travelers," the professor had told her during her first trip out here, a year and a half before. She had spent the day at the Aztec Museum, and the professor had invited her over for an after-dinner drink and a talk.

"They brought back mementos from every country they visited.

When I was a child, I had an imaginary playmate, as so many lonely children do. We read *David Copperfield* together by the *koi* pond. There were goldfish in it then."

"You were lonely when you were growing up?" She had always had Mary Clare to play with. Yet she knew about being lonely.

"My parents were distant—rather cold. And of course there was all that travel. I came to understand later that they were simply unable to be intimate with anyone but each other. A pattern, no doubt, from their childhoods. I've tried to break that pattern as I've grown older." He had sighed, then smiled. "It isn't easy, when you live alone. There's no one to practice on."

There were photos over the fireplace mantel of the professor and his wife, always together. There was a small boy, too. David. But the professor never talked about him. He had died at fifteen.

During Nicole's visit here last April he had told her more, one night when they were sitting in the garden. The sun was low, the air warm. Both Dan and Mary Clare were off somewhere, out of touch.

"In the beginning," the professor said, "Eleanor and I weren't so different from my mother and father. All we ever needed was each other. We were parent, child, lover, and friend to each other. We laughed and we played, and when we were with other people and something a bit odd was said or done, our eyes would meet in instant humor and rapport. We were a wonderful team." At this he sighed deeply. "And there can be no better relationship than that, little Nikki. You mustn't ever settle for less."

She hadn't told him about her feelings for Dan. He had guessed, from seeing them together those first days after they'd arrived. "You look at him with utmost love." It was the most direct comment the professor had ever made. And he had followed it with, "In the early blush of romance, no one sees clearly. Be careful not to overlook the obvious."

Nicole smiled and shrugged. "I see Dan's faults. I know he's not perfect. Isn't love all about accepting the other person unconditionally?"

The professor shook his head slightly. "That isn't precisely what I meant. But then . . . we can never fully know another person's relationship. How can we possibly advise?"

They didn't talk about Dan again. But whenever the four of them were together—she, Dan, Mary Clare, and the professor—there was a distance between them and him, as if he knew things about which he couldn't speak.

The memory of that silence hovered, now, like an unspoken warning above the booth in Gladstone's.

Dan was talking—answering her polite questions about his work. "We started shooting last week . . . interviews with migratory workers, illegal aliens. They've been lost in the flux of films about blacks and Asians recently, yet not much has changed for them in the past twenty years. We'll string them together with clips from newspapers, stock footage, and some new locale shots. But we're on a tight budget, so it's the personal interviews that the whole piece will depend on. If I can make them strong . . ."

He went on in that vein, looking to her for encouragement as he always had.

"That shouldn't be a problem," she said. "You're good at bringing people out. You have a knack for making them like you—for getting beneath the surface."

In his films Dan both directed and interviewed. Nicole had helped him now and then, reading scripts and making sure details of geography and history were accurate. Dan's films never glossed the surface. He supplemented topical issues with similarities in history, adding a depth and authority that reaped awards. More important, that attention to detail had brought in private funding, keeping him solvent when other young directors were foundering.

Their waitress paused to ask if everything was all right. She rested a hand on Dan's shoulder. "Need anything else?" He looked at Nicole. She shook her head. "Just a check," he said.

A noonday sun glanced through the window, heating the side of Nicole's face. She met Dan's eyes and quickly looked away. "I need to get back to the hotel."

"I'm surprised you aren't staying with the professor."

"Eleanor's niece is visiting with her little boy. He invited me, but his house isn't very big."

Dan laughed. "And you aren't at your best with chatty kids first thing in the morning."

She smiled. "As I remember, neither are you."

They had discovered that one weekend when they had taken a trip to Nagshead, to visit Dan's brother, his brother's wife, and their two kids. Nicole loved kids . . . but mostly after the hour of noon. By Sunday morning she and Dan had arranged an escape, sneaking out just after dawn to a coffee shop. They had left a note: *It was such a beautiful sunrise, we couldn't help getting out into it.* By the time they returned in the afternoon, their nerves had been soothed by eggs, Belgian waffles, and a long walk. Later, in Georgetown, that became their usual Sunday-morning routine—followed by an afternoon at a show, or the museums, or simply reading *The Washington Post* and *The New York Times.*

Nicole crumbled remnants of toast between her fingers and thumb.

"How long will you be out here?" Dan was asking.

"I'm not sure. A few days, a week . . ." The date of the return flight on her ticket was five days from now, at the end of the conference.

"I've got a great idea. Why don't you stay at my place?"

"No." She didn't look up. "I couldn't."

"Don't be silly. I've got that guest house, the one I stayed in last April. You'd have plenty of privacy. And hotels are expensive out here."

"I can afford it."

"Even so, it's been a long time. We'll have more of a chance to visit if you stay with me."

She looked at the persuasive smile, the cajoling gray eyes. *Have you already forgotten that my sister is dead?* she wanted to say. *I'm not here to visit, I'm here—*

To learn things.

Did you work your charms on my sister out here last April, get her to fall in love with you, lead her to believe that someday there might be more?

"C'mon, Nikki," Dan was saying. "I've always felt bad . . . the way we left it when I moved back here. It's not right, not even talking to each other."

She hesitated a moment longer. "Well, maybe for a couple of days."

He smiled. "It's settled, then." He gripped her hands again—his raw-knuckled, and hers narrow, yet blunt. Fine brown hairs on the backs of his fingers glinted in the sunlight. "I'm glad you're here, Nikki. I've missed you."

"Have you?"

"Very much."

There was a familiar tightening in her thighs. She pulled away. "I . . . I'll have to get my things."

"I'll go with you."

"No," she said quickly. "I'll meet you at your place. Just refresh my memory. Tell me how I get there."

A slight distancing took place. The check arrived and was split, without argument, between them. Dan drew a map on a paper napkin. "It's on the beach side, down this little street. . . ."

Nicole shoved the map into her purse and, a few moments later, followed him out of the restaurant.

Combat boots, she reminded herself. *Remember the combat boots.*

Chapter 11

Nicole glanced around the living room of the Malibu beach house. She had parked in the garage and walked down steps. More steps led from the house to the beach, some fifty feet below. Beyond the glass-walled living room was a deck surrounded by glass, a barrier against the ocean winds.

"Mary said you're subletting." In Georgetown, Dan had rented a basement flat—one room, with the shower and toilet in the landlord's laundry room.

"Yes. It's not as expensive as it looks."

"Don—your friend—he's in Spain?"

"For a year. I'm paying half the rent. For the rest, I'm housesitting."

There were gentle waves at the shore. Beyond, the ocean stretched like a blue mirror all the way to the horizon. The sky was paler blue, with streaks of white clouds.

"You can't see the smog from here." She remembered that from before; how all you needed was money, out here, to buy clean air.

"It's behind you," Dan said, smiling. "Don't turn your back too long, it might grab you."

There was a gas fireplace that was turned on by an electric switch (only in L.A., Nicole thought), and a ceramic bowl filled with tropical fruit on the serve-through counter between kitchen and living room. Mangoes, papaya, and horny yellow star fruit were piled high.

Sunlight glistened off the water and danced through the room. It tapped against the exercise bike by the window, the thirty-seven-inch television screen, the semicircular white couch, and the Native American artifacts that Dan had owned in Georgetown. In a corner stood a long, thin wooden "tube"—a Native American instrument that, she remembered, made a sound like rain. In a side wall was a large, round window of stained glass.

"I feel like I'm back in Oz," she said.

"Come on, I'll take you to the guest house."

She followed as he carried her bags through sliding glass doors onto a patio with a table, blue-cushioned lounge chairs, and clay pots full of red geraniums and giant yellow mums. A flagstone path lined with cacti and low palms led to the small white cottage. A waterfall of scarlet bougainvillea cascaded over one wall, from the roof to the ground.

"I think you'll find everything you'll need here," Dan said, opening both halves of a Dutch door. "If not, there's a store down the road."

"I'll be fine."

The inside seemed unchanged. There was one large room, broken only by a kitchen with louvered shutters over a counter. Everything was splashed with white: white stove, white refrigerator, white microwave and toaster oven. Open beams in the ceiling were painted white, and a free-standing polar-white fireplace stood in one corner.

"The sofa opens into a bed, and it's pretty comfortable." He set her bags against a far wall. "There's only one closet. If you need more room, you can put some things in mine."

"No, this is fine. I didn't bring much."

"There are extra blankets and pillows here." He opened the lid of a window seat to show her the storage cupboard. "It can get nippy by the ocean at night."

"Thanks." She brushed at her forehead tiredly. "I think I'd like to lie down awhile, if you don't mind."

"Sure. Still got a little jet lag?"

"I guess."

"I have to go out, anyway. We're editing *The Final Battlefield,* and I was out of town looking for funding. That was a waste of time. I'm sorry to leave so soon like this."

"That's okay. I'm meeting the professor for tea, and we're going to a Century Pharmaceuticals dinner after."

There was a brief flicker of surprise. "Century? How did that come about?"

"They're conducting a conference in Pasadena this weekend."

"Oh, right, I guess I heard about it." He seemed to hesitate. "I wouldn't have thought that would interest you, Nikki."

"I have Mary Clare's invitation. I thought I might use it." She met his eyes. "Somebody sent me her airline ticket, too. Do you have any idea who might have done that?"

The expression that crossed his face was hard to define. It was almost as if he had taken a physical step back. "Someone sent you Mary Clare's ticket?"

"It was probably a mistake. The travel agency mixed things up."

The gray eyes took on a sudden blandness. "I'm sure that's it." He looked around, as if searching for something to say. "Well, I'd better go. There's a phone over there on the breakfast bar, a private line. If you need to get messages, my machine's hooked up to the phone on my desk. You can give people my number . . . I'll leave the house unlocked."

"Thanks."

He touched her shoulder. "Will you be all right, Nikki? I'm worried about you. You seem—"

"I'm fine." She drew away.

He studied her a moment more. "You know, I've been wondering. Did Mary Clare . . . did she, uh, give you anything for me?"

Nicole busied herself at putting down her purse, then sat on the arm of the floral-covered sofa, crossing her arms. "Give me anything? Like what?"

"I don't know." He shrugged. "Anything."

"All her work belongs to the hospital, now, if that's what you mean. They wouldn't let me have her notes."

He rubbed a hand over his face. "I know. I just thought . . . Never mind." He turned to the door. "Get some rest, then. And Nikki —give yourself time to grieve. It's only been a few days."

She didn't answer.

"See you later, then." His smile was weary.

"Uh-huh. See you."

She sat where he had left her, on the arm of the sofa. Depleted. Unable to move except to wrap her arms more tightly about herself, as if the air had suddenly turned cold.

Mary? Did you betray me? Didn't you know how I felt about him? And did he, in turn, betray you?

Her feelings swung from anger, to grief, to sympathy. *If he made you think he loved you, then cut it off . . .*

Minutes later she heard his car start up. She roused herself, walking to the Dutch door. Cracking the top half, she stood and listened until she was sure he had driven away.

Then, moving slowly, as if in a nightmare, she tugged off her boots

and opened her suitcase, taking sneakers from it. Sitting on the edge
of the sofa, she pulled the sneakers on. Again she listened at the
open door, but heard nothing.

Hurrying back along the flagstone path, she barely noticed the
surrounding landscape, the brilliant purple blanket of ice plant that
covered the hill to the street—or the man who stood at the top of the
hill, watching.

The idea had come in a flash, while sitting at Gladstone's. *I can
find out. I can find out things if I'm there.*

Dan's bedroom was in the back, with a window on one side. It
looked out to another house a block or two away. Driving here, she
had noted that most of the surrounding houses seemed empty. And
from Dan's front window she hadn't seen anyone on the other decks
along the beach.

She brought her attention back to the drawer she had pulled open.
Socks; odds and ends; new shoelaces; some loose change.

The next drawer held jockey shorts and T-shirts, rolled up neatly.
Dan always had been surprisingly neat. Given the way he could get
wild when creatively inspired—off-the-wall, losing all perspective of
time and space—she had expected him, when first they had met, to
be messy.

"If I didn't keep certain things in order, I'd go nuts," he'd explained.

A large walk-in closet revealed tennis rackets, sneakers, sport
clothes, jeans, and shirts. Two suits—one blue, one gray—both
looking new. There was a dark-blue raincoat that she remembered
from Georgetown, and three brown cartons—a Del Monte Pineapple
and two Beck's Beer—full of books.

The other bedroom was furnished as a den, in a modern, high-tech
style. On a white desk beneath a window was a green-shaded halo-
gen lamp. Above the window were white miniblinds. Lifting a slat,
she could see across the patio to the cottage, decked with its floral
shawl. She turned back to the room.

Publicity posters of Dan's films lined one wall. Beneath them were
bookcases with research tomes: foreign-language dictionaries; text-
books on history, geography, science, religion—everything from the

pyramids to quarks. There were videotapes, too, travel tapes, which she knew he used for early research on locations. And Joseph Campbell: *The Power of Myth; The Hero with a Thousand Faces.* A complete set from the Bill Moyers interviews. Tapes they used to watch together.

There was one closet, a walk-in. With a padlock.

In Dan's Georgetown apartment, there hadn't been room for a walk-in. But there had been a large storage closet that he'd rented from the landlord, for his films and business files. He kept it padlocked so that no one—landlord or visitors—could get into it and disturb his work. He kept the key in a small carved box in the top drawer of his desk.

She opened the top drawer of this desk. Sure enough, creature of habit that he was, Dan had done the same thing here. She took the key out, laid it on top of the desk, and went through the rest of the drawers first.

Letterhead and envelopes—paper clips and staples. Rubber bands. A large bottom drawer with a pocket dictionary, maps, postcards from around the world.

That was all. She sighed, and straightened.

Closet.

She took the key and worked its magic on the padlock. When she turned the knob, the door swung open.

Canisters of film lined one wall, neatly labeled. A shelf held boxes of camera lenses, precisely aligned. A carton on the floor overflowed with old *Variety*s and other trade magazines. At the back stood a metal file cabinet.

She tried it and found it unlocked.

There were bills, receipts, and correspondence having to do with business, all neatly alphabetized. She flipped through the A's, B's, and C's, and moved quickly to the M's—looking for something, anything, that would answer questions she would otherwise have to live with the rest of her life.

Like letters. Letters from Mary to him—or copies of his letters to her. Or, possibly, more pictures. Something to verify, to make everything clear—

And the missing notebook. The one Mary Clare had given her for safekeeping. *"If anything happens to me, give this to Dan."*

It had disappeared from her house. And now something had indeed happened to Mary.

Twenty minutes later she had made it to the *Q*'s and hadn't found a thing. Nothing about Mary, and nothing that could be construed as suspicious—even if she knew what, exactly, to be suspicious of.

Disappointed, Nicole stood and flexed her legs, stiff from kneeling on the floor. She glanced at her watch. Not much time left to take a shower, change, and get to the professor's house in Pasadena—especially during rush hour.

Tomorrow. Finish up tomorrow.

She locked the closet door carefully, replaced the key in the carved box, and put it back in the drawer.

Chapter 12

"She still doesn't have the notebook," he said into the mouthpiece of the phone.

"But she's looking for it. She knows it's important."

"She can't know why."

"You don't know that. If she's read it—if she remembers what's in it—"

"I doubt she'd have understood. She's not schooled in the language, or the technology."

"Still . . . ," the other voice said. "How long can it be before she confides in someone, if she hasn't already? The very existence—"

"Don't panic. Let me handle it."

"You botched it with the sister."

"This will be different."

"Understand this. The woman must not be allowed to tell anyone."

The man sighed. He leaned his forehead against the glass window of the phone booth, tiredly. Deep lines etched his face. "I know. I know."

His hand, replacing the receiver, shook.

Chapter 13

Nicole turned onto Buena Vista, thinking again how like the east— and how unlike Southern California—this older part of Pasadena was. Trees lined a broad, quiet street, many of them over a hundred years old. Most of the houses here were large—mansions, compared to the condos of today. They were set back from the street, with broad lawns. Many had rose gardens and azaleas interspersed among palms and ferns. The professor's house was completely surrounded by dense shrubbery.

She pulled up to the curb, set the Chevy's parking brake, and climbed out, grateful for the peaceful neighborhood after the crazed freeway drive. Going up the walk, she inhaled the scent of late blooms on rose trees that led the way to the professor's door. The roses were coming back; the grass was green. Recent rains had everything flowering again.

The professor had heard the car and was waiting for her, arms outstretched. She noted that he looked older and a bit frailer—rail thin, with the white complexion of a scholar who barely sees the out-of-doors. Even his glasses seemed too large for his face, as if he had shrunk a bit since trying on the frames.

But his smile was as welcoming as ever. "It's so good to see you again, little Nikki."

She wrapped her arms around him and gave him a gentle hug, afraid she might break bones. "I've missed you, Professor."

"Come in, come in. I've got a little tea ready—jasmine, your favorite, isn't it?"

They locked arms as he led her through the center hallway, where a chandelier covered in rose silk cast a soft glow. Double doors opened into a living room with a high, carved ceiling. The French doors that led to the garden were closed, while a fire warmed the slightly chill night air.

"Sit, Nikki. Get comfortable." The professor flourished a hand toward high-backed tapestry chairs. Between them, on a low mahogany table, was a silver tea set.

"Where's Sampson?" she asked, giving a cautious look around.

Sampson was a hulking gray feline, more vicious—at least in Nicole's opinion—than any dog alive.

He smiled. "I told him you were coming, and he immediately disappeared."

"That cat and I will never be friends. He's got it in for me, you know. He's just waiting to catch me off guard."

They sat opposite each other, the professor barely making an impression on the fragile chair. His white hair gleamed in the firelight. "You are looking good," he observed. "A bit tired . . ." His voice trailed off, while his eyes remarked, *What a terrible tragedy.*

"Would you like me to pour?" Nicole leaned forward, taking up the pot. "Like old times?"

He nodded. "I remember. You always liked to pour when you were here before."

"It makes me feel gracious, like a character in a black-and-white movie, or an Agatha Christie book." Her eyes blurred as she filled the delicate china cups, hand painted with tea roses. "And jasmine tea . . . you have always been so thoughtful, Professor."

His tone was sad. "We can't change what has happened, Nikki. But Mary Clare wouldn't want us to grieve unduly for her." He glanced at the mantel over the fireplace, at an eight-by-ten-inch photograph of Eleanor with their son, David.

"You still miss her, don't you?"

"Eleanor? Very badly. She was a wonderful companion. We had the grandest adventures, until . . ." He fell silent.

Eleanor was a doctor, Nicole remembered. "You've never talked much about her work."

"No. I suppose I prefer to remember our love."

She could sense that the subject, however gently, was closed.

"As for dear Mary Clare," the professor said, clearing his throat, "she would feel, I am sure, that she has gone on to something better. Her faith was so strong."

Nicole gave a light shudder. "Spare me. That white funeral Mass was bizarre. All those nuns choraling praises to the sky."

"I wish I could have been there with you. But the doctor was adamant."

"I know." The professor had angina; he'd had chest pains recently and wasn't supposed to fly.

She dropped a slice of lemon into his tea and a cube of sugar into her own. "Did you see Mary very much when we were out here last spring? Aside from those few times we were all together, I mean."

He took his cup and balanced the saucer carefully on his knee. "It's interesting that you should ask that. We did talk on the telephone a few times, but I believe I saw her alone only once. She seemed . . ." He shrugged and gave her a wry smile, as if about to say something foolish. "Distant, somehow."

"Really? You don't mean unfriendly—Mary always liked you."

"No, not that. Perhaps secretive, although that seems a strange way to put it. Mary Clare was always so open with me."

"Until last spring, you mean."

"Well, yes. It was as if something had changed." He sighed and sipped his tea, his hand shaking slightly. "She may only have been absorbed in her work."

Nicole savored the flowery tea, holding it for a moment on her tongue. "So she didn't talk to you about anything. Privately."

He glanced at her sharply over his cup. "No . . . but why are you asking these questions, Nikki? Is something wrong?"

She sighed. "I don't know, Professor."

"Surely, whatever is bothering you can't matter now, with Mary gone."

She gave a shrug.

The professor put his cup on the low table and folded his hands delicately, placing them on his knee, precisely where he'd balanced the tea. "Even at best, life is so very short, Nikki. To agonize over questions that may never be answered . . . how can this help anyone?"

"I don't know, Professor. I just don't know." She set down her cup.

And just in time. A shriek assaulted her ears. Sampson—bigger and meaner than ever—landed on her shoulder from behind, digging his claws into her skin. She jumped, and if she'd still been holding her tea, it would have been all over her dress.

She grabbed the cat and held him up, glaring at his face.

"One of these days—!"

———

The professor drove her to the dinner in his old Thunderbird. Despite his earlier admonition, Nicole found herself unable to stop talking about Mary—her absence from the convent the week before she died, and the fact that she hadn't told Nicole she'd be gone. She told him about Sister Paula's hostile attitude . . . *"Your sister made her own rules."* And the ticket sent to her after Mary's death.

The only thing she didn't talk about was the photo of Dan and Mary Clare. The wound was still too raw.

"Let me give all this some thought," the professor said. "Some of these things can be easily explained, I'm sure. Others . . ." He narrowed his eyes.

They talked about other things—Nicole's classes, and his. "I'd like it if you would come and talk to my students while you're here. They could use some fresh blood."

"Fresh blood, huh? I'm not sure I like that metaphor." College students could eat you alive. All too often they thought they knew more than their teachers. And all too often they did.

On the other hand, the professor's students were accustomed to his brilliance. That could prove to be a challenge—something to think about, to prepare for.

Something to numb the emotions for a while.

"When would you like me to come?"

"My next class is the day after tomorrow, at two o'clock. I'm in Gardener Hall. . . ." He proceeded to give her directions.

The Century dinner was at the Ritz-Carlton hotel. Designed as a castle, it sat on acres of valuable land. Spotlights on every inch of facade illuminated their destination like a beacon. The dinner itself was long and extravagant, the speeches predictably boring. There were round tables with vases of pink roses on each, and crystal chandeliers bathed the cavernous room in an intimate glow. A chamber group played soft classical music. The menu offered a bisque of butternut squash, a salpicon of asparagus, and a light pesto with mild red-pepper coulis—along with a choice of prime rib, veal medallions, or chicken marsala.

Nicole remembered a mythology conference she had attended in Miami, and others she'd been to over the years. Sponsored by various educational institutions, the fare was generally more plebeian—chicken croquettes, baked halibut, vegetarian lasagna. It seemed as if the same people who chose the menu for grade-school lunches also chose the ones for teachers' conferences.

One thing was universal, however. The banquet rooms were always too hot. Nicole rearranged the neckline of her white dress, lifting it where it had slipped too low and stuck to her skin with perspiration. Her hair was long and heavy on her neck. She lifted that too. Turning slightly, she saw a man watching her from another table. He was nice looking, with dark brown hair and a friendly face. He gave her a flirty grin. Surprised, she couldn't help smiling before she looked away.

The professor was nodding toward the speakers' table, where five people sat—two women and three men. He leaned over and spoke into Nicole's ear.

"The woman on the right is Dr. Harriet Ilsen, head of the immunology department at Branston University in Long Beach. Are you familiar with it?"

"No."

He poked at his salad, picking out whole anchovies and setting them aside. "It's small, and very expensive. They do give scholarships, but accept only the very brightest students. Harriet should be able to talk to you about Mary's work. They always liked each other —and Harriet is on the board of Century Pharmaceuticals."

He made a face and covered the anchovies with a large leaf of lettuce. "Disgusting little creatures."

Nicole sipped her water and studied Harriet Ilsen. She had short dark hair with a frosting of gray, and a rather large nose beneath horn-rimmed glasses. Her conversation with the man next to her appeared serious rather than social. At one point Harriet Ilsen's back seemed to stiffen. She turned away and began to speak to the man on her other side, shutting the first man out.

Nicole watched her a moment more. "Anyone else?"

"To the left of the podium is John Rorrman. The one in the three-piece gray suit, red tie. He's chairman of the board of Century Pharmaceuticals."

"Did he know Mary Clare? Personally, I mean?"

"I saw them together when she was here last spring. I was on my way home from the university and thought I might catch her at her hotel room. As I was walking down the hall, Rorrman came out."

"Did you ask Mary Clare about him?"

"I believe so. Yes, in fact I remember saying jokingly, 'Are you plying your employer with food and drink to get more funding?' Because there was a table set up, you see, with appetizers."

"What did Mary say?"

"She didn't answer. She seemed embarrassed, and I felt I had overstepped my bounds. Old age does that, you know—makes you think you can say anything and get away with it." His fading blue eyes were rueful. "Sometimes it works, sometimes not."

John Rorrman, Nicole thought, didn't look as if he could be easily plied. True, his ruddy face was jovial as he chatted up the other people at the table, holding administrative court. A Good Old Boy, on the surface. But steel-gray hair, cut in a military buzz, sent the message that this was someone who could bull or bluff his way through any situation. Rorrman would almost certainly be in charge, whatever anyone might think.

Both Nicole and the professor had ordered chicken marsala, which now arrived, dripping wine sauce and mushrooms. Salads were removed. Water was replenished and coffee poured. The professor pointed out two other people whom Mary Clare had known casually: a teacher of biology at UCLA and a medical doctor from Boston, both at other tables. Neither she nor the professor knew the diners at their own table, who by now were deep in a political discussion.

The conversation droned on and on. Speeches were given. Nicole and the professor ate their meal silently, neither one of them in a social mood. A blanket of depression settled in, as heavy as the blanket of white roses that had covered the casket holding Mary Clare.

The after-dinner party was at Rorrman's house, a large estate on the beach at the north end of Malibu. Cars were lined up along the highway, waiting to pass through a wrought-iron gate. Inside the lush grounds red-coated valets hustled to move everyone along as quickly as possible.

"Nice car," a young blond surfer-type said as he held the door for her. "Fifty-eight, fifty-nine?"

"Eight," the professor answered, smiling. He patted the hood of the pale-blue Thunderbird convertible. "You will take care of her, won't you?" He slipped the valet a bill.

"You bet, Pops."

The kid slid behind the wheel. He rubbed a hand lovingly over the dash and turned up the radio. Fifties music floated from a preset station, drifting across the night air. "Cool! This is *so cool!*"

The professor smiled again as horns blew behind the kid, who nudged the gas pedal gently while signaling a universal message with his left hand.

"Eleanor and I had good times in that car," the professor said wistfully.

Nicole tucked her hand into the crook of his arm. "Do you always pay the valet something extra to park it carefully?"

"Dear little Nikki, I don't usually attend parties with valets. But there must be a hundred cars here tonight. It seemed the propitious thing to do."

They melted into the crowd along the drive, and then up steps into the modern white stucco-and-glass mansion. Invitations were checked, and Nicole showed Mary Clare's, which allowed a guest.

A huge central hall was already crowded. Doctors from all over the world had been invited—an opportunity for the host to push his latest products, the new "miracle" drugs whose major miracle was to line the coffers of Century Pharmaceuticals.

"Excuse me a moment, Nikki. I must use the facilities."

She gave her friend's arm a pat. "Go ahead. I'll mingle while you're gone."

The professor made his way slowly up broad stairs to a second floor. Nicole watched for a moment, thinking that his steps were heavy and slightly faltering. *He's not well. Not at all well.*

Sighing, she turned back to the crowded hall. People were coming out of rooms on either side with full drinks, so it seemed there must be a bar in each. She nudged her way into the room on the right, needing caffeine. Her feet hurt in the high-heeled shoes, and her energy was flagging.

She really did not want to be doing this. Even under the best of circumstances, she hated parties—hated the inane conversation and artificial peppiness they required. And what had she expected to learn, here, in this crowd?

Well, people do gossip at parties, she reminded herself. And people here had known Mary. They might drink, slip, talk.

Talk about what? Not Dan. Nicole was clear enough now to know that any answers about Dan's relationship with Mary would have to come from him. If she hadn't asked the questions yet, it was either because she wasn't sure she could trust his answers—or because she didn't want to hear them.

The bar was against a far wall, with a line of about eight people. She joined them. After a moment a man behind her spoke.

"Is this your first Century party?"

She turned, looking up into friendly gray eyes. The angular face seemed familiar. "Yes. Do I know you from somewhere?"

"Our eyes met at dinner." The man grinned.

She remembered then. He had flirted a little, while she was adjusting her neckline and hair. Automatically, one hand went to the neckline again. His eyes followed, and the grin grew wider as she discovered her dress had shifted even lower than before. She looked away, flustered.

The line moved on.

"Is this your first party here?" she asked, turning back finally to break the awkward silence.

The man shook his head. "I'm afraid not. I'm in mergers and acquisitions at Century. When Rorrman beckons, we're expected to show."

"I don't much like parties," she admitted.

"I'd rather chew on my ear."

They both laughed.

"Are you from around here?"

She shook her head. "Georgetown."

"A doctor?"

"No. I teach at the university."

"Really. I'm impressed. What do you teach?"

"Mythology. I also give a class every summer in pre-Colombian religions."

He narrowed his eyes thoughtfully. "Mythology. Let's see now, I seem to remember seeing a movie one Saturday when I was a kid, about Perseus. . . ." He wrinkled his forehead. "Ah, yes. His mother was locked up in a room of stone by her grandfather—who was afraid he'd be killed by her firstborn. But as I remember, Zeus, who was in love with the mother, wasn't about to let something as pedestrian as a lock get between him and the object of his desire. He came down through the roof and fell into her lap in a shower of gold. From that, Perseus was born."

Nicole smiled. "Sounds pretty Hollywood, but actually not far off."

"To be honest, for the longest time I thought that was how it was done—babies, that is. With a shower of gold. It sure messed up my love life."

She couldn't help laughing. "Did your movie show that after Perseus was born, the grandfather put him and his mother into a wooden box and hurled it into the sea?"

"No! Poor Perseus!"

"And that was only the beginning. Zeus saved them, and they floated to the Isle of Seriphos, where all was roses until the king of Seriphos fell in love with Danae—the mother—and sent Perseus off so he wouldn't be in the way."

"Wait a minute, now I remember." His eyes lit up. "He was ordered to bring back the head of Medusa."

"Which, after much travail, he did—picking up winged sandals and a helmet along the way."

The man's mouth turned down in a mock expression of sorrow. "I always wished I had winged sandals. I felt positively deprived in childhood without them."

Nicole laughed again. The sound was odd to her ears, and she realized that this was the first time she had felt her spirits lift in a week.

Finally, she was standing at the bar. "Coffee, please. Straight."

While the bartender poured into a tall, footed glass, she looked sideways at the man with brown hair, who was now standing beside her. She liked his eyes. They crinkled up in the corners when he smiled.

"Are you here alone?" he asked.

"No, with a friend."

A groan. "Isn't that always the way?"

She took the cup of hot coffee. "Maybe we'll run into each other later."

"Count on it."

She smiled as she turned away.

Chapter 14

There were too many people wearing too much perfume and carrying too many sloshing drinks. She couldn't find the professor anywhere in the crowd. Nicole spied a door and escaped to an empty terrace overlooking the beach. The tide was in, and the waves were lapping less than thirty feet away. She stood at the rail, a fine mist dampening her face.

From inside came the strains of a small orchestra playing society music. "Strangers on the Shore." In the center of the terrace was a fire pit with lava rocks. Deck chairs circled it, and she flopped into one, dropping her small white purse and kicking off her shoes. She rested bare feet on the cool round hearth of the pit.

There are thousands of mansions like this around L.A., she thought. *Who are these people? Where do they get their money?*

In a time when the country's population was tightening its collective belts, it seemed odd that so many got by unscathed. Or maybe they only seemed unscathed. Maybe they were dodging bill collectors every month the same as everyone else—and just knew how to hide it better.

Mary Clare had wanted to help people who couldn't afford medical care. She had had so many dreams in that direction. "You wouldn't believe the markup in medicines!" she had ranted naively but passionately, in her freshman year at Georgetown. "It's a sin—a disgrace that there are actually pills that can make people better, but they're too expensive for any sick person without insurance to buy. And what kind of age do we live in, that doctors and hospitals with the skill to do life-saving surgery can actually let a child die because its parents don't have insurance?"

Nicole, whose own work spanned the ages, knew that greed was the one constant. *You'll learn, little sister,* she wanted to say.

But she kept the warning to herself. Part of her—a long-buried part that still wanted to believe—was hoping that her zealous little sister might actually find a way to change things.

"I saw you come out here," a voice said from beside her. "Do you mind?"

The man from the bar was drawing up a chair. She hesitated only a moment. "No, go ahead. I don't mind."

He stretched his legs out next to hers. "Your feet hurt?"

She rubbed one stockinged foot against another. "It's been a long day."

"Where's your friend?"

"I don't know, I guess I've lost him for now. It's so damned crowded in there."

"And hot."

"Not to mention . . ." She searched for just the right word.

"Ambitious?" he supplied.

"Yes. Everyone is working everyone else."

"There's big money to be made. And times are tough. One has to work harder."

"But I would think that pharmaceutical companies were recession proof. The rich get as sick as the poor, and they have the cash to buy."

"The only more recession-proof business," the man agreed amiably, "is toilet paper."

She looked at him, raising a brow. "Toilet paper?"

"You bet. I was offered a great position with Kimberly-Clark several years ago. Big bucks, a corner office, job security. After all, it's the one product that everyone, even the poor, have to buy."

"I never thought of it that way. But you didn't take the job? Why?"

"Have you ever been to a sales meeting—or an advertising meeting—for toilet paper? It's hilarious. Imagine it."

She shook her head, smiling. "I can't."

"No, go on—get a picture. Say you're the CEO. You're seated at a long mahogany table in an upscale office in Manhattan, with a bunch of other stuffy three-piece suits. They've all got these wire-rimmed glasses, like Utah ministers—and they all make six figures a year. They look intelligent and relatively sober, but they're spending their days—incredibly—listening to an ad man enthuse about putting in more softness and less scent, so the average American housewife won't get a rash. Of course, no one uses the term "rash," because it's much too graphic. They use long, careful euphemisms like"—his voice lowered, taking on a somber tone—" 'dermatological reaction.' "

She laughed. "Well, somebody has to do it."

"Not me. I could just see myself meeting a woman I liked and having to explain what I did for a living." He smiled. "By the way, what's your name?"

"Nicole. What's yours?"

"Jack. Jack Blake." He extended his hand. "Nice to meet you, Nicole."

"You too."

But when he didn't release her hand right away, she felt suddenly shy. "I guess I should go in. I have to find my friend."

"Is your friend in medicine?"

"In a way. He teaches medical history."

"Will you be coming with him to the conference tomorrow?"

"I don't really plan to."

"Hmmm. So I probably won't see you again."

Her shrug was softened by a smile. "I guess not."

He gave her a grin. "Unless, of course, we make specific plans. What about dinner? May I call you?"

She hadn't meant to lead him on—only to be friendly. "I'm sorry, I don't think I'll have time."

She stood, and he did too.

"I understand. You don't know me. I could be Jack the Ripper—or even a trailside killer."

"It's not that," she assured him quickly. "It's just that the timing is bad. For me. I hope you do understand."

"Of course." He offered his hand again. "Maybe another time."

She met his eyes, relieved that he wasn't pushing. But behind his smile she saw concern.

"Look," he said, "I could tell right away that something was wrong. You don't have to talk about it, but if you feel you'd like a friend, someone to show you around while you're out here . . . Let me give you my card." He reached into his shirt pocket, handing her two. "In fact, if you'll write your number down, I'll call you tomorrow. No pressure—you can always say no."

It occurred to her that she could use Dan, or his answer machine, as a buffer—a way to avoid this man's call. It would be easier than digging in her heels right now.

She took the pen he offered and wrote Dan's number on the back of one of his cards. "I'm staying with someone. You can leave a message if I'm not there."

She put the other card in her purse and slipped into her shoes again.

"I'll walk you back in," he offered.

"No, that's okay. Stay here. Enjoy the view."

"I intend to," he promised, assessing her slim, long legs as she turned to walk away.

A blush heated her cheeks. But Jack Blake was so whimsical, so boy-next-door, she had to laugh, shaking her auburn hair and feeling her limbs go a bit soft at the thought of his eyes on her, all the way to the door.

Chapter 15

Nicole observed the party scene, feeling bone-tired. Flat.

Mary had hated these affairs as much as she. "I have to do them," she had said, "when I'm going after funding. It's politic. Otherwise, they're an utter waste of time."

Nicole agreed.

She looked around for the professor and found him at a long table of food, piling his plate high with slices of turkey and bite-sized rolls.

Her smile was weary, barely there. "Have you seen that woman you pointed out at the dinner? Ilsen, I think you said her name was."

"Harriet, yes. She was here a moment ago, and I looked for you—" He peered into her face. "Are you all right?"

"I guess. Tired. I'd like to talk to this woman, and then I wondered if we might go on home. I'm somehow not as crazy about this idea as I was."

He set his plate down and put a hand on her arm. "It's much too soon, you know. You should be at home, hiding under the covers until the shock wears off."

Blinking furiously, she looked away. "I've been hiding under covers all my life, Professor. Maybe if I'd asked more questions earlier— Look, you said Harriet Ilsen was here?"

He glanced about the room. "Yes. She was talking to . . . ah, there she is now. But, Nikki—"

"Introduce me, will you? Let's get on with this."

Still shaking his head worriedly, the professor steered Nicole toward the woman, who had just come through the door from the hall. As they approached, she glanced their way and walked toward them with a smile. The professor stretched out an arm and drew her to his side.

"Harriet, I'd like you to meet Nicole Ryan. Mary Clare was her sister."

The woman's smile faded. She took Nicole's hand in both of hers. "My dear, I was so sorry to hear about Mary. What a terrible shock."

"Thank you."

"I talked with her just a little over a week ago. If I had thought for a moment . . ." She gave a delicate shiver and dropped Nicole's hands, hugging herself. "Who could have known, with someone so young?"

Ilsen motioned to a young man who was now circling the room with a tray of drinks. When the tray arrived, she lifted a glass of red wine and downed half in two gulps. "Sorry. It's medicinal—anesthesia for the brain." She closed her eyes a moment. "God, I hate these parties."

"You knew my sister well?" Nicole asked.

"We saw each other every time she came out here. And of course, we talked on the telephone."

"Were you and Mary close? Did she confide in you?"

Ilsen's thick glasses reflected light as she hesitated. "About her work, you mean?"

"That, or anything."

The woman glanced sharply from Nicole to Professor Dirstoff, then back again. "Why? Is something wrong?"

"I just wondered if there was something she didn't tell me about, anything that might explain why she was out so late that night. Whether she was upset, or meeting someone, or . . ." Nicole stopped and steadied her voice. She realized she was saying too much, too fast. "I guess I just thought you might know something, as her friend. That's probably stupid. I'm sorry."

They were interrupted by a waiter offering hot canapés. After a distracted, "No, thank you," Ilsen turned back to Nicole. "Not at all," she said gently. "We always want an explanation when something so tragic and unexpected happens. It's part of the grieving. But aside from that, I have to admit, I also wondered what Mary was doing out on the road so late. She told me more than once that she hardly went anywhere at night, that she virtually lived in the hospital lab or her cottage."

"Yes."

"Well, as I said, she called me a little over a week ago. We didn't talk long. She seemed in a hurry."

"Did she call for any particular reason? Was she worried, about her work, or something personal?"

"She said she was sending me something for safekeeping and that she had to run. That was about it."

"Something for safekeeping . . . did she say what?"

"No, and I haven't received it, so either the mail is late, or I have to assume she changed her mind."

"You didn't think it was strange that Mary would do something like that?"

They shifted as people jostled them, passing by. The party crowd was growing thicker.

"Not a bit," Harriet said. "The thing about research scientists—myself and Mary included—is that we're innately paranoid about our work. Mary often sent me copies of her articles for safekeeping, once she'd mailed them out to a journal. There were certain things she didn't like leaving around the lab, available to prying eyes."

"She was afraid her findings would be stolen?"

"It happens all the time, I'm afraid."

"But she knew they would be safe with you?"

Harriet smiled. "I have a vault the size of a 7-Eleven in my office in Long Beach. And I'm the only one with a key to it."

"Professor Dirstoff said that you're head of the immunology department at a university near here."

"Yes. Branston, in Long Beach."

"And you're on the board of Century?"

"Yes." Ilsen broke off. "Nicole—may I call you that? Why don't you tell me why you're asking all these questions?"

There was a sound from the professor. "Tactful as ever, Harriet."

"Be quiet, Henry. There's obviously something wrong. And why did you even bring this poor young woman here tonight? She looks ready to implode. Forgive me, my dear."

"It was my idea," Nicole said quickly. "You said yourself, it's part of the grieving. There are things I need to know."

"Of course, you're right. I just wish I could be of more help."

"I've been wondering about Sister Paula, Mary's supervisor at the hospital. She seemed unusually hostile the other day. Did Mary ever talk to you about her?"

Ilsen shuddered. "Please, don't get me started on Paula. That woman is vile. Reminds me of any number of miserable, frustrated nuns I had in grade school forty years ago."

"You know Sister Paula?"

"I've had dealings with her. Part of my job on Century's board is to help allocate funding to various medical facilities around the world. As administrator of Sacred Heart Hospital, Paula always—and I mean *always*—complains that Sacred Heart is getting less money than Century's other interests. You'd think that in these days of tight money, she'd shut up and take what she can get."

Nicole looked surprised at her bluntness, and Harriet Ilsen chuckled. "It's also part of my job to be mean about these things."

"How is funding decided? I've always wondered."

"It's more than choosing straws, believe me. First I have to see that the hospital or clinic we're supporting is doing its job. Then I have to make sure it's doing it well. If there's even the slightest hint that monies are not being spent frugally, or intelligently, we go in and audit. Sometimes the problem is simple incompetence. Sometimes it's more."

"And if it's more?"

"The funding is cut off immediately."

"How many times does that happen?"

"In a given year?" Ilsen grimaced. "You don't really want to know."

"Has it happened with Sacred Heart?"

"Never. Sometimes I wish it would—then I could get Sister Paula off my back."

A new voice spoke. "What's this—ranting and raving about the good Sister again?"

They all turned to their host, John Rorrman, who was balancing a drink on a plate heaped high with hors d'oeuvres. He popped a small yellow square of cheese into his mouth and chewed.

"I just wish she'd become a Carmelite or something," Ilsen snapped. "Keep her in the gardens hoeing turnips all day."

"Harriet, Harriet. One would think you didn't like your job."

On the surface it seemed only an offhand, teasing remark. Yet Harriet Ilsen's eyes turned hard and she glanced away. There was an awkward moment before Rorrman turned to Nicole.

"Have I met you?"

She held out her hand. "No. I'm Nicole Ryan."

"Ryan . . ." Rorrman looked upward, as if searching through an index file in his brain.

"Mary Clare Ryan's sister."

The chairman's sharp gaze immediately shifted to sympathetic. "Of course. What a terrible tragedy. I'm so sorry."

"Thank you. Did you know my sister?"

"Not personally, I'm afraid. I did know of her work. She was very bright, I understand, and so young." He shook his head. "A tragic waste."

Nicole was mesmerized by the saliva that hung from his teeth in cheesy strings as he spoke. She was also stunned by the lie. She glanced at the professor. His return look said that he had noted it too. *I saw him coming out of her room,* the professor had said earlier. *Mary Clare was embarrassed. She didn't want to talk about it.*

That was last spring.

"Mary Clare was *brilliant,*" Ilsen said, emphasizing the word. "The research field has suffered a terrible loss."

Rorrman gave her a cold stare. "Brilliant perhaps, but naive. A bit idealistic." He turned to Nicole. "Forgive me, Ms. Ryan, but most successful scientists believe in teamwork. A controlled environment. Your sister was a bit of a witch doctor in the way she operated. Oh, excuse me, will you? I see someone I have to talk to." He drifted off, with a jovial nod to both the professor and Nicole.

"Witch doctor, indeed!" Harriet Ilsen muttered. "It's these pharmaceutical labs one has to watch out for, with their test tubes and five-times-removed 'cures' that make people sicker than they ever were. The real cures are already there, if they'd only open their eyes —in the earth, the flowers, the trees. The cures have always been there in a pure, unadulterated, harmless state—"

She stopped for a breath, her face reddening. "Sorry."

Nicole smiled. "Don't be. You sound like Mary Clare. But if you don't mind my saying so, not much like a board member for a pharmaceutical company."

Ilsen pushed her heavy glasses up on her nose. "Oh, don't get me started on that, either. The position was handed down by my father. I never wanted it. But now that I've got it, I do my best to be a balance wheel."

"You do an excellent job, Harriet," the professor assured her, patting her thin back.

"Do I? Sometimes I wonder. Am I a David—or merely an irritating flea on the hide of Goliath?"

The professor eyed John Rorrman, now relentlessly working the opposite side of the room. "I suspect that for this particular Goliath, you carry a quite menacing sling."

"Do you have any time to spare in the next couple of days?" Nicole asked her. "Could we talk some more?"

"Of course. Most of us attending the conference are staying at the Ritz. I'll either be there or at the corporate house in Palos Verdes over the next few days."

Ilsen took out a business card and wrote a number on the back of it. "Why don't you call me and we'll work out a time?"

"I will. Thanks."

She had lost the professor again. An old colleague had stopped him to talk, and Nicole had continued on into the huge hall, toward the front door. But the hall was packed. Something was going on at the far end, near the door. As people jolted her on all sides, she couldn't move in any direction. Wanting only to get out, she stretched her neck to see what the holdup was.

A young woman stood on a table, her blond hair swaying in a circle of light as she twisted her hips to the tune of "Diamonds Are a Girl's Best Friend." She wore a strapless red dress and long-sleeved red gloves, with a huge diamond ring on one finger. Dark-red color outlined her lips. Spiked red heels glittered with rhinestones. She was doing a parody of Marilyn Monroe.

At Nicole's left elbow stood Garrick Hale, the senator from Michigan who had recently announced his intention to run for the presidency in the next election. His image in the news was somewhat austere. Here, however, he was watching the singer, a drink slopping over one hand as he swayed to the rhythm of the music. As the singer finished, someone who had been introduced as a bank president from Oklahoma City climbed onto the table beside her. Short and overweight, he grabbed the woman before she could get away and slung her awkwardly onto his shoulder. He paused a moment with a drunken, puzzled expression as he realized he wasn't in strong enough shape to hoist them both down from the table at once. The crowd went wild.

The seduction of Hollywood, Nicole thought with a disgust born of depression. *Take almost anyone, plop them down in a party out here, and they forget who they are.*

Especially politicians. Politicians, financiers, and insurance men —always the big surprise, given the staid, responsible image they liked to portray. Underneath were salesman personalities, wanting to be liked. *I can be anything you want me to be. Just buy my line.* It seemed that politics and medicine went hand in glove. There were congressmen here, lobbyists, a governor of another state.

People drifted to a side table with brass coffee urns, and Garrick Hale worked the crowd as surely as had the blond singer. Nicole heard his voice, but couldn't see him through the crush of bodies.

"We have to increase funding for cancer research. We need a cure. Not tomorrow, but yesterday. Mothers, grandmothers, fathers, children—too many are dying from this disease that has existed for *generations.* I, for one, will exhaust every effort to increase appropriations in the next budget meeting on Capitol Hill."

John Rorrman stood listening to the senator, beaming. More public funding meant more available research money for Century labs.

The hall thinned out, and Nicole moved on, exhausted. She wished now that she had insisted on bringing separate cars. Dan's house was just down the highway from here, but as it was, she would have to go all the way to Pasadena and back.

As she waited for the professor, people she had been introduced to earlier stopped to express their sympathies a second time. Over and over Nicole heard the same words: *I didn't know your sister well, but I heard she was exceptional. Such a waste.*

One woman, a short, red-haired, motherly type who was married to a doctor, said that she had seen Mary Clare from a distance the previous spring. "She was at the King Harbor Marina with her friend, that film director—what was his name? Dan something or other, I believe. We didn't get to talk."

The King Harbor Marina, Nicole remembered, was in Redondo Beach. She and Dan had walked along there in April, the day they'd gone touring. Now it seemed he and Mary had been there together, too. Without her. She hadn't known that.

My God. My head was so in the clouds.

More weary than ever, she drifted back through the main hall in search of the professor. John Rorrman was just ahead of her, with Garrick Hale. They disappeared behind a door that had been locked earlier. "Rorrman's study," Harriet Ilsen had told her. "It's where he conducts ninety-eight percent of his business. He woos VIPs out here, wines and dines them, treats them to long sunny days by the pool . . . rents them women, of course. And when they're sufficiently off guard—whammo, they land in the arena with the king of the pride."

So . . . , Nicole thought cynically as she passed the closed door. *Let the games begin.*

Chapter 16

Driving home later along Pacific Coast Highway, it was difficult to find Dan's house. Headlights behind her were blinding. Nicole tilted the rearview mirror to shine them away from her eyes. Whoever it was shouldn't be tailgating, shouldn't have his brights on. Damn, he was almost on her bumper. She accelerated. The other car did too. If it came any closer—

She began to sweat. Jerking the wheel, she pulled abruptly into the next driveway on her right. In her rearview mirror she watched the other car—unsure why she was so afraid.

The car passed her and sped on.

She gripped the wheel, leaning her head on her hands. *Probably a drunk. What do you expect—it's after two A.M. on a Friday night.*

She looked at her reflection in the mirror. Too pale. Too strained. *Maybe Harriet is right. I am about to crack.*

By the time she arrived at Dan's house, she was shaking. She used the garage-door opener he had given her and pulled in, noting that he wasn't home yet. She parked, climbed out, and leaned against the rental car a moment, steadying herself. Then, closing the garage door, she hurried down the stairs.

There were small, soft lights lining the flagstone walk, although Dan's house was dark. She let herself into the cottage and flicked the switch by the door.

And froze.

Something is wrong.

Nicole stood motionless, like a deer on a scent. *Someone's been in here.*

For a moment she thought she was being paranoid—still nervous from the incident on the road. But then she knew what it was.

The sofa had been moved.

It stood slightly crooked against the wall. Taking a few steps closer, Nicole looked down at the rug to make sure she wasn't imagining things. No—there was an imprint where the left leg of the sofa had been a few inches to the left.

She suddenly realized how dark and lonely it was on this hill, with the closest house at least a block away. As a child she had always been afraid of the dark. She kept a night-light on in the hallway at home even now, just bright enough to light the door to her bedroom —in case anyone should be standing there in the night. It was an irrational but very real fear. That, and open closet doors.

Her eyes flew to the closet. The door stood ajar. The back of her neck prickled. Had she left it that way?

She dropped her purse and crossed the room. Taking the closet door in a firm grip, she yanked it open.

Empty.

Except for the few clothes she'd hung, it was totally empty.

Only then did she realize she was holding her breath. *Holy God. What would I have done?*

She closed the door and leaned heavily against it.

You're getting crazy, Nicole. Dan was here, that's all. He was looking for something he'd left over here.

Her eyes flicked to the dresser. She crossed over to it, uneasy. Pulling out the bottom drawer, she reached toward the back for a pair of white socks. She unrolled them.

Inside one sock was the photo of Dan and Mary Clare—right where she had put it when she packed her bags at the Ocean Palms. It was apparently untouched.

She sat on the sofa, thinking.

Then—for no reason she could possibly explain—she stood and lifted one end of the sofa, moving it out from the wall. It was incredibly heavy. An effort. She went to the other end and moved it out too.

Nothing. Either here, or along the wall.

Exhausted, she moved the sofa back. *Christ, Nicole, this is crazy. Get to bed.* She removed cushions and grasped the loops to pull out the bed. But the mechanism was stuck. The bed unfolded only partway. She pulled harder; it wouldn't give.

Damn it all, now what?

She reached down with one hand, between the springs and the arm of the sofa. Something was lodged there. It was keeping the metal hinges from unfolding.

More weary now than curious, wanting only to sleep, she pulled the mattress off so she could look through the springs.

A box. A black box.

She got her fingers around it, but it was wedged in tight. She pushed at it, hoping to knock it through to the floor.

No go.

She looked around the room. Propped beside the fireplace was a poker. Using it as a crowbar, she wedged the pointed end under a corner of the box. Leaning with all her weight, she pushed. The box popped from its tight cranny and fell to the floor. Nicole got down on her knees and reached under the sofa, pulling it out.

The black box was covered with a fine layer of dust. On its lid was embossed a small silver cross.

She recognized it now. Mary—who attended Mass wherever she was—had used it to hold her missal when she traveled. Nicole had seen it often throughout the years.

There was no lock, only a thin black cord that twisted around a cloth-covered silver button. She blew softly at the dust, then un-wound the cord and opened the box. Inside was a book, hardbound and slim. *The Maya Question.*

Nicole held it, remembering. She had taken it off her own book-shelf and given it to Mary last winter. Mary had specifically asked for it. "If you're not using it now, I'd like to read up on the Maya."

"Keep it," Nicole had said. "I have others I'm reading now."

Teaching about the Maya, the peoples who had disappeared mys-teriously from the central Mexico valley, was at the core of her summer course each year. What had happened to them was unclear still. Was their land exhausted? Their environment destroyed? There were many theories, but no certain explanations.

She had found *The Maya Question* in a used bookstore years ago and lent it to Dan briefly last year. He had been deep into a docu-mentary about the Maya; not his usual diatribe against Big Busi-ness, but a labor of love. Nicole had helped him with research—at first because she loved doing research, and then because she loved doing things for him.

The Maya Question delved into the history of the Aztecs, as well, linking their history with that of the Maya—comparing values and cultures. Dan's imagination was caught by one particularly graphic tale. Deciding that his film would be incomplete without it, he had borrowed the book, then hired an artist to read it and paint equally

graphic scenes. She remembered that she had underlined the passage for him. Flipping through, she found it.

> *The Aztecs were one of the most feared peoples ever to walk*
> *the land. They were brilliant in the arts, science, and sculpture,*
> *but their bloodletting was massive. On one horrible dark day*
> *they ripped out ten thousand hearts in the temple. They believed*
> *that this would bring them oneness with the Universe, and that*
> *oneness with the Universe was more important than individual*
> *human life.*

The artist's rendition for film had been frightening. Come to think
of it, the story had always been strong. Perhaps she could put it to
good use again.

Nicole fingered the book curiously. What was it doing here? Dan
had given it back to her long ago, and then she had given it to Mary.
And it was Dan, not Mary, who had stayed here in his friend's cottage last April—

Unless.

Had Dan and Mary been here together? All the while she herself
had been staying with the professor, thinking Dan was here and
Mary at a hotel—was Mary really here, sleeping with a man she
knew her sister loved?

Nicole's face flamed. She held both hands to her cheeks, willing
herself not to lose control.

She didn't hear Dan knock. Didn't even know he was there, until
he spoke.

"Nikki? Are you all right?"

She started, her hands jerking down from her face. "I—"

For a brief moment she thought of hiding the book. She didn't
know why.

"What are you doing up so late? I saw the light."

"I've been reading."

He came closer, his face pale, eyes strained. "Anything good?"

She showed it to him.

"The Maya Question. I remember that. I borrowed it from you
once."

"I found it under the sofa. In this." She lifted the black box with the silver cross. "Do you know how it might have gotten here?"

He looked disconcerted. "I guess . . . that's Mary Clare's, isn't it?"

"Yes."

He was silent.

"It was wedged down in the springs," she said, watching his eyes. "And it was covered with dust. It must have been there awhile."

"Maybe when Mary was out here last spring . . ."

"When we all came out together?"

"Yes."

"Was Mary . . . was she staying here with you?"

He frowned. "Of course not. You know that, Nikki. Mary stayed at a hotel."

"But she did visit you here."

"Several times. She was helping me on a film project, and we met here to talk about it."

"I guess I didn't know that."

"Well, if I remember, you were off at the beach a lot. We'd have asked you to join us . . ." His smile was too strained to be real. "Did Mary . . . did she ever mention this book to you? That she'd left it here, I mean."

"No. She never mentioned it."

"May I see?"

She handed it to him. He flipped through pages.

"Are you looking for anything special, Dan?"

A shallow laugh. "No. Just remembering. It was fun working on that Mayan project together, wasn't it?" He placed it back in her hands.

For a long moment she simply looked at him. Then she stood and walked to the window, gazing out at the light now on in Dan's study.

"Dan . . . did you love Mary Clare?"

She turned back in time to see his surprise.

"I—of course I did. Mary was a good person. Everyone loved her."

"That's not what I meant."

The mask she had seen earlier fell into place. "What are you getting at?"

"Oh, I'm just thinking that I was fighting a losing battle all along."
He shook his head, seeming both bewildered and irritated.

"When I first met you," she said, "when we started going every-where together, spending time together, I thought you were some-one who would want to explore . . . to see just how far we might go together."

His chin went up a fraction, a gesture she knew as half arrogance, half self-defense. "You never let me get that close to you, Nikki. There was always a wall."

"The wall was yours! You never gave me permission to breach it."

He stiffened, his eyes growing even more distant. "Didn't I? Well, maybe it was both of us. Maybe we both had walls, and maybe we were each other's comfort zone."

You were never a comfort zone for me, she thought.

The dream came again: the bedroom door opening, the shaft of light, the figure standing there. Trying to scream, and finding herself mute.

She woke in a huddled ball, shivering, and thought that she always had been more mute than verbal. Seldom fought for herself, for the things she needed from a relationship.

Hanging out with Dan—needing more than he was willing to give—had been like hanging out with a rock. Why had she carried on with it so long?

And why had he?

Because he was right, she thought. *I had my walls, too. And he felt safe with that.*

Just as he'd felt safe with Mary. Because surely Mary was inac-cessible. As young and inexperienced as she was, Nicole could see her falling in love briefly, even passionately—but never really shar-ing her life with a man. Never getting married and having a family. She was too devoted to her work, too much a loner for that.

We find the people we need to grow, she remembered reading once.

God help us, though, if they eat us alive before we're done.

Chapter 17

The next morning Dan appeared at her door early with a tray of orange juice, eggs, and Belgian waffles. In a tiny white pitcher were three buttery marigolds.

He grinned, setting the tray on her still-open bed. "Like old times, huh? I even went out to the newsstand and got a *Washington Post* and a *New York Times.*"

She pulled her white silk wrap together, tying the belt. Not giving him anything—even energy. Holding herself apart.

She walked to the open Dutch door. The sea stretched out beyond patio, house, and cliff, sparkling like a bowlful of aquamarines. A pale, sandy beach was already dotted with surfers and early sun worshipers.

A spicy scent of marigolds from the garden drifted over soft, warm air.

"Marigolds," she said, almost to herself. "They remind me of home, and our garden in Boston."

He stood beside her, his tone sadly reminiscent. "Mary Clare planted those one day when she was here last spring. She came from a meeting at Century, loaded down with them. She said she saw them at a nursery along the road and couldn't resist. She felt there should be something yellow against all that scarlet bougainvillaea." He smiled. "It's funny—she said they'd only bloom through the summer, but here they are, still going strong."

Nicole's strained expression stopped him.

"Sorry."

She turned away from the door, heading purposefully toward the closet. "I don't have time for breakfast. There are some things I have to do."

She took out a blouse and looked for jeans.

He stopped her, taking the blouse from her hand and tossing it over a chair. "Absolutely not. What you need is a day off, with nothing to do but relax. Besides, it's going to be over a hundred today. I say we go to the beach. We'll take a radio down and tune it to some nice mellow jazz. And"—he gave her a winning smile—"we'll take iced tea and peanut-butter sandwiches."

During the year they had spent together, they had gone to Ocean City several times when Georgetown got too hot. Iced tea and pea-nut-butter sandwiches were a craving they had shared.

"Don't do this," she said in a low voice. *Don't take us back to that time.*

He smiled patiently, pushing back her hair. "I just want you to relax awhile, Nikki. I'd like to see that haunted look disappear."

Surfers skimmed the waves, their coppery, hard bodies displaying a skill that matched any Olympic gymnast. In rhythm to their grace, the voice of Etta James poured forth from the portable radio, slow and bluesy. "It's a cool world . . ."

Nicole lay faceup on a blanket, her eyes closed behind sunglasses. *What am I doing here? I have no inner strength, no power to defend myself against him—even now.* Tears formed in her eyes. *It's been three months. Three long months. How long does it take?*

Yet it did feel good to be a blot on the sand for a while, no more than a speck in the universe. Not someone who had to deal with things, figure out puzzles, unearth answers that could only bring pain.

She adjusted the straps on the bikini swimsuit Dan had found in a back closet of his house. "The friend I sublet from had girls here all the time," he'd said, grinning because he was getting his way and feeling good about it. "I knew I'd find a suit around some-where."

She turned her head now to look at him. He too was stretched out, his eyes closed behind Ray-Bans. Her eyes drifted down, across the bare chest. A mat of fine, nearly golden hairs glistened with sweat. She remembered that she had seldom seen Dan without a shirt. In Georgetown he had thought he was too pale, too thin, to be attrac-tive, so he covered up. No longer pale, he was even thickening a bit around the middle.

"Did you know that I always found you very handsome?" she said, surprising herself.

He raised his head and opened his eyes. "No." He smiled. "Did you?"

"Yes." She rested her head back and closed her eyes. "I still do."

Now, why did I say that?

Maybe because life is too short. Too short, now, not to say the things you feel. If I'd been more open with Mary, even about the little things, more interested in what was going on . . .

And there's nothing to lose anymore. Dan is already gone. I don't have to worry about being too intense and chasing him away.

"I've missed you," he said. "Did I tell you that?"

Surprised again, she stared at the translucent sky. "Yes. But there must be plenty of . . . people . . . to hang out with here."

"No one like you. No one I have as much fun with, or can confide in the way I always did with you."

"We used to talk about everything," she agreed. *Almost.*

"Yes."

"I miss it too."

He took off the glasses and squinted at a passing blimp. It was followed by a plane dragging a sign: Bacardi Rum . . . For Your Finest Hour. Several yards away a woman in a scant bikini lay facedown on a blanket. A small cassette player beside her played meditative New Age music. The woman's fingers dragged lazily through the hot sand.

"You know," Dan said, "when I was a teenager, say fifteen or so, I was too busy for friends. There wasn't anyone to confide in. The peace movement was in full swing, and I had this camera—a home-movie camera, not video then. We lived out in the boonies of River-side on a farm, and I'd take a bus to wherever something was hap-pening around L.A. I'd go as far north as Ventura and as far south as Long Beach. Sometimes I'd camp out, be gone for days. I gave my mom one hell of a time."

"You've never talked about her much." Hardly at all, in fact.

"She was okay. A good woman. But she didn't much like what I was doing. She said I should be in school learning something that would get me a good job after graduation. 'There are already too many moviemakers in L.A.,' she'd say. I didn't listen, of course. I was too crazy for the feel of that camera in my hands. I'd shoot whatever was happening—sit-ins, peace marches—sometimes I'd get shots of people I knew, bleeding from their temples in the streets. Later I'd get the film processed and then sit and watch it in my room at night, over and over. Study it, see where I could improve it. It wasn't until later that I developed a conscience and began to see those bloody heads as belonging to real flesh-and-blood people."

She knew this about him; knew why that was. "You were keeping yourself separate," she said.

"From the trouble in the streets?"

"From something." But not the streets, she didn't think. From something he had never talked about at all.

He sat up, stretching his arm and neck muscles to ease them. He stared out to sea. "All I know is that one day I started thinking about the issues. It was like a light going on. I was watching the cops batter a young long-haired guy with their batons. He was cowering, his arms over his head, and they kept beating him, you know?" His hands worked, reflecting anger.

"I know."

"And I saw it like it had been drawn for me on a wall—the separation between government and people, the lie that government is for the people. Maybe that's the way it was supposed to be, at first . . . I don't know. Did Washington, Jefferson, and all those men who signed the Declaration of Independence—did they really believe they were establishing a kind of Utopia—a government by and for the people? Or were they just as self-serving as politicians now? Maybe they just wanted their names on a list. Some free PR."

She had forgotten how cynical he could sometimes be. Yet she couldn't help thinking he was right. Dan had a logical, reasoning way of looking at issues that would have served him just as well if he'd become a lawyer. Of course, he'd have been a public defender. She smiled.

He rubbed sand from his arm. "When I was seventeen—the summer after I graduated from high school—I hopped an old Southern Pacific up to the Central Valley. I lived in huts with the migrant workers, saw the kinds of hardships and unfair treatment they had to endure. I shot footage that summer, but never used it until this year. That's where some of my ideas came from for *The Final Battlefield,* the film I'm working on now. It begins with illegal aliens—their fight to cross the border, the risks they take—and how little has changed for them in the past twenty years. They still have to face low wages, substandard housing, unfair treatment, prejudice. And yet they keep coming. It's incredible."

"You never told me how you started out before."

He shrugged. "I guess there were too many other things to talk about. Anyway, I'm putting a twist on the migrant-worker story by relating it to today's North American worker, unemployed, having to pick up stakes and move across country to look for work. The electronic engineer slapping Egg McMuffins into a bag at a McDonald's, the CEO doing yard work, the former female boss sweeping floors." He doubled a fist and stared at it. "Do you know how long this sort of thing has been going on? How long it's been since the layoffs at the steel mills and the auto plants, when people started leaving the Midwest in droves for a better life in cities like Los Angeles and Houston? And now Houston has its unemployed, and property values are down. As for L.A., corporations are moving to Colorado, Utah, Arizona. Expenses and labor are cheaper, and they can survive—but they're leaving people out here unemployed. And all of this is happening because in government, there's too damn much fat at the top."

Nicole sat up, shaking sand from her hair. Her skin was damp with sweat, and she took one of the towels they had brought and dried it. Without thinking, she rubbed sand and sweat from Dan's back too. "Why did you ever work in investment banking if you felt like this?"

He made a sound of disgust. "Did I tell you about that? About my foray into finance?"

"Yes." Her hand slowed. "You said you'd been in it long enough to know how corrupt it was, and to get out. But from what you've just said, it sounds like you understood all that when you were barely out of school."

"Let's just say it was a family obligation. I tried it. It didn't work." He took the towel from her hand. "Here, give me that thing. I'll do you next."

She endured the gentle rubbing, trying not to show how his touch still affected her. After a minute or two, she moved away. She reached for the thermos.

"When do you finish the film you're working on now?"

"Another month if all goes well."

"Is there a problem?"

"The usual. We've gone over budget, and I need a healthy injection of funds to get us through."

She twisted the thermos cap. "You said you were out of town when Mary died."

He was silent.

"Looking for funds?"

"Something like that." His expression turned grim; the mood changed.

"Want some tea?"

"Sure."

She poured the icy liquid into ribbed plastic glasses and held one out. Sunlight struck the pink glass, shooting rose-colored circles onto the sand.

He took it, drank deeply, then dug the glass into the sand. From behind the Ray-Bans, his eyes studied her. "Why are you really here, Nikki?"

"I told you, I'm here to rest. To get away from the cold. Try to forget."

"Then why are you spending time with people from the Century conference? You never knew them before. They were Mary Clare's friends."

"I'm not exactly spending time with them. I just went to a dinner and a party. I went with the professor."

"My point is, how can you forget if you're seeing these people all the time?"

She laughed. "All the time? One night."

He stared at the surfers, then at a Latino family, holding hands as they tiptoed hesitantly into the cold waves.

"I forgot to tell you. There was a message for you after breakfast. A man."

"Really? What did he say?"

"He said his name was Jack Blake. He wants you to call him back."

"Did he leave a number?"

"The Ritz-Carlton in Pasadena. Said you could leave a message at the front desk."

She lay back, closing her eyes against the brilliance of a cloudless sky.

"Nikki?"

"Yes."

"Who is this guy?"

"Jack Blake? Just someone I met last night."

"What do you know about him?"

"He works for Century. I forget what he said."

A gull soared overhead. She could hear its wings as it swooped to land on the sand nearby.

"I hope you're not getting involved with someone you hardly know."

Dan's tone was that of a father instructing a child. She turned to him, irritated. "I talked to him at a party. That's not exactly 'getting involved.'"

"Even so—you're off balance emotionally right now. And don't take this the wrong way, but you're probably still on the rebound—"

He broke off abruptly as she lifted her head, staring at him. "I can't believe you said that." She had forgotten how tactless, how thoroughly *male* he could sometimes be.

"Sorry."

They were silent a long time. A chill settled in.

"Did this guy know Mary Clare?" Dan asked finally.

"I don't think so."

"You're not sure, though."

"No. Why?"

"I just wondered."

She turned her head and watched as the muscles in his neck grew tense with her next words. "He probably couldn't have known Mary as well as you did."

His eyes met hers without a trace of warmth. "Meaning?"

"Meaning that we were all such good friends—all three of us. Weren't we, Dan?"

The Latino family came in from the surf, the kids running and giggling as their parents flopped onto a blanket and toweled themselves dry. Nicole saw this from some far edge of her vision as the ground seemed to shift and Dan looked away.

She fingered the business card. JACK LOWELL BLAKE, MERGERS AND ACQUISITIONS, CENTURY PHARMACEUTICALS, INC. A home-office address in Century City, a 310 area code number, and an 800 number.

Dan had said, however, that he could be reached at the Ritz-Carlton in Pasadena. Harriet had mentioned that conference attendees were staying there.

"You are so obstinate sometimes," she could hear Mary saying. *"Anybody tells you not to do something, you'll do it if it kills you."*

She picked up the cottage phone and dialed.

Chapter 18

"A great cottage," Jack Blake said, hands in his pockets as he looked around. "Are you renting?"

"No, I'm staying with a friend."

"Girlfriend, or guy?"

"Guy." She gave a shrug. "Not that it makes much difference."

"He's gay?"

"No."

"Blind, then."

She laughed. "You think so?"

His eyes twinkled. "Or numb."

He had brought a small bouquet of wildflowers, and she was putting them into a tall glass of dark-blue cobalt—keeping her hands busy, feeling nervous. Wondering if she'd made a mistake, agreeing to go to dinner.

"I saw those in the hotel flower shop, and they reminded me of you," Jack said.

"I love them. Thanks."

"I was surprised when you called. I kind of expected you to use the old 'I didn't get the message' dodge."

She smiled. "I thought it might be good to get out."

"So where is your friend now?"

"He stays in the main house, actually. He left a while ago."

Jack scanned a row of books on a shelf above the kitchen counter. "These are nearly all about history."

"Yes. My friend is something of a history buff."

"Hmmm. I like reading about it, but I can't remember dates unless I can relate them to other things that happened about the same time. A teacher taught me that in college. You list all the important things that happened in the 1600s, say, or the 1800s, whatever, in art, science, and music. And you find that while Columbus was discovering America, certain masterpieces were being painted, certain preludes written. It sort of brings things to life, thinking about it that way."

She poured white wine into glasses and handed him one.

"I agree." She slid onto a wicker stool at the counter. "I use the technique in my own classes, in fact. And I try to make it fun—something the kids can relate to. Did you know, for instance, that when Cortez arrived in Central America, he was taken by the Aztecs to be a returning God? Quetzalcoatl, in fact, who had risen in death to become the morning star. So they weren't too surprised when just about the same day he arrived, there was an omen in the sky. A fiery wheel turned in circles, giving off noises and sparks. It circled the walls and hovered over the temple."

"No kidding. A flying saucer, you think?" He took a stool too, swiveling so that his knees brushed hers.

"I wouldn't discard the idea out of hand. There are other stories over the centuries about just such an event. Sometimes they occur at a time in history when great change is taking place."

Jack sipped his wine. "I wonder why."

"Taking notes, maybe. Coming back now and then to see how we're doing in terms of evolution."

"Wouldn't you think they'd give up on us by now?"

Nicole relaxed, enjoying the discussion. "I must admit, I've always wondered if we're not just an eighth-grade science experiment gone wrong."

"That's a pretty depressing thought. Do you really believe it?" He took her empty glass and put it on the counter.

"That we've been abandoned to mindless chaos by a Creator who got a D and stuck us away in a closet somewhere? I never used to. Lately, though . . ." She gave a shrug.

"I see what you mean. If I built a house and rented it out, and then I saw it burning, I think I'd throw some water on it."

Nicole smiled. "Well, maybe that's what Noah's Ark was all about."

"You know, when I was a kid back in Oklahoma, I believed in a personal God who looked after his world and us. But you can't work for a company that sells medicines without knowing how much sickness there is—and you can't watch children die without wondering why whoever put us here doesn't stop the destruction, once and for all."

"I know."

Nicole fell silent, depressed suddenly. Getting up, she went around to the sink and began to wash their glasses.

"Oh, hell, I'm sorry," Jack said. "I didn't mean to get so heavy."

"That's okay." She forced herself to smile, reaching for a towel on the counter. "Tell me some more about yourself. You grew up in Oklahoma?"

"Tulsa, ma'am." He stuck his thumbs in his belt, his stomach out, and squared his jaw. "Ah grew up punchin' cows."

"No way."

"Sho' nuff way, little filly."

"You're telling me you were a cowboy?"

"That's raahht."

"Well, I don't believe it."

He grinned. "My parents had a small ranch. 'Cowboy' is a romantic term for what I did, but it works for most women."

"I'm not surprised. The Marlboro Man."

"Would you like to go to dinner now?" he asked.

"Sure. Where are we going?"

"I had in mind a little place on the other side of PCH. Augusta's. Do you know it?"

"I've seen it, but I've never eaten there."

"I think you'll like it. There's a patio. You might want to take a sweater, in case it cools off later."

Drying her hands, she crossed to the dresser, pulling one out.

"Here, let me carry that for you," he said.

"Thanks."

The old-fashioned gallantry was unexpected. And nice, for a change.

The food was California French, light and flavorful. The wine numbed her grief—a temporary but nonetheless welcome "anesthetic," as Harriet Ilsen had called it. Somewhere during dessert, Nicole looked across the candlelit patio table and said, "This is just what I needed. Thank you."

"You're very welcome. I remember you said this was a bad time for you. Do you want to talk about it?"

She hesitated, playing with her fork. It might help to talk to someone who wasn't involved, who wouldn't get emotional along with her.

She looked at Jack, debating, and saw genuine concern and a desire to help.

"My sister . . ." It was so hard to say it. She licked her dry lips, forcing them to move. "She . . . my sister died last week."

His eyes filled with sympathy. "My God, Nicole, I'm so sorry. What happened?"

"An accident."

"That's terrible. Was she young?"

"Twenty-eight."

She was gripping the fork so hard, her knuckles had turned white. Jack took it from her, set it gently on the table, and covered her hand with his. "No wonder you've seemed down. I really am sorry."

"I thought you might have heard."

"No, I don't think so. Should I have?"

"Not necessarily. But she was a research scientist at Sacred Heart Hospital in Georgetown. Century funds Sacred Heart."

"Well, Century's a huge company, with interests all over the world." He sat back, his face clearing with the look of someone who'd just put the pieces together. "I do remember something. At the office the other day, there was talk about a young research scientist. A Mary Clare something or other. But I had no idea—this was your sister?"

"Yes. Mary Clare Ryan."

He shook his head. "I just can't imagine how difficult this has been for you."

She gave a tiny shrug, picking up her water to sip it and wet her lips again.

Jack placed his napkin on the table. He signaled for the waiter. "I'll get the check, and we can get out of here. We can go for a walk, or a long drive—"

"Mary had a car accident," she heard herself blurting out. "Her car went into the river." She looked at him, her voice unsteady as her throat tightened. "I keep thinking there's something she'd want me to do, but I don't know what."

And I'm all mixed up, she wanted to say. *I don't know whether to love her or hate her now. I think she betrayed me. But I keep hearing her voice, "Help me, Nikki. Help me." And I don't know what to do.*

"You mean you think she wants you to do something about the accident? Was there another car at fault?"

"Not that we know of. The road was icy. The police say she lost control and skidded into the river."

"How awful. I remember . . ." He fell silent, rubbing his chin.

"What?"

"When I was about eight, the same thing, just about, happened to my grandfather."

"I'm sorry. Were you close to him?"

"We were like two peas in a pod, my dad always said. My granddad was the greatest guy I ever knew."

"That's a terrible age to lose someone you're close to."

"No worse than for you, losing your sister."

The check came, and they walked for a while through a small garden behind the restaurant. Nicole pretended to relax. *Act as if— as if it's okay. It will be that way.* She repeated it twice, an old mantra from childhood.

There were stone benches here and, hidden away in shrubbery, softly trickling fountains that created a sense of peace. That helped. Gradually, Jack steered the conversation away from Mary. Nicole was grateful. He was good company—intelligent, funny, and sensitive.

After driving her back to the cottage, he thanked her for having dinner with him, opening the door with her key.

"You've been very kind," Nicole said. "Would you like to come in for coffee before you go?"

"Well . . ." He checked his watch. "That's pretty tempting. But I've got an early day tomorrow. Unless—do you need me to stay? Will you be all right?"

"I'm fine. Really. It helped to talk about it."

"I'm glad. Are you free tomorrow night?"

"I'm not sure. I'll be at UCLA in the afternoon."

"Well, I'll be in and out during the conference. Why don't you leave a message at the hotel? Only if you feel like it, of course. It's strictly up to you."

"Okay." She smiled. "And, Jack . . . thanks again."

He seemed to hesitate a moment. Then he leaned forward and kissed her gently on the cheek. "Sleep well," he said.

Chapter 19

The dreams were getting worse. Exhausted from them, Nicole slept late and awoke heavy, sluggish, barely able to move. Light from the sea reflected in through a window and struck the white beams. She closed her eyes against the sun, the interminable, damnable California sun that seemed to go on and on, no matter what horrors occurred in the world.

For the moment all that brightness was a slap in the face. Better the cold winds and rain of Georgetown that matched her mood.

There were sounds: an airplane, not too distant. A drip of water from the kitchen sink. The refrigerator turning on and off.

And scents. The wildflowers Jack had brought? No, something else. What was it?

Marigolds. The marigolds Dan had put on her breakfast tray the day before. Where were they? She looked around, thinking he had taken them away. But no, he'd left them on a little table beneath the window. The sun, streaming in, had warmed them. Their scent was heavy. Taunting.

Help me, Nikki.

She drew herself into a fetal position. "I don't seem to be doing much for you, Mary. I'm not good at this." She said it aloud, her voice a whisper, cracking. No energy for more.

After a while she glanced at her watch, a thin gold band. Mary had given it to her when she received her doctorate in mythology. Since that awful night when the police called, she hadn't taken it off.

Ten-oh-four A.M. She had to be at UCLA by two. Had to give a class. *Dear God. How will I make it through?*

By this time Mary would have been at work in the lab for four or five hours. She might be taking a break, calling to leave a message. *"Let's get together soon, okay? I feel like talking."* A pause. *"Oh, shoot, Nikki, I feel like pizza, that's the truth of it, and nobody else supports me in my bad habits the way you do."*

It wasn't very often Mary came out of her shell that way—became the kid Nicole remembered instead of the ingrown, tunnel-vision scientist. In fact, the past couple of months she hadn't called quite as often. She had seemed distracted.

What was wrong, little sister? Was it only Dan? Or was there something else? What are you trying to tell me?

She pushed the covers away and lay on her back, staring at the ceiling. Given everything she had to grieve—all the lost hours of sisterhood, of loving and sharing, of past memories and future dreams that would never come true—the question of a relationship between Dan and her sister paled. There were larger questions now.

I miss you, Mary. Tell me what to do.

She showered, letting the pounding water restore her energy. Then she made coffee. By the time she had dressed in jeans and a T-shirt, it was ready. She poured herself a cup and opened the top of the Dutch door. There was a note taped to it, from Dan.

Dear Nikki—I'll be home early tonight, around six. Let's go to dinner.

He had signed it with his flowing, somewhat arrogant *D*.

Don't hold your breath, she thought with unaccustomed rancor. And was surprised at how her feelings had cooled. It was as if some fairy godmother had appeared and waved a magic wand. With it, the final scales had fallen, remarkably, from her eyes.

These past three months she had remembered only the good times —savored and saved each wonderful moment like a masochistic knife in the heart. It now seemed a welcome relief to be remembering the bad.

Dan had always taken her for granted, waiting until the last minute to ask if she wanted to go out, or to invite himself over. At first it had seemed spontaneous and fun. But after a while she had begun to wonder if he thought she had nothing to do but sit around, waiting for him to call. Did he really think she would be available whenever he could fit her into his schedule? Or didn't he care?

It was thinking he didn't care that hurt. Finally she had sat down and written him a letter, explaining how she felt. She knew he hated getting letters like that, knew he'd rather "dialogue," as he called it. But she wasn't good at expressing her feelings orally; she needed to put them on paper.

Not that she'd ever mailed the damned letter. What good would it do? Dan had written the rules from the first: Thou shalt not expect too much. Thou shalt not talk about the *L* word, love. And the big one: Thou shalt not touch.

How do you spend so much time with someone you love and keep your hand from going out, or your arm from going around? How do you make your lips behave?

You do it with self-discipline and immense control, she had learned. And after a while, you go nuts. After a while you ask yourself, *What am I doing with this man I love and can't touch? Why am I not with someone who loves me, as well?*

She crumpled his note and tossed it into a wastebasket by the sink.

Running a wide comb through her wet hair, she looked for paper and pencil. In a kitchen drawer she found a yellow legal pad and several pens. Taking them and a cup of coffee onto the patio, she settled in one of the chairs. Rubbing her forehead, she thought, *I'm not a detective, little sister. I'm a teacher. Let's just see what we can do with that.*

An hour later she shifted in the patio chair as the sun moved to her left shoulder and heated her skin. The scent of marigolds, in their border only a few feet away, became a catalyst, urging her on.

She looked over her notes, to the circles she had drawn and placed words in—a right-brain technique she often used in teaching, for releasing ideas from the subconscious.

Mary Clare was in the center circle. And from that, spokes with smaller circles, written rapidly and without conscious thought: *Dan . . . Sister Paula . . . John Rorrman . . . Ilsen . . . notebook . . . accident . . . ticket . . . fire.*

She stared at that last word, "fire." What did it mean? It was the only word she couldn't connect to the others, couldn't see how it fit. Mary had died in icy waters—just the opposite of fire.

She began to write a paragraph from all the words, quickly, with no concern for making sense. The idea was to get down whatever rose from the subconscious and not destroy it with left-brain logic.

> *Mary left a notebook for Dan, and now it's missing. Notebook. Sister Paula wouldn't let me take the ones from Mary's cottage. Harriet Ilsen despises Sister Paula . . . but then, everyone does. Terry thought there was something suspicious about Mary's accident. Even Harriet thought it odd. And someone sent me Mary's ticket to L.A., someone who said she was Mary, transferring the ticket to me . . . two days after she died.*
>
> *A ticket agency mix-up, after all—or something else?*

She stopped writing.

She had used the airline ticket in a moment of grief and shock, wanting to get away, wanting, in her first flash of anger, to confront Dan with that photograph.

But could someone have lured her out here for some reason that wasn't yet clear? And if so, how could anyone have known she would actually use the ticket?

She looked up, irritated that she had slipped so quickly into left brain. Questions introduced logic.

But they also led to answers. What answers had she found in this short paragraph? Any?

She studied it several moments more. Now, without thinking, she began to draw spokes and circles from the word "fire." Match . . . wood . . . implode . . . explode . . . burner . . . Bunsen . . . lab . . .

Lab.

Her hand stilled. Fire—in a lab?

No . . . *explosion* in a lab. Mary's lab at Sacred Heart—the one she and Terry had talked about, the one in which Mary's mentor had died. That explosion was the reason Mary had left the notebook for Dan. She had worried that something would happen to her.

Nicole had brushed off her fears. She had laughed. "When something happens to someone you know, you always think it's going to happen to you, Mary."

But something *had* happened to Mary. And now the notebook was gone.

She needed more information. What had been going on in Mary's work, or the lab in general, at the time of the explosion?

Terry. He might know.

She gathered up her notes and went inside, setting them by the phone. But a call to Sacred Heart turned up only the information that Terry had gone for the day. She left a message on his voice mail, asking him to call her that evening.

Meanwhile, what about the professor? Perhaps he and Mary had talked about the explosion. He might know if she had suspected foul play, and why.

Glancing at her watch, she realized she'd be late for his class if she didn't hurry. Sweaty from sitting in the sun, she showered again. Applying light makeup to her face, she paused a moment, assessing herself, and thought she was feeling better.

She remembered that to get over Dan, she had thrown herself into work. The outcome hadn't been all that good; she had grown more and more tense, until finally, last month, she had blown up at that kid in class.

Ron had been right; she could admit that now. She had needed to get away.

She pulled on the long brown skirt and boots she had worn on the plane to L.A., topping them with a jacket in a contemporary style. Before leaving the cottage, she hid the yellow paper with its circles in a drawer, beneath clothes—feeling silly, like a not-too-clever heroine in a grade-B mystery.

Nicole took Wilshire to UCLA through the Miracle Mile and Century City. The drive took close to thirty minutes and allowed too much time to think. She deliberately focused on her surroundings, remembering a discussion she had had once with Dan about Los Angeles. The high rises lining Wilshire, he said, housed insurance companies, ad agencies, stockbrokers—the money makers, the movers and shakers. This prime West Coast property was owned now mostly by other countries.

"People think that Japan is the prime owner of American wealth, but the Netherlands draw those honors. After that comes Canada, then Great Britain, and finally Japan."

"Maybe the Japanese seem at the head of the list," she had suggested, "because they're noisier about their takeovers. Like a sleeping giant, they bask in an *impression* of strength."

Other countries . . . take the Finns, for instance, moved slowly
and quietly, as they had for centuries. Waiting at a light, Nicole was
reminded of a favorite tale in Finnish mythology. Wainamoinen, a
great hero of Finland (Kalevala, it was called then), passed his days
in the singing of songs. His warbling drove Aino—who was supposed
to marry him but didn't much like the idea—to throw herself into the
sea. A hare finally agreed to take on the sad task of informing her
parents of her death, but only after the daughters of the sea threatened to turn him into shish kebab if he didn't. Wainamoinen then
spent the rest of his life looking for another woman to marry. Unfortunately, nobody wanted the job. One wily woman after another
would say, "Okay, I'll marry you, but first you've got to make me a
magic mill (or whatever)." To his great distress, nobody said, "Sure,
I'll marry you, but first you've got to sing me a song."

So Wainamoinen would make the mill—which ground out riches
and food—and then he'd get left at the altar anyway. Somewhere
along the line he got the message and quit with the songs. Then one
day Wainamoinen killed a fish and made a harp from its bones. When
he played the harp, men wept—even Wainamoinen himself. His
tears fell into the sea, and it was said they became the first pearls.

Nicole smiled. Poor old Wainamoinen never did find anyone to
marry. Eventually, obsolete and feeble, he was replaced by a
younger, nonsinging hero. Wainamoinen built himself a copper ves-
sel and sailed away into the west—never to be seen again.

(It was said, however, that as he skimmed the crested waves, he
was crooning at the top of his lungs.)

Nicole had always felt sympathetic toward poor old Wainamoinen.
Maybe all he ever wanted to be was a lounge lizard in Vegas; maybe
he didn't want to be a hero at all.

The professor's classroom was at the far end of a long brick building. Nicole parked in a lot that was half a city block away and followed the instructions the professor had given her. There were trees
along the walk, and the sun was shining. Students lay on patches of

grass, either studying or sleeping. Others hurried to classes. Even hurrying, however, they looked like laid-back California kids, compared to Georgetown. Their dress was more casual, their hair longer. Winter tans complemented jeans and T-shirts, shorts and bicycle pants.

She found the professor's room and stood outside a moment, watching him grade papers. His frail form was profiled against a row of windows, through which dappled light danced. The rays of sun brought the room to life, shining on blackboards, maps, desks, and books.

"It's nice to have a break from that," Nicole said, walking in and smiling.

Looking up from the papers, he returned her smile and pushed his chair back. "Nikki! You're right on time." He stood and held out his arms for a hug. She gave him a big one, patting his back. A scent of peppermint stung her nostrils, and she remembered that the professor often carried a roll of peppermints in his vest pocket. They might be walking along a sidewalk or riding in his blue Thunderbird, and he would draw them out, offering her one. "Indigestion . . ." He would pat his chest. "It seems to help."

He stood back and scrutinized her. "They'll be pouring in any moment now, with their inquisitive little minds." He wagged a thin, pale finger. "I expect you to give them something to chew on, my dear. Shake them up a bit. I haven't been able to do that this year, it seems."

"I can't believe that. You're a wonderful teacher, you always have been."

"Oh, I have the knowledge." He tapped his forehead. "My brain is still sharp. But the inner fire seems to have been dampered a bit."

A discordant bell sounded before she could ask him about the Sacred Heart explosion. There was a sudden pounding in the corridors as students poured out of classrooms and dashed through halls.

"Few of our bells work anymore," the professor told her. "Budget cuts, I suppose. And the students have to fight for lockers. They carry padlocks with them, just in case they find one that's empty. Nothing is assigned anymore." He shook his head sadly. "I suppose that's a metaphor, somehow, for our lives in modern times."

The trickle into Room 206 began, and by the time the next bell had rung, everyone was seated and the professor had closed the door.

"This is Ms. Ryan," he said, facing the class. "She is here from Georgetown University, and I've asked her to speak to you today."

The students looked at Nicole—some with curiosity, some already bored.

There will always be the bored ones, she thought. *And they're the ones I like best. If I can just grab their attention . . .*

She was glad she had done some reading in the night.

Facing the class, she let a silence fall. The professor took a seat at the back of the room, and Nicole walked slowly back and forth, not saying a word until every eye was on her. Finally, she stopped and planted herself close to the first row, in the center of the room. She folded her hands carefully before her.

"The Aztecs," she began in a slow, husky voice, "ripped out ten thousand hearts in the temple one day. Blood flowed down the steps of the temple—*hundreds* of steps, leading into the town square. It sank into the dirt and became part of history. But if you stand there now, stand there on a dark, hot night with the thunderbolts of the gods in the distance, with torches casting shadows over the image of the dreaded Metzli, goddess of the moon"—she hugged her arms, giving a shudder—"you can still see the horrible black stain of ancient blood upon the ground."

Twenty minutes later even Nicole was feeling the drama. In this new setting, surrounded by bright new faces, her old passion for teaching had returned. She was enjoying the feel of having an audience, of being in command. The professor was nodding with satisfaction.

Nicole asked the rapt students for questions.

A hand flew up. A young woman of about twenty, with straight blond hair cut just below her ears. "Ms. Ryan?"

"Yes?"

"I thought the Aztecs were a civilized people. Did they really rip out people's hearts?"

"Absolutely. They were highly feared at that time. They were also brilliant, and in a strange way, quite spiritual. Their art, for instance, still speaks to the soul after all these centuries. Yet their bloodletting was massive."

"How could they be spiritual and still do the things they did?"

"A good question. The Aztecs believed that oneness with the universe should be held above everything, including human life. And they believed that sacrifice—the shedding of human blood—created that oneness. It was, I suppose you might say, a matter of interpretation."

"So they made sacrifices, thinking they were doing the right thing?"

"Constantly."

A serious young man with black-rimmed glasses spoke. "Is that on the same order as people who interpret the Bible in different ways now?"

Nicole craned her neck to see him. "In my opinion, yes."

"So are you saying there is no wrong or right, and that all human conduct is merely a matter of interpretation?"

"Absolutely not. What I believe is that there are explanations that much of so-called Christianity overlooks in its interpretations."

"Okay, then—take for instance the people who preach that homosexuality is a sin, because it says so in the Bible. Do you think it really says that in the Bible?"

Nicole gave an audible groan. "I'd almost rather have my own heart cut out than try to interpret the Bible. At least, not in front of thirty intelligent twenty-year-olds."

Laughter rippled through the room. But the boy rearranged his glasses and spoke again. "Seriously—if you teach about religions, you must have some ideas. What do you think about AIDS being God's punishment to gay men?"

Nicole restrained a sigh. There was one in every class. A kid who pushed, who tested. They were usually the bright ones—and all too often they wanted to show off how bright they were. An ordinary class could turn into a Grand Debate, unless you threw in a curve.

"How about if I give you an opinion based on some people I've talked to, and you tell me if you agree?"

The kid shrugged.

"There are people who believe that an autoimmune deficiency syn-

drome, transmitted through the blood, was on the planet during biblical times. They believe it was caused by the same virus that is
causing AIDS—or what we've called AIDS—today. And they believe
that the biblical injunctions against homosexuality were based not
on ethics or morality, but on a very real need to stem the spread of
that virus."

"But they didn't know anything about viruses back then."

"Correct. Which is why they were told it was 'sinful' to be homo-
sexual. Sin was something they did understand."

"Told by who?"

"There is a book called *None of These Diseases*, by a doctor
whose name, if I remember, is McMillen. It posits the theory that if
you go back through the Bible, you will find that God gave Moses
detailed instructions for cleansing the hands after handling the infected or the dead. He was taught about washing with running water, and with intervals for drying and exposing the hands to the sun.
People who had been in contact with the dead or infected were also
told to change to clean clothes immediately afterward. Now, this is
precisely the method used today in modern hospitals for killing bacteria—yet people didn't know that bacteria even existed, at that
time."

She went on, noting that she had their attention. "In Deuteronomy
twenty-three, men were told to go to a place outside their camps, to
carry a spade to dig a hole, and to bury their excrement there. This
was a sanitation method given to human beings some thirty-five
hundred years ahead of the technology we now have to support it."

She focused on the young man, making him an audience of one.
"McMillen further posits that the injunction to Abraham to circum-
cise the male was for the prevention of uterine cancer—a necessity
in those times, perhaps, because of a lack of knowledge regarding
the importance of cleansing the foreskin.

"Then, too, Abraham was instructed that circumcision should take
place on the eighth day following the baby's birth. We now know that
vitamin K, which helps the blood to clot, isn't produced in the body
until the fifth to seventh day. Therefore, the eighth day would seem
the best to prevent hemorrhaging of the blood."

She paused, her eyes moving from face to face. "Yet no one in
Abraham's time knew of vitamin K."

The kid spoke up, not bothering to raise his hand this time. "So you're saying that God came in on a cloud, or something, and told Abraham and Moses all this stuff?"

"Well, I believe that in the Bible it says that angels did it." Nicole smiled. "Personally, I've always wondered if these 'angels' weren't beings from a more highly evolved planet."

"You actually believe that?" The young man's eyes widened.

"I didn't say I believed it. I'm posing it as a theory." Her smile widened. Throw in a little *Star Trek,* you never knew where a class might go.

A female hand went up in the back row.

"Yes?"

"So let's say AIDS is the same virus, and it's been around all these thousands of years. Why is it back now?"

Nicole moved to the side of the room to see the student better. "There are many theories. But there's one I've read recently and think goes hand in hand with my particular field. It's that the excavation of old relics and ruins, into which the blood of sacrifice became saturated, may be causing it. It's widely accepted, of course, that viruses don't live very long when exposed to air—not under normal conditions. Yet, if buried in the earth, and given just the right circumstances of environment—temperature and humidity—the AIDS virus might have been preserved. This would be similar in concept to the preservation of the bodies of the Egyptians, through mummification." She smiled. "Or so the theory goes."

The kid with the glasses was back. "Has anyone every tested this theory?"

"Not as far as I know."

The students looked thoughtful.

"The rest of the theory," Nicole added, "has to do with the way the AIDS virus might have spread."

She walked to the board and began to chart various maritime paths; travel between several countries in the 1960s and seventies. Chalk squeaked on the old blackboard, its dust making her nose itch. The students, rather than being restless, were quiet and absorbed.

"In the 1970s several Aztec ruins were uncovered in Central Mexico. It was in the seventies that AIDS first began to make inroads in the United States. In the seventies, also, excavations were made in Northern Africa. This was about the time that AIDS became prevalent in Africa. The theory is that the virus may have taken up residence in people working on the excavations, through work injuries, cuts, wounds—and been passed along by them, as they or their sexual partners traveled to nearby countries."

She set down the chalk and faced the class.

"Now let's just say, for the sake of argument, that this could possibly—by some stretch of the imagination—have happened, and that these viruses were carried from country to country—"

Hands went up all around the room—yet the students weren't waiting to be called upon. Several voices rose at once.

"This is a little bit more than a stretch."

"That doesn't mean it can't be true," someone argued.

"Yeah, then why aren't scientists working on it?"

"Maybe because they haven't thought of it."

A caustic laugh. "Or maybe there's no money in it."

"Oh, Jerry, you always say that! You always think doctors are in some giant conspiracy to fleece the public—"

"Yeah, well—"

Nicole let the debate rage on. It was what she had hoped for. *Shake them up,* the professor had said. Get them talking, arguing, and see what pops up. As a teacher, it was her greatest strength. It was like sitting down to write a book, an author friend had once told her, and not knowing what you're going to put on the page. One idea leads to another, and even the most inane thoughts end in something that makes sense.

"Ms. Ryan?" A student who hadn't spoken before. "You said you read this in a book. What book was it?"

"The Maya Question," she answered, writing the title on the board. "I came across it the other night and found it fascinating reading—"

There was a crash in the room behind her.

She whirled around. The professor was lying on the floor beside a toppled desk, a hand grabbing at his throat as if he were unable to breathe.

"Professor! Oh, God!" She dropped the chalk and ran to his side, pushing through the kids who were now in the aisle. "Let me through!" The boy with the black-rimmed glasses was already there, feeling for a pulse along his teacher's neck. Nicole knelt beside him, loosening the professor's tie and unbuttoning his shirt. His eyes were open and rolling, his mouth forming words.

"Shhh," she said gently. "Don't try to talk." Turning, she yelled to the room at large. "Get some help! Get some paramedics over here —hurry!"

They had taken the professor to the UCLA Med Center.

"How is he?" Nicole asked the young doctor. He fiddled with the stethoscope that dangled from his jacket pocket and cleared his throat.

"There's definitely been damage to the heart. We're still running tests, but so far, I'd say it's mild. It helps that you got him here so quickly."

"May I see him?"

"Sorry, only immediate family for now."

"But I'm a good friend."

He ran a hand through curly reddish hair. "I am sorry. It's especially important with heart patients to keep them quiet at first. Let's give it a while, see how it goes."

She called the professor's home and broke the news to Austen.

"Oh, God, I told him to slow down. I've been telling him for months, but he never listens. . . ." There was a clattering noise in the background. "Mikey, don't touch that!" Then, to Nicole, "It probably hasn't helped having us here. But I didn't think . . . Look, I'll get a friend to look after Mikey, and I'll be right down."

Nicole paced the floor of the waiting room. On a stiff plastic sofa sat three of the professor's students who had refused to leave.

"We've all been worried about him," the girl with short blond hair, whose name was Trudy, said. "He hasn't been feeling good for weeks now. He'd be standing there giving a lesson, and he'd rub at the middle of his chest a lot. Sometimes he'd sweat, or turn pale. My grandfather used to do that, and he had a bad heart."

The studious boy with black-rimmed glasses turned out to be her boyfriend, Joel. He put an arm around her shoulders. "The professor's okay. He's stronger than he looks." She leaned her head on his shoulder.

Nicole waited by the door, hoping to see the doctor reappear with a reassuring smile on his face.

She remembered that first talk with the professor, when they were introduced in Georgetown. He had invited her to have coffee with him. Spring had landed with both feet, and they had walked along the river to an espresso shop with outdoor tables. Blossoming trees lined the banks of the river, their gentle leaves a pale green. A balmy breeze lifted paper napkins on all the tables. It touched Nicole's cheek as she looked over at this remarkable man whose books she had read, and about whom she had heard so much. No one in her adult life had had as much influence on her thinking, except perhaps Joseph Campbell.

"I never thought I'd have the chance to really talk with you," she said.

The professor had actually blushed. "I'm just a teacher," he answered with a modest smile.

"But you're a great teacher. It isn't just the way you toss out ideas, but the way you link them as common causes—or faults—in the world plan."

"Too much of teaching," the professor said, "is confined within a border of old thought forms, old beliefs. The norm is to read existing knowledge and pass it on."

"It bothers me," Nicole admitted, "that in teaching any class, I have to follow a structured plan. I've been wondering how to get around that. What I'd really like to do is give lectures, like you—something more freewheeling, where I can say and teach anything I want, the college administrators be damned."

"Well, that Utopia hasn't yet arrived," the professor said with a sigh. "I get away with a lot—like denouncing the Catholic Church in my talk here today at Georgetown, one of the world's foremost Catholic universities, in one of the world's foremost Catholic towns. But believe me, a price is always paid."

They were silent a few moments as Nicole wondered what price had been extracted over the years for the professor's progressive teachings. She felt she didn't know him well enough to ask.

"I'd like you to meet my sister," she had said. "Mary Clare is in her first year here at Georgetown, but she has a wonderful mind. I can't say I always agree with her, but it fascinates me to listen."

"I'd like that," the professor had said.

The three of them had dinner the following Sunday, and became friends from that day on.

"He's doing pretty good," Austen said, coming out of the professor's room. The anxious lines in her forehead, however, remained. Her reddish brown hair looked as if she'd been tugging at it with worried fingers. "He's only my uncle by marriage, you know, but he's always been wonderful to me."

"I'm sure he'll be all right. Do you think I could see him now?"

Austen shook her head. "I'm really sorry. The nurse said only relatives until tomorrow morning. Something about the first twenty-four hours being crucial with a heart attack. If they didn't already know you weren't a relative, we might sneak you in. . . ."

"That's okay, I understand. He is feeling better, though?"

Austen brightened. "He was talking, and his color is good. But he's worried about Sampson. He'll need to be fed."

"I've been thinking I'd go over to the house and do that. I don't seem to be much help here."

Austen gave her a grateful hug. "That would be great. Thanks. Oh, and Uncle Henry was asking for his own pajamas and a book to read. He really hates hospitals. Do you think—?"

"Of course. I'll get some things and bring them back."

Austen's smile was one of relief. "I didn't want to ask, but I hate to leave until—well, you know. Until we're really sure." She dug in her oversized purse for keys and handed them to Nicole.

"What about your little boy?"

"Mikey's with an old friend in Century City. I'll call and let them know I'll be here a few more hours."

Nicole gathered up her jacket and purse. "When you see the professor again, please give him my love and tell him I know he's going to be all right. Tell him I'll see him as soon as they let me in."

Austen squeezed her arm. "I will. And thanks. Thanks very much. You probably saved his life, the doctor said."

Nicole shook her head. "It wasn't just me. The kids were great. They really seem to care for him."

"My uncle loves teaching. Each year they make a special allowance to let him continue beyond the retirement age. Now—I don't know what will happen if he has to give it up."

"I know." It struck Nicole suddenly that she would lose an important part of herself if she had to give up teaching—it would be like losing a limb.

Chapter 20

With bumper-to-bumper traffic, the Pasadena Freeway was a veritable parking lot. Finally turning down Buena Vista, Nicole was more than relieved to see the professor's house with its familiar hedges. She pulled into the drive, nosing up to the garage. Slinging her purse strap onto one shoulder, she slid from the car.

The night air was hot; the rose trees along the path shuddered with an oppressive breeze. *Santa Anas—devil winds, tearing in from the desert.* When they were here last spring, Nicole remembered Mary saying, "Doesn't that wind just make you crazy?" She had agreed that it did. It seemed to have an adverse effect on everyone's emotional state.

Looking up, she noted that the winds were beating against the professor's second-story windows, shaking the panes, making them shimmy and clatter.

The porch light wasn't on, and she had to try Austen's keys one by one, in the dark. On the fourth try the tumbler turned. Opening the door, she reached for the light switch. The rose chandelier flickered briefly before it stayed on.

That's odd. Must be a short in the switch. She flicked it a couple of times. It seemed all right.

Locking the door behind her, she dropped her purse on the reception table and walked along the hall toward the kitchen, calling out.

"Sampson? Where are you? Cat?"

At the kitchen door she stood for a moment listening, thinking she had heard a sound. Dim light from the rose chandelier cast shadows into the room.

"Sampson, don't you dare jump out on me!" she said nervously. That cat could be especially wound up when he was hungry.

Flipping a switch, she flooded the kitchen with light. No Sampson. Well, he'd come soon enough when he heard cans rattling. If she remembered correctly . . . yes, the cat food was all here, in a bottom cupboard, neatly stacked according to flavors. The professor was a creature of habit: a place for everything, everything in its place.

She got the can opener from its usual drawer, second from the sink. As she punctured the can and air rushed into the vacuum, she glanced around—expecting to see Sampson at her heels. This was the point, when the pungent scent of food escaped, that he ordinarily appeared.

Still no Sampson. Strange.

"Sampson? Dinner!" She tapped the fork against the can as she dished the shredded beef onto a plate next to the stove. Setting the plate on the floor, she washed the fork, stuck it in the dish drainer, and pulled off a paper towel to dry her hands. Looking through the kitchen window, she could see the shapes of trees blowing in the hot wind. In the dark the leaves were faintly silver, shimmering wildly.

Come to think of it, animals got weird during the Santa Anas, too —just as they did during earthquakes. Sampson had probably gotten spooked by the rattling of windows upstairs and escaped through the cutout in the rear pantry door.

Well, he'd be all right. *Pity anyone who steps on his tail in the dark, though.*

Nicole turned from the sink, suddenly exhausted. *Better get on with it, get the professor's clothes.*

Going back through the hall, she began to climb the stairs, then paused halfway up—a hand on the rosewood banister. Was that a noise from the professor's study? It sounded like scratching. Looking back, she saw that the study door was closed.

"Oh, that's where you are!" She laughed, but with annoyance. "Sampson, how did you get locked in there?"

She ran back down the stairs, yanking open the study door. The rose chandelier cast only fringes of light on the professor's desk, the bookcases along the wall to the left, and the terrace doors, draped in white. The white moved. It swayed and seemed to beckon with the ephemeral wave of a ghost.

"That shouldn't be open," Nicole murmured to herself. "The professor always locks up when he leaves. . . ."

Uneasy suddenly, she swept the room with her gaze, slowing, then focusing on the desk in its shadows. Adrenaline pumped, bringing up a half scream. *What the hell is that? Something—someone—sitting there!*

Her hand shaking, she tried to find a light switch inside the door. Where was the damned light? Her fingers scrambled along the wall.

But there was no ceiling light, she remembered, only the lamp on the desk—and it turned on at its base.

Her vision adjusted to the dark. She could see the professor's chair more clearly now. *Oh, dear God. It's a head.*

She forced herself to be calm. *No—it's only shadows. My imagination. That damned wind is making me crazy.*

She forced herself to walk to the desk. Every muscle tense, ready for flight, she leaned over and punched the button on the base of the lamp.

"ROWWWWWWL!"

The swivel chair spun around to face her as Sampson jumped from a bookshelf onto its back, then streaked toward the kitchen. Nicole's eyes jerked from him to the chair. In it was a man, dark brown, with black hair. Menacing eyes stared through slits. A hand held something pointed, something shiny—

The terrace door flew open and crashed against the wall. Curtains billowed inward. Nicole screamed. She grabbed the desk for balance, clinging to its solid reality.

Then she laughed shakily, embarrassed. Covering her mouth, she stared.

The "man" was two and a half feet tall, a wooden carving from one of the professor's trips. Nicole had seen the idol many times before, but its usual spot was on a table along the study wall. The shiny thing he held was a razor-sharp spear.

Her face dripped with perspiration. She turned to look at the table and saw the square, dust-free spot where the idol had been. Who would have . . . ?

Mikey. Mikey, playing tricks on his mother, no doubt. Or on the professor—hoping to startle him when he came into the dark study at the end of a long day.

Nicole wiped her forehead. *Nothing but smoke and mirrors. Thank God.*

She closed the terrace door, fastening the latch securely, locking it at the bottom. Austen must have forgotten, she realized, in her rush to get to the hospital.

She carried the heavy wooden idol back to its usual place. Sampson reappeared from the kitchen, licking his lips. He smelled of beef. It was a wonderfully ordinary sight.

"What do you say we get on with things, old boy?"

For once she didn't mind that he followed her all the way upstairs, both of them glancing a bit nervously into the other two bedrooms and the bathroom.

Of course, she thought wryly as she passed the attic door, Aliens 1, 2, and 3 could be hiding out up there.

She smiled, remembering a night when she was about twelve and home alone, while her mother and Mary Clare were at Mary's school for open house. Before going to bed early she had lined the outside of the attic door with soft-drink bottles—just in case anyone came down from the attic in the night and tried to grab her.

"You see too many movies," Mary had teased her later when she saw the bottles there. Somehow, having Mary laugh at her foolishness made things all right.

The professor's room was at the far end of the hall, facing the street. It was a large room, with flowered wallpaper, a huge dark wardrobe against a wall, and an overstuffed chair in a bay window. The bed, like the other furnishings, was heavy, European in design. There were framed, hand-embroidered pictures, one of flowers in a flower cart, another of a little girl in a long dress and sun bonnet. On a wall over a dresser was a depiction of a cottage with an English garden—tall blue delphiniums bordered by pink asters, roses, and other old-fashioned flowers. It was entirely done in canceled postage stamps. A painstaking work of art, it had been signed: *by Eleanor.*

Nicole began to go through drawers, feeling embarrassed, like a Peeping Tom. The professor's clothes were simple—nothing fancy or even very new. A couple of threadbare boxer shorts had been patched, in a delicate hand stitch. Eleanor again—all those years ago, before she died? Other than that, the professor's clothes were like those of any older man, she supposed, who didn't have anyone to look after his wardrobe.

Gently, she set pajamas, shorts, socks, and undershirts onto the bed. Then she crossed to the closet, in search of an overnight case. It was a big walk-in closet, with deep recesses and no light. The corners were dark. She pushed aside suits smelling of moth balls and age, then shirts, some of them with the lingering scent of aftershave. On the floor were boxes with clothes and shoes. It took a few moments to unearth a small suitcase in a back corner, under a pile of blankets and pillows.

Dragging it out to the bed, Nicole realized it was too heavy to be empty. She unzipped it. In the suitcase was a sheaf of yellowed bond paper, nearly two inches thick. Flipping through the pages curiously, she found that they contained comprehensive scientific notes—much like the notes in Mary Clare's cottage. There were graphs, numbers, letters—and a phrase that kept repeating: Lumera 8.

Nicole became lost in the notes, wondering why they were packed away in a suitcase instead of in the professor's study. She wondered if he was still working on them or had put them away some time ago, abandoning the project. And why this sort of thing? She knew that he had a medical degree, but he had never practiced. His interest had always been in teaching, and more in history than the practical application of medicine.

Then she realized that the manuscript wasn't in the professor's writing. She had seen his penmanship in notes he had left her when she was here before and recalled its distinctive, old-fashioned style. This script was different; more delicate. More like a woman's.

Eleanor? Was this Eleanor's work? Had her grieving husband saved it all these years—unpublished notes, never to see fruition?

He had never talked about Eleanor's work. Nicole had never even thought of her as a scientist, but as a medical doctor.

She was aware, suddenly, of the passage of time. Looking up, she heard the wind howling through the attic eaves. *It must be playing with the lines outside.* The bedroom lights were flickering. *Move it, Nicole.*

There was no other luggage, so she took the manuscript and set it carefully inside the closet, back along the wall where the suitcase had been. She replaced the blanket and pillow on top, since there was no other room for them. Then she filled the suitcase with the clothes she had taken from the bureau drawers, adding a few things from the adjoining bathroom: a safety razor, Old Spice after-shave, a comb and toothbrush.

Picking up the suitcase, she left the bedroom and started down the hall.

She was almost to the stairs when the lights went out.

Shit.

The epithet sprang from a deep well of exhaustion. Tensing, Nicole jerked to a stop. Gripping the handle of the suitcase, she thought, *God, it's dark. No light from outside, no streetlights or neighbors' windows . . .*

She couldn't even see the wall, just to her right.

Sampson meowed loudly.

"Sampson?" she called out. "Cat, where are you?"

Another meow, more distant.

Where the hell was he? She didn't want to trip over him as she made her way to the stairs.

"Sampson?" She took a few steps, one hand on the wall to guide her. There was a creak on the ceiling just above her head.

In the attic? He *couldn't* be up there. The attic door had been closed when she'd passed it earlier.

But the cat whimpered again, and the sound was clearly from above.

Damn. He must know another way, maybe a hole in some wall—

On the other hand, what if he'd somehow become trapped? She couldn't leave him there, cut off from food and water. Austen might not be back until late the next day.

She set the suitcase down, and using the flocked wallpaper as a guide—her hands walking it inch by inch—she started back to the attic door. One halting step followed another, and with each one she became unaccountably afraid. She told herself aloud with every step that she was a grown-up now, and too old to be afraid of the dark. She told herself there was no bogeyman here. No one but her—and that damned miserable cat.

See if she'd ever feed him again. See if she'd ever worry one iota about his irritating, calamitous hide.

She counted the doors as she passed them—first the guest room, then Eleanor's sewing room, then the professor's bedroom. All open. Sampson couldn't be trapped in any of them.

Stop shaking, Nicole. What are you afraid of? Just keep talking. Keep talking and telling yourself it's just fine, it's okay. The end of the hall shouldn't be more than three steps away. . . .

There. Her outstretched hand felt the end wall first.

Stop. Turn left. A few more steps . . . yes, you're at the attic door. Now find the handle. Grab it.

Uh-oh. Wait. Remember what that damned cat is capable of.
She stood back, off to the side. *That's it. Now open the door.*
"RRROOWWWW!"

Sampson hurtled through the door, screeching. He landed in the hall like a stampeding elephant and would have knocked her off her feet if she'd been in the way.

Nicole shook a fist and yelled into the dark, more to hear her own voice than anything. "Damn you, Sampson! You are never going to do this to me again. You are the most foul, the most irritating, the most . . ."

From behind her came a small noise, a scent, a movement.

A breath caressed her cheek. A cold hand touched her neck. She felt the imprint of human flesh, and horror rose like a blanket, filling her throat.

Nicole began running—running down the hall, her hip bumping the banister, heart thudding. There were footsteps behind her. She screamed, tripping over the soft rug on the landing, her heel sliding onto the top step then down, stumbling, falling, grabbing the banister but falling more—two steps, three. *Oh God, let me out of here, let me out!* Her lungs squeezed shut. *No air, I can't breathe!*

Flying blindly down the stairs, she threw herself against the front door. Wrenching at the knob, she yanked it open and ran onto the porch. Through the tall swaying shrubs around the garden she could see the glimmer of streetlights, now on—and other houses, ablaze with light.

I'm safe. Oh, thank God, I'm safe.

She stumbled down the line of tree roses toward the street. She'd go to a house, find a phone, call the police—

She was nearly to the sidewalk when a hand reached out and grabbed her.

Chapter 21

Her heart actually stopped. It jerked to a halt and everything went black before it began beating again. A blinding light struck her eyes. The powerful beam traveled up and down her body, ending again at her face. Her free hand went up to protect her sight. The beam went out.

"Mind telling me what you're doing here, miss?"

Her voice, vision, and wits returned. In the glow from a streetlight, the badge was the first thing she saw, the silver badge on the blue shirt. Then another uniformed man behind the first. And a patrol car parked beneath a streetlight, half a block away. Pasadena City Police. Nicole went weak with relief. The hand at her wrist was the only thing holding her up.

"Oh, God, I'm so glad to see you!" She pointed back to the house. "There's someone in there!" She gulped for air.

The two cops looked at each other, then at her.

"Is this your house?"

The words tumbled out, one after another. "No, it belongs to Professor Henry Dirstoff. He's a friend. He's in the hospital, and his cat got stuck in the attic, and then there was someone there—"

"Okay, okay. Take it easy now," the first cop said quietly. He was Latino, and big—big in height and muscles, with thick dark eyebrows in a wide, leathery face. "Take a deep breath."

He released Nicole's wrist, and she steadied herself, drawing in air.

"That better?"

She nodded. Exhaled. "Yes."

"Okay. Now, was that you who screamed?"

"Yes."

"And you say you saw a prowler in there?" He glanced at the house again.

"Well, it was dark, and all the lights were out, so I didn't actually see him. But he touched me. He was right there by the attic door on the second floor. I was letting the cat out—" Her voice began to shake again.

"Slow down," the cop said. "Just slow down." He glanced at the other officer. "I'll go in and check."

The younger man nodded. He watched his partner release the safety snap on his holster and head up the walk, hand on his pistol grip. Then he turned to Nicole.

"May I see some identification?"

Still shaky, she dug around in her purse. Pulling out her wallet, she opened it, displaying her driver's license.

"Sorry," the young cop said apologetically. "You'll have to take it out."

She did, handing it to him. He pulled a small black flashlight from his belt, holding it up to the license. He looked it over carefully. "Maryland. Are you out here on vacation?"

"In a way. I'm staying with a friend in Malibu."

"And you know the man who owns this house . . ." He pulled a small notebook from his shirt pocket and scanned it. ". . . this Professor Dirstoff?"

"Yes. We're old friends. He was taken to the hospital a few hours ago, and I was getting him some clothes when the lights went out. Then there was a man—"

"You're sure it was a man? You said you didn't see him." His gaze moved again to the house, where lights were now on in every downstairs room. Another appeared upstairs as they watched.

"No, I didn't actually see him. It was dark. I felt his breath on my face, and then he touched my neck, and that's when I screamed, I guess. I ran down the stairs, and then out here."

She took a long, deep breath again. Her nerves were shot. He must think she was a nut.

"Don't worry. If there's anybody in there," he assured her, "De Santo will find him. You want to sit down a few minutes?"

He took her arm and led her across to the patrol car. "A neighbor called, said she thought she saw a stranger enter the house a little while ago. Must have been you." He opened the back door of the patrol car. "There's a neighborhood watch here—they keep a pretty good eye on things."

In fact, there was more than one curtain being held ajar now in surrounding houses. People had also come out in robes, sweats, and pajamas to stand on their porches. They were looking this way.

Nicole sank gratefully into the black leather seat. "You got here fast."

"Yeah, well, we were right around the corner, checking out a report on a downed power line. The Santa Anas, you know. And people around here expect us to show up fast."

She looked across the way, but couldn't see the professor's house now, beyond the trees and shrubs. "I hope your partner's all right."

"De Santo? Shit, you better hope that prowler's all right." He grinned. "Pardon my language."

She thought how young he looked, then. Younger than she—probably not too long out of the academy. His hair was short and stiff, his features still unmarked by trauma or grief.

She wondered about the man who had touched her in the house. Who was he? What was he doing there?

The police radio squawked. The young cop reached through the open window, picked up the mike, and spoke into it. "Three-two-five. What's up?"

"We have a two-seventy-thirty-five in the thirty-six block of Adams. Where are you now?"

He gave her their location. "We're checking out a possible four-five-nine here. Can you get somebody else?"

"One-oh-four's in the area. I'll see if they can take it."

"Great. Hey, Deb?" He grinned into the mike. "You free later tonight?"

The dispatcher's reprimand was embarrassed and curt. "Not on the radio, Sport."

"Ah, hell, everybody knows about us anyway."

She sighed. "Yeah, well, they do now."

He gave a chuckle. "Rafferty's?"

A brief silence. Then, with a grudging smile in the voice, "Rafferty's. Eleven o'clock."

"Ten-four."

He replaced the mike with a satisfied grin and began writing on a clipboard. Nicole sat quietly, watching leaves blow along the street, nudged by the fierce Santa Anas. She was hot and sticky—almost completely unwound. She wanted to leave, get back to the beach.

The big cop reappeared, crossing the street toward them. He was shoving his gun into its holster.

"Nobody in there now. He must have gotten out the back while we were talking in front. Probably some kid—there's a lot of that these days. They come in from other areas, park somewhere, work the neighborhoods, then meet back at the car and they're gone. Usually, they take small stuff—jewelry, cash, whatever they can stick in their pockets or a plastic garbage bag."

"You really think that's all it was?" Nicole asked. "I don't think the professor's ever had a break-in here before."

"Well, it's the times. Things are getting worse and worse."

She rubbed her face wearily. "I need to get back to the hospital. There was a suitcase in the second-floor hall. . . ." She sent De Santo a silent plea—not really wanting to go back in there alone.

"Hold on a minute." He turned to his partner. "Kid? Talk to you a minute?"

They stood a few yards away from her, conversing. Nicole heard the words, ". . . Maryland ID . . . checks with the neighbor's story . . ." Then, ". . . called from the house . . . he's at the UC Med Center."

De Santo nodded finally, and they came back to her. "My name's Leo. Leo De Santo. I'll take you back in the house. We can get that suitcase and close the place up."

"Thanks. I appreciate that."

He turned to his partner. "You call in—okay, kid? Tell them we'll be out of here in ten, fifteen minutes, more or less."

"Right."

They crossed the street. Nicole noted that neighbors were drifting back into their houses, reassured now that whatever had happened was all but over.

Inside the professor's hallway once more, she called out to Sampson. There was no response.

"There's a cat in the study," De Santo offered. "At least, there was."

She looked in. Sampson was sleeping peacefully on the bookshelf behind the professor's desk. Everything looked in order here now. No wooden idol on the chair, no ghostlike curtain, no alien human hand.

She followed De Santo up the stairs. "You say you left that suitcase in this upstairs hall?" he asked.

"Yes, when the lights went out—or actually, when I heard the cat upstairs and went back to the attic door." She halted. "That's funny."

She could have sworn she had dropped the suitcase near the top of the stairs. In fact, when she had run from whoever it was in the attic, she had been just clear enough to remember to sidestep it and not trip.

"It's not here now," she said.

"Well, you were scared," De Santo reassured her. "Maybe you just think you left it here. Maybe you dropped it over by the attic door."

They both searched there for the suitcase, without success. De Santo looked through the attic again, although he'd been up there earlier and hadn't seen it.

"Not here," he said, lumbering back down the narrow stairs. "Not any reason it should be—but then it always pays to check. How about in the bedroom?"

"No, I'm sure . . ."

Even so, they looked, through the bedroom, then the closet. The manuscript was still there beneath the pile of blankets—but no sign of a suitcase. They tried the downstairs hall, just in case it had somehow been knocked over the stairs.

It wasn't anywhere.

"The prowler must have taken it," De Santo said. "Maybe he thought something valuable was in it. You say it was only clothes?"

"Yes. Nothing but clothes and a toothbrush, things like that."

The big cop shrugged. "Like I said, a kid. Kids will take anything, thinking there might be something they can sell. If it was a good suitcase, he might've taken it just for that."

Nicole wasn't fully convinced. But with De Santo beside her, she got a brown grocery sack from the kitchen and went back to the professor's bedroom to pack more clothes.

"It was nice of you to stay with me," she said when they were through. "I don't know if I could have come back in here alone."

"Well, to be honest"—De Santo smiled—"it's not your house. And I couldn't leave you here without the owner's say-so. They wouldn't let me talk to Professor Dirstoff on the phone. Said he was doing better, though."

"You called the hospital?"

"Soon as I was sure the prowler was gone. Nothing personal, but I only had your word you were a friend. The nurse connected me with the professor's niece, and she said you were okay. Still, it pays to be careful."

"I'm impressed."

The massive shoulders moved in a shrug. "There's been a lot of talk the past couple years about cops not doing their jobs here in L.A. I just want to see they're not talking about me."

Chapter 22

"There was no sign of it," he said. "I searched everywhere."

"And the suitcase?"

"Nothing but clothes."

"Amazing. So far you have managed to fail at every turn."

"I—"

"Has she mentioned the notebook at all?"

"No. I'm sure she doesn't have it."

"Or she's too smart for us. The sister . . ."

"The sister is gone. Drop it."

"I'll give you another twenty-four hours. Then we'll have to take stronger measures."

"It won't be so easy—"

"Easy doesn't enter into it."

"—to cover up two murders."

The other man laughed. "A sister dies, the surviving sister grieves, becomes depressed . . . takes too many pills."

The caller's grip tightened on the phone. "You are the one who will blow this. You're operating out of greed and fear, not common sense."

"I'm operating from strength—not weakness."

"She's the only one who can lead us to—"

"She's the only one who can ruin everything. See to it that doesn't happen. Do what you have to do."

Chapter 23

It seemed as if the night would never end. At the hospital Nicole had to field Austen's queries about what had gone on at the house. Then she gave the professor's clothes to the unit nurse and found out firsthand how he was doing. She left a written message: *I'll see you tomorrow. Get well. Love, Nicole.*

On the drive to the beach, she encountered more traffic than she would have expected so late at night—after eleven now. She remembered that she hadn't eaten since noon.

Stop at a fast-food place? There was a McDonald's up ahead.

No. Her stomach clutched at the thought. She needed to drink some milk, take aspirin, go to sleep.

Her hands on the steering wheel were white-knuckled with left-over tension. *What a hideous night.* And no matter what De Santo had said, she didn't quite believe the kid-burglar theory. This had something to do with Mary. She didn't know why she thought that— she just did.

God, I'm tired. Too tired to think about this anymore.

She couldn't believe how her hands were trembling on the wheel. She dreaded going into Dan's garage, dreaded going down those dark stairs. She hoped the lights were on along the walk.

Mary Clare, she remembered, used to sing when she was afraid. "Whistle a Happy Tune" was the song she liked best. Their mother had taught it to them. Nicole hummed it as she pulled into the drive and punched the remote. The door swung open.

See in the car headlights? There's no one there. You're being silly.

She talked and hummed to herself all the way down the dark stairs. Halfway along an overhanging palm brushed her face—blown over the stairs, she guessed, from the wild Santa Anas. She fended it off. At the bottom of the stairs she paused, listening for the sound of a shoe on flagstone.

Nothing but the soft murmur of waves. The tide must be out.

She crossed the patio quickly. At the Dutch door she fiddled in the dark with both upper and lower locks. Damn! If she'd only brought a flashlight. *Next time.* She'd remember it next time.

The key slid through the first lock. She turned it. Then the second.

She yanked the door open, stepped in, flicked on the light, and glanced around.

Safe.

Closing the cottage door, she locked the bolts at both top and bottom. Leaning against the door heavily, she closed her eyes, standing there for long moments, breathing deeply.

Finally she sat on the sofa and pulled off her boots, wiggling her toes to let air around them. Easing her neck from left to right, she worked her hands—*open and close, open and close.*

After a few minutes she sighed and stood up, stretching. Had there been a light on in Dan's house? His car wasn't in the garage. She crossed to the window, thinking she should tell him about the professor. Moonlight glanced off the sea, outlining trees and flowers, but the house was dark.

Well, have some milk, then. Nuke it. Nothing fancy tonight. She took the opened quart from the fridge and filled a yellow mug. Turning around to put it in the microwave, she paused. On the counter was a small crumpled napkin—weighted down by a mum-sized golden marigold. She picked up the flower, then the napkin, thinking Dan must have left them here.

The name "Gepetto's" was printed on one side of the flimsy paper —and below it, a caricature of Nixon with a Pinocchio nose. Curious, Nicole turned it to the other side. Scrawled kitty-corner, as if hastily, was a handwritten note.

> *Nikki, I'm in terrible danger. Whatever you do, don't go near Dan. And don't look for*

Mary! Nicole grabbed the edge of the counter, feeling faint. The handwriting was unmistakable. Not the spare, neat penmanship of Mary's notebooks, but the same straight-up slant, the same un-looped *g* and printed *N* that she always used to begin Nicole's name.

Mary? She looked around wildly, her head jerking from right to left. "Mary, where are you?"

Then she caught herself, feeling foolish. *Mary's not here. She's gone. Hang on, Nicole, hang on.*

She stared at the note again. *Terrible danger . . . don't go near Dan . . .*

Her gaze slid to the bottom corner of the napkin. There was something scribbled there, too—the letters JMJ, and below them, a cross.

It was something Mary had picked up from one of the elderly nuns: JMJ—for Jesus, Mary, and Joseph, at the end of every letter. Ordinarily it would come after her signature, but here the last sentence ended abruptly, and there was no signature.

A conversation filtered back.

"I think it's weird, Mary, ending your letters that way. It's not like you're really a nun, after all."

Mary had stuck her hands on her hips. "It's not any weirder than dotting your i's with hearts, the way some people do. And why do people always think it's strange when you do something religious, anyway?"

The JMJ had become Mary's "personal" signature—a way of saying, *This is me, Mary Clare.*

She felt a chill. *Mary wanted me to know for certain that this was from her. If she didn't have time for both—her name and this—she'd have used the JMJ. So I'd know.*

But why didn't she have time?

The obvious answer came back: *Because someone was trying to harm her. And that someone had caught up.*

Nicole held the napkin up to the ceiling light. Mary had always dated her letters below the Cross. *Yes, here it is. . . . There's hardly any room. . . .*

The date was squeezed into the tiny remaining space in the bottom corner, and it confirmed her fear.

Nicole's fingers went numb. She dropped the napkin and watched it fall to the sink. Slowly, spots of water spread from the size of pennies to huge, angry blobs of blue across the page. The date began to fade away.

11/11 . . . November 11.

The day that Mary died.

Chapter 24

Nicole grabbed the napkin from the sink. The words were blurred, but still readable. She read them over and over, unable to stop. *Terrible danger . . . don't go near Dan . . . don't look for . . .*

What?

Don't look for what?

The blue notebook. It had to be that. Mary had left it with her for Dan, and then had warned her away. From both the notebook and Dan, the night she died.

Why? What had Dan done? And why was this note here now? How did it get here?

Still holding it, still weak, Nicole walked slowly around the breakfast bar and slid onto a stool. Leaning forward on the counter, she covered her eyes. *Please, don't let it be that Dan—*

But she couldn't finish the sentence. Couldn't conceive of an acceptable ending. *That Dan did what?*

That he hurt my sister. That he did something—something that sent her out into the night and off that road.

Her mind clutched at the next logical progression, the worst possible meaning to Mary's note. She kept hitting up against it, and finally she couldn't ignore it.

What if Terry's and Harriet's suspicions were right? What if the accident wasn't an accident, after all? What if Dan . . .

No. It was unthinkable. Dan might be many things, but he wasn't a murderer. This whole thing—this note, the marigold, finding them on the counter—it's a trick, a ghastly trick. Someone is trying to frighten me. But who? And why?

And is there anyone, now, I can trust?

It had never been in Nicole, even under the best of circumstances, simply to trust.

She slid from the stool and began to pace, remembering how it began. *Christmas, wasn't it? When I was eight? Oh, God, it's as clear as if it happened yesterday.*

She had gotten skates from her parents—secondhand, because money was tight that year. Nicole didn't care that the leather was scratched, or that it already had creases from wear. She was thrilled. After Christmas dinner she had tied the yellowed laces, zipped up her parka, pulled on her mittens, and slung her beautiful "new" ice skates over her shoulder—heading for a pond at the teacher's college, several blocks away.

She hadn't been there for a couple of years, not since her friend Judy had moved to New York. Judy's skates had fit Nicole, and they had traded off back then—one taking ten minutes on the ice, then the other. Nicole was never really good at it; her ankles were weak. But she loved it. Once she got going, she could almost believe she would one day be an Olympic medalist, spinning and leaping—being tossed into the air by a handsome boy partner. She even pictured herself in costume, and through one whole school year had drawn sketches of ice dancers on every other notebook page—spangled skirts flashing, arms gracefully held aloft.

On this particular Christmas day there were other kids at the pond already, kids from Nicole's class at school. Seeing her at the edge of the pond, they had called out: "Don't come that way, Nikki! The ice is soft there. Come over here."

Nicole looked from them to the ice, and back again. Barbara Lake, a girl she thought of as a friend, was there—all dressed up in red, her knitted hat flaking with snow. Beside her stood Billy Palmer and Tommy Dietz. They had teased Nicole about something at school the week before.

Maybe that was why she didn't trust them; she couldn't remember now. She just knew she had been certain they were lying. And the ice all looked the same to her.

Nicole took a step forward.

"No—!" all three shouted at once. "Go back! Don't come that way, you'll fall in!"

I'll fall in if I go the way you want me to, she thought.

She took another step. The ice creaked, but it always did that; it felt solid beneath her feet.

"Don't be stupid, Nikki, go back!"

She had a moment of uncertainty, feeling the slick, frozen mirror give slightly with her next step. Was it mushy? Unstable? Should she go back and take the way they had pointed to?

No. She couldn't trust them. It was a trick.

She put her weight on her right foot, pushing herself into a glide. For at least three full seconds, Nicole sailed. She was free.

Then the ice broke.

She had the awful sensation of ground giving way, of a trusted foundation collapsing. The frigid water rose to her knees, her waist, her chin. She heard the kids yelling, "Stupid . . . we told you!"

She went under. The skates, and all her winter clothes became leaden weights, dragging her down. She kicked, trying to touch bottom. But there was nothing beneath her feet, nothing but more water, dark, deep water, and she was sinking. . . .

Then the nylon parka ballooned with air, acting almost as a float. She pushed out frantically with her arms. Surfaced. Heard them yelling. Saw through a watery blur that they were holding out some sort of long stick for her to grab. Saw their hands—multicolored mittens, snow in the creases, reaching.

Humiliated, she turned away. Dog-paddling, she broke through more thin ice to reach a clump of reedy tree limbs jutting up from the black water, her arms and legs so tired now she could barely move, lungs searing with pain from the cold. With one last panicky effort she dragged herself up onto a tiny island of dirt beneath the limbs and lay there, spitting and gagging, her stomach heaving. Wretched.

But safe.

It was growing dark. She felt the other kids' scornful eyes on her. "Stupid!" she heard again, over and over—whispered now behind cold hands. And she knew they were right. She had been stupid; there was something wrong with her. Why didn't she trust people? And why was she so afraid all the time . . . afraid of the dark, afraid of people, always feeling they would hurt her if they could?

A teacher, out for a walk, saw what was happening and dragged a small rowboat from a shed, down to the pond. She paddled out after Nicole, breaking the remaining ice with an oar, pulling her into the boat, then half dragging her over to her car. She wrapped a blanket around her and drove her home. All the way from that little island to shore, Nicole had felt those accusing stares at her back. She would never forget the sound of breaking ice, or of the wind keening through slender reeds at the edge of that darkening pond. Ever since, she had been afraid of water at night. While other kids swam in the pond on hot summer nights, she sat on the shore.

And ever since, her first reaction to any new twist of fate had been, *It's a trick—someone wants to hurt me.*

She shook her head, as if trying to shake the childhood pain away. Staring at the note again, she thought: *I can interpret this in so many ways. But the truth is, the last person I can trust right now is myself. I'm too close, too upset. Too afraid.*

She wished there were someone she could talk to. Someone who knew Mary, who might know what had been going on. If only the professor weren't ill.

What about Harriet Ilsen, then—from the party the other night? She seemed intelligent, with a cool eye for the facts—and she had been Mary's friend.

But, no. If Ilsen had known that Mary was in danger, she would have said so long before. Wouldn't she?

And how do I know she was Mary's friend? Because she said so? What if there was some sort of conspiracy. . . .

Yeah, like Barbara Lake conspiring with Billy Palmer and Tommy Dietz to have me fall through the ice.

Get a grip, Nicole. Haven't you learned your lesson yet?

She crossed to a front window, pulling the curtain slightly aside. Fog had moved in, but she could still see across the patio. A light had come on in Dan's house. Its reflection glanced off the white patio table.

I can't believe Dan would actually have harmed Mary. But what if —purposely or not—he involved her in something? Something that put her in danger?

There seemed, finally, only one thing to do. And she had avoided it far too long.

Crossing to the dresser, she searched through it for the socks that held the photograph of her sister and Dan. Unfolding them, something seemed different about the way they were rolled. But she must have done that herself; the photograph was still there. Tucking it and the Gepetto's cocktail napkin into her skirt pocket, she pulled a pair of soft brown sandals from the closet and slipped them on.

As she crossed the dark patio, the scent of marigolds was strong. A toe caught on a flagstone, and she nearly fell. Reaching out, she grabbed the back of a damp metal chair to right herself. There was a small scrape of sound as metal slid against stone. She caught her breath, realizing only then that she was deliberately trying to make a quiet approach, hoping to take Dan by surprise. She didn't know why.

There were no cars passing by on the street above, and no light anywhere, save the dim one issuing from Dan's house. The moon had disappeared with the fog, and you wouldn't know the sea was there past the bluff, save for the dull *slap, slap* it made against rocks.

A gull, squatting on Dan's roof, flapped its wings. Nicole stifled a scream.

The patio doors were closed, the drapes drawn. She looked down at the latch, saw it was in the open position. She reached for the handle. Sliding it sideways, quietly, she listened.

Dan was talking with someone. But she heard only his voice, followed by brief pauses. The words were clipped and tense. He seemed to be pacing.

"I'm telling you, she won't be any trouble. If she is, she goes—it's as simple as that."

Another silence followed. He was on the phone.

"No. We can't force her . . . she's the wrong person to try that with. If she thinks we're trying to control her in any way . . . blow the whole deal sky high."

His voice faded in and out as he moved about the room. Nicole pushed the door open farther. The drapes billowed inward from the damp breeze. She froze. Had he seen?

But the conversation continued. "I'll get back to you tomorrow, soon as I know what effect . . . no, there should be some response . . . may not let on. Hold on."

She was standing with one toe on the door's track when Dan whipped the drapes aside. The look he gave her was frigid; as if he had torn a mask from his face.

"I'll have to call you back," he snapped into the cordless phone. He clicked it off, grabbing Nicole's wrist and pulling her in. "What the hell are you doing? How long have you been here?"

She stumbled into the room, then yanked herself free, rubbing her wrist. "Well, I'm so goddamned sorry!" she said angrily. "I didn't realize you had anything to hide."

Abruptly, he changed. "Oh, damn . . . I'm sorry, but you startled me. Did I hurt you?" He reached for her wrist again, turning it gently, looking for marks. Somehow that was worse than the original pain. She pulled away.

"I was talking to my backer—on a new film," Dan said. His smile was boyish, the old charm falling into place easily. "I guess you heard. He was giving me a hard time."

She didn't respond.

"I, uh . . . well, I'm not proud of some of the tactics I have to use out here in Hollywood." He motioned to the round glass dining-room table. "Sit down, I'll get us something to drink. Wine? I've got some nice chardonnay from the Napa Valley. I remember you always liked chardonnay. . . ."

Don't let him pull you off track, Nicole. He's good at that, at covering truth with illusion.

She watched his face. "I'd rather hear more about these tactics. And the woman you were talking about, the one you might have to force into doing something."

He pulled a wine bottle and two glasses from a cupboard. "An actress. Cheryl Stark—you know, she was nominated last year for *Seductions.* I'd like her to do the narration, because she's got that great, sympathetic tone and style. But she's insisting on top billing and appearance on screen as host. I didn't want a star on screen for this particular piece. It's about natural disasters and I don't want to give it the Hollywood look. I like her voice, but physically, she doesn't have the right image for something this serious. . . ."

It was a lengthy explanation. He seemed nervous—rattling on and on. Pulling the cork from the wine, he broke it and had to insert the corkscrew a second time. Finally, he was pouring chardonnay for both of them. Coming around the counter, he held out a glass. Nicole shook her head, her eyes never leaving his face.

"You said something about different tactics. Does that mean you're losing your values here? Beginning to sell out?"

He shrugged and set her glass on the table. "I'm not sure I even know what 'selling out' means anymore. There are things you do for a greater purpose. . . ."

He sounded more like a lawyer than ever. Reason and logic above all else. No real feeling. *God, how cold he can be.*

He left the sentence unfinished and took a chair across from her, glancing at his watch. "Did you just get home?"

"A while ago."

"Was there any special reason you came over?"

Nicole hesitated—unsure, now, how to proceed. "I guess I felt like talking."

He leaned back in his chair. "How was your date?"

"Date?"

"Didn't you go out with that guy you met at the conference, or something? Blake, I think his name was."

"Jack Blake. No. I've been at the UC Med Center. The professor had a heart attack."

His eyes widened. "Professor Dirstoff? My God, what happened?"

"He collapsed while I was talking to his class at UCLA."

"That's terrible. Is he all right?"

She was amazed at how quickly his emotions had switched . . . from anger, to charm, to worry.

"They say it was mild," she answered.

"Well, thank God. I haven't seen the professor lately. I'll stop by when he's feeling better."

She was silent.

Again he glanced at his watch. "Uh . . . anything else on your mind?"

She'd have to say it. Get it out, no matter how hard. "I've been thinking about you and Mary."

The eyes went blank. "What about me and Mary?"

She reached into her skirt pocket for the note. Hesitating only a moment—feeling the weight of its possible consequences in her hand—she held it out to him.

Dan took it, turning the napkin front to back, seemingly bewildered. "What is it?"

"Read it."

"Nikki, we're both too tired for this." He sighed. Then his eyes began to scan the words. His fingers tightened on the note. "Where did you get this?"

"It was on the kitchen counter just now, in the cottage."

"I don't understand. Who is it from?"

"It's Mary Clare's writing."

"Mary's?" He looked at it again. "Are you sure?"

"Yes."

"But how did it get in the cottage?"

"I have no idea. Look at the date."

He glanced at the note again, not finding it.

"It's in the bottom corner, beneath the JMJ."

He held it up to the light. "Eleven-eleven." His forehead creased. "I don't—"

"Mary died November eleventh."

He shot her an angry look. "I *know* that, Nikki! I damn well remember when Mary died. But how could— Where the hell did this come from?"

Nicole reached over and slid the note from his fingers, shoving it back into her pocket.

"Funny you didn't ask first what it means. Mary says she's in danger. She warned me away from you."

He reached for his wineglass and drained it. His arm jerked, the straw-colored fluid spilling down his chin, onto his shirt. With deliberate care he set down the glass and wiped his mouth with the back of his hand. "I don't want to talk about this."

Her voice hardened. "Too bad. I do. Why was Mary afraid of you, Dan?"

He swung to his feet, an angry red flushing his face. "That's enough, Nicole."

She rose too, matching his anger. "What was going on between you and my sister?"

"Nothing! Nothing was going on between me and Mary. What are you talking about?"

She pulled out the photograph. Held it up for him to see. His hand reached out, a finger touching the celluloid image of Mary. His mouth moved with her name, and his eyes closed briefly. Several seconds passed before the mask fell into place once more.

Dan shrugged. "It's a picture of me and Mary. So what?"

"So what? So you look like you're on your goddamned honeymoon!"

His jaw hardened. "How can you possibly read something like that into an ordinary photograph?"

"Well, Dan, you've got your arms around each other, and your cheeks are touching. It was incredibly easy."

"Christ, Nikki! We were on a fishing trip, down off Redondo. There were other people on the boat. Mary caught a fish, the first of her life, and she was jumping up and down, laughing. I grabbed her to hug her. It was a hug of congratulations, that's all. Someone on the boat snapped the picture." He stood, almost toppling his chair as he shoved it away. "Mary and I were friends—that's it. Period. And I don't know why she wrote that note."

She grabbed his arm as he headed for the door. "Oh, no, you don't! You aren't walking away from this. You always want to talk until I start getting close to the truth, then you get scared and run."

He shook himself free. "Look who's talking about running. You always did this. Just about the time we might be getting close, you'd find something to argue about. You'd throw that wall between us— the same way you did when I told you I was moving out here. You didn't want to talk about it, you just ended the relationship. One day we were together, the next it was over. You gave me no choice."

She stared at him, astounded. *"You're* the one who moved away!"

"I asked you to come with me."

"Like hell you did!"

"Well, I tried—you just didn't give me a chance."

Her eyes widened. "That's *crazy!* You never—not in an entire year did you give me even one sign that you wanted our relationship to develop into something more."

"I most definitely did. You just didn't see it."

"Oh, really? Tell me when. When exactly did you say any words to that effect?"

"Dammit, Nikki, why do you have to nail things down all the time, talk about them, put them in neatly labeled boxes? Can't you ever just go with your feelings? Do you have to analyze everything to death?"

"Analyze? Because I'd like to hear something in clear, concise English once in a while? *'Nikki, I love you. Nikki, I care about you. Nikki, I don't want to lose you.'"*

"I told you I loved you—more than once."

"Right, as a friend. You always added that."

"Well, goddammit, I thought you knew I felt more."

"Well, goddammit, you never *said* that!"

"Because you didn't want to hear it. If I'd said it, you'd have run a mile."

She shook her head, stunned at the direction the conversation was taking. "I don't know where you got that idea."

"You've been running from relationships all your life, Nikki. Ever since you were a kid. Hell, you don't even like men."

"Don't like—" She was outraged. "That, coming from someone I cared about, gave my love and loyalty to for a solid year—with, I might add, very little in return?"

"Yeah, well, you and I—maybe we were perfect for each other. Maybe the minute you let down your walls, I threw up mine. So we both got what we wanted. We were safe. We never had to worry that we'd get too close."

"That's not true. I wanted—"

She had wanted to be close. It was only he who had run from it. *Wasn't it?*

She shook her head. "This is insane. I don't want to talk about this —I came over here about Mary. I want to know what you did to her, what you got her involved in."

But he wouldn't let it go. "You came over to throw up another wall, Nikki. The other day when we were on the beach, I knew that you were starting to have feelings for me again. I was feeling things too. But dammit, I also knew you wouldn't let it last."

It was too much. "I can hardly *have feelings* for someone who was fucking my own sister!"

He blanched, rocking back as if she'd struck him. "That doesn't even begin to come close to the truth."

But she hardly heard, wasn't listening. Things were coming out, things she'd never meant to say but couldn't hold back. "Everything I ever wanted, Mary got. All the love, all the attention. Even our mother liked her better, I knew that, it was always that way—"

Dan grabbed her shoulders. "Stop! Stop it right there, Nikki. No, don't turn away—*think*. If you really believe that, tell me why. Why did your mother like Mary better?"

"I—" She wrenched away. "How the hell would I know?"

"You *do* know. *Say* it."

She began to pace. "Mary was a more likable child, that's all. She got better grades, and even so, she was more fun. She wasn't serious back then."

"Forget Mary. Tell me about you. And while you're at it, tell me about your father."

She faced him, her mouth suddenly dry. "What about my father?"

"To begin with, you never talk about the man."

She wet her lips. "I barely remember him."

"Kids always have some memories, especially about a father who's died. Do you ever miss him? Wish he were back?"

"I told you, dammit, I don't *remember.*"

"Like hell you don't. Mary was six years younger than you, and she remembered."

"Well, maybe she had a better memory!"

"Or she wasn't as adept at blanking things out."

Heat rose in her face. Her shoulders tightened, her back muscles began to spasm. "What the hell does that mean?"

"Mary learned to face what had happened and deal with it—unlike you."

Nicole hugged herself, feeling cold. "This is ridiculous."

"So let's get back to why your mother liked Mary better. She liked her better because . . . Finish the sentence, Nikki. Say it right out. Your mother liked Mary better because . . ."

Her fists clenched. "Shut up! Just shut up!"

"Because Mary was the one your father never touched."

A heavy silence fell. It was as if the room had been filled with something dark and menacing, some awful black presence so appalling it couldn't be named. Nicole's vision seemed to fail.

When she could speak at last, her voice was small and frail, not much more than a child's whisper. "You don't know anything about that. How can you stand there like some . . . some two-bit psychiatrist . . ." Her eyes filled with tears, and she covered her shaking mouth.

"I've done three documentaries on child abuse," Dan said softly. "I've talked to women in shelters, to children in treatment. You never wanted to talk about those films. I wondered why. And I asked Mary."

Her eyes widened; she was stunned. "Mary told you?" *Mary knew?*

"She was relieved to get it out in the open. She said she was always afraid to talk to you about it because your defenses were so strong. She was afraid if she broke through them, things would never be the same between you. Meanwhile, she was lonely. She never felt really connected to you."

Nicole's hands went to her cheeks. "Stop it! Don't say that!"

"You've built this image of yourself, Nikki—Nicole the Untouchable, the university teacher controlled by her intellect. You reason everything out because that's what you learned to do, to save yourself as a child. Even now you never make decisions based on the way you feel. You don't trust your emotions. Christ, Nikki, anyone who's ever studied the subject can see what's been going on with you. If you had done anything as a child based on the way you felt, you might have killed the man. Now you keep us all at arm's length so you won't have to risk being hurt again."

She barely heard him, still lost in the terrible thought: *Mary knew.* She couldn't get past that. *All those years, Mary knew.*

She didn't realize she had said it aloud.

"She knew," Dan said, "and she felt guilty."

"Guilty? Why?"

"Because the reason your father left her alone was that he had you. Mary had to live with the fact that all those years, you were the only thing that stood between her and him."

"No—" Tears filled her eyes.

"She was also very much afraid. Because she knew that when she got older, he'd have her too. It was a blessing he died when you were fourteen. And your mother—Nikki, didn't it ever occur to you to wonder why your mother died at such a young age?"

Nicole shook her head numbly, only part of her understanding. "My mother had cancer."

"But why?"

"Why? For God's sake, people get cancer! How do I know why?"

"Some people think it's a disease of despair. There are things a person can't face, circumstances they can't live with anymore. Guilt, depression—people get sick from those things."

"Are you implying that my mother knew all along?"

"Think about it, Nikki. Mothers almost always know, at some

level. Maybe yours did, maybe she didn't. But the result was the same. You weren't protected. And you never felt taken care of."

"She tried. . . ."

"Possibly. But did she try hard enough? Or was she afraid? Did she look the other way?"

Nicole turned to the window and stared out at the fog. She felt as if she were falling, the same dread sinking sensation as falling through the ice all those many years ago.

Because the people you were supposed to be able to trust . . .

Her eyes closed. Against their darkness she could see her childhood room, and an eight-year-old Nicole under the covers, afraid to breathe. The bedroom door opening softly; a shaft of light from the hall slanting over her bed. *Move!* she is screaming inside herself. *Get up! Don't let him do it again!*

She saw herself not moving—not getting up, not running. Instead letting it happen, over and over, year after year, until all the trust had eroded away. Not just for him, but for everyone.

An overwhelming depression struck her. For years the horrors of her childhood had been shoved into a box in the corner of her mind, labeled: DO NOT OPEN IN THIS LIFETIME—OR POSSIBLY EVEN IN THE NEXT. Now, Dan . . .

Her thoughts took a hard, protective turn. *Remember the lesson, at least. You still don't know who you can trust.*

Abruptly, she straightened her back, lifted her chin, and faced Dan. "You've managed nicely to swing this conversation away from Mary's warning about you—and onto me."

"Nikki—"

The telephone rang. Dan turned in irritation.

"Go ahead." She folded her arms. "Must be important—someone calling this late."

He gave her a look, then grabbed it up. "Hello!"

He turned his back to her slightly. "Yes. It's going just fine. But I can't talk now."

A distinctively female voice came from the receiver. Dan gave a soft chuckle.

"No, not now. I'll call you later."

He hung up and turned back to Nicole. The kitchen light was harsh on his face, revealing new lines. He gave her a tired smile. "Sorry about that. My backer again. You remember how it is at the beginning of these projects? Constant back and forth, checking into things."

"Yes." She remembered. "I remember that you never seemed to have time for me—back then, when you were starting a new project. You were always off and running with whoever the fresh blood was . . . the new producer, camera person, script girl . . ."

"You were jealous."

"Don't reduce it to anything so simple. I may have been insecure, but you were insensitive. There's a saying—just because you're paranoid doesn't mean you aren't being followed."

And Dan was still not someone she could trust.

"Nikki . . . what are you trying to do?"

"Speak the truth for once, I guess."

He ran exasperated fingers through his hair. "Dammit, you're throwing up that wall. Again."

"And why does it have to be that I'm 'throwing up a wall'? Isn't it possible I'm just seeing things clearly—maybe for the first time?"

"No. You're shutting out the way you *feel.*" He clenched a fist. "And you're so damned suspicious. Look at this, tonight. You stood outside my door eavesdropping on a private phone call. And then that note. Instead of showing it to me right away, you try to lead me into some sort of trap—"

"*Trap.* An interesting choice of words. And you know what, Dan? It looks very much like it worked."

"What are you talking about?"

"That story you told me, explaining the photograph—how Mary had caught her first fish and was so excited, you hugged her? Well, guess what? Mary didn't catch her first fish with you last spring. She caught it at the age of six. I remember the moment clearly. My father had me cornered in the cabin of his friend's sailboat while Mary was out on deck reeling in a twelve-inch flounder."

Dan's eyes shifted momentarily. *Caught out.* Then rage took over. She saw it move through his head like a rogue wave. "I'm out of here!" He grabbed keys from a small glass dish on the table and, brushing by her, stormed out the door.

Nicole stood motionless as it slammed, then shuddered on its hinges. She heard Dan run up the steps, heard the car peel out of the garage. Then—more awful than all the rest—she heard the silence. For within the silence lay the unspoken words: *What really happened to Mary?*

He never did ask that, she remembered. *It was almost as if he knew.*

Chapter 25

Nicole's heavy steps took her not to the cottage, but out on the bluff. She stumbled over loose rocks and clumps of weeds, unable to find the path in the dark, and too numb to care. At the edge of the bluff a cold wind blew, tangling her hair. She stood gazing blankly at the waves that moved in slow, lazy lines toward shore, then at the moon, which was low on the horizon and almost obscured by fog. Tears ran unchecked down her face.

I don't know what to do now, Mary. I'm so confused. And I miss you, I miss you so much.

She dropped to the ground, ignoring the dampness and cold, and drew up her knees, burying her face in her arms. *It's such a mess. Did you see, Mary? What he did? He reached inside my soul and yanked out all the pain I've been hiding there for years, without any thought for how I felt, or what it might do.*

He used it, Mary. Used me. He didn't want me to see that he's hiding something. But I know it's true.

And you . . . what did he do to you?

I need answers, Mary. And people who aren't involved in this. People who can help.

Tell me who to trust.

The wind blew, and if she thought she heard answers in its keening, they were garbled, unclear. Her shoulders began to shake, and she let it all out—all the grief and confusion, past and present, crying until it frightened her, until she wondered if she'd ever be able to stop.

When she finally had the strength to raise her head and wipe her face on her sleeve, the moon had passed out of sight. Nicole was stiff and chilled to the bone. Her throat hurt; her eyes were nearly swollen shut.

But her head had begun to clear.

I know one thing. I know that I have to fight back.

She eased herself up, bent nearly double by the cold ache in her joints. Slowly, she straightened her back until her spine was upright, until she felt new courage begin to pour through.

Moments later, at the cottage, she saw that only an hour had passed out there on the bluff.

In her heart she had moved forward light-years.

Inquest

Chapter 26

From the cottage phone Nicole called the Ocean Palms Hotel and reserved a room. She checked her watch: after one A.M. "I'll be there in about an hour," she said.

Next she called the business office at the Pasadena police station. "I'd like to reach an Officer De Santo," she told the woman who answered. "My friend's house was broken into earlier tonight, and he answered the call. I'd like to talk to him about it."

"Do you have new information on the crime?" the woman asked.

"No. I'd just like to ask him some questions, if that's all right."

"Sure. But we have two De Santos—Leo and Luis. Where was the break-in?"

Nicole gave her the address on Buena Vista. "My friend's name is Dirstoff. Henry Dirstoff."

"On Buena Vista? Let's see. . . ." Papers rattled. "That'd be Leo. Sergeant Leo De Santo. His shift was over a little while ago, but I can ask him to call you when he comes in tomorrow. That'd be around four."

"Well . . . I wonder, would it be possible to reach him at home in the morning? I'd really like to talk to him before that."

"Sorry, I can't give you his home number. If it's important, I could call him for you," the woman said helpfully. "He'll probably get back to you. Leo's good that way."

"It is important."

"Okay, give me your name and number. If I can reach him, I'll give him the message."

"Thanks. It's Nicole Ryan. I'll be at the Ocean Palms Hotel in Santa Monica." Nicole read the number from her address book. "Please ask him to call me first thing in the morning, if he can."

She tossed her suitcase onto the sofa and packed quickly, including Mary's black case and the book she'd found in it, *The Maya Question*. Making a last quick check around, she wondered if she should leave the cottage keys on a table, or in Dan's house. Almost without thinking about it, she shoved them into her purse.

It was while she was closing the double Dutch doors behind her that the idea came to her. *The woman on the phone. Was she the same person he'd been talking to earlier, while she was standing outside his patio door? Had he lied about it being a backer? And did he originate that call?*

She left her suitcase on the patio. Moving quickly, she crossed to Dan's house and let herself in through the sliding glass doors.

The cordless phone was where Dan had left it, on the dining-room table. She pressed the talk button, then punched the redial.

"Hullo," a sleepy female voice said.

"Uh, hello . . . is Joyce Robinson there?"

"Sorry, you've got the wrong number."

"Is this 555-5804?"

"No."

She could hear the phone shift, knew the woman was getting ready to hang up.

"Wait, please." She spoke quickly. "Can you tell me what number I reached? I'm calling long distance. I'd like to get credit."

A sigh, the voice still husky. "You've got 555-6012. It's a private home."

A click, and then a dial tone.

Nicole wrote the number on the pad that hung by the phone. She tore it off and stared at it. Then she shoved it into her purse.

With one last glance around the patio, she wondered why she had thought this house, this setting, so beautiful at first. Even the sea, stretching out there into the vast darkness, seemed menacing now. As if the tide might rise, and with one massive, angry wave, carry her away.

Chapter 27

The hotel room was nearly identical to the one Nicole had left two days before. She quickly unpacked, then called the Med Center, asking to be connected to the unit the professor was in. A different nurse answered, but she seemed up-to-date on the professor's condition. "He's doing well—better than expected, in fact. He has a strong will to live."

"Is his niece there?"

"Yes. She's spending the night."

"Can I see him in the morning?"

"Better give it until evening. That'll be twenty-four hours, and we'll see how he's doing then."

"Thanks. Give him my love, will you? And please tell him I called. Nicole Ryan."

"Sure."

"Oh, and one other thing. I've just moved into a hotel, and I'd like to leave the new number, in case you need to reach me."

"Of course."

Nicole read it aloud. "Would it be too much—could you pass it along to the professor's niece, too, if you see her?"

"I'd be glad to."

"Thanks."

She called down to the night desk clerk. "Is the concierge on?"

"Not until seven in the morning. May I help you with something?"

"I need something to write on. Some lined paper, if possible."

"Of course. I'm sure I can find you something in the manager's office."

Within five minutes there was a hotel employee at her door with not only paper but pencils. Until four in the morning Nicole sat at the table overlooking the 3rd Street Promenade, writing.

"It was nice of you to come all this way to meet me," Nicole said. It was a little after one o'clock, and she and De Santo stood in the lobby of the Ocean Palms. "I'd have driven to Pasadena."

He shrugged. "I like coming out here to the beach on my days off.

It's good for people-watching." They walked outside, and he glanced down at her. "Don't take this wrong, but you look like you could use a good strong cup of coffee."

"I could. I was up all night."

"There's a little sandwich shop down here with the best coffee around. That okay?"

"Perfect."

He turned left on the sidewalk, leading the way to a small restaurant with a low white fence around an outside patio. They took a table, and a waitress appeared with water.

"Two coffees?"

They both nodded. "Please."

"Anything else? Danish, a sandwich?"

Nicole shook her head, and De Santo said, "Maybe later. Thanks."

The coffee came. It was rich and strong, as De Santo had promised. Nicole added cream and sugar, drank deeply, then studied her cup. She felt ill at ease, unsure how to begin.

"You, uh . . . you probably don't get a lot of calls from people you've met on the job."

He smiled. "More than you'd think. Especially in domestic disturbances. People see cops as peacemakers, the first person they call for when things get rough again." He gave her a sharp look. "Is this about the break-in last night?"

"It could be. But I don't even know why I think that. It's sort of gut level, and I could be all wrong." She rubbed her brow tiredly.

He shifted position, leaning back in his chair and stretching out his legs. "I'm not in any real hurry. Why don't you drink your coffee and relax a little, then we can talk."

She gave him a grateful look. "Thanks."

De Santo's dark eyes lazily scanned the passersby. Nicole finished her cup. It was quickly refilled.

"There's a strange, awful dichotomy about this place," she observed.

"The Promenade?" He glanced around the enclosed street, lined with restaurants, bookstores, clothing shops.

"Yes. There's obviously been money spent to make it attractive— all these black iron benches, trees, flowers, old-fashioned lampposts. But then you have that, over there."

She nodded toward the doorway of an empty store across the way. A bearded man was stretched out, sleeping, his head resting on a travel-worn duffel bag. He was dressed in ragged khakis.

"And that woman," she said softly. At a nearby table a thin, very old woman sat with a cup of coffee. She was dressed in a thirties-style chemise, faded red, with tassels. On her cheek was a large black beauty spot. Her head was nearly bald. The few wisps of hair she had left were bleached to a bright, coarse yellow. The woman mumbled to herself, peering suspiciously over her cup.

"It's L.A.," De Santo said. "Here, they're getting to be the norm."

"You said you come here to people-watch. Doesn't it make you sad?"

"It's not always what I'd call fun. But I study, I learn. It's important to know the people you're supposed to be protecting."

"But you work in Pasadena."

He gave a shrug. "People are people. There are some with money and some without. Some who'll commit crimes and some who won't. Once you get a fix on certain things, there aren't a lot of surprises."

"There must be some."

He sighed, lacing his fingers over his stomach. "That's true. There are always the ones who fool you."

Nicole drank her coffee and studied him—a solid man, with hard-muscled arms and only a bit of thickening around the waist. She guessed he didn't sit in a patrol car munching doughnuts when things were quiet. He'd be the type to get out and about, see what was going on, make things happen. Leo De Santo had the look of someone who'd struggled in life to get where he was; the face a bit worn, the hairline receding, but eyes that were gentle and not yet embittered. Seeing him in daylight, she guessed he must be in his forties. She wondered how he had managed to keep from being hardened by his line of work.

The heavy-lidded eyes were on a street performer at the moment —an old black man with gray hair and a stained gray suit. The cuffs of the pants were frayed; the seat almost worn through. A battered suitcase for donations was on the sidewalk before him, and they had seen him set it up, priming the pump with a handful of quarters, dimes, and two one-dollar bills. The man was playing a sax, and so far as Nicole could tell, not even Getz in his prime had done better.

The man's audience was thin, however, his prospects not too good. On a weekday in November there were few people on the Promenade. Nicole knew from her previous stay here that on Wednesdays there were crowds at the west end, for the farmer's market. But up this way some of the shops had closed down, victims of the continuing recession. She wondered if there would be a major revival of the Hare Krishnas on the streets. With Krishna being the god of the lower classes, and the former middle classes being relegated to that position now, people would be looking for something. Or someone. A guru, a god.

De Santo was watching her quizzically. She smiled.

"I teach mythology. And I was thinking that maybe what the world needs now is a Brahma—a god of energy. According to legend, when the present age of the world is over, water will cover everything. Then high above it, Brahma will appear on a lotus stalk to carry out his periodic task of creating the earth anew."

"A clean slate?" De Santo shook his head. "I don't know. Before me, my dad was a cop—one of the first Latinos on the force. All my life has been focused on fixing up what we've already got."

"A Vishnu, then." Nicole smiled. "Vishnu corrects or removes evil. It's his job to attack and destroy the forces of injustice."

De Santo brightened. "I like that better. Vishnu, huh?"

"His wife was the goddess of beauty and wealth. Have you got a wife, De Santo?"

"Not lately. At least, not so's you'd notice." He sighed, and from his expression she knew there was trouble at home, and that he didn't really want to talk about it.

"If you're feeling better," he said, leaning forward and folding his arms on the table, "I do have some word on the break-in at your friend's house."

"Really?"

"Yeah. I don't know how this fits into your own thoughts on the subject, but we caught the guy we think did it. A kid. He was making the rounds, and another patrol spotted him three blocks away. He was carrying a trash bag with jewelry, cash, a few wallets."

"What about the professor's suitcase?"

"He didn't have it on him. But he couldn't have carried it around very easily. My guess is he took it back to the car, then moved on down the street, figuring we were busy with you. These kids are pretty casual. They don't seem to sweat it out too much, just do their thing and move on."

"You didn't find the car?"

"Not yet. And the kid's denying everything, including being at that house."

"So you don't know for sure it was him."

"No." De Santo studied her a moment. "Ms. Ryan, what's going on?"

She set the heavy white cup on its saucer, carefully. Staring into it, she tried to think how to say what she had to say without coming across as a nut. "I don't really know. I guess I was hoping you might be able to get some information for me. I need someone completely objective—first, to look at what I think is going on and tell me if I'm crazy. And if I'm not crazy, then I need help finding out who killed my sister."

There, it was out. Just like that. Someone killed my sister.

Nicole felt herself wanting to cry from the relief of having said the words. Laughing slightly, she dabbed at her eyes with a paper napkin. "I'm sorry. I didn't mean to do this. I just don't know who else to trust."

De Santo slid his own, cleaner napkin over to her. "Here. Cry all you want." He shrugged his massive shoulders and gave her a kind smile. "Hell, nobody's here to see. Or the few people who are, are so out of it, they wouldn't know if you stood on the table and did a belly dance."

She couldn't help laughing. "I don't think we have to worry about that." Then the tears started again, and she wiped at them some more. Her hands shook. "It's just that things have been getting so crazy. But I'm sorry . . . taking up your time this way. I know you have to go to work."

De Santo shrugged again. "Not until four. And not much happens up in Pasadena. If it does, I've been around twenty years—long enough to know they'll get by without me." He grinned. "For a while, anyway."

"Even so. I want to get this out before I lose my courage."

He leaned forward. "I'm listening. You said you think someone killed your sister?"

"I don't know. I think it's possible."

"When did this happen?"

"Last week . . . a week ago Tuesday."

"What happened?"

The question was gently put, but she could see the coplike curiosity behind shrewd eyes.

"It was supposedly an accident. Her car went off a bridge, into the river."

"The police investigated?"

"Yes."

"And they were satisfied it was an accident."

"Yes."

"Where did it happen?"

"In Georgetown. Maryland. I live there, and Mary did too."

"But you think the police might have overlooked something. Can you tell me why?"

Nicole pulled the cocktail napkin, with Mary's note on it, out of her purse. She handed it to him. "This was in the cottage where I was staying last night."

De Santo read it through, then looked up at her, his dark brows knitting. "You're sure this is your sister's handwriting?"

"If not, it's a good forgery. It looks just like Mary's, and it's signed the way she always signed her letters, with that JMJ and the cross" —she pointed to it with a fingertip—"here at the bottom."

He studied the note again, turning it front to back, then front again.

"I suppose other people knew she signed her letters with this JMJ?"

"Yes. You're right, anyone could have done that. I just thought—"

"What?"

"I thought that since she did that instead of signing her name, it might be some sort of message, something to tell me it was really from her."

He set the note on the table, holding it down with one thick finger. "Well, I think the first thing you should probably do is send this through a lab for analysis. You'd need something else you know for sure is in your sister's handwriting. And if it is from her, and she was in danger—who is this Dan she says not to go near?"

"A friend out here. He lives in Malibu now, but Mary and I met him in Georgetown. We, uh, we've known each other a year or so."

"A close friend?"

"I used to think so. I was staying at his house until last night."

"And you moved out? Because of this warning?"

"That . . . and other things."

"Did you show him this note?"

She nodded.

De Santo studied her. "You can't be too afraid of this guy or you'd have come to me first—or to the police, somewhere."

She glanced away. "I guess so. I don't know."

"You were personally involved with him?"

Nicole hesitated, then decided there wasn't much point in tap-dancing around the facts. "We were friends. I fell in love and he dumped me."

"I'm sorry. Recently?"

"Three months ago."

"So you don't have a lot of reason to trust him, going in. And then along comes this note."

"Yes."

"Even so, you showed it to him."

Irritation flickered. "Why do you keep saying that?"

De Santo leaned back in his chair. "Just wanted to make sure I understood."

"Understood what?"

"How he fits in, that's all."

Nicole rubbed her forehead. "I'm sorry. I didn't mean to snap at you."

"Tell you what." He took out a small spiral pad. "Give me his full name and address. I'll run a check on him, see if we come up with anything."

"You mean something criminal?" She couldn't keep the note of surprise out of her voice.

"Well, you did say you only knew him a year. That's not very long these days. You ever meet his family?"

"No."

"Ever talk to anybody who knew him as a kid, lived in his hometown, went to school with him?"

"No, but—"

"Like I said, I'll run a check."

She met his eyes, then looked down at her hands. The nails were cutting into her palms. She eased her fingers open and rubbed the sore tissue. Giving De Santo the information on Dan, she sipped her coffee moodily.

"I, uh . . . I think he was having an affair with my sister."

With a start, De Santo looked up from his writing. "This guy, Rossi? You think he and your sister, the one who wrote the note—?"

"Yes."

He dropped his pen and let out a soft whoosh of air. "Kid," he said after a brief pause, "this is the way it looks to me. You've got too many things to deal with at once. First you've got the grief over your sister's death, and now, not knowing for sure what happened, you got fear. Not to mention a lot of anger. It's tearing you apart. And it's got to be confusing as hell."

Nicole set her coffee down and rubbed her eyes. "I guess that's why I needed a clear head, someone to look at all this objectively."

De Santo nodded. "Okay, then, let's move on. The note warns you not to look for something."

"I can't be sure, but I think that might mean a notebook—one Mary gave me to give to Dan in case anything happened to her."

"She was worried something was going to happen?"

"Yes. There was an explosion in her lab last summer. Mary wasn't there, but a friend of hers was, another scientist. She died in the resulting fire. After that, Mary gave me the notebook."

"You weren't worried about her yourself?"

"Not at the time. Mary was like that from childhood—she'd worry when things happened to other people. I thought that was all it was."

"So what was in this notebook?"

"Mary said it was research for a film Dan was working on. She helped him that way sometimes. We both did."

"You didn't look inside the notebook?"

"No. I thought she was just being silly, and I remember I was in a hurry that day. I stuck it away in a bottom drawer, and then I just plain forgot it."

"Where's this notebook now?"

"I don't know. When I remembered it the other day after the funeral, it wasn't there."

De Santo sighed heavily and shifted position. "Okay . . . Is there anything else?"

"Right after the funeral last week, an airline ticket appeared at my door." She explained about the Express Mail envelope, the call to the travel agency.

"I thought the agency had simply made a mistake, and I wanted to come out here anyway, so I used the ticket. But now I'm wondering if someone purposely sent that ticket because they wanted me out here."

"Do you know why that might be?"

"No. I can't even begin to imagine."

"And this incident at your friend's house last night. You think it's connected somehow?"

"I—it's just a feeling. And you were right, I've had a lot to handle. I may be—oh, I don't know, looking for shadows under the bed." She gave a short, bitter laugh. "I just remembered . . . I accused Mary of that, the day she gave me the notebook."

De Santo picked up the cocktail napkin and looked at it again. "Gepetto's. You ever been there?"

She shook her head. "I've heard of it, but no."

"What about your sister?"

"As far as I know, she never went to bars. She didn't even go out, usually, at night. She lived near her lab and spent almost all of her time between the two. Mary was . . . different."

"Kind of a loner?"

"Yes, but not in a bad way. Not weird, I mean. She was focused on her work, and she was deeply spiritual as well. Her closest friends were the nuns at Sacred Heart."

De Santo put the note between them and folded his arms on the table again, leaning toward her. "Look, kid. You could shrug a lot of this stuff off, maybe. Put it down to coincidence, misunderstanding, whatever. But this note?" He glanced down at it. "Whoever entered the place you were staying last night and put it there was clearly sending you a message. And I don't want to scare you, but I think you're damned right to take it seriously."

Nicole felt a flicker of fear. Yet at the same time, De Santo's words somehow set her free. "I guess I needed to hear that from someone else."

They were silent a few moments, drinking their third coffee refill. Finally De Santo said, "First thing is the handwriting analysis. I can run it through our lab if you get me a sample you know is your sister's for sure."

Nicole was surprised. "You'll do that for me? You'll help me?"

"Sure, it's easier for me. And as soon as I get in this afternoon, I'll put a call through to the Georgetown PD. See what kind of investigation they did, and if they had any doubts about the accident. Sometimes individual cops will have questions, but there's no way to prove anything, so it never goes anywhere."

She felt her eyes tear again. "I can't thank you enough."

"Well, you've been dealing with too much, like I said. That's what's been driving you nuts. It's important to take a slow, steady course, one thing at a time."

He reached into his back pocket and pulled out a wallet. "There is one thing I'd like you to do for me."

"Of course."

He searched through the worn leather wallet and drew out a business card. "Here. Check this guy out."

Nicole scanned the card, then glanced up in surprise. "I don't understand."

"Look, you gotta learn to take care of yourself. Even if that business last night had nothing to do with you, it's a crazy world out there. Now, you're doing okay, all things considered—but the way I see it, you're pretty near the edge."

"You're right," she admitted. "I am. But this?"

"It'll be good for your self-confidence. We'll just hope you don't need it for anything else."

She glanced at the card again. "This is just down the street."

"Friend of mine. I stop in there all the time." De Santo stood, the heavy, competent hands on his hips. "Anything else before I take off? Anything you need?"

She rummaged in her purse. "Would it be possible to find out whose number this is?" She drew out the slip of paper with the phone number of the woman who had answered the redial on Dan's phone.

De Santo took it. "The prefix looks like Beverly Hills. Sure, I can find out for you. Is this part of all this trouble?"

"I don't honestly know."

"Okay. I'll get back to you on it."

"I can't tell you how much I appreciate all this," Nicole said again.

"You're an easy lady to do things for, Ms. Ryan. And I don't like the idea that there's somebody out there twisting your life around." He glanced at his watch. "I'll call Georgetown soon as I get back to the station. Meanwhile, can you get that sample of your sister's writing?"

"Yes." She could ask Terry to send some of Mary Clare's notes from the lab. He could overnight them.

"I'll let you know what I find out tonight from Georgetown," De Santo said. Then, when you get the sample, we can meet again. That sound okay to you?"

"It sounds great." She took the hand he offered and held it a moment. "But do me a favor? Call me Nicole. Or Nikki. Ms. Ryan sounds like a schoolteacher."

"I thought you were a schoolteacher."

She smiled. "That doesn't mean I want to sound like one."

"Okay." De Santo grinned. "If you return the favor."

"You want me to call you Leo?"

"Hell, no. That always sounds like my mother, calling me for dinner. I was thinking . . . what's that guy's name? Vishnu?"

"Whose job it is to attack and destroy the forces of evil?" Nicole's smile widened. She slung the strap of her purse over her shoulder. "Perfect. But Vish, I think. It suits you better."

Chapter 28

She stood on the sidewalk five blocks from the sandwich shop, looking at the business card De Santo had given her.

Then she glanced up at the sign above the storefront studio: KUK KIDO. Beneath it were smaller letters: SELF-DEFENSE CLASSES . . . MEN, WOMEN, CHILDREN . . . TAE KWON DO . . . RAPE PREVENTION COURSES . . . AIKIDO . . . KARATE. Taped to the window were faded magazine covers: One, *Inside Karate,* offered these articles: Take Control . . . Submission Techniques that Work . . . Pure Power! . . . Build Confidence, Self-Respect, Self-Control.

And to think that just last night I made a resolve to begin fighting back. Nicole laughed softly. *I didn't quite have this in mind.*

Well, the place looked affordable—the sign's paint was peeling, and the windows were dusty. Glancing in through the half-open door, however, she saw that the interior, including the red-carpeted floor, was sparkling clean.

She ventured in, feeling like someone else, someone she no longer knew. Certainly not the Nicole Ryan that Dan had accused her of being, the uptight schoolteacher afraid of her own shadow, afraid of her past. Someone she was seeing only a cautious glimpse of—as if she'd invited herself for dinner, but hadn't yet decided whether to set a place at the table.

A glance around the long, narrow room revealed a row of chairs along one wall, and above them an American flag. On either side of it were larger signs, both titled: PRINCIPLES. Listed below the title on one sign were the words: *Compassion, Modesty, Respect, Self-Confidence, Harmony.* On the other: *Courtesy, Integrity, Perseverance, Self-Control, Indomitable Spirit.*

The opposite wall was mirrored, and a third, back wall held a poster-sized white-and-blue emblem with the words, "The World Tae Kwon Do Federation." A royal-blue curtain covered the doorway to another room.

"May I help you?"

A slender young man approached her from behind the curtain. He was Japanese, with hair clipped short and brushed back on top and sides, skimming his neck to the collar in back. Loose white pants were topped by a white shirt, which was gathered with a woven black belt. His feet were bare.

"I'm Nicole Ryan. Sergeant Leo De Santo referred me to you."

"Leo!" The young man smiled. "A good man. I'm Ken Ito. What can I do for you?"

"Well, Sergeant De Santo thinks I need to learn to protect myself, I guess. But I don't know how long I'll be out here. Is there, uh, such a thing as a crash course?"

The young man smiled patiently. "There are what some call 'crash courses,'" he said in careful, slightly accented English. "But much of self-defense is instinctive. It is something you learn over a period of time. I can give you basic moves, and you can learn to carry them out. But the rest—reacting with the proper move at the proper time? One cannot rush these things."

"I just want . . . look, I know it sounds silly, but say someone tried to grab me in a dark room. I want to be able to get away. Even if this person is bigger and stronger. I want to know what to do."

Ito nodded. "I'm holding a Basic Impact class for women here next week. I highly recommend it. Meanwhile, if you prefer to start now, we can work one-on-one each day. What I would do is teach you self-defense based on timing and technique, rather than size and strength. I can take you rather quickly to a point where you know the right moves. You will also gain self-confidence, which will be important in carrying you through most situations." He paused. "Have you had a frightening experience recently?"

"Yes." She didn't elaborate, and he didn't ask her to.

Ito nodded. "A fresh fear, then, is something you will need to overcome. But it's good that you want to do this, because otherwise that fear would spill over into other areas of your life, such as work and relationships. Fear affects everything we do."

"Are you saying that self-defense is almost a kind of therapy?"

"Not almost. It very definitely is, depending on your need, of course. Many people take classes solely to improve their self-confidence in sports. Some need to increase their attention span—for book work, as in accounting." He smiled. "Again, there is a mental process involved. Until we begin, there is no way to predict how quickly you might progress in that."

He gave her a questioning look.

"Well . . ." She still felt kind of silly about it. But if De Santo thought it would help . . .

"I guess I should make an appointment."

Ito moved to a desk by the front window, glancing through an appointment calendar. "I have a class in tae kwon do at five. Would you like to observe? This is not what I would do with you, precisely. I would focus more on simple defensive moves for your purposes. But watching a class might make you feel more at ease. Then you can decide."

"I guess you know this feels awkward." She smiled.

"Of course." His gentle tone indicated that he understood completely. "But once you have learned a discipline, no situation feels awkward. You will go into even the darkest corners armed with a sense that no matter what happens, you will land on your feet."

She grinned. "Like a cat?"

He shot her an answering grin. His black eyes flashed. "Like the great Ohonamochi, who descended into Hades but met every test and fought his way out."

Ah, a fellow lover of the ancient tales.

"I don't remember that story," she said. "Will you tell me sometime?"

He bowed slightly. "Of course. It will be my pleasure."

"Well . . ." Nicole sighed. "Let's do it, then. No time like the present."

"No present like time," the young man corrected gently. He took her hand in both of his and grasped it.

In that moment Nicole felt both gratitude and hope. She might still be in deep water, but she had been thrown a life preserver—no, two. Ken Ito and Leo De Santo. She was no longer alone. It made a difference.

Chapter 29

While she waited for Ito's class to begin, Nicole walked along the Promenade. Stopping at a phone booth in front of a restaurant, she pulled out her calling card, and dialed Sacred Heart Hospital in Georgetown. It took two evening operators and three transfers between extensions to find that Terry Asher, again, had left for the day. She remembered that the night she had gotten the news about Mary, she had found his home number in the phone book and jotted it down on the only thing at hand—her checkbook. She pulled it out and riffled through the registry until she came to the number. It was below the last entry, Shearson's Market.

She dialed.

"Ritz-Carlton Huntington," a female voice answered. "How may I help you?"

Nicole blinked. "I'm sorry, who is this?"

"Ritz-Carlton Huntington."

She was certain she had dialed Terry's number. Maybe she still had the Ritz, and Jack Blake, on her mind. "I'm sorry. I guess I dialed wrong."

The operator disconnected. Nicole tried again. This time, when another female voice answered, "Ritz-Carlton Huntington," she asked, "Which Ritz-Carlton is this?"

"You've reached our hotel in Pasadena, California, ma'am."

"I don't understand. I'm trying to locate a friend back east, in Maryland. I'm certain I dialed his number there."

"He probably has call forwarding," the woman said helpfully. "Is he attending a conference here? Many of our business guests have their home calls forwarded automatically."

"Oh."

But Terry, out here? Why hadn't he mentioned it the other day? "Can you see if you have a Terry Asher registered?"

A brief pause. "Yes, ma'am, we do. Would you like to be connected?"

"Please."

The phone rang several times. No one answered.

"Sorry, Mr. Asher seems to be out. Would you like to leave a message?"

"Yes. Please ask him to call Nicole Ryan after seven tonight." She followed with the number of her hotel.

"I'll see that he gets the message," the operator said.

"Thanks."

She hung up, still wondering what Terry's unexpected presence out here could mean.

Her stomach was growling; she'd forgotten to eat. Nicole bought a hot dog from a vendor and walked down to the park overlooking the beach. Sitting on a bench, she noted that shoreline signs had been posted:

DANGER
WATER UNSAFE FOR SWIMMING.

Dan had talked about the pollution problem here. Manufacturers were dumping toxic waste, and home owners along the banks of waterways had installed illegal sewer hookups. The raw sewage from both those sources ended up in the waters where children and others who couldn't read the warning signs—or for lack of education, ignored them—were even now swimming.

If you can't trust the ground you walk on, she thought, *or the water you swim in or drink . . .*

The scene with Dan the night before replayed in her mind, over and over. She kept trying to make it come out differently, but nothing worked. Mary had known what was happening with their father all those years, but couldn't trust her big sister enough to talk to her about it. Now she was gone—and they'd never be able to talk.

Nicole finished the hot dog, crumpled the napkin in her fist, and sat thinking until the sun drifted low over the horizon. Finally she glanced at her watch. Nearly five; she should be heading back. She tossed the napkin into a wire trash bin.

Nearing the school, she began to acknowledge that she was more than a little nervous about this whole idea. She had never known anyone who was studying the martial arts, and never seen a real class. Her picture—admittedly born of ignorance on the subject—was one of five-hundred-pound sumo wrestlers. Or—from television, which she hadn't seen much of since high school days—young Asian men in high-flying kicks yelling *Aieeeee!* as they trounced the enemy, à la Bruce Lee.

It was therefore a shock when she walked into the studio a few minutes before five and found it overrun with women. They seemed to span all ages, from twenty to sixty, and all were dressed in the white martial-arts uniforms. Some had white belts, some yellow, red, or brown. All twenty or so were going through exercises on their own—warming up, it seemed. On occasion someone would address Ken Ito as Master Ken, or sir. Several were taking positions a few feet apart, facing the mirrored wall.

Nicole made her way along the side of the room to a chair against the wall. Several of the women shot her friendly smiles. After a few minutes she spotted Ken Ito, and he nodded and smiled, acknowledging her presence. She saw him speak to a woman behind him, who looked Nicole's way. After a moment the woman came over and introduced herself.

"Hi, I'm Linda Webber. Ken says you're starting classes tomorrow."

"It looks that way." Nicole held out her hand. "I'm Nicole Ryan. I hate to admit it, but I'm a little nervous about all this."

"Everybody is when they first start. Kenny said to make you feel comfortable."

The woman had shoulder-length ash-brown hair, held back with an elastic band. Bangs fell over her forehead, accenting deep blue eyes in a thin, angular face. Her entire body, in fact, was all long, gawky-seeming angles—yet she moved with the grace of a dancer. She wore the uniform of white pants and shirt, but attached to her red belt was a beeper.

Nicole eyed it curiously.

"I'm a nurse anesthesiologist," Linda Webber said, smiling. "I'm on call for surgery. In fact, we're all nurses—we come from hospitals all over West L.A. for Kenny's class."

"I had no idea there were so many women taking martial arts," Nicole said.

"Well, you know, it's pretty rough in the city these days, and when you work a night shift—" She gave a shrug.

The class was forming, nearly everyone standing straight at even intervals, facing the mirror. "Looks like I've got to go. But don't be nervous, okay? You'll love it. And Kenny's great."

"Okay. Thanks." Nicole smiled and watched her join the class.

The tae kwon do was a revelation. There seemed to be a formal structure to it; a beginning, middle, and end. At the beginning, students held their fists low in front of them, together, then bowed, slapping their palms against their outer thighs. Ken Ito called for "basic form," and they took positions, thrusting first one arm out straight, then the other, their legs widespread, knees bent, as they stepped forward, then sideways, in something resembling a square. At intervals they shouted out at the completion of a thrust or kick, everyone shouting something different and displaying different levels of power. From one young, shy-seeming woman came a tentative *"Uhhh,"* from another with a serious, intent look, a forceful *"Eeeupp!!"* and a grin.

Not once did Nicole hear a screaming *Aieeee!* although Ken Ito encouraged the women to use their voices for *chi*—which she came to understand meant power. Pressing his palms on his stomach to demonstrate, he said, "Bring it up from here. To yell gets the power out. It can also scare your opponent. Many times the only thing needed to defend yourself is the yell. Your opponent may run."

At one point they paired off for sparring, and Linda Webber, off to the side, watched the other women's positions. Apparently more advanced, she helped Ito to correct them as they worked. She taught one woman to kick higher, aiming for her opponent's face. "Just be careful not to really connect." She laughed.

The "opponent" gave a relieved grin and flicked her short blond hair back, wiping a sweaty brow. Linda watched, gently correcting the arm movements next. A rectangular pad was strapped to her forearm, and she held it out before the woman with the brown belt. The woman let out a forceful yell and kicked high. The side of her foot connected with a loud slap against the pad. Linda complimented the woman, and she grinned, looking proud. *Chi.*

There was a short break in the middle of the hour-long class, but no one chatted. The women sat on the carpet, backs against the wall, resting. Some, along with Linda, did slow, easy stretching exercises.

Soon after the break Linda's beeper went off. She glanced at Ken, who nodded, and then she headed quickly for one of the curtained doorways. A couple of minutes later she appeared in jeans and a T-shirt, breezing toward the front door. "Got to run," she said softly to Nicole. "See you tomorrow?"

Nicole gave a nod. "Tomorrow."

After class she asked Ken about the price of one-on-one lessons. He gave her the price per lesson, and then per week. By the week was more reasonable. "Martial arts is a lifetime commitment," he reminded her. "But give me two weeks, and I can get you to a point where you will feel comfortable, at least, defending yourself."

"Two weeks it is, then," Nicole said. By now she was committed—if for no other reason than that she wanted to know more about this power, this *chi*. She wasn't sure she had ever experienced such a thing. But it was time.

They agreed on a schedule: every afternoon at four. And if she liked, she could stay anytime for the five o'clock class in tae kwon do. She could join the nurses for beginning lessons.

As she left, a strange new emotion stirred. Nicole recognized it, again, as hope.

"What do you think of this, Mary?" she whispered.

And the words came back: "One step at a time. It will all come clear."

Chapter 30

He inspected himself in the mirror. He was getting old. Not as old as Joe would be if he were alive today, but old enough.

Not as smart as Joe would be, either. Or as popular. Even now.

Well, popular was an idea he'd given up on long ago. Joe had been the football hero, the Navy hero, the "real man" in the family.

Joe had died in Nam, being a Navy hero. Now he wasn't anything.

I tried. I tried to take his place, do what was expected of me. But *damn* the old man. Damn the legacy he left me with.

His dad had worked in a bank. He made a lot of money over the years. But he was never satisfied, never felt like a success. His dad was short, with a short man's fears. Somehow he had missed passing them on to Joe. But his younger son had soaked them up like a sponge, even though he'd grown to be six feet tall.

His height alone was cause for hate on his father's part. "Boy, you've got all you need to make it. What the hell's wrong with you?" And he'd smile that mean smile, the one that said what he really meant was, "I'm glad that inside you're nothing but a little shit like me."

He had learned the hard way, however, that height isn't enough to get a boy through school—or a man through the world. You needed more. In school you had to find some way to be popular. Either you had to be good at sports—or at girls. Well, he wasn't much good at sports. When you got beaten up at home night after night, it wasn't much fun getting your legs kicked out from under you on the playing field each day.

Girls were something else. Early on he'd learned that there was something about him girls just liked. And he'd somehow instinctively developed a technique, one that didn't require too much investment of feeling. He'd hang out with girls and kind of woo them—just generally turn on the charm full blast, knowing he was reasonably good-looking, had a great sense of humor, and could pull it off. From high school on he could get girls to do almost anything for him. Sex was easy. "Just get over here and do it," he'd order, all man, unzipping his fly and letting his swollen cock fly free. And they would. Later, when sex took a backseat to career, they'd type his résumés. Do his wash. Cook his meals.

Not that he didn't manage a good flying fuck with them now and then, too.

Lately, however, he had hunkered into a celibate mode. Girls were just too damn much trouble—and so, for that matter, was sex these days. Besides being dangerous, it kept you from getting where you wanted to go. So when things got too hot, he'd pull a disappearing act. Girls didn't like that—but they had to learn. He had to be his own man.

Besides, cutting out was better than what his old man did. He'd come home drunk on weekend nights and beat his sons senseless. Joe first, because he was always the one to stick himself out in front, to bravely take the brunt of it. By the time he got to his second, younger son, good old Dad would have his substitute dick, the gun, out, and he'd be waving it around—his real appendage being far too small and limp to do much with, burdened with alcohol or not.

Meanwhile, nobody ever knew what it was like at home. Their mother covered up, and to all appearances they were a nice, normal Ozzie and Harriet family. When Joe died a hero, their congressman came to pay a sympathy call. It was an election year, and Joe's plane had been downed by "friendly fire." A U.S. fighter pilot had gotten his signals mixed, thought he was shooting at an enemy plane, and brought his buddy Joe down instead. Friendly fire was an embarrassment to the government anytime, but during an election year, anathema. The congressman was sent to smooth things over—to keep the family from making too much of a fuss in front of the reporters who were already nosing around.

He asked if there was anything he could do, anything the family needed. The old man fixed him with a crafty eye and said, "I've got one remaining son. I want him to go to college, and I've got the money to send him. But I want him accepted by the best." The sly, shaggy brows punctuated the next line. "I want him to have what you've got."

Not that the old man really cared. He just wanted to grab the government by the balls and yank as hard as he could.

Next thing Number Two son knew, he was accepted by Harvard. From there he was on his own. But again, he was smart. He aced all the tests and used his skills at making people like him. His room-mate, Rick, was from a wealthy family, owners of a large pharma-ceutical company. That first fall he and Rick spent long hours getting to know each other. They'd hang out in the dorm on Saturday after-noons with chips and beer. Outside, the ground was covered with fallen leaves—brilliant swabs of yellow, orange, red. He'd loved the New England autumn, being from California with its brown hills and bare, ugly tract homes. The dormitory hall would be filled with the sound of televisions blaring—some football game or other. He kind of liked that too. It made him feel somehow a part of all the things he'd missed in high school.

Meanwhile, in their room, he and the rich kid would be yakking about pharmaceuticals.

"The pharms," Rick had informed him, "are the only companies that are going to last out the next recession. And it'll come, believe me, they always do. There'll be a false upswing in the eighties, and then—POW!—it'll all be over. While other companies are laying off, the pharms'll be hiring. It's a world-class industry, and the U.S. has always been the international leader. Shit, the U.S. pharms have got more major drugs in the pipeline than any other country in the world. Listen—have you got any idea of the markup on drugs?"

"Yeah," he had agreed, "but you've got the government to deal with. And one of these days they'll have to do something about prices." He had been reading up on the pharmaceutical industry, much the same way he'd read up on girls—trying to figure out how best to use whatever knowledge he could gain, to get what he wanted. Knowledge was power, after all.

"There's already talk about putting price controls on prescription drugs," he said. "People are saying they should take away tax cred-its if the drug companies raise their prices above an approved level."

"Fuck people," the rich boy muttered. "They don't get how it works. The reason the pharms are the most successful companies in the world, even during recession, is because they set prices high enough to put a ton of money back into research and development.

Right now the pharmaceutical companies in the U.S. are spending billions of dollars a year on R and D. And you know what it costs to bring even one successful new drug onto the market?"

"I'd say somewhere in the millions."

"You got it, buddy. And rising every day. Fuck! The government starts fucking with profits, the pharms'll stop doing R and D, then they're not going to be world leaders anymore. They'll be paying less taxes, hiring less people, exporting less drugs . . . Shit, give the government half a chance and it'll mess the whole thing up."

It would also mess up Rick's chances at inheriting a vast fortune. Rick was going into medical law. His future was laid out, nice and bright: He'd work for his father's business, get to know it, and one day inherit. As long as the pharmaceutical companies did as well as they were doing now, Rick would be okay. He'd never lack for a job, for money, for women—any of it.

A friend like that was worth cultivating. Worth the six-packs of beer that were bought every Saturday from his own limited budget. Worth the nights of study, helping Rick cram on constitutional law. Worth giving up girls for a while, to focus on what was important— the future.

Somebody had said—who was it?—"The richer your friends, the more they will cost you." And he had invested seven long years on this one.

But the plan worked. Sometime before graduating from Harvard Law, Rick had held out the brass ring. "Why don't you come to L.A. and work for us? With government sticking its nose up our butts every time we even stop to pee, we'll be needing people with a mind like yours."

So they went to L.A. together, and that's where their closeness came to an end. Rick went to the top floor of his father's twenty-story corporate headquarters, acquired a key to the executive wash-room, a private dining room, and a staff of secretaries—none of whom he had the good sense to fuck. He himself was assigned to a small cell on the fourth floor, with a host of other corporate drones.

But he was smart. He watched patiently as Rick married a girl from a good family, bought a house in Glendale, and stuck an Ameri-can flag on the lawn. Rick had the requisite two children—one boy, one girl—planted rosebushes around the American flag, and dreamed of moving to a farm one day. As he neared his thirties, he got too comfortable. He lost his edge.

In short, Rick was a great disappointment to his father, John Adams Rorrman. Chairman of the board of Century Pharmaceuticals—with realistic aspirations for its becoming the largest and wealthiest pharmaceutical company in the world—John Rorrman needed a son he could trust, one who would take up the cudgels against congressional interference. Especially now, as the voices in favor of price fixing became more insistent.

At a small sit-down dinner one night in Malibu, with only a handful of family and friends, John Rorrman had looked beyond Rick—glanced over his head, in fact, as if he were invisible—and found his son's old Harvard roommate ready and waiting to take his place.

A week later they met at Rorrman's private club, surrounded by old brandy, old men, and old cigars. "I've been watching you," Rorrman had said, "ever since you roomed with my son. I've looked over files you've worked up on competitors, especially the one on Garso International. You found out what new drugs they were working on, and even that they haven't filed all the necessary papers yet for the FDA. We can use that to slow them down while we get our own production in gear. I especially like the way you seem to take a backseat at meetings and parties, keep a low profile. People like you right away—they like that you get them to talk about themselves. And you know . . . there aren't many who see how shrewd you really are." Rorrman's smile was ingratiating. "I hope you take that as a compliment."

He had nodded, his own smile carefully humble. Things were finally going according to plan.

"So what I've been thinking, boy, is that I'd like you to do some special work for us now. Not that you aren't good at what you do. But what we need is someone who can infiltrate other companies, the way you did with Garso. And we need to know what's going on in the government—we've got to have access to their files." Rorrman had frowned, stabbing his cigar into a cut-crystal ashtray. "The goddamned investigators almost got us last year for selling those outdated drugs to third-world countries. We need to know what they're *planning months ahead of time. Knowledge is power, son. And with your talents . . . I'd say the sky's the limit."*

Corporate investigator . . . that's what Rorrman had called it. And his new work began the following month. The only change anyone in the company saw was that he now reported only to John Rorrman.

He began to make new friends in business, and—because L.A. was a movie town and much of the local power base lay within that industry—in Hollywood. He moved back and forth between the two worlds with ease, taking on shadings of each like a chameleon. The stories he told about his background, of course, changed with each telling. To some he had been raised by a single mother, to others he'd grown up in a happy family, on a farm.

He frequently traveled across the country to broaden his future scope of influence. He met people in New York, and of course in Washington. Occasionally, when the situation called for it, he would take on another identity. To a certain set of friends he was an up-and-coming exec. To others he was pure Hollywood—right up to the lingo, the dress, and the attitude.

He had even learned how to write a bit. To write, to schmooz, to handle a camera . . .

That, in particular, had come in handy of late.

Some might say that he still wasn't as smart as Joe would be if he were alive today. Joe would do what was right—what was brave—regardless.

"I'm not that brave," he thought. "I still hate the killing."

Killing women, especially, stuck in his craw. But he'd have to do it to this one, just like he did with the sister. She wasn't giving him anything. And if she ever figured out what was going on, if she ever talked—

Besides, Rorrman wanted her dead. And for him, the Old Man's word was law.

Old Man. Funny, that's what he used to call his own dad. When had Rorrman made the slide into that particular base?

Chapter 31

Nicole swung open the heavy glass door of the Ocean Palms Hotel. Her thoughts were on everything that had happened that day. Now that she'd committed to the self-defense classes, she felt better. Meanwhile, she had to call Terry, if he hadn't phoned her back yet—and if he didn't have something with him in Mary's handwriting, she supposed she would have to call Dan. Surely Mary had written letters to him now and then. In looking through his house that first day, she hadn't seen any—but then, she never really finished her search.

She wondered what reason she might give Dan for wanting a sample of Mary's writing. Should she tell him about De Santo, that he wanted to take it to the police lab for analysis of the note from the night before?

And why not? Why shouldn't he know what she was doing with it? If he had nothing to hide . . .

She moved briskly through the small lobby, past the splashing fountain, and headed for the brass-plated elevator.

"Nikki?"

She turned, surprised. Standing in the lounge area a few yards away was Jack Blake. "Jack, hi!" A hand went to her hair, smoothing it awkwardly. "I didn't expect you to be here."

He was dressed in jeans, a navy-blue sweater, and running shoes. She noted that he looked younger and more relaxed this way. His brown hair was ruffled from the wind, making him look kind of shy and cute.

"I left a message on your friend's machine," he said, "out at the beach yesterday. When you didn't call back, I thought I'd stop by on the chance I might find you in."

"How did you know where I was?"

"I called again this morning. Your friend said you might be here. I must say, though, he didn't sound very friendly."

"He—well, we're having some problems. I thought it might be better if I left for a while."

She tucked her blouse in. "I'm sorry about last night. I have a friend who became ill—the man I was with at the Century party where I met you, in fact. I was at the hospital, and then by the time I got home, it was late. . . ."

"Well," he said, smiling, "how about tonight?"

"Oh . . . I don't know if I can. I've got so much to do."

"You've got to eat," he said. "We can go somewhere nearby, and I promise not to keep you out late."

"I just don't think I'd be good company."

But his crestfallen expression was both funny and touching. And he was right—she did have to eat.

"I guess it might do me some good to get out." In particular, to get out with someone who wasn't connected to everything that had been going on. She could talk about other things, get her mind off all her troubles for a while.

"But I have to call the hospital first and see how my friend is. And I'd like to visit him, if only for a few minutes. He's at the UCLA Med Center."

"Sure, we can do that. I'll drive." He reached for her arm.

She laughed. "Not so fast. I've got to change. And I need to make some calls before I go out. Do you mind waiting down here a few minutes?"

"For you? Not at all."

She pretended not to notice that his eyes were all over her, checking her out as she walked to the elevator.

The red light, signifying a message, was flashing on her phone. She called down to the desk.

"You had one call, a Sergeant De Santo. He asked that you call back as soon as possible."

She wrote down the number, pressed the hook, and dialed.

"Police department, Pasadena," a woman's voice said.

"This is Nicole Ryan. I have a message to call Sergeant Leo De Santo as soon as possible."

"Just a minute, I'll try to patch you through."

She was put on hold. Checking her watch, she saw it was six thirty-five.

There was a crackle of static followed by a couple of clicks. "Nikki?"

"Hi. I can hardly hear you. I'm returning your call."

"I'm out on patrol, but it's pretty quiet. I've got a few minutes. Look, I want to call you back from a pay phone. Are you at the hotel?"

"Yes, but what—"

"Five minutes okay?"

"Uh, sure."

There was another abrupt click as De Santo hung up. Nicole stared at the receiver curiously, then set it down.

While she waited, she changed into clean pants and a dressier blouse, washed her face, and brushed her hair.

The phone rang.

"Yes?"

"Are you alone?" De Santo asked.

"Yes."

"Good. Listen, I'm gonna talk fast. And I don't want you to talk about this to anyone else, okay?" His voice was tight; he sounded harried.

"Of course. What's going on?"

"I spoke to some people back in Georgetown. And believe me when I tell you I couldn't find out a damned thing. I asked for the cop on duty that night and got his lieutenant. The lieutenant passed me on to the captain. And nobody gave me a straight answer—except to say that they can't talk about your sister's accident. Now, that kind of silence usually means there's an investigation under way. But if that's the case, I don't know why they wouldn't talk to another cop about it, just in case I had something to add to the pot. The only other thing I can think of . . ." He hesitated. "Did your sister have anything going on that the government would be involved in? Was she in any kind of trouble?"

"Mary? Not that I know of. I mean, certainly not with the government."

"Well, the reason I ask is because it's real strange. There's been a gag order—that much I'm sure of. It could have come from the DA's office if they're investigating the crime. But, Nikki, the cops I talked to didn't even ask me any questions. If they were investigating a simple accident, they'd have been all over me wanting to know why I was calling, what I knew about it. It wasn't like that. Somebody told them not to talk to anybody at all."

"What do you think it means?"

"My guess is some other agency's involved. FBI, maybe."

"But what could the FBI possibly have to do with Mary Clare?"

She heard a police radio squawking in the background, then a male voice—De Santo's partner, the young cop, she guessed. "Leo! We've got a call. Come on."

He muffled the receiver. "Give me a minute!" he yelled, then came back to her. "I don't know, kid, but I'd say something big is going on."

"So what do we do now?"

"I tried to reach that Sister Paula you told me about. She's not at the hospital, or the convent. I left a message. And about Dan Rossi —I ran a preliminary check through the DMV. Didn't come up with a thing, not even a moving violation. Usually people've got *something* on their records."

She heard his partner call out again.

"Look, I gotta go. But I've got some other ideas—like credit checks on Rossi, see if I can find out where he went to school—"

"UCLA. Didn't I tell you? He got a degree in film."

"Sorry, kid. Not according to the registrar's office."

"But they must have made a mistake! That's what Dan said . . ."

"We'll see. Meanwhile, I'll make some more calls to Georgetown tomorrow when it's not so late back there. And before I forget, what about that handwriting sample?"

It took her a moment to answer. If Dan had lied about his past . . .

"Nikki?"

"Oh, sorry. The person I thought I might get it from, Terry Asher, seems to be out here at the conference now. I doubt he'd have any-thing with him. But I thought of someone else, a Harriet Ilsen. She's an old friend and colleague of Mary's. I thought I'd go out to the Ritz-Carlton in the morning and look for both her and Terry."

"Good idea. What about Ken Ito—did that work out?"

"Yes. In fact, I think it'll be great. I've got my first class tomorrow at four."

"I'm off tomorrow. Why don't I meet you there? We can bring each other up-to-date, if I don't talk to you before."

"Great."

"Nikki, look—be careful, will you? I don't like the feel of this, not any of it. What are you doing tonight?"

She smiled. "Don't worry, Vish. I'll be all right. I'm going out with a friend."

Chapter 32

"I know a great spot," Jack said. "It's an old abandoned hotel, high up in the hills above Malibu. From one side you can see the city lights, and from the other—with the moon the way it is tonight—you can see the curve of the coastline, all the way from Malibu to Palos Verdes."

"Sounds wonderful." She noticed, however, that they were heading up the coast, rather than toward Westwood. "I do have to see my friend at the hospital first. Did you forget?"

"Oh, right . . . I guess I thought you'd changed your mind. Isn't it almost past visiting hours?"

She glanced at the dashboard clock. "Seven-twenty? I don't think so. Anyway, the nurse said it might do him some good if I came and talked to him for just a few minutes. He seems agitated, she said. He asked for me."

"Do they . . . uh, think he won't make it?"

"No, in fact she said he's doing quite well, physically. He's probably worried that he might have to give up teaching, especially since he's already past retirement age."

"That's too bad. Where does he teach?"

"UCLA. Medical history, just part-time in recent years."

"Have you known him long?"

"About six years or so. He came to give a talk at Georgetown, and we became friends. I've stayed with him when I've been out here before. He has a wonderful old house in Pasadena."

Remembering her last visit to that house, she wondered if she'd ever feel as relaxed there again. She was glad Austen was staying there, and that she wouldn't have to keep going back to feed Sampson.

Jack swung the car into the right lane, then onto Wilshire, heading toward Westwood. She leaned her head back against the Mercedes' soft leather cushions. A Chopin sonata drifted from the six-speaker stereo. A digital thermometer on the dash showed that the outside temperature was sixty-nine. The inside, climate-controlled air was a pleasant seventy-two.

"You're awfully quiet," Jack said.

Nicole smiled. "I was thinking that this car is like a fort." There was even a button on the driver's side that locked all the doors automatically. Her little MG at home was fun to drive, but its canvas top was weathered; it flapped and threatened to fly away at anything over fifteen miles per hour. And the locks hadn't worked right in years.

"There's been a lot of crime on the streets lately," Jack said. "Carjackings, and people being shot while they're in line at drive-in restaurants—even pulled from their cars and robbed at red lights. It's strange. I was a rebellious teenager in the seventies, and I came out of that era scorning luxury cars and gated apartment houses, all the trappings of the rich. Now I wonder if we aren't all going to end that way, building barricades around ourselves for safety."

"I'd hate to think that was true."

"Me too. Actually, this is a company car. I love it because it's so comfortable to drive . . . I never quite thought of it as a fort." He braked for a red light and grinned. "But given its Germanic origin, maybe that was the original intent."

"Does Century give all its executives luxury cars?"

"Only after we've been there awhile. You should see what they give their scientists."

She raised her eyebrows.

"Most successful pharmaceutical companies," he said, "don't spare much when it comes to key employees."

"Doesn't that drive up prescription prices?"

"I guess they feel it's a good investment. There's a fearsome amount of competition in pharmaceuticals. Everyone's afraid the other guy will find the magic bullet—the panacea for all the world's diseases. Whoever finds it first will patent it, and the best the rest can hope for is to ride their coattails with something that's similar, but not as well received by the public. The public will want the drug with the 'name,' the one they've read about in all the papers."

"I think the public is getting smart about that. We're buying more and more generic drugs, to save money."

"Some people are. But you know—how many times have you gone into a supermarket and picked up a can of Del Monte peas, rather than the store brand? Something in you says they're better quality, maybe because of all the commercials you saw growing up. Remember 'The valley of the Jolly Green Giant, ho ho ho'?"

She laughed. He was right. As a student she had thriftily purchased generic brands. But once she was fully employed, she had switched back, often, to buying products that were more highly touted. She doubted it was a disease peculiar to the television age. Her grandmother had bought Campbell's soup because of the Campbell Kids ads in her women's magazines.

"So companies like Century," Jack said, "who are determined to stay on top, are fiercely competitive. They buy the best equipment, and they treat their research scientists like gods."

"I know you're right about the competition. My sister told me a while back about someone in Canada who shot three of his scientific colleagues. He claimed they had stolen his findings and published them behind his back."

"The old 'publish or perish' mandate. Happens all the time."

"Mary said that every thirty seconds, twenty-four hours a days, manuscripts arrive at the desks of research journals around the world. Apparently, many are fakes—data that's been contrived in some way to present a picture that isn't true."

Jack moved into the left lane, rounding a white stretch limo. On either side rose the glittering high rises of Century City, like sentinels guarding the canyons of the rich. Century Pharmaceuticals' corporate offices were in one of those high rises; Nicole remembered hearing that somewhere.

"It's risky, faking test results," Jack observed. "Another scientist reading the article will try to replicate the experiment and find that it fails. The author who lied about the data can lose his career, his funding, and his reputation."

"I just wonder how many are never caught."

"I'd say there's a goodly number."

"And these are the people we're giving money to, and depending upon, for a cure? It's frightening."

A few minutes later they were near the campus. Nicole started to give Jack directions through the heavy traffic to the Med Center.

"Not to worry. I know a shortcut." He wove expertly through back streets, residential areas with mansions that had been built in the early part of the century. Before she knew it, they were at the crowded Med Center parking lot. Jack slid into a space near the entrance, marked Private. "I have meetings here with administration sometimes," he explained. "I've gotten to know which of these slots are hardly ever used."

Again she had the feeling of being cushioned from the real world —a world that included aggravation and discomfort over the minor details of life, as well as fear. When she opened the door, she found Jack was already there, helping her out.

An old-fashioned thing to do. And Nicole—who had put herself through college and built a career alone, who had her own apartment, her own credit cards, and all the other paraphernalia of liberated, female life in the twentieth century—found that she rather liked it.

She was disturbed, however, by the professor's emotional state. The nurse assured her, as she had on the phone, that physically he was improved. Her name was Constance, and she had short, glossy blond hair that swung energetically as she bustled about.

"We'll be moving him to a private room in the morning. You'll see. He'll do fine once he's in more normal surroundings." She hurried out, scanning the bank of monitors in the central kiosk, checking other patients' status as she moved from one glass cubicle to another.

Sensors were still strapped to the professor's chest, and an IV tube ran to a needle in his right hand. There were no flowers; the environment in this unit was as carefully controlled as in Jack's Mercedes. But childlike hand drawings were tacked to the white cotton of a folding screen. They were signed *To Uncle Henry from Mikey*. There was a flowery card from Austen on the nightstand, and one with several signatures—apparently from students. Nicole wished she had thought to bring something.

"I hear you're going to be all right," she said, taking the professor's free hand and squeezing it gently. "The doctor says you're really strong. And your nurse says you're a pill—which is supposed to be a sign of increasing good health."

The professor didn't smile the way he might have once. "I hear there's been some trouble at my house. Are you all right, Nikki?"

She patted his hand. "I'm fine. And your house is fine. But I'm surprised they didn't wait to tell you about it when you were stronger."

"Austen asked them to wait, but the police needed information."

"Is that what has you worried? The prowler?"

"A bit. I was concerned about you. And I'm grateful you're all right, little Nikki. But there are so many more things to think about here." He sighed. "There has been much too much time to think."

She tried to soothe him, stroking his hand. "What's wrong? Can I help?"

His small smile was rueful. "Only by listening, if you will. I can't talk to Austen about this, she's too close. And I've never given much weight to the Catholic version of confession—bringing in a middle man, so to speak. But now that I'm faced with the very real possibility of death, I think it might be good to go into the next life without so many burdens." He sighed. "Will you play my mother confessor, Nikki?"

She smiled. "Of course. But I can't believe you would have anything that awful to confess. You're a good man."

"We all have things we hide, Nikki. We pack them into a knapsack and carry them over our shoulders, hoping we'll never have to open that sack as we make our way down the road. Yet invariably we do. Perhaps that's all life is about, that knapsack of crimes and failures —and what we'll do with it in the end."

She squeezed his hand reassuringly. "Tell me. I'll listen and I'll understand, the same as you've always done for me."

Tears slid from the professor's eyes. Embarrassed, he raised his right hand to wipe them away. Around the IV needle the tissues were badly bruised. For the first time she realized how frail he looked— the white skin laced with veins, the cheeks hollow and slack from the gravity of age. She took a Kleenex from the nightstand and dabbed gently at the tears. Then she put it near his side, where he could reach it later. The professor smiled tiredly, nodding his gratitude.

"It's so hard to know where to begin."

"That's all right, take your time. I'm in no hurry." She heard herself echoing Leo De Santo, when she had needed to talk. It was her turn now.

"David . . . ," the professor began softly, then swallowed, his lower lip trembling.

"David? Your son?"

"Yes . . . mine, and Eleanor's."

"I remember you told me he died many years ago." Never anything more.

"Yes. And I don't want you to think that what happened to David was Eleanor's fault. She was so good . . . a wonderful human being. But I'm afraid that when it came right down to it, we weren't the very best of parents. Like our parents before us, we were much too absorbed in ourselves." He gave her a look that said, *Please understand.*

"Go on," Nicole murmured.

"I don't mean this as an excuse. It's just that when David was born, parents didn't know as much about the effect on a child of that kind of neglect. We thought that if we gave our son a nice home—not major luxuries, but a large room to keep his hobbies or baseball trophies in, perhaps a garden, a good nanny, kind neighbors, excellent schools . . ." The professor paused, coughing and catching his breath. He dabbed at his mouth with those thin, white fingers. Nicole's heart ached for him. She waited quietly until he began again.

"We . . . we thought he would be all right. It wasn't until David turned fifteen that we realized how lonely he had always been. He started to 'act out' as they say. He was picked up for shoplifting, first, and then we found that he wasn't attending school. He had forged a note with my signature, saying that his mother and I were taking him out of the country for a couple of months, to travel. He even brought home a pile of books and homework assignments, to study on the 'trip.' The principal's office had mailed us a release, of course—which David intercepted and signed."

Her friend's voice caught. For a moment his eyes closed as he struggled to regain his composure. "I'm sorry. This is even more difficult than I imagined it would be."

Nicole patted his arm. "It's all right . . . really, it is. Don't try to rush it, we've got all the time in the world."

His smile was faint. "You are a good person, Nikki. Far too good."

He sighed. "We were devastated, of course, when we learned about David. Someone suggested a psychologist, and we didn't know what else to do. We went . . . all three of us. And Eleanor and I tried, we really did, from then on."

"I'm sure you did."

"The psychologist said that we had been 'absent' parents. Not that we traveled, the way my own parents did. We were at home most nights with David. But our minds—we had so many wonderful things to learn, so much study and professional growth to attend to. I had just turned forty when David was born, and I suppose I was going through some sort of midlife crisis. That's when I stopped practicing medicine and began to teach. I threw myself into teaching and loved every minute of it. I barely noticed David growing up, never went to his little open-house nights, never even saw one of his classrooms over all those years." He blinked back tears. "Most young fathers these days wouldn't believe that. They're so involved now, it seems."

"What about Eleanor?" Nicole asked gently.

"She tried—she honestly did. She didn't mean to neglect David. But he was born so late, and by then her career was in full stride. Eleanor didn't think of the things other women think of when they become mothers. She lived, it seemed, in her lab.

"The psychologist explained what all this had done to David, shutting him out of our lives. And as I said, we did try. But by then it was already too late. We found . . . we found our little boy . . . our precious little boy . . . on the floor one day. He was dead. A drug . . ."

The professor's face filled with pain. His skin became ashen. Bleeps on the monitor were erratic now, and Nicole, worried, reached for the call button. But the nurse was already on her way in the door. Nicole gripped her old friend's hand—careful not to bruise it, but knowing she would have to leave, and anxious to reassure him.

"You did the best you could, Professor. If that psychologist were here now, he'd tell you that. We all do the best we can. We have to forgive ourselves for the rest."

The nurse checked the monitor and her patient in one swift glance. She touched his cheek, then the IV, examining it closely. Holding his frail wrist, she felt the pulse.

"I'm sorry, you'll have to leave," she said to Nicole. "He'll be all right—but he's overdone it. He needs to rest."

The professor's lined face was worried, anxious. "I must finish. . . ."

Nicole leaned over and kissed the dry forehead, stroking back the white hair. "I have to go. But we'll talk more tomorrow, okay? Just don't worry. You're a good man. You did your best. *Believe* that. I know it's true."

"But I need to tell you the rest. . . ."

The nurse gave them both a firm look.

"Tomorrow," Nicole whispered. "There isn't anything that can't keep until tomorrow."

The professor's eyes closed as he shook his head slowly back and forth. "You don't understand, Nikki. I am still paying for it . . . still trying to make up for it."

His anxiety—and the curious words he'd used to express it—followed her all the way to the door.

Chapter 33

The Mercedes purred softly to life. "You've been quiet," Jack said as he negotiated the parking lot. "Is your friend all right?"

"I think he is. But we were talking, and he became upset. I had to leave."

"You were having an argument?"

"No, nothing like that. He was talking about things in the past, about his son, who died, and his wife—the kind of relationship they had. He seems to feel he needs to make up for past sins."

"Are they that terrible?"

"Not at all. But the professor has always had high moral standards. It's natural, I think, that he'd review his life at this time, given the state of his health."

"Were you able to reassure him?"

"I'm not certain. I tried."

"Well, we have about a twenty-minute drive. Why don't you just lean back and relax?"

Something warm and dreamy—by Liszt, Nicole thought—drifted through the car's plush interior. As they left the city and began climbing the hills above Malibu, there was almost no need for headlights. The moon was a huge white disk, illuminating the dark highway. Far to their left, the sea was dotted with sailboats out for a moonlight cruise.

A memory came back, unbidden.

Boston. Another sailboat. Mary's first catch.

A friend of their father's had taken their father, Nicole, and Mary out for a sail one warm summer day. Mary was six. She was at the rail with a fishing rod, pretending to fish. Nicole had gone into the cabin to get a soft drink.

At twelve, she was bursting out of last year's swimsuit. She had thought herself fat—but the truth, she knew now, was that she'd merely been developing. The friend and her father were drinking beer by the wheel. And there had been someone else. Who?

A radio blared—a Red Sox game. Nicole pulled the tab off a can of Coke and turned to go back out on deck. Her father was standing just inside the cabin door. He was drunk, smelling of beer. He stum-

bled forward and put an arm around her, a hand on her breast. The too-narrow swimsuit top slid down. He groaned and squeezed her nipple, pushing her back against a refrigerator, shoving himself hard up against her. She tried to squirm away. "Don't, Daddy. Stop it!" His beery mouth came down, cutting off the words. His chin was stubbled with an hours-old beard. It scraped her chin, leaving it raw.

That was what she remembered, afterward: the sores on her chin, the crusts of blood. The rest became vague, surreal . . . a hand shoving, hurting, prying into places where it had no right to be.

There was a sharp cry from the deck. Her father, startled, released her just enough. Nicole spun around. Mary Clare—with no life jacket—had leaned too far over the rail. She was falling, hanging on by one hand. Nicole shoved her father aside so hard, he fell. She ran outside and dived for the rail, just in time to grab her sister by the waist and drag her back. Falling to the deck with her precious burden, she held her close and rocked her . . . wanting more than anything to protect her, to keep her safe.

"You ninny," she reprimanded through her tears. "I told you to be careful."

Mary's green eyes were clear and excited. "But Nikki, I caught a fish! A big fish! Did you see it? It was so beautiful, all blue and silver and shiny!" Her face was flushed, her hair—more reddish blond than auburn in childhood—was tangled from the brisk salt air. "He got away, though," she said sadly.

Nicole didn't have the heart to berate her further. "You're lucky he didn't have you for dinner, Mary Clare." She hugged her sister close. "Now stay here. Stay right here by me."

The two of them sat beside the main mast, huddled together, for a long time afterward. Nicole shaking, Mary not fully understanding her sister's fear.

The grown up Nicole remembered, now, who the other person had been on the boat. A woman. Someone she didn't know, someone young and pretty, in a skimpy bathing suit. Her teasing laughter had been muffled by the sound of the ball game. Her fingers had stroked the other man's hair, his neck and chest, then idled down to where his suit began.

Her father had watched that, watched them with lust in his eyes, just before he had found Nicole in the galley.

Dear God, where was my mother? Where the hell was she? If she had been there . . .

A surge of unfamiliar anger shocked Nicole, snapping her back to her surroundings.

"It must have been difficult," Jack was saying. "At the hospital." He looked at her, his voice concerned.

The anger slipped away. She felt tension leave her shoulders. "No, it's not that. I've been thinking about my little sister."

"The one who died in the accident? What was she like?"

"Well, I think I told you, she was a research scientist. She worked at Sacred Heart Hospital in Georgetown."

"That's right, of course. Did she enjoy her work?"

"Very much. She was devoted to it."

"And you and she were close?"

"Yes."

"I'm sorry. It's especially hard when someone young goes so quickly. You don't have time to prepare."

Nicole closed her eyes tightly, willing away the image of Mary being forced by some monster into that dark, dark, water. "You know, I don't think I can talk about that tonight."

Jack made a right turn onto a side road. It was narrow, the trees on either side forming a rough arch that nearly touched the top of the car. There were no lights up here, no nearby houses. Jack turned off the climate control and with one flick of a button rolled down all the windows. A soft breeze lifted Nicole's hair. On either side of the road, in deep shadows, small animals moved. A deer, its eyes bright and wary . . . and a rabbit, its fuzzy underside of tail a flash of white in the dark.

"It's pretty isolated up here," Nicole observed.

"But beautiful, don't you think? Away from all the city noise."

"That's true."

Jack braked to avoid another rabbit as it darted across the road, then accelerated. Nicole smiled. He wasn't a particularly good driver. The acceleration was jerky. Impatient.

"Since the hotel up here closed," he said, "the area has been reclaimed by wildlife. Last time I was up here, I spotted a cougar."

She gave a shudder. "You come here often?" An old singles'-bar joke.

"Now and then. Sometimes I have to get out of the city smog to think. I swear that stuff kills brain cells."

They rounded a curve and came out into the open. To the left was a rise, a small hillock. To the right, nothing but chaparral—a dense thicket—and more trees. Before them, the road stretched farther up the mountain. Moonlight brushed the tops of trees, turning them a pale silver.

Jack pulled the car to a stop. "We're here. Stay close, now." He grinned. "I'll try to protect you from the bears."

"Bears?" Nicole glanced around nervously.

"As in lions, and tigers . . . you know."

"Oh. Right." She laughed and reached for the door, but it was locked.

"Not yet. First I want you to close your eyes. I'll lead you. The effect is much better that way."

"The effect?"

He smiled. "You'll see."

"Well . . ." Covering her eyes, she heard him get out and come around to her door. She heard it open. Then he was leaning in, his breath on her cheek, a hand on her right elbow. "Just keep your eyes closed. That's right." She turned her legs, stepping out of the car.

"Good. Now move around the door." She took a few steps and heard the heavy door close behind her.

"Great." Jack's hand tugged at her elbow, and Nicole sensed they were rounding the Mercedes to the other side of the road. She felt herself being led up a slight hill. There were loose stones and dirt beneath her feet.

She started to take her hands away. "Wait a minute. I don't really like not being able to see."

"No, don't." Jack covered her eyes with one of his hands. "Trust me. It's better this way. Much better."

"I don't know . . . it's been a long time since I played Blindman's Bluff." She was embarrassed by the slight quaver in her voice. But Jack's arm was firm around her waist; he was urging her ahead with a reassuring grip.

"We're almost there," he said. "A few more feet."

At last they stopped. "Now, keep your eyes closed, okay?" She did, and he dropped his hand. "You have to count to ten first. Then look."

Her laugh was uncertain. A sense memory flooded back—something about being a child and frightened, yet doing as she was told.

"Jack . . ."

"Trust me, Nikki. It'll be worth it. One . . . two . . . three . . . ," he prompted, a smile in his voice.

Oh, why not. She gave a soft laugh. "Four . . . five . . . six . . ." An aeon of time passed. ". . . nine . . . ten!"

Whew.

She opened her eyes.

Before her lay the coastal curve. Moonlight dazzled, revealing palatial mansions lining the beaches of Malibu, Santa Monica, Venice. Tall hotels were emblazoned with light. On the beaches, fire pits dotted the sand with golden flames. Waves crashed into white foam, and from there the ocean stretched all the way to the horizon, as if a bucketful of diamonds had been tossed onto gray silk. More brilliant lights—red, yellow, blue, green, white—stretched south to the curve of Palos Verdes.

Nicole looked up. Overhead were hundreds of stars—the first she had seen since arriving in L.A.

"Jack, it's wonderful! A truly outstanding surprise." She turned to thank him for bringing her here, for sharing this with her.

But he wasn't there.

"Jack?" She laughed uncertainly, looking back toward the car. "Where are you?"

He didn't answer.

"Jack?"

There was no sound but the hoot of an owl, and a crackle of underbrush from across the way.

"I don't think I like this game," Nicole said, afraid suddenly. "Jack, tell me where you are."

"Over here, Nikki."

"Where?" She turned on her heel, making a half circle.

He laughed. "Across the road."

She couldn't see him there. "Are you . . . Jack, are you there by the trees?"

"Yes. Come on over."

"I . . . I'd rather not. Why don't you come back?"

"It'll be worth it," Jack said. "Honest. And it'll only take a minute. C'mon, Nikki. Come over here."

Again, the sense memory. *Come here, Nicole. Do what I tell you.*

Nicole shivered. Yet she obeyed. Her feet moved in Jack's direction; almost of their own volition they took her across the road.

She entered the chaparral, pushing aside the first low, prickly brush. Her foot struck something solid. She looked down and saw stone. A stone walk, half-submerged by dirt and overgrown weeds.

"Jack . . ." She tried to see through the dark beyond surrounding trees. "Where are you?"

His voice was low and teasing. "Just follow the yellow brick road, Nikki."

Her stomach knotted; her skin grew clammy. *This isn't fun anymore. I feel sick.*

Her head hurt and there were pictures flashing before her eyes. Terrible pictures. She saw the pond, the bright red flash of Barbara Lake's snow hat, the smirking boys. "Come *this* way, Nikki . . . *this* way."

"But I can't trust them," she heard herself say in a tiny, childlike voice. "I can't trust anyone. They'll hurt me, just like—"

She began to shake. And it was clear, suddenly, that the one thing she must *not* do was follow this walk. She drew in a breath, whirled in the opposite direction, and dove deep into the woods.

"Nikki, no! Don't go that way!"

Branches whipped her face as she ran, but she hardly felt them. Jack's voice followed her, growing closer.

"Nikki, follow the path! It's not safe that way!"

Not safe that way, safe—

Her running feet came down on air. Then she was falling . . . falling . . . into a huge, vast hole that had no visible bottom. Nicole screamed. She tried to right herself, grab for a handhold behind her, somewhere, anywhere.

Nothing.

Like falling through the ice. Again.

Then her arm was yanked, hard. The next thing she knew she was flat on the ground. Jack Blake was kneeling beside her. "For God's sake, Nikki! I told you—" His hands touched her face, brushed back her hair, cradled her head. "Why didn't you listen?"

She fought for breath, for control. Jack held her for a moment against him as they both looked down into the gaping cavity in the ground. "There have been wreckers up here," he said, "tearing things down. This used to be storage below the kitchens. My God, when I think—this hole must be three stories deep. You could have been killed!"

Gathering her wits, she was angry then. She shook herself away from him, pushing to her feet. "I didn't want to come over here at all! Why did you insist? You must have known—"

He ran shaky fingers through his hair. "I didn't expect you to come this way. I thought once you were in the woods, I could lead you."

"Lead me *where?* What the hell kind of game are you playing, Jack?"

On his face was a look of hurt. "No game, Nikki. It was an adventure."

"Adventure? Jesus, God—"

"Oh, hell, let me show you."

He took her hand, tightening his grip when she tried to pull away. "Trust me, it's okay."

With her feet dragging reluctantly, he led her back into the woods, to the stone path. The stones were wobbly, insecure—and Nicole no less so. Seconds later the path widened out onto a terrace. Beyond the terrace was the skeleton of a small Spanish-style hotel. Arched doors led to what was once a lobby. There were no longer windows, and the gardens on either side of the terrace had grown wild.

On the terrace, however, was a round, cloth-covered table. In its center was a bowl of flowers, banked by two brightly lit candles. A silver bucket held a bottle of champagne. There were curved concrete benches on either side of the table.

Nicole stared, brushing the side of her hot face with a hand.

"I set it up this afternoon," Jack said. "I remembered how much you seemed to enjoy the dinner the other night at Augusta's, out on the patio. And you've been going through a rough time—I thought this might help."

He gave an apologetic shrug. "I suppose the champagne's warm. I didn't know you'd have to make a stop at the hospital first. But everything else should be okay."

Taking Nicole's hand again, he pulled her over to the table. From beneath it he took an insulated icebox. In it were cold chicken, French bread, assorted cheeses with apples and grapes. Red plastic plates and silverware.

He set them one by one on the table. "I put the bread in the box so the animals wouldn't get to it. It feels pretty cold. Well, it'll go with the warm champagne—which I didn't put in the box, because I wanted it to look impressive went I brought you here." His smile was boyish. "It's not exactly the Ritz. But I thought you'd like the view."

Suddenly Nicole began to laugh. And cry. Maybe it was relief—or just realizing the absurdity of her fears. Either way, she couldn't stop laughing, even as tears rolled down her face. She brushed at her eyes.

Jack smiled uncertainly. "Is something funny?"

"I was thinking of the view I'd have had from that pit. Jack Blake, you are one hell of a date."

He joined her in the laughter then. Taking her shoulders, he turned her around, so that her back was to the hotel. "Look."

Through damp eyes she looked across the terrace and saw, beyond it, parts of the coastline again. But now she could also see the city. Los Angeles and its millions of twinkling lights lay at their feet. It was the same view as from the observatory—but more.

"They built the hotel," Jack said, "so that from the terrace you could see all the way from the San Fernando Valley to Palos Verdes. Malibu is pretty much out of sight from this angle, but there's Santa Monica and Venice. Farther south is Playa Del Rey, then Manhattan, Hermosa, and Redondo Beach. Those hills all the way to the south are Palos Verdes. They block the Port of Los Angeles, and Long Beach."

"It's so beautiful," she said, relaxing at last.

"We lucked out. Not only did the Santa Anas the past few days blow the smog out to sea, but we've got a full moon, too."

"And you did all this—" She gestured to the table. "You did all this earlier today?" She shook her head, amazed. "How did you know I'd even be free for dinner?"

"It was worth the risk."

She looked at the old hotel, the candles and flowers. She looked at

Jack Blake with his anxious desire to please, and then at the stag-
gering, mind-blowing view of the City of Angels.

This time, the thought of combat boots didn't even cross her mind.

The chicken was cold and moist, with a hint of garlic; the champagne warm enough to douse them with a foamy spritz when it was
opened. They sat across from each other on the stone benches. Can-
dlelight shadows danced. The air was warm, and the stars very
bright. Nicole knew suddenly why she had been so burned out in the
past year. There hadn't been enough fun.

Jack dabbed at his mouth with a napkin and set it beside his
plate. "How long will you be staying out here, Nikki?"

"I'm not sure. Why?"

He smiled. "I'd like to get to know you better."

"I'd like that too." But when he leaned across the table to kiss her,
she eased back.

"I'm sorry," she said awkwardly. "I hope you don't think I'm playing games. This is really wonderful"—she gestured about the terrace—"but I'd like to take things a little slow just now."

"Is there someone else? The man whose house you were staying
at?"

She gave a shrug. "We were friends for a long time."

"And now?"

"Now there's a whole other set of issues. And I guess I don't really
want to talk about him right now."

They were silent for a time. Nicole regretted spoiling the mood of
the evening. On impulse she grabbed the half-empty bottle of champagne. Holding it in both hands, she looked purposefully across the
table at Jack. Another moment and she was shaking it. Then her
thumb left the mouth of the bottle. Jack gaped as the spray struck
him right in the face.

"I can't believe you did that!" He was openly astonished.

Reaching across the table, laughing, he grabbed for the bottle,
wresting it from her hands. She laughed and jumped to her feet,
running across the terrace. He chased her. She could feel moisture
on her back, on her hair. When she reached the low wall on the city

side and could go no farther, she spun on one heel and surprised him, grabbing the bottle back. Feeling behind her with one foot, she leapt onto the stone wall, so she'd have the advantage of height. She shook the bottle and pointed it at his face.

"I've got you now," she warned, narrowing her eyes. "And I take no prisoners."

Jack stood only three feet away—utterly sober. An expression crossed his face, of fear and something else she couldn't fathom. "Come here," he said tensely. He held out his arms.

She lowered the bottle. "What?"

In the moonlight she could see his worried eyes as clearly as the beads of perspiration that clung to his forehead. He moistened his lips with his tongue, as if he'd found them suddenly dry.

"Come here."

She leaned forward and let him take her off the wall. Gently, he set her on the ground. Then his arms went around her and he held her close. He was shaking. "Look."

She turned her head, looking back. Beyond the wall, the ground fell away into canyon. The sheer drop was several hundred feet deep.

Her knees went weak. "I thought . . ." Their approach from the other side had been up a gentle slope.

"The terrace was built facing a precipice, so that nothing could ever block the view."

She felt the champagne bottle slide from her hands, heard it roll along the tiles. "This has not been a good night for heights."

"No." Jack looked off into the distance. "This night hasn't worked the way I'd planned it at all."

Chapter 34

The immunology panel was held the next morning, in the ballroom of the Ritz-Carlton. It was the largest meeting room in the hotel, but even so, the crowd overflowed into the halls. Double doors were left standing open so that people outside could hear. As Terry had said, immunology was hot. Everyone wanted to know what was new, from pharmacologists to research scientists, from sales reps to doctors. And, of course, journalists.

Maids and other uniformed hotel employees paused in the over-flowing halls, curious to see what had drawn such a crowd. Disap-pointed not to hear the voice of a Liz Taylor or an Arnold Schwarzenegger, they would quickly move on.

Liz had appeared, in fact, the day before, to plead for funding for AIDS research. Like the Century party in Malibu, this panel carried an element of glitz. The *Los Angeles Times* and the *New York Times* were represented, as were *Time, Newsweek,* and other periodicals that normally gave only minimal space to scientific news. In addi-tion, reporters had arrived from *People* magazine, *USA Today,* even *National Enquirer.* There were camera crews from the local news, the networks, and CNN.

Would an important cure be announced? Not likely; such an an-nouncement would almost certainly have appeared in a medical journal prior to the conference. But one never knew. It was best to be on the scene, grab whatever slice of hope was offered and feed it to the public like wedding cake—let them slip it under their pillows at night; they could at least dream of happy times to come.

Nicole elbowed her way through the crowd, knowing from other conferences that there was almost always a single seat available, that people were often put off by the thought of crawling over as-sorted legs to get to it. She hoped to find one close enough to see Terry; a call to the hotel that morning had yielded a brief and unsat-isfactory exchange.

"Hi," she had said when he answered. "What on earth are you doing out here?"

He sounded brusque and hurried. "The Century board asked me to attend. Sacred Heart had to be represented in some way, and since Mary . . . well, they asked me to talk about her work."

"Oh." She was surprised. "I didn't know that you knew that much about Mary's work." She remembered him saying, *Mary kept her postdoc studies to herself.*

His tone was cool and strangely defensive. "When you work side by side with someone as long as I did with Mary, you pick some things up by osmosis. I guess the board thought I knew enough to tell people what she was working on."

She had the feeling that he hadn't intended to return her call. She pressed to meet with him for coffee after the panel, but he made excuses. "I'm still tired from the flight. I think I'll just come back to my room and lie down."

"It won't take long," she had persisted. "I'd just like to ask you some questions about Mary."

He had finally agreed. But even then she thought that if she didn't show up in the audience and grab him right after his talk, he might disappear.

The panel began late. The crowd—over four hundred in all—grew restless. It was warm in the ballroom, and many fanned themselves with programs and informational handouts. From a seat toward the front but far to the left, Nicole scanned the audience. Mostly men, and the majority had taken their jackets off because of the heat. This left a sea of white shirts and ties. Here and there was a dot of color —women in blue, red, lavender, beige.

Her gaze slowed, then returned to one bright green shirt in the row behind her, off to the right. Not female; male.

Dan Rossi. Their eyes connected and held a moment. He was the first to glance away.

She shifted her gaze to the stage and wondered why he was here. Was he planning a film on AIDS? He had talked about that once, long ago.

Dan had called late last night while she was out with Jack, and then again early this morning. She had ignored both messages. There was nothing he could say—nothing she could fully believe.

A rapping sound from the front of the room claimed her attention. Her eyes focused on the stage, a raised platform with a long table. The speakers had mounted the platform and were taking seats. Harriet Ilsen stood holding a gavel, flanked by four men, two on either side. Terry Asher was at the far left, the end closest to Nicole. Before each speaker was a glass of water, notes, a pad, and pencils. Terry leafed through an expanding file folder. He drew out a sheaf of papers.

The room quieted and Ilsen began. "The board of Century Pharmaceuticals, Incorporated, is proud to have as its guests today such distinguished research scientists in the field of immunology as David Fontner from Rockefeller University in New York City"—she nodded to a tall man with an ascetic look, who smiled—"Paul Verbling from San Francisco State"—a nod from the heavyset man beside him—"Terrence Asher from Sacred Heart Hospital in Georgetown . . . and of course, Lawrence Mahabius Secrist, from MIT."

There was a burst of enthusiastic applause at the last name. Cameras flashed in the direction of Secrist. *I've heard of him before,* Nicole thought. *Must be some star in the scientific firmament.* Ilsen smiled and turned the floor over to him.

Star or not, as a speaker he was dull and unimaginative. Nicole sighed. She settled in for a long, tedious morning.

Drifting, she thought of the Emily Dickinson poem, something about hearing a fly buzz when she died. Then she realized the buzzing was only the third speaker, droning on and on. She slumped down in her seat, and folding her arms, she gazed at the ceiling and let her mind roam.

What a strange night, last night, up in those hills with Jack. Her emotions had spanned everything from fear to desire. *There's something about a shared fear. It heightens tension until it becomes sexual, until it can be satisfied in only one way.* And she had to admit, she had wanted him after he'd pulled her off that ledge.

Yet Jack had driven her back to the hotel, kissed her on the cheek, and left her with the promise of a call tomorrow. She had stood leaning with her forehead against the inside of the door, limp and groaning with frustration. Then she had ordered food from room service—cheese, crackers, an apple, sourdough bread, hardboiled eggs.

She had eaten everything in sight and finally, her senses dulled, she was able to sleep.

Jack Blake was different from any other man in her life. He stirred something that had lain dormant over the years of being an academic. When he had led her, eyes closed, to the view on the hill and left her there, some part of her had enjoyed the uncertainty—the flicker of fear.

She remembered being a teenager and having a boyfriend with a motorcycle—a crazy, reckless kid. She had delighted in riding behind him without a helmet, her hair flying. Even now she hated wearing seat belts. And her little green MG? It was so old, it was always breaking down—sometimes in the night on her way home from late classes. She could afford a new car, but didn't bother to buy one.

There was something in her that liked operating without a safety net. Nicole wondered what that was.

The third speaker wound up his presentation to a polite smatter of applause. Last to speak was Terry.

He looked nervous, unused to this sort of public gathering. Mary had told her once: "Terry is a competent scientist, but he's not comfortable with presentations. And he doesn't publish enough. If he doesn't break out soon, he'll be passed up for promotion. It's too bad."

Well, things had apparently changed. Terry stood. Reading from notes, he began to speak.

"I'd like to talk about a new finding." His voice quavered at first, then quickly took on strength. He scanned the room with self-assurance. "There hasn't been time to publish this, but I believe it to be important enough to talk about today. In fact, I don't think I would be out of line in saying that by all early indications, this is very close to being the magic bullet we have all been looking for. By targeting the immune system, strengthening it to a level that will prevent infection or disease from ever taking hold . . ."

As he continued, there was a buzz throughout the audience. Cameras flashed. Journalists who had been standing idly along the walls began to edge closer to the stage, writing furiously.

So this is what Mary was working on, Nicole thought, feeling proud. She actually did it! She succeeded at finding the drug she had talked about for so many years—the one that would prevent illness, rather than simply curing it. *A magic bullet.*

Terry continued, describing the drug's properties, its protocol, and the preliminary testing that had been done. Nicole waited for him to mention Mary's name.

The moment never came.

As she watched with growing disbelief, the audience came to life. People leaned forward in their seats, jabbing their hands wildly in the air. Terrence Asher, in a few short minutes, had elevated himself from the position of new kid on the block to rising star.

"If it's all right with Ms. Ilsen, I'll entertain questions now."

Terry looked toward Harriet, whose expression was stiff with obvious rage. His eyes flicked back to the audience, and ignoring her lack of response, he proceeded to acknowledge the raised hands.

"What's the name of this new drug?" one reporter asked.

"I've called it Lumonex. Its primary property comes from the bark of a little-known tree in South America, called the lumenaia."

"And you're saying this new drug can cure cancer? What about AIDS?"

"Lumonex isn't actually a cure—it's a preventive. In layman's language, it works by fortifying the immune system before disease or infection can take hold. But yes, I'm hopeful that even after cancer and AIDS have appeared in the body, Lumonex will effect a 'cure,' so to speak, by restoring the immune system to the point where healing can then take place."

"Without surgery?"

"You mean no chemo? No radiation?"

"Yes," Terry answered firmly. "The body should heal itself rapidly with Lumonex."

Another swell of excited comments from the audience.

"How long before this is available to the public?" a reporter demanded.

"That, of course, depends on any number of factors. How much funding is available, how soon we can implement human testing . . . These things take some time."

"Is this your own discovery, or was it a team effort?"

"Some of my early findings were based on research from other sources, of course, as is always the case. But, yes, you can say that the final result—Lumonex—is my own discovery."

Nicole heard a commotion as Dan Rossi pushed past people behind her and made for an exit door.

Reporters, photographers, and television crews with minicams flocked to the front and surrounded Terry. Harriet stood, her face now an unemotional mask. She was forced to close the panel.

A star had been born. Could a Nobel prize be far behind?

Nicole tried to swallow her outrage, but it filled her throat to the point of pain. She waited until the crowd had thinned and Terry, nearly alone at the head table, was gathering up his papers to leave.

"Not so fast!" She stormed onto the platform.

He looked at her briefly, then glanced away. "I'm sorry, Nikki. I don't have time—"

"Damn you, Terry! You never even mentioned my sister's name."

"Please." He flicked a glance around the now-empty stage. "Please, lower your voice. You have to understand. Mary is not here to finish the work. I am."

"You stole my sister's notes—everything she devoted her life to!"

His expression was stony. "Do you have any idea what this publicity can do for Sacred Heart, for funding everyone's work?"

"Everyone's work? You mean *yours*. And you've stolen to do it!"

"That's a lie. Mary was employed by Sacred Heart. Her work belonged to the hospital. By no stretch of the imagination can it be called stealing."

"It's stealing if you take all the credit for yourself. It'll be in all the papers tonight: Terrence Asher, research scientist at Sacred Heart Hospital, Georgetown, announces major discovery. God, Terry, how can you do that? Didn't you care about Mary at all? What about giving her credit for all the hard work she did at night, alone, with no one to help her? The hours and hours . . ."

She thought of the volume of notebooks in Mary's office, in her cottage. The nights she had dedicated to study, never going anywhere, never seeing anyone—putting aside her own life for the sake of a drug that would keep people well, make them whole.

Her eyes narrowed. "You don't even *know* that much about Mary's discovery," she guessed suddenly. "You read from her notes just now, like a script. Immunology wasn't even your field."

Asher's narrow chin went up defensively. "On the contrary. I've always been interested in immunology. But with Mary working on it, I had other things to do."

"You mean you had to do other things because you didn't have the brilliance to come up with anything like this on your own!"

He flushed angrily. "I don't have to listen to this."

In his anxiety to leave he jerked around on his heel and dropped the accordion file. It landed with a thud on the carpeted floor, spewing papers in every direction. He knelt quickly to pick them up, shoving them back into the file.

Nicole's gaze fell on something familiar—something blue.

"Stop." Her voice was harsh.

Terry looked up.

"What is that?" she demanded. Amid the papers was a blue notebook exactly like the one that Mary had left with her for Dan. She bent down quickly and picked it up, flipping through it. The notes were in Mary's handwriting.

She stared at Terry. "This was in my house in Georgetown. How did you get it?"

Terry grabbed it back, shoving it deep into the accordion file. "It belongs to Sacred Heart now."

"You mean to *you*, don't you? You aren't speaking for Sacred Heart. I want it back, Terry. Mary left that to me."

"You'll have to talk to Sister Paula about that," he said smoothly, glancing behind her.

Nicole turned. The nun was only a few feet away.

How long had she been listening?

"She wants Mary Clare's notes," Terry said. His smug, confident tone conveyed that he was certain of the nun's response.

Sister Paula addressed Nicole. "I believe we have already had this discussion."

"You don't understand. This isn't part of my sister's work—this is something she left specifically to me. She asked me to keep it for her."

"May I see the object in question?" Sister Paula fixed her heavy-lidded gaze on Terry.

He hesitated. Then he reached in, searched among the papers, and pulled out the blue notebook—holding it up but out of reach.

"I'd like to *see* it, please." Sister Paula's voice was hard.

Reluctantly, he handed it over. Paula glanced through it. Several emotions crossed her face—first anger, and finally, indifference. She looked at Nicole.

"These are simply ideas, jotted down at random. I doubt they hold much importance. Still, as I've said before, they belong to Sacred Heart." In one smooth motion she tucked the notebook into her habit's deep pocket. Terry flushed in protest, as did Nicole.

"I told you, that rule doesn't apply in this case," Nicole said angrily. "My sister left that notebook to me."

The nun gave her a cold, implacable smile.

"I'll fight you for it," Nicole said. "I'll take you to court."

Sister Paula arched a dark brow. "You could do that, I suppose." Her mouth twisted into an arrogant smile. "But the papers that Mary Clare signed upon employment with Sacred Heart are clear. If there is anything of her work in this notebook, it belongs to us. The matter is closed." She whirled on one heel, her rosary beads clacking against the white habit as she walked away.

Nicole couldn't remember ever hating someone so thoroughly. She watched the nun's haughty, retreating back, and then looked at Terry, who wedged his folder under his arms and stalked out of the room. Her hatred was complete. It was pure.

She would bring these people down.

Help me, Nikki. Help me, she heard.

I will, little sister. Trust me. I will.

Revenge

Chapter 35

Nicole was so wrapped up in despising Terry and Sister Paula, she didn't notice Harriet Ilsen at first. The woman had been standing off to one side, taking in the argument.

She approached Nicole, a scowl on her face. "That woman is despicable. Have I said that before?"

"Yes. But thank you for saying it again."

"I take it she refused to return something that belonged to you?"

"A notebook. Mary Clare wanted me to have it."

"I couldn't believe my ears," Ilsen said. "Terrence Asher . . ."

"He actually stole my sister's work."

"I know. And he was so blatant about it, so self-serving. I wanted to jump up and shout *thief,* but I was too stunned."

"Harriet, he said that the Century board invited him to speak."

Ilsen made a scornful sound. "He called yesterday and virtually pleaded with me to let him appear on the panel. He said it would be a tribute to Mary Clare. I had no idea. I'll have to speak to the board, of course. But to prove plagiarism won't be easy. Not now, with Mary gone."

Nicole glanced around, noting that hotel employees were beginning to clean up, to straighten chairs and vacuum in preparation for the next event. "Look, can we get out of here? I'd like to talk. Do you have a few minutes?"

"There's a coffee shop. We can go there."

Several booths were empty, one overlooking the lush Ritz gardens and an expanse of rich green lawn that stretched several hundred yards to a ridge of trees. They settled in and ordered coffee. Nicole hesitated. How much was safe to say? She felt surrounded by enemies. Yet Harriet Ilsen was on her side against Terry and Sister Paula; surely she could be trusted.

"You said you knew that Terry had plagiarized Mary's work," she began. "How do you know?"

Ilsen nudged her thick glasses farther up on her nose. "Well, as I told you the other night, Mary and I were friends. We had many talks about her work, both on the phone and whenever she was out here.

She was disturbed that there were pressures on her to complete her preliminary testing and publish the results."

"Pressures from whom?"

"Sister Paula, principally. But of course, she spoke for Century."

"Why Century?"

"My dear, don't you know? Century virtually owns Sacred Heart— and the Sacre Coeur Order now."

"No . . . I didn't know."

"Mmmmm. Well, it's sad how that all came about. Century was my grandfather's company. He founded it in the early nineteen hundreds when pharmaceutics was a young, innocent industry by today's standards. Feel-good drugs were only beginning to be researched. Many were opium based, and that was thought to be fine. In fact, it was a time when one of the major ingredients in Coca-Cola was cocaine." Her smile was ironic. "The ads, in all innocence, promised an increase in energy. We were only beginning to discover, as a nation, the ill effects of certain drugs."

Their coffee arrived, and Harriet paused to add sugar. She stirred, a brief flicker of anger crossing her earnest face. "My grandfather had immigrated from Sweden to Baltimore. A Protestant by birth, he converted to Catholicism when he married my grandmother. He sincerely wanted to help people, and in his early conversion fever he donated large sums of money to the Order of Sacre Coeur. At that time, the order consisted of only a handful of nuns from France who were trying to establish a hospital in this country. They came to America to heal." She gave a wry laugh. "And of course to win souls for the Church. My grandfather wanted to help them. He built the hospital in Georgetown with Century funds, then established an ongoing trust for Sacre Coeur. That way, no matter what happened to him, the nuns would always be taken care of."

Harriet removed her glasses, which had slipped down again. She rubbed the bridge of her nose and gazed myopically at Nicole. There were tired lines beneath her eyes.

"Then my grandfather died. And my father—he was an artist. He simply wasn't interested in pharmaceutics, and it wasn't long before Century was in trouble. My father sold shares. Before he knew it, the company was a large corporation—the Century Pharmaceuticals you see today. I'm on the board only because it was written into the original bylaws that someone from the family would always have a seat on the board. Rorrman hates that, of course. He hates me. He'd like to see me gone." Her smile was bitter, and her pale-blue eyes took on a rebellious light. "So would our dear Sister Paula."

"I'm not sure I understand the extent of the connection between Sacre Coeur and Century. You said the company owns the Sacre Coeur order now?"

"Just about. What began as a simple trust to ensure ongoing donations to Sacre Coeur has become a truly tangled web. Over the years other donors dropped out, and Century, with future profits in mind, increased its contributions. At this time the order is almost completely funded by Century. In return, all of the order's hospitals and labs, worldwide, belong to Century. All research scientists have to sign papers on employment saying that their work and the patents for any and all discoveries belong to Century."

Nicole frowned. "When Sister Paula wouldn't let me take Mary's notebooks from her cottage, she said they belonged to the hospital. I had no idea that meant, in effect, Century Pharmaceuticals."

"Yes, well, Mary may not have realized that at first, either. But the papers she signed upon employment at Sacred Heart Hospital contain a fairly recent clause in very fine print. That clause states that Century is the parent company, so to speak, of Sacre Coeur. Thus, anything belonging to Sacre Couer . . ." She gave an elaborate shrug.

"My God. That gives Century all kinds of power over the order."

"And over Sister Paula. As I've said before, I understand why she needs to be tough. I still don't like her. Not one whit."

"So given all this, Terry Asher must be Century's fair-haired boy right now—thanks to Mary. Harriet, what can you tell me about my sister's work? I didn't understand all of the terminology in Terry's speech."

"I doubt that even Terry understood half his presentation. From where I sat, he seemed to be reciting from notes that he'd cribbed last night."

Ilsen took a sip of coffee, made a face, and added more sugar. "Mary was working with a compound derived from the lumenaia tree. This is a tree that's indigenous to South America, and a tea made from its bark has been known for centuries to create euphoria.

The compound—also called lumenaia—is essentially a mood elevator. But the tree is difficult to grow, and up to now lumenaia has
been unprofitable to market in its pure state. It's also highly meta-
bolically reactive. One concoction made from the bark may give a
mild sense of relief from woe, while another might send a person
into a three-day stupor, or even, in an overdose, lead to death. The
reaction appears to depend on the chemical makeup of the individual drinking the tea."

"I've read about these herbs, in my own studies," Nicole said. "In
fact, Mary and I had several conversations recently about the shamans in South America, and the way they're introducing research
scientists to natural remedies."

Harriet nodded. "Ordinarily, one might take the pure lumenaia
extract and use small, relatively inexpensive amounts of it to come
up with a derivative. The derivative might then be marketed as a
tranquilizer or mood elevator—such as Valium, say, or Halcion. But
as Mary explained it to me, lumenaia's reactivity makes it difficult to
work with in this way. For that reason science has pretty much left it
alone."

Ilsen sat forward, her expression becoming more animated with
the telling of the story. *She knew Mary well,* Nicole thought. *Better
than I. She was involved in Mary's work; she understood her.*

"Mary told me over a year ago," Harriet said, "that she had come
across old studies on lumenaia. As I'm sure you know, Mary was
always intrigued by the connection between laughter and healing.
Norman Cousins wrote of it extensively, and scientists have been
studying the phenomenon for years. Well, in the bark of the mood-
elevating lumenaia tree, Mary found a natural substance that is
identical to that triggered by the brain during laughter—the substance now believed by science to promote healing. In laboratory
tests on rats, she found that lumenaia actually prevented tumors,
HIV, leukemia—all the immune-system diseases, even the common
cold—from ever taking hold."

Through Harriet's eyes Nicole could picture it. Mary up late on a
Friday night, working in the lab, her eyes burning from lack of sleep.
She could see her studying blood samples in test tubes, discovering
the wide-ranging potential of lumenaia for the very first time.

Her eyes welled. "She must have been so excited."

Harriet smiled. "More like ecstatic."

"But she never let on. A major breakthrough, and she never told me a thing."

"Oh, Nicole, please, don't take that personally. There's an innate secretiveness in researchers—we're truly strange. And aside from that, there were problems with the drug. Mary didn't want to talk about it or publish until she had the kinks worked out."

"But she told you."

"Only because I'm on the Century board, and she thought I might help."

"You mean to deflect the pressures to publish her results?"

"Yes. Mary called her preliminary drug Immu-Phor. *Immu*, of course for immunity, and *Phor* as in euphoria. Immu-Phor really might, eventually, be the magic bullet that scientists have so long been hoping for—the one drug that will not simply cure, but prevent all the diseases of the immune system."

Ilsen's mouth tightened. "And Immu-Phor is the drug Terrence Asher presented today, calling it Lumonex. Every word he said was straight from Mary's notes, from months and months of agonizing, bone-weary research on her part. There's just one minor detail Asher left out, and it happens to be the reason that Mary hadn't yet released her findings to the public herself."

There could be only one reason, Nicole thought. "She didn't feel it was safe yet."

"Exactly. As it stands, Immu-Phor must be taken on a daily basis. It must be active in the bloodstream twenty-four hours a day, three hundred sixty-five days a year. And you can't get the immunity factor from the drug without the euphoria. Which brings us back to the reactivity of lumenaia. Given its potential to put certain users into a stupor, we could end with a nation of zombies—of people staring at their belly buttons in order to remain disease free."

"Not to mention a nation addicted to uppers," Nicole said, "trying to counter the side effect. Which apparently doesn't bother Terry Asher."

Harriet made a gesture of disgust. "Believe me, this happens all the time. The ethical scientist will hold back, while someone out for immediate glory runs to the finish line in stolen track shoes."

"Are you certain, though, that Mary hadn't ironed out the problems with Immu-Phor? She was supposed to talk today. Maybe she was going to present her findings herself."

"No. I talked with Mary about it briefly, when she called me a couple of weeks ago. She was still working to equalize the drug in such a way as to make it safe. Meanwhile, she was adamant about not releasing her findings today. She was afraid that public pressure would encourage Century to put the drug on the market too early— that they'd go for a quick fix rather than a safe one."

"What about the FDA? It would have to pass tests, wouldn't it?"

Ilsen gave a snort. "Don't get me started on the FDA. Look at Prozac, Xanax, Halcion. Hell, look at Valium. All FDA-approved drugs that have been found to have serious side effects. Yet they're on the market, earning billions of dollars a year. Mary felt that given enough pressure from both Century and the public, the FDA would be swift to approve Immu-Phor, regardless of its side effects. There would be warnings in small print on Century's detail sheets, and that would be that."

"I suspect Mary was right. Don't you?"

"Absolutely. And until she had the drug perfected, she hoped to keep it secret. Unfortunately, Rorrman has known about it for months. All researchers at Sacred Heart Hospital are required to make a monthly report outlining their work and findings. The reports are presented by Sister Paula, in a monthly meeting with Rorrman. He was far too excited, Mary told me, when he learned about the possibilities for Immu-Phor. A drug to prevent cancer could make Century the most powerful pharmaceutical company in the world." Her expression was wry. "It would also line the pockets of Rorrman and the rest of the board—myself included—with gold."

"But if Rorrman knew about Immu-Phor—if Mary had to write up a report on it, and all of her findings belonged to Century—why did he need her to agree? Why didn't he simply release the news about Immu-Phor to the papers himself?"

Harriet's smile was tight. "Mary was very cautious—and very clever. Her early reports limited her findings to Immu-Phor's potential. After learning of Rorrman's reaction, *never once* did she include a formula, or even enough detail for Century's own researchers to come up with a formula. This was a constant source of irritation to Sister Paula, who had to explain just why her subordinate was being so difficult. You can well imagine Rorrman's anger. But Mary was stubborn. 'John Rorrman would just as soon turn us into a sleeping society,' she said more than once. 'He's not getting Immu-Phor until I know it's safe.' "

"But if he owned her, so to speak—owned her work—couldn't he have taken her to court for her notes?"

"As a matter of fact, Rorrman finally brought the issue up in a board meeting. I was in complete agreement with Mary, and I managed to convince the board that we'd be better off letting her work on the formula until she perfected it."

"That must have endeared you to Rorrman."

"He was livid. But he had to go along."

Or maybe not, Nicole thought with a start. "Harriet, what if he didn't go along?"

Ilsen's glance was sharp. "Meaning what?"

"What if . . ." Nicole couldn't bring herself to say it. Some sort of conspiracy? With Mary dead and her formula for Immu-Phor in the hands of Terry Asher—a man who wanted the glory and the funding more than the good of the public—things couldn't be better for Century. They now had what they wanted. And Mary couldn't do a thing about it; she was out of their way.

The formula has to be in the blue notebook, Nicole thought. That's where Mary hid it. And she had wanted Dan to have it for safekeeping if anything happened to her. She must have thought that with his anticorporate, antiestablishment value system, he would somehow find a way to protect it from Rorrman.

But how did Terry get it? Did he actually break into my apartment and take it?

She couldn't imagine his having the nerve to do that.

Then a thought occurred, and almost immediately she knew she was right.

"Harriet, when I met you the other night, you said that Mary was sending you something important. Did it ever arrive?"

"No. Why do you ask?"

"That small blue notebook that Terry had just now. The one I wanted, and that Sister Paula took."

"Yes?"

"Mary gave it to me a few months ago for safekeeping. She told me that if anything ever happened to her, she wanted me to get it to a friend of ours. But then the notebook disappeared. Harriet, I've got a feeling Mary's formula was in that notebook, and she got nervous and took it back. Maybe she came over to ask for it one day and I was out—I don't know. But I think that's what she was planning to send to you."

But again, how did Terry get it? And why would Mary have changed her mind about wanting Dan to have it?

Because she had stopped trusting him. That's why she wrote the note: Don't go near Dan . . . and don't look for . . .

The notebook. That had to be it. Everything fit.

"She wanted you to give this notebook, with her formula in it, to someone?" Harriet asked.

"Yes. A friend of ours. She said it was research for a film."

Ilsen peered through narrowed eyes. "Film. Is this Dan Rossi we're talking about?"

"Yes. Do you know him?"

"I've met him. And I know that he and Mary were friends."

Nicole hesitated a moment. She had told Harriet more than she'd intended. Yet the woman seemed completely aboveboard. She too had revealed secrets. "Harriet, I wonder if you'd look at something." She reached into her purse and pulled out the photograph of Dan and Mary Clare.

Ilsen took it and rubbed her eyes. She held the photograph close, leaning slightly toward the window to cast more light on it. "My God. They look . . ."

"Like they're in love," Nicole finished.

"Yes." Ilsen set the photo down between them and sighed. "Well, I had no idea it was that serious. Mary never mentioned it, not at all." Deep worry lines creased her face.

"You look as if the idea disturbs you."

"I . . . I probably shouldn't say. It can hardly matter now."

"Please, Harriet. Whatever you're thinking, it could be important."

"Well . . . Mary and Dan were seen together quite a bit when Mary was out here last spring. There was gossip among colleagues, in fact. You know how people chat."

"This was in April?"

"Yes. Mary was here for an immunology conference at UCLA."

Nicole's mouth tightened. "I know. I was here, too."

All those messages on the professor's answer machine: *"Hi, Nikki, it's me—Mary. I won't be at the hotel tonight. I'm staying over with a friend."*

"I dismissed the gossip as just that"—Ilsen looked down at the photograph, shaking her head—"because Dan Rossi was dating Kitty Rorrman at the time."

Nicole blinked. "Dan was dating someone? In April?"

"Yes. John Rorrman's niece, Kitty."

"You're sure this was in April."

Harriet nodded. "When Mary was out here for the conference, yes. She and Dan were seen together frequently, but he showed up at a major Century function with Rorrman's niece. They were quite close —touchy-feely, holding hands . . ."

Nicole rubbed a hand over her eyes, bewildered. *Where was I while all this was going on? At the beach? Out with the professor, having coffee? What kind of an illusion was I living?*

"Did Mary know about Rorrman's niece?" she asked.

"I have no idea. But seeing this photograph, I can't help wondering how Kitty Rorrman fit the picture, so to speak."

Dan betrayed Mary with her. That's how she fit. Damn him!

Nicole drummed the tabletop with her nails. De Santo had said not to tell anyone of her suspicions. But Harriet had a level head, and she had clearly been on Mary's side. If anyone could help her sort this out . . .

"Harriet, two nights ago I was staying at Dan's house in Malibu. When I got in, I found a note from Mary. She warned me away from Dan—and the letter was signed the day she died."

Ilsen's eyes widened. "What do you think it means?"

"I don't know. But everywhere I turn, there's evidence that Dan Rossi isn't the man Mary and I thought he was. And now you tell me he was involved with the niece of a man who apparently was Mary's enemy."

"Nicole, have you talked to anyone about this note?"

"I showed it to Dan—who tap-danced all around the issue. So I took it to a sergeant on the Pasadena police force. He's been very helpful, even to the point of calling the Georgetown police to see if there was anything questionable about Mary's accident. He ran up against a brick wall. It seems there's been some kind of gag order placed on Mary's case."

"But if Mary died in an accident, there shouldn't *be* any case."

"Exactly."

Ilsen drew back and stared. "You don't think that Dan Rossi—"

"No. Oh, God, no, I didn't mean that. It's true I don't know what to think about Dan anymore. Things keep coming up—like this business with Rorrman's niece, and the note from Mary. It's got me going in circles. But the circles keep coming around to Century, Harriet—and John Rorrman. If Rorrman wanted Mary's formula that badly—" She spread her hands. "Well, he's got it now—via Terry and Sacred Heart—both of whom, you've just told me, virtually belong to Century. And Mary isn't around to cause a fuss."

"Good Christ, Nicole! You're right, of course. But I can't believe—" Harriet caught her breath, her face paling. "Murder?"

"What do *you* think?"

"I just don't know. Not that I'd necessarily put it past John Rorrman. But I certainly can't believe the rest of the board is involved. And even if all this were true—"

"A couple of nights ago, Harriet, there was an incident at a friend's house here in Pasadena. You know him, in fact. Professor Dirstoff."

"Henry? Yes. I've been meaning to go to the Med Center to see him."

"I was with the professor when he had the attack. Afterward I went to his house to pick up some things for him. There was an intruder. If the police hadn't come, or if I hadn't run—well, I don't know."

"You think this . . . intruder . . . was after you?"

"Maybe not. But there have been other things. I've had a feeling of being followed, of my things being gone through."

"But if Rorrman has the formula now, and Mary is out of the way, what could anyone possibly want from you?"

"I don't know, Harriet. Maybe it's just that they don't like my asking questions."

Ilsen sat back, looking tired and wan. "I'm sorry. I'd have told you what I knew sooner, but I had no idea. . . . What are you going to do?"

"Whatever makes sense, I guess. I'm taking it one step at a time. But you know, I have the strangest feeling this all goes back to that visit out here six months ago."

Harriet sighed. Looking down at the photograph again, she picked it up and studied it sadly. "If only Mary had confided more. And what stories this little piece of celluloid might tell, if only it could talk."

She brought the photo closer. "Wait. My eyes aren't good with small print. What are these letters?" She pointed to the wheelhouse.

"I think they're the last two letters of the name of the boat they're on. *AH*. That's all there is."

"Hold on." Harriet pushed aside her coffee cup and reached for her briefcase, opening it on the table. Her short, unpolished nails shuffled through a stack of colorful brochures. "Part of my job at overseeing funding for Century is to contact philanthropists as possible donors. We offer them 'incentives,' you might say, to set up grants for company-based research. This is one of those incentives." She slid a red presentation folder across the table. Embossed on the front, in gold, was the name CENTURY PHARMACEUTICALS, INC.

Nicole gave her a questioning look.

"Open it."

She did so, pressing the folder flat on the table. Inside were two oversized, full-color postcards of the type mailed out to clients for promotional purposes. Beneath each was a formally printed description of amenities offered.

Nicole studied the postcard on the right. It depicted a long three-tiered cruise ship. *Century I* was the name across the bow.

"That one is docked at Marina Del Rey," Harriet said. "Rorrman takes doctors on cruises twice a year. There's gourmet food and entertainment aboard. In fact, if you remember the blond woman who was doing a Marilyn Monroe impersonation at the party in Malibu—she's hired by Rorrman to perform on the cruises. The doctors eat it up, and Rorrman calls it medical education. What he's educating them to do, of course, is prescribe Century's drugs to their patients. The costs of the cruises are then passed on to the public in the form of inflated drug prices."

She gave a shrug at Nicole's expression. "I know, I know. I'm after the board all the time to put a stop to it. But the best I can do is be a watchdog, I can't do a thing if they outvote me."

Nicole looked down at the postcard again. "I don't understand what this has to do—"

"Look at the other one."

The postcard on the left was of a smaller boat, a moderately sized yacht. On its bow was the name, *Haokah.*

"That's the original corporate yacht," Harriet said, "before Rorrman got it into his head to buy the *Century I.* The *Haokah* is docked at King Harbor, in Redondo Beach—close to our company house in Palos Verdes, where we host visiting executives."

"Haokah," Nicole said thoughtfully.

"The Sioux thunder god—but you probably know that. I remember Mary saying that her sister taught mythology. Well, my grandfather loved the old legends, too. He named this boat *Haokah* in the thirties. When Rorrman took over, he wanted to rename her the *Century I.* I said that sounded too much like real estate—and for once, I won." Her eyes held a satisfied light. "Of course, a year later the board gave him permission to buy the cruise ship, which he took great delight in christening *Century I.*"

Nicole fingered the postcard. The wheelhouse looked exactly the same as the one in the photograph of Dan and Mary Clare. There were distinctive markings—an unusual bowed trim around the windows being the most remarkable.

"Haokah was a god of opposites," she said, almost to herself. "He laughed when he was unhappy, and cried when he felt joy. The two sides of his face were entirely different colors."

So you never knew who he really was, she thought. *Like the man with the two-sided hat.*

Like Dan.

"Would Dan and Mary Clare have been alone on this boat?" she asked Harriet. "Or with other people?"

"I'd say that the rumors about the two of them had to start somewhere. They might have started that day. If there was a small company party on board, for instance . . ."

"Is there any way I can find out for sure?"

"Of course. Our captain lives in an apartment at the marina. I can call and ask him to go over and look it up in the ship's log. He keeps excellent records. We even use them for tax purposes."

"Harriet, I'd like to go down there and talk to him myself. Maybe he remembers something about that day—something that could help me figure out what happened to Mary. Would that be all right?"

"Of course."

"And another thing. I need a sample of Mary's handwriting. Do you have a letter from her, a note, anything I might have?"

Harriet glanced at her watch. "Tell you what. I'm hostessing a party for visiting executives in Palos Verdes tonight. It won't be as 'Hollywood' as the one in Malibu, and in fact it may be quite boring. But why don't you come down? Bring some clothes and stay overnight. I'll find you a letter of Mary's, and bring it to Palos Verdes with me. Then in the morning we can go out to the *Haokah.* I'll be sure to have Captain Nealy there."

"That sounds great."

"It's settled, then. Good. And you know, I've been thinking of something else as we talked. There's someone I'd like you to meet."

"Really? Who?"

"Someone who might be able to help you with all this." Harriet's brow knitted. "I'm worried about you, Nicole."

"Well, I'll be there. What time?"

"Make it around eight. Here, I'll draw you a map."

Nicole watched as Ilsen fashioned a quick sketch of the coastline on a piece of notepaper. "Sepulveda shouldn't be too bad at that hour. It goes south past the airport, and then into the beach towns. At the southern end of Redondo Beach you turn right on Palos Verdes Drive. In five minutes or so you'll be at Malaga Cove, and you wind up this hill . . ."

Finishing the instructions, she wrote the Palos Verdes phone number below them and handed the map to Nicole. "Meanwhile, do be careful."

She does look worried, Nicole thought. *And much of it must be for Century. If Rorrman was involved in a conspiracy to wrest Mary's formula from her, Harriet has a monstrous problem on her hands.*

They paid for their coffee and parted—Nicole with a sense that she had found another friend in her search for the truth about Mary Clare. She crossed the hushed lobby, her mind on the talk with Ilsen. A doorman held the door for her, and she turned left, toward the self-parking lot where she had left her car. Out of the corner of her eye to the right, she thought she saw Dan. She turned that way, curious.

It was Dan, approaching a car with a valet standing by. He was talking quietly to the woman beside him, his arm lightly around her shoulders as they walked. At the car he went to the driver's side and she to the door opposite. Dan looked up, as if sensing Nicole's presence. His head turned. He seemed to look straight at her before ducking into the car.

The valet held open the passenger door. Sliding in next to Dan— gathering her heavy white skirts with one hand, and smiling—was Sister Paula.

Chapter 36

The car pulled away, turning at the end of the drive. Nicole stared after it. Dan and Sister Paula going off together, acting like old chums? And Sister Paula smiling?

She had never seen a smile on the woman's face before. What the hell was going on?

Nicole checked her watch. It was past two o'clock, and she had her first session with Ken Ito at four.

She drove down 110 with her foot hard on the accelerator, her mind running to keep up. Dan—who had been dating John Rorrman's niece even as he was romancing Mary last April—was on his way somewhere with a woman who had always been hostile to Mary. Not only that, but a woman who ran Sacred Heart Hospital, who needed capital and had every reason to want to please John Rorrman and the Century board.

The evidence against Dan Rossi kept piling up. She wondered how she could ever have believed in him. Was love truly so blind?

Nicole parked in the Ocean Palms parking lot and walked the five blocks to Ken Ito's studio—anxious about this first lesson, but even more, to see De Santo and tell him what she now knew.

In the storefront studio she found Ken talking to an artist, who was dressed in jeans and a splattered T-shirt. He was painting the inside of each plate-glass window in an abstract but recognizable martial-arts design. Most of each window was already covered in white. Splashed across the white were kicking figures in black and gray, with touches of red.

Ken turned to Nicole. "Hi. Nice to see you." He gestured with pride to the windows. "How do you like what we're doing here?"

"I love it." She noted that the artwork effectively prevented outside passersby from looking in. The studio now seemed warmer, and somehow more inviting.

"Did you do the windows down the way, at the eyeglass place?" she asked the artist. It had portholes, with glasses hanging in it like fish.

The young man stood back and gave her a smile as he surveyed his work. " 'Fraid not. I just stopped by looking for a loan, and Kenny put me to work."

Ken Ito smiled. "It was serendipity. I've been wanting to do something with that window, and when Jason came by, it felt right."

He led Nicole to the back of the studio and pulled aside the dark-blue curtain. "This is the changing room. You'll find clean uniforms on hangers. Please help yourself to whatever fits you best. You will want it loose and comfortable, yet not so long that you might stumble over it as you move. Take a white belt from the shelf above."

He crossed over to a row of lockers and held one open. "You may use this for valuables while you are here. In five years, we've never had any trouble." He gave her the combination.

She thanked him, and he stepped out, closing the curtain behind him. Nicole looked around. The room was large, with separate curtained dressing rooms for changing. There was a mirror in each cubicle, and a chair.

She used the combination and placed her purse in the locker. Then she scanned the white uniforms, taking one that appeared to be her size. Undressing, she hung her skirt and blouse on an empty hanger. She stepped into the soft cotton pants and found they fit, then the top, which had wide, long sleeves and crisscrossed in front. Tunic length, it covered her hips.

What else? She reached up to the shelf and chose a white belt, tying it loosely. Then she assessed herself in the mirror.

She couldn't help laughing. *Nicole Ryan. Karate Kid.*

Well, she thought, *let the games begin.*

Now, where had she said that recently—and why?

The class was only an hour, but it seemed to last forever. As she and Ken worked, Nicole was astonished to find that in the middle of great stretches of concentration—of complete focus on the lesson— long-forgotten snatches of her childhood came back. Once she had challenged a teacher in psychology class: "You say that people don't remember the bad stuff that happened to them as children—like mothers not remembering the pain of childbirth. But I remember *only* bad stuff. Or even when I remember something 'good' now and then, it seems to be surrounded, or attached to, something bad."

"What you don't understand," the teacher had answered, "is that the bad things you remember *are* the good, relatively speaking, of course. The other—the part you can't remember—must have been much worse. It's too painful to remember that, so a gentle, protective amnesia takes place."

It was frightening, Nicole had thought, that things could have been even worse.

But now she knew it was true. In strobelike flashes she remembered nearly smothering on her bed . . . being touched, unable to move. A dreadful weight, pushing her down. *"Daddy's little girl . . . do it for Daddy, Nikki. Here. Ah, yes, that's good . . . right here."*

She had felt as if the ground were opening up beneath her feet. Just like on the ice pond. Suddenly betrayal was everywhere.

During one of these flashes of memory, she lashed out in anger when Ken demonstrated a hold that grabbed her from behind. He hadn't yet taught her to strike backward at his gut with her elbow, yet she did so automatically.

Ken was pleased. "As children, women are seldom taught to fight back or to yell. It is good that you are getting over that inhibition so quickly. I always like this time—the first time a woman defends herself."

But Nicole was doing more than simply overcoming inhibition. Given a venue for releasing rage, she felt old hostilities pour forth in a tidal wave of emotion. She was honestly angry—not at Ken, of course, but at something.

He saw this when he pushed her off balance the first time. The move wasn't meant to hurt, but to give her the feel of being overtaken. He had leveraged her balance gently, so that she tumbled to the floor.

Nicole jumped to her feet and stopped just short of smacking him. Again Ken was pleased at the quick reaction, yet he asked her now to temper the anger. "Self-defense requires intellect and self-control. You cannot be in control and angry at the same time."

She stood back, wiping her brow and panting. "But I'm stronger when I'm angry."

"Stronger, but not smarter. Whatever it is that you are angry about, feel the anger when you aren't here. Let it rage. Stand on the beach and howl at the sun if you must. But then before you come here, tuck the anger beneath your belt. Let it lie in your gut like a sleeping child, one who is not allowed to attend the adult party because such a thing would be inappropriate for the child."

Nicole would try to do this, but at times it felt as if the child sat secretly in wait, watching the party through a banister at the top of the stairs while planning how best to wreak havoc on the scene below.

De Santo had still not appeared, but Linda, the nurse she had met the day before, came in early and observed for a few minutes. When Ken had to answer the phone, he left them with instructions to spar together. Nicole was afraid of hurting her female partner—more so than with Ken, who didn't seem fazed by anything she might do. "Harder," Linda urged, "kick harder!" Nicole aimed high with the inside edge of her right foot, whacking the cushion strapped to Linda's arm. But there wasn't much power behind the movement. When he came back, Ken demonstrated a better stance to level a kick from. Nicole was startled at the power he gave it, and that Linda was even left standing. She was intimidated by the thought that he would one day aim a kick like that at her, and told him so.

"We'll work on that in class," he said. "It's important to get over the fear of being hurt. That fear could make you hold back before striking. It could lose you valuable time, give your opponent the edge."

Along with a few beginning martial-arts techniques, he was teaching her some of the self-defense moves from the Basic Impact course. One technique, called the "chicken beak," was similar to the old child's game of casting shadows on the wall.

"Take the ready position," he said, standing opposite, playing the part of opponent.

After only forty-five minutes Nicole knew the ready position: arms straight out, one hand slightly ahead of the other, strongest leg behind the other, ready to kick. "If you step back with your right foot," Ken said, "put your left hand out front. Now hold your fingers together, as if you were making a shadow of a chicken beak on the wall. Aim for the eyes and jab as hard as you can. The point is to do damage, not to simply make your opponent mad. If you make him mad, you'd better be prepared to follow through."

He had her jab her fingers against her palm, to feel the impact.

Even though her nails were short, it hurt—more than she would have thought.

"You can also use the flat of your forward hand. Slam it against the nose, or if the opponent is too tall, slam upward beneath the chin. You can actually kill someone that way."

He said this casually, which at first took her aback. "I was hoping I could just learn how to hurt someone. You know, enough to get away."

Ito smiled patiently. "You can do that, of course. We have a class especially for that situation."

"Really?"

"It's called *Run Like Hell.*"

Nicole laughed. But she got the message.

He reminded her seriously, "You are learning to defend yourself against rape or death. The most important thing isn't the move you choose to make, but your willingness to make it. You must be prepared to damage your attacker as much *or more* than he intends to damage you. It is the same principle as with a weapon. One should never point a gun to scare someone. You must intend to shoot."

And again, if someone should grab her from behind: "Try to put some distance between you and him first. Get one hand up along your cheek if there's time, to create space between his arm and your face. Step forward a bit, if possible. Then you can do one of several things. You can slam your fist straight back at his groin—" He demonstrated on himself. "Or, if you've got the space, you can twist slightly to the right and stomp on his instep. Try it on yourself. See how much it hurts."

Nicole did. She grimaced, coming down on her foot harder than she meant to. "Ow!"

"After you stomp on the instep, you can use your elbow at his gut as you did earlier, or your flattened palm beneath the chin or at the nose. You can also use the chicken beak at the eyes, or any number of moves, which we'll practice over the next two weeks."

Toward the end of the hour, Nicole saw De Santo out of the corner of her eye. He was standing off to the side, hands on hips, looking pleased—even proud. By the time class was over she was thoroughly exhausted. It had never occurred to her that self-defense would require so much energy. She slid to a sitting position against the back wall, sweat streaming from her hair, her forehead, her neck, and between her breasts.

She had learned to straighten her uniform, kneel, bow—all the small but important disciplines of the martial arts. Whirling about in her mind were terms like "ax kick," "roundhouse kick," and "chi." There were others, too—alien words she didn't know how to spell but that sounded like *shuh, eeupp,* and *pwaro.*

"Pwaro," she finally came to understand (and thank God for it), meant "rest."

When she had changed, Leo was at the front door, talking with Ken. He saw her approach and broke into a grin. "You did great, kid. How about some coffee?"

Ken Ito looked pained. "You are a bad influence, Leo. Coffee, coffee, all the time . . ." He turned to Nicole. "I would recommend juice."

She smiled and thanked Ken for the lesson.

"Do you feel all right about the way it went?" he asked.

"Yes, I do. It was tough—but I'm looking forward to tomorrow."

"You learn quickly," he said. "You have a natural instinct for survival. Tomorrow we'll touch again on overcoming your fear of harming the attacker."

"I thought I did pretty well at that."

Ken's soft brown eyes surveyed her thoughtfully. "I rarely have anyone begin lessons who is quite so . . . ready."

She wasn't sure he meant that purely as praise. But she had to agree he was right.

"Let's go to Congo Square," De Santo suggested as they headed out the door. "It's right up the block, and we can get coffee *and* juice. Keep Kenny happy."

"Great. I've got a lot to tell you, Vish."

His look was sharp. "Go ahead."

She brushed her hair back, feeling tired. "Why don't we get that coffee first? I've got to get to Palos Verdes tonight."

"P.V.? What's up?"

"I've been invited to a party. I'll tell you about that, too."

The Promenade after dark took on a different order of life—from young partying yuppies arriving in heels and suits at expensive restaurants, to fading hippie types in bizarre outfits. Panhandlers moved in quickly on anyone who was dressed even the least bit smart. Homeless huddled in Salvation Army clothes on fancy wrought-iron benches and wandered in and out of sidewalk cafés, hoping to pinch a dime.

Congo Square was one of those cafés. There was a self-service bar at the back, and lining the walls along each side were sofas, chairs, and end tables that looked as if they might have been purchased from the local Goodwill. Nearly every seat was taken. At a couple of long tables, young people were deep in conversation. Others read books or were feverishly writing; they looked like the kids she taught. One man alone in an easy chair was dressed in a long white robe, a turban, and brown hiking boots. Standing lamps were from the fifties, original issue, battered and standing askew.

"This is so . . . California, Vish," Nicole said. Part of her was intrigued. The other half felt out of place. She remembered Ken's advice about juice, but shrugged and ordered a cappuccino. Sprinkling it with chocolate from a shaker can, she thanked De Santo for treating. They escaped outside with their foam cups and began to walk along the Promenade.

A few doors down, street performers—a drummer, a bass player, and a clarinetist—played jazz. A tiny woman, alone on the fringes, whirled in a dazed, erratic dance. One of her legs dragged, as if damaged. She wore a flowing orange dress and hat. There were objects dangling from her dress—toilet-paper rolls, pieces of netting, feathers, metal objects. She looked, Nicole thought, like a fish lure.

The woman reminded her of something. "Kenny says our bodies store memories, Vish, in the cells. That's why we have backaches, stomachaches, headaches. Do you think that's true?"

"If Kenny says it's so, it probably is."

"I wonder what kinds of memories that poor woman is storing." She nodded to the fish-lure lady.

"You're sounding kind of troubled, kid."

"Yeah, well, I guess Kenny's class is bringing out all sorts of things."

"Memories, you mean?"

"He said I was using my body in ways I never had before—and that as I did that, memories were released."

"Bad stuff?"

She gave a shrug. "Pretty much."

"Well, if you want to talk about any of that, I can lend an ear."

"Thanks. Maybe later?"

"Sure. Anytime."

They skirted a small group of people who were watching a street magician.

"I learned some things about my sister today, Vish. I think this could be important."

His cappuccino gone, De Santo dropped the cup into a trash container. "You did better than me, then. I'm still working my way through that gag order in Georgetown. What have you got?"

Nicole told him about the immunology conference, about Terry's announcement of Mary's discovery, and claiming it as his own. Then about the blue notebook, and the talk with Harriet Ilsen.

"According to Harriet, Century wanted Mary Clare's formula for Immu-Phor, but she refused to hand it over. Terry has the formula now. So, therefore, does Century. And there are billions to be made on this drug—regardless of the fact that it could anesthetize the world."

"Holy shit. I mean, no wonder there's an investigation going on. But who ordered it, I wonder? And why the gag order?"

"I have no idea. But Harriet wants me to meet someone tonight. She thinks this person may have some ideas."

He stopped and gave her a sharp look. "This Harriet—Ilsen, you said? What do you really know about her? If she's on the board of Century, God knows what she could be up to."

Nicole frowned. "I felt she was on Mary's side. I trusted her."

De Santo shook his head, irritated. "I asked you not to talk to anyone else about this, kid. Look—"

Nicole faced him squarely. "I'm not a kid, Vish. It felt right talking to Harriet."

He opened his mouth to argue and was met with a determined expression. He sighed. "Damn, I may regret sending you to Kenny. Okay, you're a big girl—you can take care of yourself. Even so, I'd better run a check on this Harriet Ilsen. And maybe it's time to dig into Century as well."

The tension eased. They began to walk again.

"What I don't get is, if this drug—Immu-Phor, you called it?—if it keeps people from getting sick, wouldn't that put the doctors, the hospitals, and for that matter, the drug companies out of business? Why would Century want that?"

"I suppose it's only a matter of time before someone discovers a similar drug. Century certainly is realistic enough to know the possibility exists and to plan ahead. If they're the first to get the patent and corner the market, they'll not only survive, but soar. Others might not."

"So you think maybe this Terry guy was paid by someone in Century to steal your sister's formula?"

"Harriet thinks John Rorrman wouldn't be above doing that. But she can't believe the whole board is involved."

De Santo shook his head. "You know, kid, the more I hear about all this . . . I keep going back to that gag order and where it came from. Georgetown is really D.C., isn't it? Mostly politicians. And if anybody's pulling strings in a town like that, it's probably somebody on Capitol Hill."

"I never thought of that, Vish, but it does make sense. Especially given the way politics and medicine shake hands."

"Did your sister know anybody in politics?"

"Not that I know of, not directly. But then, I didn't know all of her friends."

De Santo's brown eyes were thoughtful. "Century . . . wait a minute. They're in Century City, aren't they?"

"That's their corporate headquarters."

"Sure. I've got a friend in that division. And I'm remembering something."

He looked around, then took her arm, leading her over to a phone booth. "Hold on, kid."

He lifted the receiver and dropped a quarter in the slot, punching in a number. A few seconds later he spoke into the receiver. "Bobby? It's me, Leo. You awake?"

He listened, then rolled his eyes. "Sorry—I hate to interrupt you juicing your vegetables. You getting in shape for a run?"

A pause, and then a sorrowful shake of the head. "I don't know, Bobby. I kind of miss the old days when you could find any cop you knew at a doughnut shop. Hey, buddy, I need to know something. You remember Century Pharmaceuticals—something that happened last year sometime? Yeah, that's it. What exactly came down on that?"

He was silent, listening. His forehead creased in a frown. "And Century was involved somehow?" He nodded. "Yeah. That helps, but I need more. Can you find out and get back to me? Great. Yeah, either at the station or home. Soon as possible. Thanks, buddy."

He hung up, the worry lines deeper than they had been before.

"Let's sit down a minute. Sometimes I think better when my feet aren't so damned tired."

They settled onto a nearby park bench, and De Santo faced Nicole. "Okay, kid, here it is. Sometime last year there was a man in France who was kidnapped and killed. Some newspaper mogul over there—"

"Newspaper mogul! Vish, when I went through Mary's things last week, there was a clipping about a journalist who was kidnapped in France."

She told De Santo about the box of mementos, and how odd it seemed that Mary would save an article like that. "But what's the connection between that kidnapping and Century?"

"Bobby says the French police contacted the LAPD because they had reason to believe someone close to Century Pharmaceuticals was involved. There was never enough evidence, though, to book anyone."

"Did they suspect any one person, in particular?"

"Bobby didn't remember. He wasn't on the case, he just heard about it. He's going to ask around, quietly, and call me."

Restaurants around them began to fill up. De Santo glanced at his watch. "It's almost six. You said you have to get to P.V.?"

She nodded. "Around eight. I'd better go."

"What's that all about? You never did tell me."

"Harriet Ilsen identified the boat Dan and Mary were on when that photograph was taken. It's the old Century corporate yacht. I'm staying at the corporate guest house tonight, then in the morning I'll talk to the captain and look at the ship's log."

"What are you hoping to find out?"

"I don't really know. Maybe nothing, other than the fact that Dan Rossi and my sister had an intimate cruise together one day last April. But I can't help thinking now that there's more to it. I want to find out if anyone else was on the boat that day."

"This Harriet Ilsen, she lives in P.V.?"

"No, Long Beach, I think. But she's hosting a Century party tonight."

De Santo's worry lines deepened again. "I'm sorry, but this worries me. Given what we've found out so far, it feels like you're heading into a nest of vipers."

"I'll call you if anything looks the least bit off. Okay?"

"Is that a promise?"

"It's a promise."

He gave her a grudging smile. "Okay."

She stood and dropped her empty coffee cup into a trash can. De Santo eased his heavy frame off the bench with a groan.

"Do you have the number down there?" he asked. "If I hear anything important from Bobby, I'll give you a call tonight. Otherwise, I'll catch you at your hotel tomorrow."

Nicole took out the notepaper Harriet had given her. De Santo wrote the Palos Verdes phone number on the back of the receipt for their coffee, stuffing it in his shirt pocket. Then he walked her to the door of the Ocean Palms.

"Look," he said, laying a hand on her shoulder. "I know you don't want to hear this—but don't get too cocky with all that *chi.*"

Nicole smiled and leaned forward, giving him a light hug. "Don't worry, Vish. I'll be okay."

At the front desk she found a message to call the nurses' station on the professor's floor. Alarmed, she returned the call as soon as she got to her room.

"Is something wrong?"

"Not at all. Your friend is gaining strength. In fact, he's sitting up, and he'd like you to bring him a book."

"Of course. Anything in particular?"

"He asked for something called *The Maya Question.* He said you'd know which one he meant."

"I do. I can bring it right now, in fact." There was just enough time to squeeze in a visit before heading down to Palos Verdes.

"Why don't you wait until tomorrow?" the nurse suggested. "He's doing well, but we're planning to get him up and ambulatory in the morning. I'd like to see him get plenty of sleep tonight."

"All right. I'll be there tomorrow," Nicole agreed.

She took *The Maya Question* from her suitcase, thinking it odd that the professor had asked for this particular book. But then she remembered that she'd been quoting from it when he had the attack. It must have stuck in his mind.

Chapter 37

She had been to Palos Verdes before. When they first arrived last April, Dan had shown her the beach towns and these hills above them.

"This is where the truly rich live," he had said. "Not just the Hollywood types, but the business leaders—the movers and shakers. The ones who had sense enough to get out of town back in the fifties and sixties and buy cheap down here."

Nicole couldn't see much; it was a bit after eight, and dark. But as she wound up into the hills above Malaga Cove, the lighted houses became more and more elegant, the view decidedly expensive. With smog still out at sea, courtesy of the Santa Ana winds, the entire Los Angeles Basin was visible below, to her left. On the right, houses covered the hills, interspersed with trees, other greenery, and swimming pools.

She rounded a bend that took her away from the vista and into the trees. Slowing, she flicked the overhead light on and glanced quickly at the sketch Harriet Ilsen had drawn. *A half mile or so farther,* she thought. But it wasn't that far before she knew she was at the Century executive compound. Cars lined the curbs on both sides. People dressed in party garb were walking uphill along the street.

Harriet had told her to pull into the driveway. A valet would be there. "Nothing fancy, just a kid who lives nearby. I like to give him things to do." He would have instructions to park her car in the garage, since she'd be staying overnight.

She was glad she didn't have to hike up the hill. She was tired, and the session with Kenny had left her sore in muscles she hadn't even known were there. Aside from that, she was wearing the white dress again, not having anything else fit for a party, and that had called for heels.

What the hell am I doing here tonight? she wondered, feeling suddenly depressed. I should be in bed, sleeping. I could have driven down in the morning.

But Harriet had called just before she left. "I wanted to be sure you were coming tonight. It's important."

Sighing, Nicole pulled into the driveway of a mansion that looked like a mini–White House. It sprawled into wings on either side, and was lit up by spotlights discreetly nestled into gardens. Surrounding trees were highlighted as well, and ground-level lanterns illuminated overflowing tubs of white gardenias lining a semicircular drive. A young kid in a white shirt and red vest—no more than sixteen, she guessed—came up to her with a smile.

"Hi. I'm Nicole Ryan. Harriet said you'd park the car?"

"Sure, Ms. Ryan. Just leave your keys. No problem." He smiled and opened her door.

"I have a bag in the back."

"It'll be in your room, waiting for you. You just go on in. Ms. Ilsen's expecting you."

Nicole took her purse and slid out, thinking: A plain old gray Chevy rental car, and I'm getting better service than those BMWs I passed down the road. Maybe it *is* all in who you know.

And much as she despised it, she understood the seduction of big money. It wrapped wool around one, a protection from the world.

The scene wasn't an exact replica of the one at Rorrman's house in Malibu the other night—but close. The valet called ahead on a two-way radio to a butler, informing him of Nicole's arrival. Harriet, in a simple black silk dress and a rope of pearls, met her at the door. Her eyes were tired, but her brown hair glimmered with highlights. A light fragrance surrounded her. *White Shoulders,* Nicole remembered. The perfume her mother had used.

It made her uneasy. She wasn't sure why.

Harriet drew her inside. "I didn't want you to have to wander around looking for me. Don't you hate arriving at a party where you don't know a soul, and no one greets you? For the first twenty minutes you wonder if you're at the wrong place."

"Most women head for the powder room to repair their war paint," Nicole said, smiling.

"So they can come out again and face the enemy," Harriet agreed. She patted Nicole's arm. "I knew you and I thought alike, the moment I met you."

She drew Nicole down a vast hall, lined on one side with windows that overlooked a pool and gardens on a lower level. Catering staff drifted in and out of rooms with trays of hors d'oeuvres and drinks. Women in sequined dresses and men in formal wear chatted in clusters, balancing assorted goodies on napkins. Glasses set down on mahogany tables were quickly scooped up by attentive wait-persons before they could leave rings. Chamber music played.

"There's a powder room here at the end of the hall," Harriet said, steering her along the relatively quiet corridor. "If it's busy, there are five—count 'em, five—upstairs." Her tone was predictably caustic. "It was Rorrman's idea to have a separate manse just to impress the out-of-town execs. He says it motivates them, gives them a standard to aspire to so they'll work harder. My grandfather used to say if they weren't self-motivated, they didn't belong at Century."

At the door to the powder room Harriet gave her a hug. "As soon as I can break away from my duties, we'll talk some more."

Nicole hugged her back, gratefully. "Thanks, Harriet."

The older woman left her with a rustle of silk. "I'll be in the east wing. Any of the servers can show you the way."

Nicole waited a few moments until the powder room was free, and then stood surveying herself in its gilt-edged mirror. Her white dress was only a little rumpled from the drive. It had a smudge near the shoulder, however, that she hadn't seen when she put it on.

Her cheeks were pale, and she pinched them, the way her mother had taught her to as a child. *To bring color to them, Nikki. You don't want to go around looking like a ghost. Men despise that, you know.*

A scent drifted through her memory. *White Shoulders.*

I hate that perfume. I really hate it.

But why?

Her eyes, reflected in the mirror, widened.

Mother. Mother bending over my bed, kissing me good night. Leaving that imprint of White Shoulders on my sheets. "Mom's night out with the girls," she would say, laughing and looking happy. "Daddy's baby-sitting so I can play."

Then, after she was gone . . .

Nicole covered her hot cheeks. *Dear God. It went on for years!*

A wave of hatred engulfed her as she thought of her mother's laughing face, that tossed red hair, those pale pink lips. *Why did she leave me? She must have known. What was so important that she had to leave me alone with him?*

A hand went to her long auburn hair and smoothed it. In her mind, it became *his* hand. Stroking. *"Daddy loves his little girl. You love Daddy, don't you? Give me a little kiss. That's right, honey. Now give me one here. C'mon, Nikki, do it for Daddy . . . right here."*

At eight years of age, she remembered now, she had wanted to kill. To kill, and kill and kill.

By twelve she was numb to it. She did as she was told. Because if she refused . . .

"If you don't like me anymore, Nikki, maybe I'll just go across the hall and visit Mary, Mary quite contrary."

So she had given in to it. To *that*. And later, when Mary had come to live with her in Georgetown, hints of those memories had surfaced at odd, unexpected times, creating a distance that she couldn't explain.

Dan had said that if their mother loved Mary more, it was because Mary was the one her father hadn't touched. Was that true? And if so, had her mother felt jealous—or merely guilty because she never did anything to stop it?

Nicole squeezed her eyes shut and gripped the vanity for balance. *The truth is, I'll never know. I'll never be able to get to the truth, because everyone is dead.*

She clenched her fists. *Everyone except me. And I've got to survive. I will, goddammit, I will. I swear I will never let myself be abused again, never again let any man have power over me like that. I have got to be my own person. I've got to take care of myself.*

And I still have to take care of Mary.

She opened her eyes and straightened. Squaring her shoulders, she flicked back her hair and tightened her jaw. Someone was knocking on the powder-room door.

"Anyone in there?"

"I hope so," Nicole said softly to herself. Then, with more certainty, "Yes. I'm here. And I'm on my way out."

There were no Marilyn Monroe look-alikes at this party, no paparazzi, and the chamber music was almost too restful. A sonorous rendition of Pachelbel's *Canon in D* was putting her to sleep on her feet. Harriet was trapped in a corner, responding with barely concealed boredom to a group of Japanese men. Nicole rubbed her eyes wearily. If Harriet hadn't specifically said that she wanted her to meet someone, she would have asked to be shown to a room for the night. In fact, she was seriously thinking of doing so, anyway, when a commotion at the door caught everyone's attention.

Entering on the arm of one of the most beautiful women she had ever seen, was Dan Rossi.

The woman was as tall as Dan, with a mane of tawny blond hair that reached nearly to her waist. She wore tight faded jeans, artfully torn across the thighs. They were topped by a white T-shirt snug enough to show off her figure, and over that an open jean jacket, a hand-painted eagle on the back. High-heeled black boots with a fringe came nearly to the knee of her long slender legs. From her ears dangled earrings made of bits of feathers, turquoise, and glass. The turquoise matched the woman's eyes.

Nicole hated her on the spot.

What the hell was Dan Rossi doing here—and with someone like that?

The question was answered a few moments later when Harriet brought them over to the window to where Nicole was studying the view, hoping not to be noticed.

"Nicole, you know Dan Rossi, I believe?" Harriet's smile was tight, uncertain. "And this is Kitty Rorrman. Kitty is John Rorrman's niece."

So this is the woman you betrayed my sister with, Dan.

Nicole acknowledged the introduction with as much grace as she could muster. She forced her fingers out of the fist they had formed and extended her hand. The other woman ignored it, saying nothing.

Up close, her light turquoise eyes were brittle, the pupils nearly nonexistent. Nicole had the sense that if you removed every trace of the woman's makeup, there would be nothing beneath it. No skin, no flesh, no soul.

Hiding a slight shiver, she turned to Dan. "This is the second time today that you've surprised me. Didn't I see you earlier with Sister Paula?"

He looked blank. "Sister Paula? I hardly think so. We're not exactly on friendly terms."

"You looked pretty friendly to—"

"You must have seen someone else." He turned from her abruptly, his tone cold. "Kitty, why don't we go find a drink?"

Harriet lifted a hand to beckon. "No need. I'll get one of the waiters."

"No, really, I think I see someone I should talk to."

Dan tugged at his companion's arm and pulled her away. "See you later, Harriet," Kitty Rorrman said. "Nice party." Her words, husky as if from sleep, trailed behind her, flat and emotionless as her eyes.

Harriet stared after their departing backs. "Well, I must say—I didn't know they were still seeing each other. Nicole, I'm sorry. But I thought it'd be less awkward for you if I brought them over."

She watched them mingle, Kitty seeming completely at ease with the assorted executives and their families.

"She must do this a lot."

"Attend parties?" Harriet gave a scornful laugh. "It's about all she's good for, if you ask me."

Nicole wondered. If she weren't mistaken, Kitty Rorrman was the woman who had answered the phone when she had pressed the redial at Dan's house.

"What's the story on her?" she asked.

"Well, to begin with, she has more money to spend than is good for any young woman her age—thanks to her dear uncle John. Her parents are back in Connecticut. Kitty came out here to live with her uncle four years ago when she was nineteen, hoping to hit it big in Hollywood and become an overnight star. She did work as an extra in a couple of movies, but for the most part she hangs out on the fringes of the industry. She mingles with the celebs, and travels with them. I suspect she's deep into drugs, as well."

"From the look of those eyes, I'd say you're probably right. What do you think she and Dan are doing together?"

"Well, I hate to say it, but it's widely known that Kitty likes to buy her men. That is to say, she isn't looking for love. She simply pays for a body and then dumps it. I've heard her called by various unflattering names—The Black Widow Spider is one."

Nicole shivered again. "And Dan is with her. You know, Harriet, the more I see of Dan Rossi lately, the less I like him."

"I'm so sorry. I didn't know he'd be here tonight."

"It's all right. But you know, I really am tired." She glanced around. "You said you wanted me to meet someone. If he's not here yet—"

Harriet hooked her arm in Nicole's. "As a matter of fact, he just a few moments ago sent word from the kitchen that he'd come in the back way. We're to meet him upstairs in my rooms."

"You certainly are being mysterious about this person," Nicole commented as they climbed the stairs to the second floor.

"I don't mean to be. It's just that I don't want anyone overhearing us. This whole matter should be confidential, just between you, my friend, and me."

They left the music and chatter far behind as they traversed a long hallway into the west wing.

"Here we are," Harriet said, opening a door on the left. Beyond it was a large sitting room, softly lit by a Tiffany lamp on a desk in one corner. A bay-shaped window spanned an entire wall. There were no curtains; thousands of lights twinkled in the valley below.

Before the window was a grouping of chairs, a low coffee table, and a blue and white-striped sofa. On it was seated a man. As they entered, he rose and turned to greet them.

"Hi, Nikki. Hi, Aunt Harriet."

Nicole didn't know whether to stare or to laugh.

"Jack?" she said at last, confusion in her voice. "Jack Blake?"

Chapter 38

"Don't tell me you two already know each other." Harriet smiled indulgently.

Jack walked over to Nicole and put an arm around her waist. He drew her into the room. "Reasonably well, I'd say."

"You might have told me," Harriet complained with a mock pout of her lower lip. "Here I've been going on and on about you, Nicole, and he didn't say a word."

"And spoil my fun? You know how I love to tease you, Aunt Harriet. Your nose turns red when you're surprised."

"It does not!" she protested. But her look was that of a fond, indulgent mother.

"What's going on?" Nicole asked. "Is Jack the person you wanted me to meet here tonight?"

"He certainly is. But I had no idea—how well do you two know each other, anyway?"

"We just met," Nicole said.

"We've been out a few times," Jack amended.

Harriet looked from one to the other and gave a wise smile.

"Here, both of you, sit down. I had coffee sent up." She crossed to a sideboard where a silver coffeepot, cups, cream and sugar, and a bottle of brandy had been left on a tray. Carrying it over, she set it on the low table.

Jack settled into the sofa, but Nicole stood looking at them both with questions in her eyes.

"*Aunt* Harriet?" she said pointedly to Jack.

"Not by blood," he admitted. "But I've been around so long . . ."

"Fifteen years is it, now?" Harriet added, pouring coffee.

"At least."

"Jack seems like family," she said. "And there's no one in the company I trust more than Jack to keep an eye on things. This is confidential, of course—just between us. Jack has brought me valuable information over the years, information that has helped to forestall certain of John Rorrman's moves that would have been disastrous for Century."

She leaned forward and touched Nicole's hand gently. "I hope you don't mind. I asked Jack to come here tonight because I want him to look into our suspicions about Mary's death, and her work."

"I'm just . . . so surprised." Nicole looked from one to the other.

"Well, I for one am glad you two already know each other," Harriet said. "It will make it easier for Jack to look after you."

"What do you mean?"

"Nicole, after our talk today I felt certain you needed protection until we know what's really going on. If someone actually harmed Mary, your feelings of being in danger yourself could be very real."

"But I still don't understand what Jack might have to do with that."

He set his coffee on the table and pressed his hands together, tapping his chin with a steepled finger. "Aunt Harriet would like me to stick close—to keep an eye on you until we understand the situation better."

"And I want him to look into it personally. I hope you don't mind," Harriet said again. "I don't mean to push you into something you don't feel comfortable with. It's just that I trust Jack." She turned to him. "What exactly would you need to get started?"

"More coffee would help. Beyond that, anything Nikki knows and wants to tell me." He threw her a questioning look.

Harriet refilled their cups. "A little brandy?" She lifted the bottle next to the coffee carafe and poured a dollop into both her own cup and Jack's.

Nicole shook her head. "I don't . . ." She sighed and leaned her head back against the chair. "Oh, why not."

Jack Blake was indeed a surprise. But it might be helpful to have him involved. Harriet was proving to be a good friend.

Unused to the brandy, Nicole felt a bit fuzzy. She had yawned several times in bringing Jack up-to-date—repeating the same story she had told De Santo, then Harriet. It was a story she was beginning to weary of telling.

"I just don't see why anyone would harm *me*, at this point. Now that Terry Asher's got the formula, that means Rorrman and the Century board have it too."

"I would agree," Jack said, "if you hadn't come to Los Angeles asking questions. And now you say you've brought the police into it. Rorrman could be afraid you're making too many waves."

"All I want to know is what happened to Mary."

"I understand that. But, Nikki, we may never be able to prove anything one way or another. You could spend your life agonizing over it. Do you agree, Aunt Harriet?"

Harriet rubbed her nose. "I suppose you could be right. Sometimes when something is done, it's done . . . and if we can't change things, we have to let go."

"I don't think I can do that," Nicole said firmly. "I have to at least try."

Harriet flicked a glance at Jack. "If you feel that strongly, then by all means, we must do what we can."

"Along those lines . . ." Jack hesitated.

"Yes?"

"Well, you may not want to hear this. But this Dan Rossi—this friend of yours and Mary's—"

"What about Dan?"

"I know you've cared about him in the past, Nikki. Maybe you still do. But after we talked last night . . . look, I know I didn't have any right to, but I was worried about you. I've been asking around about Rossi. And what I've heard isn't good."

Her eyes flicked from Jack to Harriet, and back again.

"What have you heard?"

"Apparently, he's in deep financial trouble. He's halfway through a film project and he's run out of bucks. The person I talked to said Rossi has let it be known around town that he'd do anything—and I mean anything—to rake in some cash."

Nicole frowned. "I never . . . Dan and I were friends for more than a year, and I never knew him to be like that."

Harriet spoke. "I don't know the man, really. But just playing devil's advocate—you saw him downstairs earlier with Kitty Rorrman. Was that the man you used to know?"

"No, but—"

"Nikki, the cover of the book may look the same," Jack said, "but the contents may well have changed. This is something you've suspected for a while, isn't it?"

She was silent.

"I knew he and Mary Clare were friends," Harriet said in the breach, "and I assumed he must be a nice person. But Hollywood has a way of changing people. So many who start out with pure motives and fresh ideas become prostitutes for their art." She leaned toward Nicole and squeezed her hand sympathetically. "I'm not saying this happened to your friend. But you may have to consider the possibility."

"Just to pose a theory," Jack added, "what if Rossi began seeing Kitty Rorrman with the hope of landing financial backing from her for his project? She's been known to invest heavily, and not very wisely. And suppose Rorrman saw that his niece's involvement with Rossi could open doors for *him?* He must have known Rossi and your sister were friends. From what Harriet tells me, there was talk about them being more than that, in fact."

Nicole glanced at Harriet.

"I'm sorry," she said. "But I thought he should know. It seemed important, after everything you told me this afternoon."

"I think Rossi's involvement with your sister is damned important," Jack said. "If she trusted him, it follows that when she began to get nervous about Rorrman getting his hands on the formula, she'd have told Rossi—and maybe even given him a copy of the formula for safekeeping in case anything happened to her. Rorrman, banking on that, may have sent Kitty out to meet Rossi and wheedle —or steal—the formula from him."

"And you're suggesting that if Dan had the formula, he might have sold it to Kitty to keep his film going?"

Jack's gaze was steady. "What do you think?"

Nicole rubbed her temple, where an ache had begun. "I still can't believe it. Or maybe I don't want to. And for that matter, Dan didn't have the formula, so far as we know. If it was in the blue notebook, Mary gave it to *me* to hang on to."

"But you said it disappeared."

"Well, Mary had a key to my apartment. I think now that she must have come over and gotten it and was planning to send it to Harriet. She may have thought it would be safer in Harriet's vault."

"But Harriet never got it. It somehow fell into the hands of Terrence Asher." Jack sat on the edge of the sofa. "You're resisting looking at the obvious, Nikki. Mary probably sent it directly to Rossi, who sold it to Kitty. She gave it to Rorrman, who brought Asher out here to announce the discovery as his—and Century's—own. Don't you see? It all fits."

Nicole was suddenly overwhelmingly tired. She sank back in the chair. "But there was the note from Mary. And then, Sister Paula . . ."

"What about Sister Paula?"

"Oh, nothing." She shook her head. "I'm sorry. It just gets more and more confusing."

Harriet rose briskly, patting Nicole's shoulder as she stood. "It's late, and I know you must be exhausted. Why don't we suspend all this for the night? Let Jack mull it over, see what he comes up with. We can talk more tomorrow."

"I'd like to make a couple of calls," Jack said, rising. "I need to cancel some appointments." He crossed to the phone on Harriet's desk.

"And I have that letter you asked for," Harriet told Nikki. "For the handwriting analysis." She pulled it from a drawer in the desk. Nicole stood, taking it.

"Mary sent it to me after her visit here last spring," Harriet said. "It's short—a thank-you for my hospitality while she was here."

Nicole glanced at the note, saw the familiar JMJ below Mary's signature, and felt a pang. She tucked it into a pocket. "Thanks, Harriet."

"You do look tired."

"I guess I really could use some sleep. That brandy knocked me for a loop."

Harriet put an arm around her shoulders and hugged her. "I'll show you to your room right now. Unless you'd like to wait for Jack . . . ?"

"Yes, let's give him a moment. I'd like to say good night."

The two women stood looking out the broad window together. Moonlight illuminated the L.A. Basin all the way to Mount Baldy in the east, and the Malibu hills to the north. Nicole imagined she could almost see the abandoned hotel where she and Jack had been the night before. Directly below, the coastline formed a white crescent along Redondo Beach, Manhattan, and then northward to Venice and Santa Monica.

"This is a rare sight," Harriet said. "But these are the days—and nights—that keep me here. In Southern California, that is."

She pointed to the closest marina. A cluster of masts stood like slender white toothpicks. "That's King Harbor, where the *Haokah* is docked. You can't see it from here. There are restaurants and a hotel in the way. But we'll go down there in the morning." She gave a delicate yawn, covering her mouth. "Sorry."

"At least I can blame the brandy," Nicole teased. "You never even touched your coffee."

"Didn't I?" The woman laughed softly. "The truth is, I seldom drink when I'm around Jack Blake. I do believe one imbibes to alter reality, don't you? And Jack is such a fascinating man, one hardly wants to alter him. He's good-looking . . . smart . . . and *very* attentive."

I'm seeing another side of her, Nicole thought. *A more relaxed, more feminine side that Jack has brought out. Funny how we don't really know people until we see them in a variety of situations.*

"Are you—are you in love with Jack, Harriet?"

The woman blinked. "Good God, no! But I do care for him. Since the time he joined Century, he's been like a son."

"What's that you're saying, Auntie dear?" Jack had left the phone and was standing behind them.

Harriet smiled. "I was telling Nicole that she'll have a chance to see the *Haokah* in the morning."

"Sounds good."

"In fact, since the two of you know each other so well, I think I may let you go down there without me. That way you can talk further, and I can take care of my wretched hostessing duties."

"Is the *Haokah* going out tomorrow?"

"Strangely enough, Rorrman hasn't scheduled any cruises this time. He must have thought they'd get in the way of all his damnable parties."

"Fantastic," Jack said with a wicked grin to Nicole. He twisted an imaginary mustache. "I can play Captain Hook and you can be Wendy."

She laughed, forgetting her worries for the moment. Funny how Jack Blake had a way of easing her mood, even at the worst of times.

Chapter 39

Her sleep that night was restless. An unfamiliar bed, noises in the hall—other overnight guests, settling in late. Wakefulness gave her time to think. She wondered how the professor was doing. What a strange conversation they'd had the night before. David and Eleanor, all those memories flooding back now . . .

A flood of sunlight on her face woke her, and later there was a substantial brunch served in a dining room with wall-to-wall windows. Catalina Island nestled into the sea before them, looking a mere stone's throw, rather than twenty-six miles, away.

While her guests devoured fresh fruit, scrambled eggs, and sausages, Harriet telephoned the *Haokah*'s captain. He was on twenty-four-hour duty and lived in an apartment at the marina, only steps away from the dock. He agreed to meet with Jack and Nicole on board.

A man in his sixties with a heavily lined face, he was waiting for them in spotless white uniform when they arrived.

"Captain Nealy," Jack said, "this is Nicole Ryan. She'd like to look around the *Haokah,* and if you don't mind, ask you some questions."

The captain nodded and extended a hand. "Ms. Ilsen told me you were on your way. Anything I can do, I'll be happy to help."

Nicole looked at the name *Haokah* above the wheelhouse. From here she could picture the exact spot where Dan and Mary Clare had stood. This was the boat—she was absolutely sure of it now.

"My sister was a passenger on this boat last April. She and a friend, Dan Rossi. I wondered if you might remember them."

"Your sister's name was Ryan too?"

"Yes."

"Well, the names aren't immediately familiar, but then I'm kept pretty busy when we're out at sea. And we've had a lot of guests on the *Haokah* since then. It was a busy summer."

She showed him the photograph. "This is my sister, with Dan Rossi."

"Hmmm. The faces are familiar. But I think you might find out more from the log for that month. Ms. Ilsen asked me to have it ready for you."

He took them inside the large cabin, which was outfitted with a navy blue sofa, several comfortable chairs, and maple side tables, all bolted to the floor. Lamps were bolted to a wall. Against the opposite bulkhead was a large captain's desk with a barometer, a globe, and a row of books. A clock ticked on the bulkhead above the desk.

On the desk a large leather-bound book lay on a green ink blotter. The captain opened it and leafed through the pages. "April . . . April. Here we go. Do you have a specific date?"

"Between April seventeenth and the twenty-sixth. My sister was out here during that time."

"Well, April twenty-second was a Sunday, and we often take guests out on Sundays. Ryan and Rossi, you say? Here it is. We did go out that day. A small party, though, not the usual."

"How small?"

He turned the book her way, running his fingers down the lined page. "Mr. Rorrman, of course. And his niece, Miss Kitty—" His face turned red, and he caught himself. "That's what some of the crew call her—after the madam in that old TV show, *Gunsmoke.*"

Nicole couldn't help smiling. "Whatever fits."

The captain's finger moved down the listed names. "Here's a Mary Clare Ryan—I guess that's your sister. Yes, and a Dan Rossi, too." He hesitated, then glanced uncertainly at Jack.

"Say whatever you want, you're among friends."

"Well, we hardly ever go out with just a couple of guests. Mr. Rorrman likes to take as many as possible—that way he gets as much as he can out of each trip, in terms of a payoff in publicity for the company." He stared at the log, thinking. "If I'm not mistaken, that was the day Miss Kitty got so out of sorts. When we got back to port, she came up here snapping at all of us—saying the *Haokah* needed a good cleaning, that we hadn't been keeping things up. That wasn't at all true. I figured she had some bee in her bonnet about something else and needed someone to take it out on."

His tone was offended. "We take good care of the *Haokah*. We would never let her fall into disrepair."

"I'm sure you wouldn't," Jack assured him. "But is that all you remember about that trip, or was there something else?"

"Nothing specific. I just remember the whole day seemed strained. I was glad when it was over."

"Well, thanks for your help. May I show Ms. Ryan around now?"

"Of course. Ms. Ilsen said you might not have time for a cruise, but I had planned a brief run just outside the breakwater today— a routine mechanical check. Would you like it if I did that while you're here? You'd get to see a bit of the view from that perspective."

Jack looked at Nicole. "What do you think, Nikki?"

She shrugged. "I guess. How long would it take? I have an appointment in the city."

"A half hour or so, no more," the captain said.

She smiled. "Okay. That would be nice."

They followed the captain out, and Jack leapt down onto the dock, untying the ropes that held the boat fast. He tossed them up, and Captain Nealy caught them, securing them along the *Haokah*'s deck. When he was back on board, the captain revved the heavy motor and began to inch the ship out of its berth.

Jack and Nicole stood at the prow as they motored south toward the exit from the harbor. Pelicans shared the breakwater to their right, and beyond were men fishing on the rocks. To their left was a three-story pink hotel, the *Portofino.* Next to it, a restaurant, then a pier lined with more fishermen, and a coffee shop. Its sign read: POLLY'S ON THE PIER.

Several seals swam in the water around the boat, but most of them converged on the pier, barking and begging for scraps of food.

This is a working harbor, Nicole thought, with fishing boats and tugs, *yet at the same time, a playground for the rich.* She tried to picture Mary on this boat, enjoying that day with Dan. Her serious sister, who never had time to play, and scorned all things material.

A fishing boat, the *City of Redondo,* glided by. Gulls flocked around it, thick as mosquitoes on a summer night. Tourists stood at a seawall. They snapped pictures and waved.

The *Haokah* eased into a channel that led to the sea. It glided slowly toward a long barge bearing a white-and-orange crane that was easily five stories high. At the top of the crane was a sign: Connolly Pacific Co.

"They're still building the breakwater," Jack said. "You see that restaurant over there, the Blue Moon? It was washed away in the last big storm. Hopefully, the breakwater will prevent that from happening again."

"My, you certainly are a good guide," Nicole said, amused at his earnest tone.

"Well, you should know these things if you're planning to move out here."

"Move? But I'm not."

"It's a great place to live—lots of sunshine. You could do worse."

She laughed. "Are you a realtor, too?"

"No." He grinned. "I'm just hoping."

"That I'll move out here? Why?"

"Because I'm out here more than I am in the east. I'd like to keep seeing you, Nikki. In fact, I'd like a lot more than that."

She glanced away, focusing on the barge.

"Hey," Jack said softly, "come back. What are you thinking?"

She sighed. *About Dan. And the mistakes I made with him.*

"Look at that," she said to change the subject. The jaws had come down from the monster crane and landed with a resounding crash on an adjacent barge piled high with gigantic boulders. The jaws grasped a boulder the size of a compressed car and began to lift it. The crane, on a swivel base, turned toward them. The boulder began to swing their way.

She grabbed Jack's arm. "It's going to hit us!"

He smiled, putting his arm around her shoulders. "Not to worry. They know to the inch how much room they've got to maneuver."

Indeed, the boulder missed them by a good fifteen feet.

"I can't believe how big that crane is," she said. "And that man in the catbird seat—he must be at least two stories above the ground! And look at that—"

Jack was clearly enjoying her excitement. "It's a monumental task, building a breakwater."

"What do you think he makes at a job like that?"

"Probably a lot more than I do," he said with a rueful grin. "Would you like to ask him?"

"No, of course not, don't be silly—"

Too late. He was already motioning to Captain Nealy. "Do you think you could pull alongside that barge?"

"No problem." The captain swung the *Haokah* in that direction.

"Come along, woman." Jack grabbed her hand and pulled her toward the prow.

"Jack, no! I only wondered. We can't actually bother the man."

"Why not? As Captain Hook I can do anything!" He tugged harder. "Furthermore, as Wendy, it's your job to do my bidding."

Laughing, she let him lead her to the prow, where they stood as the captain eased closer to the barge. Jack called up to the man in the catbird seat. "Ahoy, there! Can we ask you some questions?"

The man cupped an ear and shook his head. "I can't hear you."

"That's okay. All we want to know, really, is how much money you make."

"Jack, don't!" Nicole whispered, flushing with embarrassment. But she couldn't help laughing.

The man shook his head again. "Wait."

They watched him transfer another boulder to the breakwater and drop it with a loud *BOOM* into place. Then he shut the motor off and came out and stood on a small deck. It was suddenly very silent. "Some problem?"

Jack's mouth twitched. He leaned toward Nicole's ear and muttered, "I didn't really want him to stop the damned motor."

She laughed. "Don't mind him," she called to the man above them. "He's the curious type. But now he's shy."

The man, who wore a hard hat, an orange vest, and sported more meat on his muscles than a wrestler, stood with hands tucked into a wide leather belt and grinned. "I could drop one of these rocks on him. Take care of that real fast."

Nicole wasn't so sure he was kidding. She tugged on Jack's arm, laughing. "Let's get out of here."

Jack, his expression bland, waved at the man and yelled, "Thanks anyway." He motioned to Captain Nealy to go on. As the *Haokah* pulled away, the catbird operator looked after them, still grinning.

"You are too much," Nicole said. "You'll do anything, won't you?"

The gray eyes were steady on hers, and serious. "Well, that remains to be seen."

———

She should have been able to relax after that and forget for a while. Jack had made her laugh more in one morning than she had in a week. But she was tired, and her thoughts kept returning to Dan and Mary, on this boat with Kitty and John Rorrman. What had transpired here?

She looked down into the water as the *Haokah* plowed into open sea, and shivered. *I'm trying, Mary. Vish is trying, too—and now Harriet and Jack. Maybe together we'll be able to sort it out.*

"Are you okay?" Jack was at her elbow.

"Yes, I've just been thinking. Are we going back in soon?"

"I just asked him. He's turning around now, and we'll be back at the harbor in ten minutes or so. Would you like to go inside? We can get something to drink."

Back in the cabin she sat on the sofa. Jack made sure she was comfortable. "What would you like? Wine? Brandy."

"No, just some juice, if there is any."

"Sure." He pressed a section of paneling that masked a wet bar with a refrigerator beneath. Reaching in, he pulled out a carton of Minute Maid.

"Presto, chango," Nicole said. "I'm impressed."

"Harriet's grandfather had a lot of compartments built into the bulkhead, to conserve space. He designed the *Haokah* himself. Some say there are secret panels all over the ship, although no one's ever admitted to finding any."

"It would figure, though. Haokah was a god of secret emotions. With him, nothing was as it seemed."

He handed her a cold glass of orange juice and sat in a chair across from her. "What's wrong, Nikki? You seem down suddenly."

She sipped, then stared at the pulpy juice. "I don't know. Maybe I just have too many things to think about. And to do."

She drank again, deeply, and set the glass down. "A nurse from the professor's floor called last night. He wanted me to bring him a book, and I told her I would. I have to get over there today."

"A book? If he's reading, he must be doing pretty well."

"Physically, yes. But he's worried about something personal—not to mention the break-in at his house. I wish they hadn't had to tell him about that."

"Was anything valuable taken?"

"We won't really know until he gets out of the hospital and looks around for himself."

The captain called down that they were coming back into harbor, and they went outside to stand by the rail. The *Haokah* glided gently between the two ends of breakwater.

The giant crane was now in a resting position. A worker ran along a catwalk spanning its "neck," which stretched out over the water, easily a hundred yards in length. At the end, where the jaws were, he called back to the operator: "You're right, Baby's got a broken tooth. You want to change over now, or later?"

The operator called back, "Better do it now."

The worker made his way back along the catwalk to a platform. The crane began to move toward a flat barge, where a backup set of jaws lay among ropes and other equipment. The operator set the crane down gently, and a crew on the barge took over.

"Why don't we go somewhere for lunch?" Jack suggested. "I know a great place with a view. And I'd be fulfilling my assignment to keep an eye on you." He grinned. "I can't believe Harriet is actually grateful to me for doing the one thing I've been wanting to do since we met."

He was impossible and charming, and she enjoyed him thoroughly. Nicole glanced at her watch. A little before noon.

"I have an appointment at four this afternoon. That leaves me just enough time to get to the Med Center and see the professor first. I'm afraid lunch is out."

They drifted between boats in the marina, down the channel toward the *Haokah*'s oversized berth.

"You said the professor asked for a book. Anything in particular? Harriet's set up a huge library back at the house. She says it lends some class to an otherwise crass operation."

"He asked for *The Maya Question*. It's an old volume of mine that I'd given to Mary and then found a few nights ago in Dan's cottage. I was quoting from it in the professor's class when he had the heart attack."

"Wow! Must have been an exciting plot."

She laughed. "Gory, anyway. It's about the Mayans and the

Aztecs, and how the Aztecs killed so many people in the temple one day—"

She broke off. Jack was gazing blankly at the surrounding boats, deep in thought.

"I'm rattling on," she said. "You don't want to hear about this."

He focused back on her. "On the contrary, I'm enthralled."

"Uh-huh."

They both laughed.

"We'll tie up the *Haokah*," Jack said, "then we'll get the book and I'll drive you to Westwood."

"Thanks, but I've got my car at the house."

"Leave it there. This way I can keep tabs on you."

But she was too tired for company; she wanted to be alone for a while.

"I've got a lot to do," she said, smiling. "I have to go to the hotel first and change, make phone calls—"

"I can hang out while you do those things. I promised Harriet, you know."

"But it's broad daylight. I'm more likely to be mugged by a carjacker than anyone from Century Pharmaceuticals."

"Even more reason."

She was irritated, suddenly. *Dammit, I can take care of myself. I'm not some helpless female. I'm not a child.*

The captain killed the *Haokah*'s engine. Nicole stood by while Jack leapt to the dock to secure the boat. The Captain started down the steps from above, but Nicole motioned to him. "I've got it!" She picked up the lines and tossed them to Jack. For a brief instant she resented Harriet's having brought him into all this. She liked him—possibly even more than that. But she didn't want to be smothered.

As quickly as the resentment had flared, it faded.

I've always been this way, she thought—*wallowing in the feeling of being cared for, and then—the next moment—casting it aside. I would be miserable to live with.*

On the drive back to the house, a certain tension set in. She wanted to relieve it, but didn't know how. At the house she left Jack at the foot of the stairs and inquired after Harriet—who, she was told, was having lunch at the country club with a Japanese doctor who had been at the party the night before. Leaving a message of thanks, she dragged her own suitcase to the waiting car, under the protests of an eager butler who nearly had a stroke insisting he'd gladly do that for her.

Nicole slid into the driver's seat. A glimpse in the rearview mirror as she adjusted it revealed a gloomy Jack Blake watching from a balcony above the graceful white portico of Century's "White House."

She headed north, feeling free. Although why the thought occurred to her in just that way, she couldn't say.

Chapter 40

Nicole dropped her overnight case and purse onto the hotel bed. There had been one call: "From a Sergeant De Santo," the desk clerk had said. "Just a few minutes ago. He left word that it was urgent." She reached him at home.

"I just tried you in P.V.," he said. "They told me you were on the way up here."

"What's wrong?"

"Terrence Asher is dead."

"Dead? Terry? I don't believe it! How?"

"An automobile accident. They said he was driving drunk."

"Vish, as far as I know, Terry hardly drank at all."

"Well, maybe he was celebrating his new discovery. Anyway, that's how the coroner's calling it for now. There'll be an investigation."

"This doesn't feel right, Vish."

"I agree—and I want you to start being more careful."

For a brief moment she wondered if she'd been foolish, not letting Jack come back with her.

"I ran that check on Harriet Ilsen. She comes up clean. I'm still working on Rorrman. Everything go all right down there?"

"Yes. It was fine. I learned some things about Mary and Dan, but I don't know what they mean."

"Well, Bobby got back to me about Century and the French police. It seems a woman drowned last spring in the Seine, a known prostitute. The French police suspected the drowning was a cover-up, and that death had probably occurred during an S and M scene that turned sour. She wasn't all that popular with the gendarmes, so they weren't real aggressive at following up. But then a French newsman turned up a connection between the pross and our very own, very venerable Senator Garrick Hale. You know him?"

"You bet I do. I saw him just the other night, in fact, at a Century party in Malibu. He was meeting with John Rorrman."

"Doesn't surprise me a bit. Well, this journalist claimed to have proof that Hale was with the pross just before she turned up dead. It was sick stuff, he said, not the usual fun-and-games thing.

He figured the senator paid someone to make it look like she'd drowned. He was going to print a major exposé—and next thing you know, he's kidnapped. Gone. Vanished. No one's heard from him since."

"So what's the tie-in to Century?"

"When the journalist disappeared, somebody on the French police —a friend of his—showed up here in the States asking questions. Apparently, Senator Hale had an ironclad alibi for both the night the prostitute died, and the night the journalist disappeared. Guess who provided the alibi?"

"Don't tell me."

"You got it, kid. John Rorrman."

"You think he lied, Vish?"

"No. Hale was seen at Century functions both nights. But Senator Garrick Hale is an old, old chum of John Rorrman's. Rorrman's been investing major sums from Century coffers into Hale's campaigns since he was nothing but a raw boy running for his first local office. It's no big secret he's been grooming Hale for the presidency."

"And if Hale was exposed now as a killer, all those campaign contributions would go down the tubes along with him."

"Not to mention Rorrman's hopes to have a pal in the White House."

"So what happened with the investigation?"

"Not a damn thing. The French police never had anything but circumstantial evidence that Rorrman was involved, or that Hale had the prostitute killed."

"Damn! And now Terry Asher—another automobile accident. But what would Rorrman have to gain from that? He wanted Immu-Phor released to the public, and Terry had already done that."

"I don't know. There's got to be some other motive—something we can't see yet, maybe because we're too close."

Nicole glanced at the clock on the nightstand. "Look, I have to get to the Med Center, then I'll be at Ken's around four. Will you be there?"

"Not today. I'm going to hang with the guys on the Asher investigation, and in between I'll make some more calls back east. But, Nikki, I mean it—you be careful. If anything happens, call me, okay?"

"Yes," she said softly. "Don't worry. But thanks."

Hanging up, she took *The Maya Question* from Mary's black box with the cross on its lid and packed it into a tote bag she'd bought in the gift shop downstairs. Then she tucked her shirt into jeans and headed out the door.

Chapter 41

"He's much better physically," the nurse on the professor's new floor told her. "He seems to have a strong will to live, almost as if he's got some mission and can't let go until it's carried out."

"That's good, isn't it?"

"Ordinarily, it would be. But he's disturbed about something, and we're worried about a setback. Emotions do strange things to the body. I hope you can cheer him up."

The professor indeed looked stronger. He and other ambulatory patients were enjoying the sunshine on a rooftop terrace. There were white tables and chairs shaded by striped umbrellas. Pitchers of ice water and juice decorated the tables, along with tiny bouquets of flowers.

He half rose as she approached, and an off-white throw cover began to slide from his lap. Nicole walked more quickly. "Don't get up. You look great sitting there, your face all pink from the sun."

The professor smiled, and she leaned over, kissing his cheek.

"They want us to think we're on vacation at some luxury spa," he complained as she helped him tuck the blanket around his legs once more. "Supposedly we won't mind, then, when we see the bill."

Nicole laughed. "You're as much a curmudgeon as ever."

She sat across from him. "I'm so glad to see you looking this much better. I was worried about you the other night."

"Oh, I'm not going anywhere." The professor sighed. "I don't have enough plenary indulgences lined up yet, little Nikki. I need to do a good deed first—to work my way out of purgatory."

She leaned forward and took his hand. It was cold. "I know the other night you were thinking about the past, and David. Professor, you have to let it go."

"There is no past, Nikki, not really. Everything we do, from birth to death, is connected by some ethereal thread. And we never know, when we do something, whether it will have a good or bad effect on our lives. History has taught me that."

"I know. We've talked about this before. But we also agreed that we couldn't carry guilt about the past with us, didn't we?"

"Not guilt, no. But, Nikki, there comes a time when wrongs have to be righted, or other wrongs are committed. I'm guilty of not righting a wrong early enough. I hope you will believe that I meant no harm to anyone." His shoulders moved in a tired shrug. "Of course, you know what they say about the road to hell . . ."

He glanced down at the tote bag Nicole had purchased as she left the hotel. Made of black canvas, it lay on the table with its decorated side up. A guitar, boots, a marshal's badge, and wanted posters had been hand-sewn onto the canvas. One of the posters read: $500 Reward—Jesse James—Dead or Alive.

"Is that to make me smile?" he asked.

"I thought you might like it. You asked for a book, and I thought if people brought you others, you could use this to take them home in."

"It has a nice whimsical touch. May I see the book?"

The Maya Question? Here." She reached into the bag and drew it out, pausing to wipe a bit of dust from the cover.

The professor leaned forward. "Hand it to me, please, Nikki."

Bewildered at his urgency, Nicole did as he asked. His worried eyes scanned the book, then met hers as he clutched it to his chest.

"In case anything happens to me, I have to trust that what I'm about to tell you won't put you in danger, that you'll know the right thing to do."

"Professor . . ."

"Please, just let me explain. You'll understand when I'm through." He took a deep breath. "Nikki, before our David died, Eleanor was working on a new drug. A mood elevator. It was from the bark of the *lumenaia* tree in South America."

"The *lumenaia?* But that's the drug Mary was working on! The one that inspired her studies about laughter and the immune system. It led her to Immu-Phor."

"Precisely. Mary found Eleanor's notes on *lumenaia* when she was here a year ago last summer, attending a seminar at UCLA. She asked if I had an extra suitcase that she might use to carry books home. Since I never travel these days, I told her she was welcome to look in my closet and take whatever she could find."

His voice was becoming thin. He reached for a glass of water and took a sip.

"When Mary found those papers—oh, dear God, I didn't know what to do! It had been so many years since I'd hidden them away in that suitcase, I'd forgotten they were there. But Mary was holding them in her hands when I got home that night. She was nearly fever-ish with excitement. She knew immediately what they might mean to her own work."

Nicole also remembered those papers—taking them out of the suitcase, putting them on the floor in the back of the closet.

The professor continued. "Mary asked if she might take the notes and work from them. She would give Eleanor credit for her findings, of course. But I had promised Eleanor when she was dying that I would never let those notes see the light of day."

"Why?"

The professor looked down at his folded hands. They were shak-ing. *"Lumenaia,* Nikki, is what killed our son."

"David?" Nicole's voice went soft, despite her surprise. "David died from *lumenaia?"*

Her friend blinked away tears. "Eleanor had a small laboratory in the house, the room that is now a sun room, in the back, overlooking the azaleas. As a small child, David would sit in a big overstuffed chair and read in the sunshine while Eleanor worked. It was a place where he felt very comfortable. He had been taught as a small boy never to touch anything in the lab, of course. He was always so good about that. But he absorbed a great deal. He learned about drugs and how they worked."

The professor's eyes closed briefly. When he opened them, they were filled with pain. "Something changed in David when he was fifteen, when he first started suffering from depression. One night after a particularly bad argument with David over his attitude, Elea-nor filled a vial with *lumenaia.* She was bringing it to her lab here at UCLA for further testing—hoping to dilute its effects enough to make it a safe and valuable mood elevator for patients with depres-sion." The professor reached for the water again, his hand shaking. After wetting his lips he said, "I'm sure she was thinking of David, and of trying to help him. But there never was time. We found David on the floor of the sun room the next morning . . . an empty *lumenaia* vial beside him. He was dead."

"My God." Nicole brushed at tears that sprang to her eyes. She grabbed her friend's hand and held it tight. "Professor, I know you've always felt that David committed suicide. But don't you think it's just as likely he took the *lumenaia* hoping it would cure his depression? You said he had learned what drugs could do. And he must have known the benefits of *lumenaia,* as well as the dangers. Perhaps he miscalculated. The thought of suicide may never once have entered his mind."

The professor's chin shook. "It's a possibility, of course. The question haunted Eleanor until the day she died. I agonize over it even now. Not a day goes by that I don't ask myself, was David trying to treat his symptoms—or simply to overdose and end his life? Someday perhaps I'll see my dear boy again." He gestured to the hospital surroundings. "Possibly sooner than I'd expected. Then I might know the answer to that awful question."

Nicole leaned forward and took his hand from the glass. She stroked it, noting the fragility, the thin blue veins. She searched for the right thing to say. "I'm so sorry. But you have to believe that you did the best you could as a father. You can't blame yourself."

"Perhaps not entirely. Not about David." He drew his hand away. "But I do blame myself, Nikki, for Mary Clare."

"Mary?" For a moment she wondered if her friend, in his weakened state, had become confused. "I don't understand. Why Mary Clare?"

"Nikki, it's true that when Mary wanted to take Eleanor's notes, I refused. It would have been breaking a deathbed promise to my wife. But Mary had all of that afternoon with those notes before I came home. And she admitted to me recently that she had carried Eleanor's formula, all the pertinent information, in her head until she could write it down. She apologized—but from the moment she found those papers in my closet, she realized the effect *lumenaia* might have on the immune system."

His fingers picked absently at the throw cover on his knees. His head was bowed. "If I had destroyed those papers long ago, Mary would never have found them. She never would have discovered Immu-Phor, and she wouldn't have been hounded—perhaps even killed for it."

Nicole drew back, feeling a slight shock. "You think Mary didn't realize . . ."

"I've had a great deal of time here to think."

"But, Professor, you can't assume responsibility for Mary's death. She was doing what she was trained to do. She could no more have forgotten Eleanor's notes . . . You couldn't have stopped her from using them."

"I should have thrown them away years ago, as Eleanor asked me to."

"But—"

"Wait. The formula . . . Nikki, we must protect it from the wrong people now."

"I'm sorry, Professor. I'm afraid it's too late for that," Nicole said gently. "Terry Asher—Mary's former colleague at Sacred Heart—made Immu-Phor public yesterday. Here, in Pasadena."

The professor shook his head. "No, that's not possible."

"But he found a notebook of Mary's—"

"A notebook she had given to you?"

"Yes. How did you know?"

Her friend's smile was faint, but real. "Only half the formula was in that notebook, Nikki."

"Half?" She shook her head, bewildered.

Picking up *The Maya Question*, the professor held it against his chest again.

"When Mary was here last spring, she seemed worried. She told me that if anything should happen to her, Rorrman's greed and *lumenaia* might be the cause. She said she had deleted essential values in the formula from her files at the hospital lab and hidden half the formula in a notebook she was giving to you. The other half is in this book. *The Maya Question* was hidden, she said, where it might never be found—or if found, it would at least eventually land in your hands rather than those of Sacred Heart and Century. Even if they were to discover its existence, she said, you could legally claim it as yours, since it was once a personal gift from you to your sister."

He fingered the book. "When Mary died in that accident last week, I didn't suspect anything at first. I grieved for Mary—and for your loss, of course. But—and I know this was criminally selfish—I was greatly relieved to think that *lumenaia* had been laid to rest once and for all. I believed *The Maya Question* to be packed away in a box with the rest of Mary's personal belongings, where it might not be found for years. And I felt I had kept my promise to Eleanor, never to let her work become public."

The professor's pale face became tight with anxiety. "Then you showed up, asking questions. And imagine how shocked I was when you began to quote from *The Maya Question* in my classroom the other day! You said that you'd been reading it the night before. To me that meant only one thing. The book was now out in the open where anyone might find it. Not hidden, not packed away. Then you had that experience at my house—a prowler. What was he looking for, I wondered?"

Eleanor's notes, she thought now. "But professor, the notes were still there when I went back into the house. I had tucked them into the back of the closet."

His tense, thin shoulders relaxed. "So they weren't found. Thank God. I'll admit, that had me worried." He passed a hand over his eyes. "Nevertheless, I put my suspicions about that incident to-gether with the other strange things you said had been happening to you. And I began to wonder: Had there been foul play in Mary's death? Was she forced to reveal the importance of Eleanor's findings to her work? If so, what else might she have told? About the exis-tence of *The Maya Question?* And if so, and they suspected you had the book—would they now come after you?"

Nicole had a terrible thought. "You said you were shocked when I began to quote from *The Maya Question,* Professor. So shocked you had this heart attack?"

He was silent.

"I'm so sorry—I had no idea. I thought I was being a clever teacher, inspiring your students with a wild, gory tale."

"As indeed you did." The professor gave a weary smile and handed the book to her. "I'm feeling rather tired, however, little Nikki. If you wouldn't mind, take this and turn to the back cover. You will need to remove the endpaper carefully. And do try to keep what you find out of sight."

Nicole turned her back to the patio and opened the book on her knees. Sticking a fingernail under one corner of the back cover, she began to tear the thick paper lining away. Beneath it were three sheets of airmail paper, tissue thin and weighing less than an ounce. The sheets were folded into quarters. Nicole slipped them out, set the book on the table, and spread the papers flat on her lap. They were covered with words . . . symbols . . . numbers . . . all in Mary's tiny, painstaking handwriting.

"The other, essential half of Immu-Phor," the professor said quietly. "Use it to save yourself, Nikki—in whatever way you deem fit."

Chapter 42

All the way to Ken Ito's, Nicole agonized over what to do with the terrible burden of Mary's formula. Give it to Harriet? Hope she would do what was right?

Or keep it to herself for a while, perhaps forever. If Immu-Phor had indeed been responsible for two murders—Mary's and Terry Asher's—how much more harm might it do?

She was nearly late for class. She ran into the locker room, and as she undressed, she wondered where to hide the formula during class. There was no one here who would be interested in Immu-Phor—but even so, she owed it to Mary to be careful.

We've never had any problems here, she remembered Ken saying. She finished dressing, throwing her purse, with *The Maya Question* in it, onto the top shelf of her locker. Then she shoved clothes in front of it and secured the combination lock.

She stood before Ken Ito in her white uniform, relieved not to have to think, for this next hour, about what she should do.

"I'm making moves in my sleep," she told him, taking the ready position.

"That is very good. Self-defense needs to enter your subconscious, where it will then be available to the conscious mind when you need to call it forth. Today we are going to concentrate on getting you over your fear of being hit."

The moves were rougher, and at first she felt intimidated. Her arm was padded, yet when Ken's foot came flying at her, she flinched. Shock waves traveled up her arm—like striking a funny bone.

"You turned away," he reprimanded gently. "It hurt more than it should have because of that."

They did it over and over, until finally she stopped flinching and stood waiting, hopping the way a prize fighter might, moving toward his advancing foot with relish.

Painful memories came again, but this time she had too many things on her mind. They flashed through her consciousness and left, like the frames of an old movie. As they did, she acknowledged them, allowed them to fuel her anger, removing fear. *Fear and anger can-*

not live in the same house, she remembered reading somewhere. She found it to be true.

After the first half hour they took a short break. Then, finding herself restless to get back to the lesson, she urged Ken on.

"You're doing well," he said as they faced each other again on a thick mat. "We'll try something new. I'll try to attack you, and I want you to put your hand out here"—he held his out, to show her—"the way you normally might to fend off an attacker."

She did exactly as she was told, thinking *no, this isn't a new move, we've done this before.* But then he lifted her arm in one swift, hard motion, twisted away, and flipped her to the floor. Shocked, Nicole jumped to her feet, fists flying. Without thinking she gave a fierce *eeeeeuh!* and punched her teacher in the gut.

Ken felt the power of the blow, even though he was padded. He bent slightly, grabbed his stomach, and groaned. Then he straightened, rubbed his offended abdomen, and smiled. "You took me by surprise," he said. "That is excellent indeed."

Satisfied that she hadn't actually hurt him, Nicole realized that for the first time she was feeling her *chi.* She gathered strength and confidence as they continued the workout.

"You promised to tell me a legend," she said a few minutes later, as she slapped her foot against his arm. "About Oho . . . Oho . . ."

"Ohonamochi." He kicked her back. She grunted and reversed—a roundhouse this time.

"Ohonamochi is the earth-god of my people." He moved around her, approving her stance with a nod. "He is so worshiped"—his kick went higher and harder this time—"so worshiped that every year the gods come together to do him honor, and no one is left in heaven for a time." His dark hair fell over his forehead as he pivoted away. "Stand a little closer next time. Don't be afraid to get near me."

She did, and slammed her foot on his padded arm as hard as she could.

"Much better." He grinned.

She paused to wipe her brow with her sleeve, then began again. "So what did Ohonamochi do to earn this great honor?"

"He entered into Yomi—that's Hades, or hell—where several

tasks were given him to perform. He performed them all well, and with the loving support of his wife, was allowed to flee from hell."

"There's always a woman behind the man," she grunted, breathing heavily now.

He kicked her padded chest, nearly knocking her down.

"Damn!" She regained her balance and shook her hair from her face. "And the heros are always given tasks to perform. You are giving me difficult tasks today, Master Ken."

"Perhaps they will free you from your own personal hell."

After class she walked back to the Ocean Palms. Moving briskly across the lobby, she approached the hotel clerk.

"Do you have any glue I can borrow?"

"I don't believe we do up here. . . ." The woman rummaged around in a drawer below the counter. "No, I don't see any. But I'm sure they have some in the business office. I can have it brought up to you."

"Thanks."

She had only enough time to wash her face and change into more comfortable jeans and a navy-blue T-shirt before the bellhop appeared. Nicole thanked him and locked the door. She took *The Maya Question* from her purse and set it on the table by the window, back cover open. Carefully, she glued the endpaper back into place. She carried the book over to the dresser and wrapped it in a sweater, cramming it far back into the drawer.

Then she sat at the table by the window and wrote a brief note. She sealed the note—along with Mary's letter to Harriet for the handwriting analysis—in an envelope addressed to Leo De Santo, in care of the Pasadena police station. She then called down to the concierge and asked for a messenger.

"I need someone you've used before and know well. Someone I can absolutely trust. This is urgent."

"Express Courier is excellent, we use them all the time. I'd say they're completely trustworthy."

"How soon can you get someone here?"

"I'll have to call, but I'd say twenty minutes. A half hour at the very most."

"Fine."

She called the Pasadena police station, asking for Leo. Within seconds they patched her through.

"I was just getting ready to call you, kid. I've got some news, but I'm afraid it's not all good."

"Just hit me with it, Vish. I'm not in a mood to screw around."

A slight pause. "Kenny must be doing you some good. This is the best you've sounded since I met you the other night."

"I'm finding my *chi*, Vish—my *chi.*"

"Uh-huh. I hope I won't regret this."

"Why were you about to call? What have you got?"

"It wasn't easy, that's why it took so long. I had to call in a favor with an old friend in the D.C. department. He contacted a buddy of his in Georgetown, who was willing to talk."

"Did you find out what all the secrecy is about? Was there really a gag order?"

"You bet. And it did come from high up. Look, kid, I'm sorry, but they agree your sister's death was not an accident. In fact, they think she was held captive several days before the killing—at the townhouse of our friend Senator Garrick Hale, in Georgetown."

"Hale, again! My God, Vish."

"They had a lead on Hale last week—or at least on his house. The FBI moved in immediately and placed a gag order on the case so they could investigate without interference from the media. Some top players in politics were worried about a scandal, given that the senator's just announced his intention to run for the presidency next year.

"Anyway, the townhouse was closed up, because the senator's been staying at his place in L.A. But they got a search warrant and went in a couple of days ago. There were fingerprints all over the place that matched your sister's. Like I said, kid, I'm sorry."

Hale—who was suspected of murdering a prostitute in France with sexual fun and games. Sick stuff, Vish had said. Dear God. What would a man like that have wanted with Mary? And what did any of this have to do with Immu-Phor? Or had they been on the wrong track all along?

"Vish, why haven't they arrested Hale?"

"That I can't say. This is all my friend knew, or at least all he'd tell me."

"You know, I just don't get it. I don't see how Garrick Hale fits in."

"Well, we know Hale and Rorrman are buddies. Maybe Hale loaned Rorrman the townhouse. He's been in L.A. a lot. He could've closed his eyes to whatever was going on."

"I guess that's possible."

"I'll keep working it at this end," Leo said. "Meanwhile, you got anything else?"

She hesitated. "Yes. But I can't tell you on the phone."

"Okay. We need to meet?"

"No. You'll understand in an hour or so."

"Hmmmm. Okay. Well, one more thing, in the meantime. My friend got someone at Sacred Heart Hospital to talk. It seems that just before Terry Asher left to fly to California a couple of days ago, he was bragging—quietly, of course, and only to this guy—that he had a major promotion coming up. Something in the Century labs, rather than the hospital."

"I'll be damned. A payoff, Vish, for stealing Mary's formula. It fits."

"Looks that way."

"And I hate to say it, but there also seems to be a link between Dan Rossi and John Rorrman. Or I should say, between him and Rorrman's niece, Kitty."

"Ah, yes, the infamous Miss Kitty."

"You know her?"

"Only by reputation. She's in the papers all the time, on the arm of some rising young god of the silver screen."

"Vish, you know that phone number I gave you to trace?"

"Yeah, I've got that next on my list to do."

"That may not be necessary. I'm all but certain it's Kitty Rorrman's. I just wonder what she's doing with Dan."

"Does he wear pants?"

"Please."

"I'm serious. It's like that with Miss Kitty."

"Even so. In Dan's case, I suspect he's getting more out of it than a roll in the hay."

"You want me to look into it? Talk to some people?"

Her voice was hard. "No, I think I'll do that myself. It's time Dan Rossi and I had another talk."

"I don't know, kid. If he's involved with Miss Kitty, it's only one tiny step from there to Rorrman himself. You'll want to be careful."

"I'll be okay. I've got my *chi*, remember?"

"You also, if I'm hearing you right, have a healthy load of anger in your gut. I hope Kenny told you the story about the sleeping child."

"The one who wasn't allowed to come to the adult party? You know something, Vish? My sleeping child is beginning to resent being left out for so long. She's telling me it's time to wake up and join the grownups downstairs."

When the courier came, she watched him place the envelope to Leo in a locked briefcase.

"I appreciate your taking so much care."

"We sometimes deliver valuables from hotel guests to banks, jewelry stores, stockbrokers," he explained. "The desk clerk told me this was important."

All the comforts . . . you only have to be able to pay for them. But she'd better cut back; her nest egg was diminishing fast.

She stood for a moment at the window, gathering strength for her next move. In her mind's eye she saw Mary, ending her life as a prisoner in a strange house in Georgetown. "Looked like she'd been there several days," Vish had said.

Monsters.

Her anger grew, and she allowed it to, tucking it under her belt, as Ken had advised, rather than punching her fist through the window as she would have preferred to do. *Save it. It will be there when you need it.*

She gathered her purse and car keys and was heading out the door when the phone rang. She went back and picked it up.

"Yes?"

"Nikki, it's Jack."

"Jack, hi. Look, I'm sorry, I'm on my way out—"

"Nikki, I called to tell you something."

There was a strange note in his voice.

"What's wrong?"

"I'm afraid it isn't good news. I was at the Med Center a little while ago on business for Century. In fact, I just missed seeing you there. I looked into your friend's room to see if you were still around, and—I'm sorry, but it seems he's taken a turn for the worse."

She gripped the receiver. "He isn't—"

"No, not dead. But they doubt he'll make it through the night."

"I don't understand. When I left him, the nurse said he'd be all right."

"Well, I don't know if this has anything to do with it, but Dan Rossi was there shortly before he took that turn for the worse. I saw him leaving the room."

Dan, you bastard! What have you done? "I was just on my way to talk to Dan Rossi," she said roughly. "I'm leaving right now."

"Well, call me afterward in Palos Verdes, will you? And Nikki, be careful. If Rossi's in league with Rorrman—"

"Warn *him,*" she said, and slammed down the receiver.

Chapter 43

The traffic north on Ocean, then PCH, was an abomination. She floored the accelerator, zooming around slower cars and through yellow lights. In Malibu it took far too long to make the left turn on PCH to the road that led to Dan's house.

Approaching his drive, she remembered that she still had the garage door remote. She grabbed it from the glove compartment, but parked outside at the curb. Stepping out, she jabbed the remote to see if Dan's car was inside. The door swung open—the garage was empty. No matter. That would give her time for a few preliminaries. She ran down the stairs as the garage door groaned shut.

Letting herself in with the keys she hadn't returned, she crossed the living room, heading straight for Dan's office. At the desk she opened the top drawer and grabbed the carved box that held the closet key. She opened it, took the key, crossed the room, and twisted the key in the padlock.

Opening the door, she crossed to the file cabinet. It was unlocked as before. Last time she had stopped at the M's. This time she knew what to look for. She'd been thinking about it all day.

She went straight to the R's. *Reference, Reviews, Rights*—amazing how organized he was, how predictable—yes, here it was. *Rorrman.*

Inside the file she hit paydirt. Two letter-size envelopes and a seven-page contract. The heading at the top of the first page of the contract was CENTURY PHARMACEUTICALS, INC. She scanned down and saw a figure: $150,000. Further on there were other, higher figures—payouts and escalations. An indented paragraph described what the money was for: a private industrial film detailing the plight of pharmaceutical companies as to research and development, loss of government funding, increased taxes, unfairly imposed ceilings on drug prices . . .

She flipped through to the last page. The contract was signed by John A. Rorrman. The date was the previous May 1.

So Dan had been planning the move out here for a full two months before he'd told her about it in July. She replaced the contract, then opened one of the envelopes, drawing out a single piece of paper. A check from Kitty Rorrman for $100,000. It bore yesterday's date; yesterday, when Dan had arrived at the party in Palos Verdes with Kitty on his arm. The memo in the lower left-hand corner read, "For The Final Battleground." Dan's latest film.

So Jack and Harriet were right. He had been working Kitty for her cash, and he was in bed with Rorrman as well. He'd sold out—gone back to Big Business. The question was, what did he give in return?

Dan didn't give away pieces of himself—not to anyone. And in all the time she'd known him, he had never bartered with sex. But he did return favors. He was good about that.

She opened the second envelope, knowing instinctively what she would find. Even so, she felt a chill as she drew the blue notebook out and held it in her hand. She thumbed through it. One word leapt from the pages. *Lumenaia.* She was holding the other half of Immu-Phor.

Nicole's hand shook.

How did Dan get his hands on it? She had assumed that Terry had gotten it back from Sister Paula yesterday and was killed for it. But that would mean—

No. Dan *couldn't* have killed Terry. He simply couldn't.

Still holding the check and the notebook, she folded her arms on the open file drawer and rested her head. *I'm so damned tired.*

"Nikki, what the hell are you doing?"

She jumped. Then she rose and turned, meeting Dan's eyes. "Housecleaning." She held up the check and notebook.

His voice was cold. "How did you get in here?"

"In the closet? I remembered where you always kept the key. For once my memories worked for me rather than against me."

"What are you doing with those?" He stepped toward her and reached for the notebook and check. She pulled her hand away, holding it behind her.

His face flushed with anger. "Nikki, you've got to give that note-book to me."

"Oh, really. Why?"

"Because you aren't safe with it! Look at what's happened so far. Mary, Terry, Professor Dirstoff—"

"Tell me, Dan. What exactly do you know about the professor?"

He fell silent.

"It seems he's taken a turn for the worse, and it seems you were there today, just before that happened." She slammed the file drawer shut with her foot.

"Nikki, I didn't do anything to him."

"Don't lie! I *know*."

A tic developed beneath one eye, and she wondered what she had seen as charming in that face.

"What is it you think you know?" he said harshly.

"You've been needing money—bad. You were out of town trying to hustle it up when I first got here. You've even been working for Rorrman. You've got a contract to do a film touting Century Pharmaceuticals as the savior of all mankind. You sold out."

The tic worsened. A finger went up to rub it.

"But that wasn't enough, was it, Dan? You needed funds to finish *The Final Battlefield,* and you worked Kitty Rorrman for that. She's already paid you in advance, hasn't she? In return her uncle gets Mary's formula."

She held up the blue notebook. "Only thing is, Dan, you've got only half the formula here. You knew that, and you knew Mary had told the professor where she'd hidden the rest. You went there today and tried to force him to tell you where it was."

"You've got it all wrong, Nikki. I was working *with* Mary, not against her."

She pushed past him, toward the door. "Well, isn't it a good thing she's not around to dispute that now."

He grabbed her arm, his fingers biting into her skin. "Listen to me, dammit! You've got it wrong!"

She wrenched away. "Get away from me! I am *not* wrong. Mary trusted you, at least for a while. She must have told you she'd split the formula up and that the professor knew where the other half was. And now he's had a setback. You may have killed him, Dan, and all because of your goddamned greed."

"That's not—"

He tried to grab her again, and she broke away, hitting up against the file cabinet. "Damn you! Jack Blake saw you at the hospital. He saw you coming out of the professor's room. You got to him. He may be dying, and it's all your fault."

"I'm telling you, he was all right. It's true I was there, but he was all right when I left him."

"I don't believe you. I think you've been lying all along."

"Nikki, who fed you this crazy story?"

"That doesn't matter."

"Jack Blake? Tell me you don't trust him. You can't, Nikki. He works for Century. He probably works directly under Rorrman."

"He works for *Harriet.* Harriet trusts him. She doesn't trust you at all."

"Hell, Nikki, she could be in on it too. Her grandfather founded Century. She's probably got her own agenda, hoping to take back control if she can release Immu-Phor under her own name. They've been lulling you into a false sense of security, Nikki."

"They've been protecting me, Dan. It just took me a while to realize they were protecting me from you."

His tone was desperate. "Look, I've been worried about money, that's true. Anxious, even. But not enough to hurt the professor. And that check from Kitty—why would I have filed it away, if I meant to cash it? For that matter, if I knew I was getting money from her, why would I have gone to Georgetown looking for it?"

Everything in Nicole went still. "Georgetown? You were in Georgetown? That's where you were when Mary died?" She paled and shrank against the shelving that held the film canisters. Not Mary . . . he couldn't have done that too.

Her voice shook. "What other kind of work have you been doing for Rorrman? What's the going price for murder these days?"

"That's it, dammit! I'm not listening to any more of this."

"Tell me you didn't kill my little sister, Dan." A sob caught in her throat.

His hand came up and covered her mouth. "Stop it! *Stop* it, Nikki!"

He pressed his weight against her, muffling her breath. She fought and he pressed harder.

Someone else had done that, pushing her down, muffling her cries. . . .

Nicole bit his hand. At the same time her heel came down on his instep. He yelled and let her go. Twisting, she shoved him away. "I'm getting out of here."

He flung an arm in front of the door, barring her path.

"Get out of my way, Dan!"

She gave him another shove, using all the power she could summon. He stumbled sideways, knocking down the free-standing shelves. Heavy film canisters rained on his shoulders and head. He was half buried beneath their weight. Nicole ran out, slammed the closet door, and slid the padlock through its hasp. She snapped it shut.

She could hear him banging on the door. "Nikki, dammit, let me out! Open this door!"

She ran to the phone on the desk, yanked out her address book, fingers shaking, and punched in the number for the Pasadena police. The dispatcher answered after three rings.

"Leo De Santo. Please hurry! It's urgent!"

"One moment."

The pounding continued as she was put on hold.

Hurry, hurry. I have to tell Leo. Whatever happens to me, somebody has to know.

Static. The sound of the patch going through.

"Hello?"

"Vish?"

"No."

Oh, my God. A strange voice. She gripped the receiver. "Who is this?"

"This is Officer Luis De Santo. Who's this?"

"There are two De Santos," the dispatcher had said days ago. *"Leo and Luis."*

"I need Leo. Can you get him for me, please? Hurry!"

"Hold on."

More static. The operator again. "Sorry. I thought you said Luis. Leo's in the middle of a call right now. Can he get back to you?"

The banging on the closet door was louder now. She could barely hear the woman's voice.

"Never mind!" She hit the flash button for a dial tone with one hand, and with the other, rummaged in her purse for the number of the Century house in Palos Verdes. *God, let him be there.*

Jack answered the phone himself. "Nikki, where are you? I've been worried."

"I'm at Dan's. Jack, I've got the notebook, the blue notebook, with Mary's notes in it. Dan hid it away in his closet. Jack, he must have killed Terry for it, and Mary."

"Nikki, it's okay. Calm down. Are you alone?"

"No, Dan's here. I—I locked him in the closet."

"All right, listen, I want you to get out of there. *Right now.* Come down here, but not to the house, there are too many people around. Harriet and I will meet you on the *Haokah.* We'll fix the gate so it's left open for you. And, Nikki, bring the notebook with you."

"I've been trying to call Leo. I need to tell him what I've found."

"Leo De Santo? From the Pasadena police? He called here. He said he'd be out of touch for a while, but that he had some information that would blow all this sky high. I told him we'd meet him on the *Haokah,* where we'll have some privacy. You, Harriet, and me."

A panel on the closet door splintered. Dan had hit it with something hard, something that sounded like metal.

The file cabinet.

She had left the padlock key in there, on that cabinet. If he made a hole big enough, he could reach through to the lock—

"I've got to get out of here, Jack. I'm on my way." She dropped the receiver, leaving it hanging.

Running from the house, she jammed the blue notebook into the back pocket of her jeans. As she reached the car, she heard running footsteps on the stairs.

Chapter 44

He never really wanted to hurt Nikki. He had tried to get her to stop—to forget the whole thing. Accept what had happened and move on. Damn her soul! Why had this one particular woman had such an effect on him? He never had this problem before.

And that sister, too. It wasn't all that easy with Mary Clare, he had to admit. This damned new weakness of his had started with her.

Mary Clare. So beautiful, so intelligent . . . yet such an innocent. She had fought back with everything she had. When the drug began to take hold, she fought to keep her secrets. Instead of drifting away, going with it, she kept saying things—things from the Bible, or some prayerbook, over and over—left-brain stuff, difficult passages, not prayers. She knew enough to focus with the left brain to try to disable the drug's effect on her bloodstream.

But he had used the newer one, the one Century scientists were still testing. More powerful than any other that had ever hit the market, there was no way to fight it for long. She had gone under at last, and that was when he had learned that she had split the formula up. Stupid Asher. When he found that blue notebook in the lab, he thought he had it all. He even tried to hold Rorrman up for a fortune. Never even took the time to test it out first, to find out that it wasn't all there.

That's what happens when you get too eager, too greedy . . . too sloppy.

He tried never to be sloppy. That was something his father had beat into him. "If you're going to do something, do it right," his father would say. "None of this half-assed shit."

The only time recently he had done anything sloppy was that last day with Mary Clare.

"No more than half a cc every twenty-four hours," Rorrman had warned. "More than that could kill her. We don't want her dead before she spits out the formula."

He was so careful at the senator's house in Georgetown. For four days he kept her half-under, trying to learn her secrets. In her lucid moments she fought him like a tiger. He finally had to tie her down. But then she had talked him into letting her go to the bathroom, and

Christ, she'd been holding it for a whole day and night. "I can't go with my hands tied behind me." *She stood there naked and shame-faced, shivering, the tiny veins in her legs blue, her whole body puckered with goosebumps from the cold.* "I just can't."

He didn't hate the kid. Didn't really want to hurt her. Kind of respected her, in fact.

All he wanted was that goddamned formula.

He should have been more careful. That last night—after the bath-room, when she broke free and ran away—he got scared. That could have been the end of everything. But he kept hearing his father say, "You goddamned sloppy kid. You blew it again." *When he found her on the street it was like Christmas morning, everything he'd asked for sitting right there under the tree. He thought for sure he had her then. The drug was still in her bloodstream, she was confused, dis-oriented. Vulnerable.* "Come home with me, Mary Clare."

But she had fought her way through the mental fog. "That's not my home." *She had run.*

Into that bar. Gepetto's. But she still wasn't sure what she was doing, who he was—enemy or friend. The drugs told her friend. Gut instinct said run.

She went with her gut. Made a beeline to that convent. And shit, if there hadn't been some big deal going on at the church, some all-night vigil, there would've been all those nuns there. She'd have told them everything.

As it was, he was in the convent waiting for her. Alone.

"Jack?" Nicole stood on the dock below the *Haokah*. The yacht seemed completely dark. "Harriet?"

The ramp was down, though. They had put it down for her. They must be aboard. She ran up it, landing with both feet on the deck. "Jack! Harriet! Where are you?"

No answer.

She began to feel uneasy. The boat rocked gently beneath her feet as she made her way along the side, toward the cabin door. She steadied herself with one hand on the cold rail. Beneath her Nikes the deck was damp and slick.

God, she hated this. This night, this dark water. It didn't help much that there were boats on all sides. There was no sign of life on any of them. No one in the marina at all, so far as she could see. Where was the harbor patrol?

And where was Jack?

She opened the cabin door. Service lights from the dock offered dim illumination. She remembered a light switch just inside the door and felt for it. *There.* She flicked it. Nothing.

Damn. Wasn't there a generator, or an electrical hookup to the dock?

She stepped into the cabin. "Jack, Harriet, are you here?"

Something snaked around her ankles. It tightened, cutting the skin. She stumbled, falling to her knees. She screamed.

"Easy does it, Nikki. Keep it cool."

Jack was beside her, shoving her flat on her face, yanking her arms behind her back. Within seconds her hands were bound. Then her feet. He flipped her over. She saw a piece of wide gray tape come down. She tried to scream once more. Too late.

"Sorry, Nikki. Can't have you making any more noise while we're still in harbor."

Jack's hands slid over her clothes, searching. They paused at her back jeans pocket. "Ah, ha. What have we here? The elusive blue notebook. It's had quite a journey, I'd imagine, from Asher to you."

He yanked it out. Then he stood, flicking his brown hair back from his forehead with his fingers. The gray eyes were cold.

"Now, just relax. We're taking a little ride."

He left her there. She heard him leap onto the dock, heard ropes being dropped. Then another leap as he landed on the deck again. The boat gave beneath his weight, swaying slightly. His footsteps pounded up the stairs next to the cabin. She heard him above her. Then the rumble of the engine. The *Haokah* began to move.

Oh, dear God. Somebody help me. Somebody help me, please.

Chapter 45

No one was going to help her. Nicole knew that now. They were somewhere out at sea, or at least far out from the harbor. The sky outside the cabin windows was dark. The moon had vanished behind clouds.

There was no sign of Harriet. She and Jack were on the *Haokah* alone.

She had trusted the wrong man. Taken the wrong way onto the ice —once again.

Idiot. Dammit, Nicole, you're an idiot.

Well, she'd have to get herself out of this one. *Think.*

Think what?

About Mary.

Oh, poor Mary. This man killed my sister.

She felt anger then, more than fear.

I will not let him kill me. I'll get him, Mary, for both of us.

The boat had stopped, the engines were silent. She heard a grinding sound, like a motor-driven winch. *The anchor. He's weighing anchor. What next?*

She heard him come down the stairs. The cabin door opened. He touched the switch, and this time light flooded the cabin from a lamp on the wall. Nicole blinked.

"All right, Nikki. It's time."

He yanked her up, propped her into a corner of the sofa, and ripped the tape from her mouth. She cried out as her skin burned. Her back arched in a spasm of pain. Her arms and legs, still bound, began to cramp.

But she had a chance now. She could talk to him, reason with him, argue her way out.

She looked up, blinking back tears. "Untie me, Jack. This really hurts."

"Not until you tell me where the other half of the formula is." His thumbs were hooked arrogantly into the waistband of his jeans. Beneath the short-sleeved T-shirt, his muscles tensed, ready for any move she might make.

"I don't know what you're talking about, Jack. The formula is in the blue notebook—you already know that. It's all there."

"Not quite. That's why we need to talk."

"Untie me first. Then I'll tell you whatever I know."

"I don't think you understand, Nikki. You aren't in a position to barter. You are going to die. That's a given."

A wave of horror engulfed her. She struggled to come out of it, lifting her chin. "There's no point in my telling you a goddamned thing, then. Why should I? That's crazy."

"Not at all. You wanted to help your sister. Isn't that what you said? Well, the only way you can help her now is by giving the world Immu-Phor. That way her work won't have been in vain."

Nicole's eyes flashed. "Mary died protecting that formula from you. I'd rather her death not be in vain."

"Rorrman's already got the Century labs working on the half from the notebook. Fortunately, Asher thought to copy it before Paula took it away."

"Fine. They don't need my help, then. They'll come up with the rest."

"But think how many lives you could save by giving them the missing half now. The world needs Immu-Phor, Nikki."

"I don't give a fuck what the world needs! I won't die trussed up like an animal."

His eyes widened in mock surprise. "I do believe that's the first time I've ever heard you swear, Nicole. I didn't know you had it in you."

Her voice rose. "Fuck you, Jack Blake. And Rorrman, and Century, and fucking Sister Paula—"

"Sister Paula?" He laughed. "Did you really think she was in on this?"

"Wasn't she?"

Keep him talking. Buy time. Maybe someone heard me scream in the harbor. Maybe help will arrive.

"Not by a long shot. Sister Paula knew about Immu-Phor, of course. Your sister had told her all about it. And Rorrman had promised Sacred Heart Hospital a considerable amount of funding if Sister Paula could convince Mary to turn over the formula. Paula tried. She argued that Century's scientists would work on it further, that they had better equipment and could perfect it more quickly. Mary refused. She felt—and rightly—that Century wouldn't improve on the formula, but peddle it as is.

"Sister Paula didn't agree. Still, it was a simple difference of opinion between the two of them. Then, after Arnault died in the lab fire, Paula had her suspicions. She wondered if the explosion was meant for Mary." He laughed. "She was right. Rorrman hired a couple of amateurs to do the job. Of course, if I'd known, I would have explained to him that terrorist tactics always backfire.

"Anyway, Paula pulled up the drawbridge, manned the moats, and wouldn't talk to Rorrman about the formula anymore." He shook his head in what seemed like genuine admiration. "That is one mean, but smart, nun. She's been getting in my way, trying to get evidence against me. And I've got to tell you, she's next on my list."

Nicole tried to work some space between her wrists and the rope. No go. There wasn't a breath of slack. "What happened to Terry Asher?"

"Asher was a stupid man. He found the blue notebook in the lab the night before he spoke out here. It was in an envelope addressed to my dear Aunt Harriet, and it had fallen behind a desk."

"So I was right. That's what Mary was sending her for safe keeping."

"Except that she apparently left it in the lab the night I grabbed her. Either she forgot it or thought it'd be safer there."

Had it really fallen behind that overflowing desk Mary shared with Terry? Or did she hide it there, on some gut-level instinct before Jack had gotten to her?

"So Terry found the notebook and decided to profit from it."

"He realized its importance immediately. He called Rorrman and bargained for a major position with Century. A lab of his own, a staff, the latest in equipment. Said he was tired of being at the bottom rung of the research field, tired of scraping for a living."

"But he was already a Century employee, by virtue of working at Sacred Heart. Rorrman could simply take him to court for the notebook, couldn't he?"

"Asher had worked for Sacred Heart since he was a young lab

assistant just out of college. In his early contract with Sacred Heart, there was no clause saying his work belonged to Century. Somehow Century overlooked updating that contract the way they had other employees of Sacred Heart. So, unlike your sister, Asher didn't legally have to turn the results of his work over to them."

"So Terry got what he wanted from Rorrman, came out here, and made his announcement. But then Sister Paula . . ."

"Took the notebook from him. I didn't know that, of course—you didn't tell me that, Nikki. So I went after Asher for it. You know what he told me? He realized even before he gave his big speech to all those reporters that part of the formula was missing. He was winging it, confident that with what he had in the notebook, he'd come up with something workable on his own."

Jack curled his lip in disgust. "He was beside himself when I showed up. A real twit, that guy. No balls at all. He pleaded that he didn't have the notebook—but I found the copy of the formula on him. He cried just before I stuck the needle in. *'Please don't do that,'* he said. *'Please don't.'* I hate weaklings. You know what my dad used to say?"

Her tone was laced with sarcasm. "No, Jack. What did your dad used to say?"

"No guts, no glory, Jack."

She laughed scornfully. "Real original."

The skin around his eyes went taut. "It's gotten me through a lot of things."

"What things? Being a killer? What kind of life is that?"

"Don't moralize with me. You sound like—"

"My sister? Did she ask you that too? She always had an eye for a fool."

His face flamed. "You're pushing it, Nikki. Be careful."

"Well, isn't that what you'd call it? You still have only half the formula."

"On the contrary. You're going to give me the other half, Nikki. Tonight. Before you die."

She laughed again, more bravado than real courage. "It's pretty obvious I don't have it on me. Or do you plan to make a strip search?"

"A delightful idea, although not at all necessary. You'll tell me what I need to know."

"Not until you untie me, Jack. That's final."

His eyes flickered again with surprise. "You are becoming a very interesting challenge, love."

"Fuck your challenge. Untie me, or I don't tell you a goddamned thing."

Outrage had brought back her *chi.* She could feel it, a physical sensation churning in her gut, giving her strength.

Jack stared at her a moment. Then he stood, crossing to the built-in bar. Feeling along the paneling beside it, he pressed until a hidden panel the size of a wall safe swung open. Reaching in, he pulled out a small black case. He snapped it open, taking out a small bottle and something long and thin.

Nicole licked her lips. They were cracked and dry. *A syringe.*

"This should quiet you down nicely," Jack said. He pierced the bottle's rubber stopper and drew the clear liquid into the syringe. "Nicely indeed." He smiled, walking toward Nicole. The needle glinted in the cabin light as he depressed the plunger slightly, letting out air. Nicole's gaze fixed on the single bead of liquid that balanced at the needle's sharp end, broken only when Jack shoved the point against her temple.

Chapter 46

She had thought he was going to kill her right then. Instead, he had used the syringe to intimidate, to keep her still as he untied her. It was part of his game, she knew now. Cat and mouse: a promise one minute; jaws tightening around a fragile neck the next.

"Better now?" he asked.

"Much."

The clock on the bulkhead ticked softly. Nearly midnight. Nicole sat unbound on the sofa with Jack across from her, his arms stretched out on the soft arms of an easy chair, fingers loose on the syringe.

"As I was saying, I never meant for this to be so difficult for you. I like you, Nikki, I really do. It will pain me greatly when the time comes for your burial at sea."

"Thanks. I'd hate to be someone you loathe."

"Meanwhile, we have a mystery to untangle."

"Maybe you do. Not me."

He smiled. "But, Nikki, you're the one with the clue."

"I can't think what you mean."

With his free hand he reached over to a drawer in an end table by his chair. He pulled out a book. *The Maya Question.*

"It's in here, isn't it? The missing half of Mary's formula."

She hid her surprise and smiled. "If it is, then you don't need me anymore. Why don't we just go back to shore and I'll go on home. . . ." She half rose.

Faster than she could blink he was there beside her, the point of the syringe pricking her cheek. His other hand gripped her upper arm.

"I could make this so much harder for you, Nikki."

Her knees gave, but his iron grip kept her from falling. The needle jabbed more deeply into her skin. She gave a soft cry.

"This is the same drug I used on Mary Clare. It's not—shall we say —fully tested? An eighth of a cc too much, and your sweet little sister went into convulsions. Would you like to hear about that? About the way she bit her tongue in two, how she screamed and screamed. . . ."

Her vision went momentarily dark. Tears filled her eyes.

"So much blood. She was dead before her car went into the river, of course. Not long before—an hour at the most. I had to work fast. It had to look like an accident, I couldn't afford an autopsy."

She tried to wrench away, but he shoved her backward onto the sofa. Bending over, his face was hard. His finger caressed the plunger of the syringe.

Nicole's eyes blazed. "Go ahead, dammit! I don't care what you do anymore. Kill me the way you killed Mary. Just get it over with."

He knelt with one knee on her lap, pressing down against her pubis. "Not yet, Nikki." He shoved her chin up and held his lips to her left eye, the needle to the right. Drawing the sharp metal down, he stroked her cheek, her neck, her breast. Pausing there, he drew slow, deliberate circles around her nipple. "I need a win, Nikki. And you are going to give it to me."

She began to shake. "Stop . . . stop it, Jack."

He pulled back enough to smile into her eyes. "You like the excitement, don't you? You don't want to admit that. You're horrified even to think it. But you like what I'm doing to you now. You feel like that little girl, the one who was touched in all the wrong places. . . ." He held the needle against her breast while his free hand moved down between her legs and caressed. "You hate it . . . I know you do . . . but it's turning you on."

With a scream of rage she struck the flat of her palm beneath his chin. He fell back, but was on his feet, upright, instantly. The syringe never left his hand. He laughed, shoving her back against the sofa with a foot.

Nicole's face twisted. "Why didn't I see it? Why didn't I see how sick you are?"

Jack's voice was gentle, almost wooing. "Mary didn't like being touched, either. I guess Daddy diddled her too. And that's why our little Mary, Mary, Quite Contrary lived like a nun."

She stared, unable to hide her confusion. "How do you know our father's name for Mary? What makes you think he—how do you know *any* of these things?"

He eased back into the chair across from her again, one leg nonchalantly crossed over the other knee. The syringe rested in one hand on the arm of the chair, his thumb on the plunger.

"It was easy, Nikki. Your sister kept a journal. A personal journal." He smiled at her dazed expression. "You didn't know that, did you?"

She clenched her fists, working them open, then shut. Staring at them, wondering what had happened to her newfound *chi.*

"Where is Mary's journal? What did you do with it after you read it with your filthy mind and found out all our family secrets?"

"Sorry, I destroyed it when I'd finished with it. Wouldn't do to have anyone find it in my possession. Too bad for you, though. I bet you'd like to know what your little sister had to say about you."

She didn't answer, wouldn't give him the satisfaction of hearing her pain.

"Oh, what the hell." He shrugged. "Your sister felt she had let you down, Nikki, that she'd withdrawn too much, not given you enough of her time."

Nicole's eyes stung. "She wrote that?"

"And that she was beginning to realize how important you were to her. Rorrman was pressuring her about the formula, and she was afraid something might happen to her. She hoped that if anything did, you'd get this journal and know how she felt."

"But you destroyed it. And I'll never see it now." *The one thing Mary left me, the most important thing.*

"Other than the information in the journal, I managed to get only a few words out of Mary. Words about a blue notebook. She thought she was talking to you, at that point. 'Give it to Dan,' she kept saying. 'Help me, Nikki. Help me.' "

Nicole steeled herself. She would not cry. "The note, the one on the cocktail napkin, in the cottage the other night. You put it there?"

"Of course."

"It said to stay away from Dan."

He smiled. "Your clever little sister wrote that while she was on the run from me. I suppose she knew I'd be after him next and didn't want you involved. I found the note on her . . . later."

The thought of Jack's hands on Mary was too much. Tears spilled, hot on her face.

"That was when I knew I could let her go," he said, "to her reward, so to speak. I wasn't getting anything more out of her, and I thought then that you had this blue notebook—and possibly even the other half. Mary never did tell me where that was."

"You searched my apartment for the notebook?"

"Of course. While you were at the funeral. I couldn't find it, and that had me worried for a while. I finally decided you must have hidden it somewhere. I planted mikes, hoping you'd talk to Rossi about it on the phone. You never did. Meanwhile, I was under pressure from Rorrman. I couldn't just follow you around until you decided to dig the notebook up from wherever it was and mail it off to Rossi."

"You sent me the ticket?"

He smiled. "Good for you, Nikki. Mary's ticket to Los Angeles was in her purse the night I grabbed her. I gave it to a woman I knew and asked her to call the travel agent, to say she was Mary Clare Ryan. She thought we were playing a joke on a friend.

"With a free ticket to L.A., I figured you'd get the notebook from wherever you'd hidden it and take it to Rossi in person. I could grab it either in Georgetown before you left, or out here."

"But what if I'd sent back the ticket? I almost did, you know."

"Not a chance. I knew you were burning out. And I guessed that with your sister dead, you'd want to get away."

"You knew I was burning out? How?" She had barely realized it herself.

"It was a few months ago that Rorrman first assigned me to getting that formula from Mary. The first thing I did was study up on her —and her family. I knew where you worked and lived, I knew your habits, and I even went through the records at your local library. A few months ago you started taking out fiction instead of your usual research tomes—thrillers by Ludlum, Le Carre, MacInnes, Clancy, Clark. Most were chockful of international intrigue and even a bit of romance—escapism, one might say. Then I followed you one Saturday to the travel agency you used. You were asking questions about Mexico, about accommodations there in the winter." He smiled, pleased with his cleverness. "Planning some time off during the school year, love?"

She didn't respond.

"At first I thought a sabbatical, but you hadn't been at Georgetown long enough for that. And you never did follow through on the trip, so I thought perhaps the yen to get away had passed. Then, last month, when you blew up at that kid in class—"

Her eyes widened. "You knew about that?"

He gave an elaborate shrug. "I know the size of your shoes, Nikki. I know every place you've ever lived, every house, every apartment. I know your grades from grammar school and high school. I know you were tested in eighth grade and found to have a genius IQ, which you've mostly underused—and I know you were badly abused by a bastard of a father who—"

"That's enough!" She leaned forward, her hands knotting into fists. "Who the hell are you, Jack Blake?"

He smiled. "I'm a man with two hats, Nikki. Red for one side of the road, black for the other."

Her mouth fell open.

He laughed. "I thought you might appreciate that. One of your favorite myths, isn't it? And now, my dear sweet Nikki, I think we've wasted quite enough time."

He held up *The Maya Question.* "You gave me the clue when you said the professor was asking for this book in particular. You didn't hide it very well in your room, I'm afraid. Still, I've had only a short time to study it. There are passages highlighted. Must be a code, something only you and your sister would know. Did you play spy games in childhood, Nikki? Most of us did. I remember we would assign certain meanings to certain words in books, or pick the third letter, or every other vowel. . . ."

Nicole let her fists relax. "The formula's not in the book, Jack."

"Of course it is, Nikki. I managed to get that much out of the professor, although he really wasn't cooperative at all."

Hatred seared her gut. "So it was you. You went to the hospital, twisted the professor's arm for information, and then when he had a setback, you told me Dan was responsible."

"Just to deepen your suspicions about Rossi a bit—and make you trust me more."

"Well, you've blown that. You really think that after all this, I'd tell you where the missing half of the formula is?"

"I already know where it is. It's in this book. All I need is for you to reveal it to me."

"I'm telling you, Jack, it's not. It was on tissue paper, hidden underneath the lining inside the back cover. Look for yourself. See where I tore the lining off, then glued it back on?"

A look of uncertainty entered the gray eyes. He placed the book on his knee and opened it with one hand. Turning to the back, he studied the endpaper, running a finger over it. Impatient suddenly, he stuck a nail under the lining and ripped it off. His face darkened with anger.

Nicole smiled again. "Nothing. Just as I told you. See?"

"Where is it, Nikki? What have you done with it?"

Deliberately, she taunted him. "Don't like being outsmarted by a woman, huh? Doesn't feel good, does it?"

He flung the book to the floor and jumped to his feet, leaving the syringe on the arm of the chair. Standing over her, he grabbed her throat. His voice was tight with rage. "I need that formula, Nikki. I need it tonight."

"People in hell need ice water." Her laugh was shallow, constrained by the hands tightening on her throat. "That wasn't very original either, was it? Like 'no guts, no glory.' The things our fathers teach us . . ."

He slapped her. Her head snapped to the side. She twisted it back and spit in his face. In the second of surprise that gained her, she formed a chicken beak with her fingers and slammed them into his left eye.

Jack screamed. He fell back and grabbed for the eye with both hands. Swaying, he drew them away. Nikki saw blood welling in the socket. Her stomach heaved. But she threw herself forward and yelled, as Ken had taught her to do. A deep, guttural scream welled up from her diaphragm, flooded her chest with strength, and bellowed from her mouth as her feet hit the floor. "Eeeeeeeeuh!" For the second time that night her palm hit the underside of his chin. As he rocked backward, her foot slammed into his groin. He staggered back, then forward, clutching himself. She struck with the heel of her hand against his nose. Bone crunched.

Jack fell, gripping his face and moaning, twisting into a fetal position on the floor.

She ran around him to the chair, grabbing the syringe. She held it out with one hand, keeping the other ready, and pointing it at him from six feet away. "Get up, Jack! Get the fuck up!"

He was still writhing in pain. She stepped closer and kicked him in the thigh, just hard enough to get his attention. "Get up now or we'll end this right here." She slammed the needle down against his neck, letting it prick the skin.

"Don't! For God's sake, don't, Nikki! Give me room—I'll get up!"

She eased up on the pressure but kept the needle at his neck. Jack struggled painfully to his knees. Moving back a few feet, Nicole maintained a cautious stance.

Jack's eye still dripped blood, but she could see that she hadn't put it out. She had held back at the last second, too squeamish to give it all she had. Even so, she had done serious damage. He knelt and swayed, trying to focus on her.

"All right, now, you're going to play Captain Hook again," Nicole said. "Won't that be fun? You even have the eye for it now. Maybe when we're back in harbor, we'll get you a patch—after we check in with the local police."

He stood slightly bent, one hand on the eye, the other covering his groin. His face was a ghastly white. "You bitch. You goddamned fucking bitch."

"Enough with the compliments. Outside." She gestured with the syringe. When he didn't move fast enough, she yelled, "Now! Get your ass out there!"

She didn't know the person she had become. She recognized the rage, however. It came from a small child who still lived within her and who was ready to kill now, if that was what it took to keep the grownup woman safe and alive. *Let them try to hurt me, ever again. Let them just try.* As Jack stumbled toward the door she kicked one foot at the small of his back. "Move!"

They were outside. "Up the steps, Jack. Get up there."

She followed a safe distance behind, watchful for any move on his part that might send her flying backward down the steps. "Lights," she snapped as they stepped into the wheelhouse. He reached for a switch in the wooden "dash" below the window. Dim green lights came on, casting sickly shadows on his face. To either side of the wheel were instruments. She spotted a small black box with switches and a microphone. A radio.

"Turn the radio on."

"It won't do any good—"

"Turn it on!"

He flicked a switch. Nothing happened. No lights, no static. "I disabled it before you got here." His voice was still thick with pain.

She swore. "Stand back." She motioned him toward the bulkhead, to where he wouldn't be able to reach her. Keeping the syringe pointed at his face, she tried every switch on the radio. Still nothing.

She glanced through the damp, water-spotted window. Black all around; no lights visible in any direction.

No, wait, a red light flashing way off there, to the right. And a blue one. Could be King Harbor Marina.

There was a compass on the instrument panel. It was pointing north. Right, then, had to be east. Maybe not King Harbor, but east would be shore.

"All right, get over here."

She backed off and motioned him to the wheel, standing only close enough to watch his hands. "I'll give you one chance to get us safely back into harbor. But I'd just as soon kill you as look at you now. If you do anything stupid, I will."

He clenched the wheel with both hands, leaning on it. In the green light his face was haggard, the blood slowly oozing from his left eye. A thick black goo rimmed the socket. He flicked the switch that started the engine. Then, another. The anchor groaned as its electrical winch raised it from the deep. He turned the wheel, pushed a lever. The *Haokah* began to move. Nicole steadied herself and glanced at the compass. They were heading east.

So far, so good.

"I'm really surprised, Nikki." Jack's voice was strained—weak—but tinged with praise. "You are one tough lady. I never dreamed—"

"Stuff it," she snapped. "You can't work me anymore."

Two classes, she thought. *Two lousy lessons. Kenny would be proud.*

"Even so . . ." Jack shook his head.

She took a step closer and shoved the syringe at his ear. "Shut the fuck up. No, wait, I take that back. Talk to me, Jack. Tell me about Mary. Tell me how you got your filthy hands on my little sister. Entrance me with that as we cruise on back to shore."

He shook his head again.

"Nikki, trust me . . . you don't really want to know."

"Talk!" she yelled. Her finger, wet and shaky, slid over the plunger. One fraction of an inch, the smallest motion of her thumb, he could be dead. She wanted to do it. She wanted it so bad.

He must have sensed it. He wet his lips and spoke quickly. "I was back in Georgetown a couple of weeks ago on another job for Rorrman. His friend Senator Hale had decided to back the bill that puts a ceiling on drug prices. I guess Hale figured it would earn him support in his upcoming presidential campaign. But Rorrman was angry. He sent me to talk to the good senator, remind him of past favors, of old sins covered up."

Nicole lowered the syringe slightly, easing back against the bulkhead. "You did this sort of thing a lot for Rorrman?"

"Sure. It's what he hired me for."

"You never really worked in mergers and acquisitions."

"I did in the beginning—and I still play the part, for all anybody knows. But for the past few years, no."

"And these old sins of Hale's. Did he happen to commit them in Paris?"

Jack gave her a look of surprise.

"I know about Hale and the prostitute who supposedly drowned," she said. "So do a few other people. They know Rorrman helped him cover it up by hiring someone to dump her in the Seine. Looks like that someone was you. But it's all coming out, Jack. It's only a matter of time before they get to you. Especially if I turn up dead now, too. Everybody knows I've been seeing you. Cops, Dan Rossi, and what about Harriet?"

He laughed softly. "Harriet thinks I've had to fly back east unexpectedly on business. She's used to that. 'Tell Nikki I'm sorry not to say goodbye,' I said. 'Tell her I'll be back in a couple of days.'" He smiled, his face relaxing as he boasted of his conquests. "Aunt Harriet was disappointed we wouldn't be seeing each other tonight. She was matchmaking a bit, I think."

"Harriet doesn't know about you? She doesn't know you're a monster?"

"I can't say I like your assessment of my character, Nikki. But no, I'm the apple of dear Aunt Harriet's eye. She thinks I'm a marvelous guy."

"Poor Harriet."

"Women like me," he said simply. "It's a skill, you might say, that I've always had."

"Past tense, Jack. When all this comes out in the papers, you'll look like the slug you are. It'll be my gift to the female world." She glanced at the compass. Still due east. "Meanwhile, tell me more about Mary."

"Well, as I said, I had just met with the senator in Georgetown. After we talked, he left for his place in L.A. So I knew his townhouse was empty when Rorrman called and told me to grab your sister. She was refusing to announce her findings on Immu-Phor at the Pasadena conference, saying she still wasn't ready. Rorrman had some major financial deal in the works, something with Japan. Century needed the publicity and status that Immu-Phor would bring. It was essential to the outcome of Rorrman's deal."

"He told you to 'grab' Mary? You were supposed to force the formula out of her?"

"Whatever it took. And I knew I'd have to take her where I could have her to myself for a while. I thought of the senator's empty townhouse."

"How did you get Mary to go with you?"

"The same way I got you to, Nikki, my dear. It was easy. I actually met Mary for the first time during one of her trips to California last year. Another party at Rorrman's house in Malibu. At the time, I didn't know anything about Immu-Phor, but you just never know when someone's going to come in handy. So we had some talks, some laughs. I told her how much I admired the work she was doing on the immune system, that I'd read her articles in *JAMA* and the *New England Journal of Medicine.*"

She felt her throat constrict. "So she went with you willingly. She thought you were a friend."

"By then, yes. I 'ran into' her at the hospital as she was coming out of her lab. I told her I was there on Century business, that I was glad to see her. I'd been thinking about our talk in California, I said, and I had some ideas about how she could get funding for her work. We made plans for dinner. When I offered to pick her up at the lab and drive her back right after dinner, she accepted."

"Mary didn't like driving at night. Did you know that?"

"Of course. Anyway, instead of taking her to a restaurant, I drove her to the senator's house. I told her the senator was there and he'd invited us to dinner along with some other people. I told her he was part of my plan to get funding for her work, and I thought it'd be a good idea to go."

"She believed you?"

He shrugged. "She knew Harriet and I were close. She had no reason not to trust me."

It was all Nicole could do to keep her voice even. She knew that if she lost control, she'd lose any advantage she might have. "So you drove Mary to this house and you tried to make her talk with that drug, and when she wouldn't, you gave her too much and—" She swallowed, trying to relieve the painful lump in her throat. "You killed her with it."

"Oh, not right away. Like I said, before things went bad, she almost escaped. She said she had to go to the bathroom, and I knew she really did. I'd had her tied up a long time. I thought there were still enough drugs in her system that she'd be pretty docile, that it'd be okay. But she faked me out. When she came out of the bathroom, she was carrying Hale's straight razor. I had taken her clothes, and she couldn't find them. She held me off with the razor while she got some of Mrs. Hale's things out of the closet and put them on—a red dress, a fur coat. There was a purse with some money in a dresser drawer, and she took that too.

"I caught up with her on the second-floor landing, but she tripped me. I fell down two flights of stairs and was out for a few seconds. When I came to, Mary was gone. I got Jimmy—you don't know him, he's just somebody I use to drive for me now and then. He was in back, in the kitchen. We went after her.

"When we found her, she was still confused by the drugs. Running blind, just trying to get away. I didn't want her screaming or anything out there on the streets, so I tried to coax her back to the house. She was clear enough, though, to run for it. She managed to get to a bar, and I followed her in. I hoped I could convince her— that she'd understand it was the right thing, coming back to the house."

Keep him talking, Nicole reminded herself. *Don't think about the way your hands are shaking.*

She felt dirty, just being near Jack Blake. Worse than that, she was afraid. Afraid that if she didn't turn him over to the police soon, she would kill him.

"Tell me how—"

The words were barely out when the boat lurched violently. Nicole was slammed with massive force against the bulkhead. Then, as if propelled by some inner demon, her body flew forward against the instrument panel. Her hand hit something sharp. A nerve screamed in agony, her fingers opened. She dropped the syringe on the panel. Through a red haze of pain she saw Jack's face, rigid and determined in the green glow as he reached for the syringe with one hand and the wheel with the other, twisting it sharply back and forth. The boat canted—lurching from side to side. She pitched back, then forward again. She grabbed blindly for the instrument panel, for the wall, for anything to cling to, but her feet no longer supported her. They had slipped out from under her, and she was sliding . . . sliding . . . toward the outside deck.

As if she were falling through ice.

Chapter 47

Nikki, don't go that way! Nikki, don't, it's not safe. Come this way, come back. . . .

The voices were all around her. In the black, icy depths it was all clearly before her: friends from school, the pond, her skates slipping out from under as the ice gave way.

Swim, Nikki, swim!

She struck out with both hands, trying to doggie-paddle to the surface. But the water was too deep. Too suffocating. It filled her lungs, and with it came panic.

I don't want to die. Help me, Mary. Help me!

Never in her life had she prayed so hard. Never before had she asked Mary for help. It had always been the other way around; she had been the one to support, to protect.

She kicked her feet, striking out again. And still she didn't surface. Her lungs ballooned with pain.

Mary, I can't hold my breath. Help me, I'm going down!

A sweet, sweet scent washed over her. The spicy scent of marigolds.

Mary, oh God, Mary? Is that you?

A face swam before hers, surrounded by a halo of auburn hair. Pale white hands reached out and touched her cheeks. They paused there a moment, then slid beneath her arms. The ghostly figure held her close. Impossibly, a warm, soft breath caressed her cheek. Nicole began to rise as the figure pulled her up, up, to where there was light, a dim light from the moon shining down through the waves.

She broke through, gasping, paddling wildly to stay afloat. She blinked water from her eyes and shook her hair back to see.

No one. No Mary.

She was alone.

Several hundred yards away, the *Haokah* was circling, its spotlights sweeping across the surface of the water. *He's making sure I drowned. But he can't see me this far out.*

"Swim to shore!" a voice said. *"You can do it, Nikki, go!"*

It seemed impossibly far. The lights were mere pinpoints, and nothing between here and there except—

A buoy. She saw its blue light rocking gently, about halfway between her and shore.

She swam toward it, gliding quickly and silently through the dark water. Trying not to think of the depths that lay below.

"Just get away! Get away, Nikki! Don't let him do what he did to me."

The buoy had seemed close, but it took her eons to reach it. Now and then she rested, floating on her back while she caught her breath. The *Haokah* continued to move, its ever-expanding circles of light coming closer.

Ahead, the buoy rose from the water. It became a dark, moving blur, capped by a small blue light. She focused on the light. Only a few more strokes . . .

She was there.

Thank God. She reached up a hand. *I can hang on and rest a few moments, regain my strength.*

"AAAAAAARRRT! AAAAAAARRRT!"

Nicole jerked back her hand and screamed.

There were bodies all around her suddenly, long furry bodies full of hair, skin, teeth. A horrible stench. Something slimy. They dove from the buoy and came up beneath her, over her legs, nudging her, bumping her, pulling her down.

Sea lions. Oh, God, help me, they're attacking.

She screamed again. "Get away! Oh, God, get away!" Her head went underwater. She beat them off, kicking and paddling, then surfaced for air. She tried to pull herself up onto the buoy. "AAAAAAAR-RRRT!" A sharp sentry had been left behind. Another one cuffed her from below.

Do they think I'm food?

In terror she struck out for shore, not worrying now about noise. She put every ounce of strength she could muster into her strokes, kicking out with her legs as hard as she could to discourage the sea lions from coming near. For several moments she kept her head underwater, going for speed. But then she had to breathe, and when she raised her face to the side to gulp in air, she was cheek to cheek with a dark, furry sea lion, swimming alongside her. She felt something at her toes. A nibble. A bite. Wet, leathery flesh slithered along her belly. *Dear God, help me. Help me, please!*

Her fingers struck something hard. She looked up, dazed.

A barge. *I'm at the barge with the crane.*

A huge tire hung against the side. She scrabbled for a handhold, casting a quick look back. A dark seal-head bobbed in the water, not five feet off. And the *Haokah* was heading this way.

Nowhere to go but up. She began to pull herself out of the water, wedging one foot onto the inner rim of the tire, then the other. She stood on the rim. Then she reached higher, felt the upper edge of the tire and the chain that it hung from. She jammed her toes into ridges along the side of the barge. One mighty push and she had grabbed the chain.

Sharp points of rusted metal dug into her palms. She slung a leg over the tire's upper edge. Pulling herself up, she lay sideways on it. Her head throbbed; she could hardly breathe. From the neck down she was numb from the icy water. She had to rest.

"No time, big sister. Get going, Nikki. He's close at your back."

Another massive pull on the chain shot pain through her arm sockets. But then she was standing on the top of the tire, her hands now easily touching the deck. She felt for a handhold. Her fingers touched a ridge. One last superhuman effort and she was up and over. She lay on her stomach, her face against something cold and metal, her chest heaving.

A miracle. I don't know how I did that. Where did I find the strength?

A scent of marigolds.

"Remember it, Nikki," she heard. *"Remember that strength. You don't ever have to be afraid again."*

Her stomach and chest burned from the friction of the climb. Her arm and leg muscles were weak, nearly useless. She was alive—but would she ever be able to move again? She tried to flatten herself against the deck, hoping that Jack wouldn't see her. She could hear him calling now, the words deceptively soft as they drifted across the water. "Nikki, Nikki . . . I know you're alive. I heard you scream. Where are you, sweet little Nikki?"

She raised herself as much as she dared and looked around. Fifty yards or so across the water were the restaurants. But they were dark now—not a sign of life. Even the parking lots were dark. Streetlights, some distance away, cast a murky glow on the opposite side of the barge. Here on the ocean side it was dark like the back of the moon. Gaining strength, she began to inch forward. Her hand struck a jumble of ropes, metal rods, bird shit. Her knees slid in oil. Around her rose the smell of diesel, of rusted copper, and steel.

She paused, rubbing her palms on her wet jeans and thinking. A barge was like an island. You could hide only so long. Sooner or later Jack would find her—he could turn the *Haokah*'s searchlights on the barge, or bring one on board.

So she couldn't just hide, like a rat in a hole.

Take the offensive, Kenny would say.

But how? And with what?

The *Haokah* was closer now, its searchlights turning this way.

"Think, Nikki, think," she heard.

Instinctively she scanned her mental inventory of old legends. The hero or heroine always found the villain's weakness and used it to his or her advantage. What were Jack's weaknesses?

Physically, his nose and eye were badly injured; his depth perception would be off. Emotionally, he'd be in a panic now, unsure of his ability to find her, to stop her before she got to the police. He might be sloppy, might make some fatal mistake.

But she couldn't count on that. She had done bodily damage—but not nearly enough. Remember what Kenny said? *We have a course for that: It's called Run Like Hell.*

Jack would be determined to get her. If not for Rorrman's sake, then to salve his own ego.

Ego—that was it. He seemed to have an inordinate belief in his powers over women, his ability to persuade. Could she use that to lure him? Like Lorelei, who sang her songs to entice sailors to their destruction?

She glanced around. If this were a movie, she thought, I could run up those stairs to that platform, turn on the crane, and scoop up the

Haokah—Jack and all. Leave him hanging there until the cops come. The visuals—as Dan might say—would be great.

But this isn't a movie. And I don't know how to operate any of that stuff.

Think, dammit, think.

Jack had stopped calling. Nicole twisted her head around and saw the *Haokah* bobbing just outside the breakwater, near the buoy with the sea lions. The searchlight scoured the breakwater. It moved through the channel, nearly touching the barge. She began to crawl again, toward a large mass of equipment and machinery. Pulling herself up beside a clawlike object, she stood in its shadow, looking around.

There must be something she could use. But everything was alien: a Caterpillar tractor, huge bullet-shaped weights, rusted anchors, winches, objects whose names she didn't even know.

Behind her rose the formidable structure of the crane. Its base was round and black, housing for the crane's mechanism, she supposed. Stairs went up an orange-and-white rectangular structure, to the catbird seat. From such close proximity, it looked higher than ever.

To the left of the catbird seat was the root of the mammoth crane itself, which had been lowered into a horizontal position for the night. It resembled a duck with a hundred-foot-long neck, its orange head, or beak, pointing downward now to the sea.

All right. This is what you've got to work with, Nicole. A mess of rusted junk, a considerable amount of bird shit—she rubbed her hands on her jeans again—*and your wits.*

She moved closer to the stairs that led up to the crane.

She could hide up there, way out on the beak where the steel jaws were. She could follow the same catwalk the worker had taken earlier, when the jaws had broken a tooth. But Jack would certainly think of that. And if he found her there, she'd be trapped. He could follow her, force her off that precarious point into the sea.

Remember the legends, Nikki. Your mind is your best weapon.

A few feet away a long length of rope hung from a hook. She inched toward it, careful to stay in shadows. Touching the rope, she fingered it thoughtfully.

Remember the Will Rogers experiment on old Quetzalcoatl, and how you hog-tied Ricky Morehead in class? There are lots of things you can do with rope, Nikki. You got really good at it, remember?

She looked up at the crane again. The length of the floor of the catwalk looked reasonably solid. But on either side huge spaces gaped between criss-cross girders.

Her eyes narrowed. *That could work.*

She looped the hemp over one shoulder. Glancing down, she saw a steel rod lying at her feet, perhaps six feet long. *A pry bar.* Not pointed and sharp, like the harpoon Opochtli carried, in her kitchen at home. But it had a lethal look.

"*That's right,*" she heard Mary say. "*Go fishing, Nikki. Not for a whale—but a monster.*"

She picked up the steel rod, hefting it.

Moving quietly back toward the stairs leading up to the crane, she looked again for the *Haokah.* The searchlights were off now, the boat nearly invisible. She wouldn't have known it was there if she hadn't been looking for a dark shape on the surface of the water.

Was that shape closer now? Yes.

Her stomach clutched with fear. Her palms grew wet. *I can't do this.*

"*You can, Nikki. You can.*"

Repositioning the heavy rope on her shoulder, clenching the pry bar, she began to climb the steps to the crane. She didn't stop at the first level, but climbed to the very top. There she stood on a large, flat platform, catching her breath. Above her, on a pole, an American flag whipped tautly in a stiff breeze. On another pole a red light blinked. Other than that, the platform was bare.

She looked to her right, to the neck of the crane. From here it resembled a long white road, its weblike girders and catwalk gleaming. Its orange duck-head was barely visible in the darkness, hundreds of feet away, out over the water. Metal cables were strung along the sides as handholds. There were cables on the floor of the catwalk, too.

The air was hot, drying her face and clothes. *The Santa Anas.* She licked her lips, tasting salt. Her hair was drying too; it blew into her face. She placed the rope and pry bar silently on the deck of the platform and made a braid, knotting the end for lack of an elastic.

Looping the rope over her shoulder once more, she tied one end to her belt, so that if it fell, she wouldn't lose it. To free her hands, she stuck the pry bar through her belt like a sword, but in back, out of her way.

She stepped out onto the catwalk. The winds picked up and she grabbed a guiderope. She couldn't remember ever having been so frightened. Beneath her feet, the floor of the catwalk consisted of a metal grid with small diamond-shaped holes. She wouldn't fall through. But now that she was up here, the spaces looked farther apart on either side than they had seemed from below.

Hand over shaking hand on the guiderope, she took a few more steps, then looked out toward the breakwater. The *Haokah*—where was the *Haokah?* She couldn't see it now. No lights, no black form. *Where was it?*

"No time to think or be afraid, Nikki. Just keep moving. One foot in front of the other, careful now, and hang on. Pretend you're only two feet off the ground.

"Remember when we were kids? Remember how we'd stick a two-by-four on a couple of old wooden sawhorses and pretend we were tightrope walkers in the circus? 'There's plenty of room for your feet, Mary,' you'd say. 'Just don't look down.'"

The farther she got from the platform, the stronger the winds became. Cables clanged against wet metal; the crane swayed. The catwalk felt slippery beneath her feet, and there were snakelike cables to watch out for. *"Pay attention, Nikki. Don't slip."*

She quickened her pace. Another few feet and she was more than halfway along. *"That's it. Keep going now."*

She was nearing the end when she heard, and felt, a bump.

Clutching the guiderope and a girder, her legs straining for balance, she forced herself to look over the side. At least two stories below she saw the deck of the barge with its heap of rusted metal, the hook of an anchor standing out in sharp relief. Her glance fell to the side of the barge. Jack was tying up the *Haokah*.

She looked back to the ducklike head of the crane before her, gauging her distance. *Almost there. It's time.*

She removed the rope from her shoulder and set it on the catwalk, squatting down.

"Careful, now. Don't let him hear you. Don't let him see."

Leaving one end of the rope tied to her waist, she fashioned the other end into a noose.

She heard him call. "Nikki? I know you're here. It was a stupid move, Nikki. You'll never get off this barge alive."

She looked up and saw that the moon would soon appear from behind clouds. She would have to count on the darkness, count on Jack not to look down, not to see—

So many things.

She positioned the noose, hiding it carefully between the cables at her feet. Then she began to inch forward again, pushing the remainder of the rope out of sight along the sides as she went along.

She was somewhere here, he knew. He could feel her presence. Her fear. Where would she hide?

Use your skills, Jack. Your knowledge of women. What would a woman like Nikki do?

With no need for stealth, he made quick work of searching the deck: the tractor, the heap of rusted metal, the doors leading to the various structures. All were locked; none looked as if they'd been pried open. Still, he had to check. She might have found an open door and gone in to hide, locking it behind her.

He found a crowbar on the deck and used it to pop the door of the smaller structure at the prow. Nothing. No one. Then the other, midway along. Still nothing. The third door he came to was at the foot of the crane. A metal hatch, it wouldn't pop. He put all his weight on it, but the damned thing wouldn't budge.

Okay, okay. Stay cool.

But the pain was almost unbearable. She had broken his nose, and God knew about the eye. He couldn't see a damned thing out of it.

The bitch. Where the hell was she?

"Nikki!" he bellowed, wincing at the red-hot fire that shot through his face.

He looked up.

Was that— Yes, a movement out there at the end of the crane.

Laughing softly, he checked the inside pocket of his windbreaker.

The black leather case held the syringe intact. All he needed was to get close enough.

He began to climb the stairs.

"Nikki," he called softly. "I know you're up here. Why don't you make this easy for both of us? All I want is to talk."

He was at the top of the stairs, stepping out onto the platform.

Nicole inched back into the relative shelter of the duck-head, just before the jaws. Relative, because it was enclosed on either side—relative, because there were dark waters visible through the grate at her feet. This time she didn't look down.

Instead she watched Jack, approaching the catwalk. He knew exactly where she was.

She tried to swallow, but her mouth had gone completely dry. She couldn't even wet her lips. They shook. A soft sob of fear escaped her throat.

"Nikki, I heard that. Hey, come on, don't cry. All you have to do is tell me where you hid the rest of the formula. That's all I want."

She was silent.

"I can make it so it doesn't hurt, Nikki. Not like Mary."

He stepped out onto the crane, not clutching the guiderope as she had, but moving toward her with self-confidence.

He's used to this sort of thing. Used to physical danger. Either that, or he doesn't care.

"I don't want you hurt, Nikki. I just need the win."

She found her voice. "Why?"

"It's a personal thing."

"Yeah, well"—her laughter was soft, but harsh—"this is pretty personal to me."

"But you haven't got a choice, Nikki. You might as well tell me. Like I said, you'll be doing something for Mary, getting her formula out to the world."

She laughed again. The winds carried it away.

"Okay, look, you're right. But Nikki, it's Rorrman who wants you dead. I can fix that. I can give you money, lots of money, and you can go away and hide. I'll tell him I killed you, you drowned at sea. He'll never know."

His argument was warm and persuasive. "I wanted to do that with Mary. If the drug hadn't gone bad . . ."

"That makes a real big difference, Jack. Knowing you meant well."

The moon slipped out, and she could see him clearly now. The white, angry face, the blood-encrusted nose and eye. His brown hair blowing in the breeze. He was just past the center of the crane.

Please, God, don't let him look down.

"You trusted me before, Nikki. Trust me again. I care about you. Let's just get off this thing." He gestured at the apparatus surrounding him. "Christ, Nikki, this is crazy! Look where we are. Let's just go down and talk. It'll be all right."

Nicole stepped out onto the catwalk. "Come and get me, Jack." Her right hand held the pry bar at shoulder height, like a harpoon, a lance.

His voice grew soft. "You won't use that thing, Nikki. You're a schoolteacher—not a warrior. And even so, I'd take you with me."

The wind whipped her hair, loosening strands from her braid. Lights from the harbor—too far below—made her dizzy. For a moment she wavered. Then her shoulders squared.

"Being a schoolteacher has its benefits, Jack. I've been thinking about Metzli."

Confusion crossed his face. "Who?"

"Metzli. See, that's what I mean. I know the old stories, and I respect their teachings. That gives me an advantage."

Jack shook his head. "You're losing it, Nikki." The wind howled.

"Metzli was the Aztec goddess of the moon. When darkness surrounded the universe, she decided to make a human sacrifice. She threw a leper into a fire and walked with him into the flames. Pretty hard on the leper, wouldn't you say, Jack? But it worked. Night disappeared and the sun blazed forth. For light to be born"—she raised the pry bar, tightening her grip—"the darkness had to die."

He laughed softly. "You won't be able to do it."

"Take you into the flames, even if I have to go with you? Try me."

"You're insane."

He took a step closer. Then another. She looked down at his feet. *Three more steps.* That would do it.

One . . . two . . .

Jack paused, foot raised. There was something in his face. He *knew.*

God, don't let him know. Move, *Jack.* Do *it. One more step, one more . . .*

But his eyes were on the rope tied to her waist. "What is that?" he said softly. "Nikki, what have you got there?" His gaze fell, following the length of hemp as it snaked along the side of the catwalk in his direction.

Then his eyes widened with the shock of recognition. But too late —he was midstep, the weight of his body carrying him forward, unable to stop.

That's it, Jack.

Three!

Nicole dropped the pry bar and grabbed the rope at her waist. With a violent jerk she pulled it taut. The rope came free of her waist, and at its other end, it looped around Jack's feet. He began to fall sideways. She jerked it again and again, pulling it tighter. Stretching out his arms, Jack tried to grab on to something to break his fall, but there was nothing but air. With a hideous scream he hurtled toward the pile of rusted metal on the deck.

The point of the anchor sheared his neck. Blood spilled.

For a moment Nicole thought she would faint. She grabbed a guiderope and hung on, afraid she would follow Jack over. Her stomach heaved. Dry heaves—there was nothing there but fear.

She drew herself together.

Make sure. Make sure.

She ran along the crane's catwalk, hand skimming the guiderope, stumbling once and falling, but righting herself, no longer afraid. From the platform she clambered down the two flights of steps, clutching the rail for balance.

At the foot of the hill of rusted metal, she paused, wiping her face with the back of her hand. She began to climb, cutting her hands and knees on jagged steel, not caring, just wanting to make sure.

She stood over Jack. His eyes were open, staring blindly. She reached to check for a pulse in the neck, but there was no neck, only blood, and the barnacled point of an anchor pricking the sky.

The wind tore at her hair. She pushed it back. Tears began to flow.

"I got him, Mary Clare. I got him."

She knelt on the blood-soaked pile of rubble and cried.

Epilogue

With all the cheerful nuns gone, the cemetery seemed more like what it was, a place to bury dreams, along with flesh. A place to put "The End" to a life's story.

Nicole stood above Mary's grave, huddling for warmth in her green coat. She had been talking softly for ten minutes, telling her sister everything that had occurred since the last time she'd been here.

"But you know all this, don't you, Mary? You were with me all the time."

She pulled her hood closer, protecting her face from the light snowfall. A crunch of boot on frozen ground caused her to turn. The welcome sight of Leo De Santo met her eyes.

"Vish! What are you doing here?"

He wore a black leather police jacket, and his cheeks were spotted with color from the cold. He didn't look at all happy with the weather.

"The Georgetown P.D. wanted some info on what's been going on, so they can close out the case from this end. The FBI too." He shrugged. "Guess I could've given it to them over the phone. But I had a few days' leave coming. I kind of wondered how you were doing."

"How did you know I'd be out here?" she asked, looking around the cemetery.

"You weren't at your apartment, and some guy named Sanders over at the college said you'd just left his office. I took a guess."

Nicole shook her head. "You are one in a million, Vish."

"Yeah, sure. You know, I really like that name, Vish. I just don't know that I've lived up to it. This time it was you who attacked and destroyed the forces of evil."

She was silent.

"It's okay, kid. You did good."

"It did feel . . . satisfying, at some level," she admitted.

"Uh-huh. Next thing, you'll be telling me you want to be a cop."

"Hmmmm. Do you think they've got any use for a storyteller? A purveyor of tales?"

"Hell, Nikki, you read the papers. What do you think?"

She smiled. "Speaking of telling tales . . . Vish, I seem to have arrived at the vast old age of thirty-four without having much discernment. I trust the wrong people and don't trust the right ones."

"Don't be too hard on yourself, kid. You were mixed up in something that even stumped the F.B.I. And this guy, Dan . . . you had a history with him. He wasn't straight with you about a lot of things from the first, so when it looked like he was one of the bad guys, what could you be expected to think?"

"I could have trusted him. I'd known him so long. Don't you think it's odd that I didn't trust him?"

"I think that from what you've told me this last week about your childhood, you had good reason to fear people you should have been able to trust. And I think that screwed everything up for you. You need to talk to somebody, maybe."

"I know. I'm planning to. Vish, I said it felt good to get Jack Blake. But I'm having some problems with it, too."

"I thought you might."

"I can't help thinking that in the old days heros slew villains all the time. That was what made you a hero, for heaven's sake. So why don't I feel like a hero?"

"I don't know, kid. In my twenty years on the force, I've had to ask that question of myself twice. I still don't have an answer."

"I don't even know how I was able to do it. It was so . . . so ancient a thing. I went out there deliberately, hoping he'd fall into that snare. I wanted revenge."

"He didn't have to follow you. The guy was a madman, Nikki. You met him on his own terms."

"That's what worries me. In the legend of Lorelei, the sailors she lured to their destruction were condemned to wander with her for all time." She gave a shudder. "I wonder if I'll carry Jack with me forever."

A woman walked by on the path, holding the hand of a small boy. He carried a fistful of white chyrsanthemums to place on a grave. It would be Thanksgiving soon.

A terrible time to lose someone. Nicole looked away, blinking, and Vish cleared his throat.

"Uh, you know, that gag order? It wasn't just that they were worried about a political scandal with Hale."

"No?"

"They told me a little while ago, the Bureau's been investigating Century Pharmaceuticals ever since that reporter showed up over here from France asking questions about Hale. Seems he went to the FBI first, then the LAPD. We dismissed it. The FBI, though, turned up the connection between Senator Hale and Rorrman. They started looking into everybody close to Rorrman—and guess what they came up with on our friend Jack Blake?"

"What?"

"He ever tell you he had a grandfather who died when he was eight years old?"

"Yes, I seem to remember—a car accident, he said. Something like Mary's."

"Yeah, well, it wasn't any accident."

"No accident? Vish, he was an eight-year-old kid! Why would he do something like that?"

"We may never know. But the FBI came up with all kinds of shit on that guy. He was pretty twisted from way back. But he fooled people, you know? He had a way with him. Some friends and family had their suspicions, but they never really wanted to believe he could be responsible."

"My God. How long has the FBI known about all this?"

"They've thought for months that he might have been the one who drowned that French prostitute, but they couldn't get anything on him. He was pretty clever at living a double life. Then, with you and your sister, he began making mistakes."

"I can't believe how blind I was, Vish."

"You have to give yourself credit, kid. You were real smart, sending me that note by messenger. Telling me the formula was in the locker at Kenny's. Hell, it was smart you even thought to hide it there."

"I figured whoever was after the formula would search my room at the hotel. They'd gone through things at Dan's cottage when I was out there—or at least, I thought they had, one night when I got in and things were slightly off-key."

"That note you found there from your sister? It was her handwriting."

"I know. Jack put it there to turn me against Dan, so that if I found the blue notebook, I wouldn't give it to him."

"Well, Rorrman's been arrested and charged with conspiracy in Terry Asher's and your sister's murders, as well as that of the French prostitute. With your testimony added to the case the FBI's already been building, they should have enough to put him away for a while. But then, you know how those things sometimes go."

"Yes. But he's lost Century. Harriet's stepped into his shoes, and she'll make sure Mary's formula gets into the right hands now. She's promised it'll go to a hand-picked team of scientists she's worked with personally and trusts. Immu-Phor won't be released until it's safe."

De Santo looked out across the graveyard at the wet, bare trees, the lowering sky. He shivered. "Damn, it's cold here. You coming back to California? You gonna try to work things out with Dan Rossi?"

"I don't know if that's possible, Vish—or if I even want to. But I'm coming back, as soon as I wrap things up with the police here. I'd like to take some more classes with Kenny, get to know Harriet better, live in the sunshine awhile."

"Rossi was only doing what he thought was right, Nikki. Trying to protect you from it. Maybe you should give the guy a break."

"Maybe."

"Look, I'm gonna leave you alone here. I just thought I'd ask if you'd like some dinner tonight. I could pick you up at your place, say around eight? We can talk some more."

"Sounds great. But, Vish, I want to thank you now, for everything. For being there when I needed you, and for Kenny. I felt as if I was drowning, and you came along and threw me a life preserver. You . . . you give cops a good name."

"That's all I ever wanted to do, kid. All I ever wanted to do."

She watched him as he walked away—a big man, in more ways than one. How fortunate she had been. In that smog-ridden, chaotic, crazy city of lost angels, she had stumbled across someone who genuinely cared about people. More than one someone, in fact. Harriet Ilsen, Kenny—and the professor, who had only been doing his best to keep a promise to a woman he'd loved. With Jack dead, and the formula safely in Harriet's hands, he'd begun to recover again. In fact, he'd be leaving the hospital this week. She had told him she'd be taking off work until the beginning of spring term. Meanwhile, she wanted to stay with him awhile, help him out until he was back on his feet.

It surprised her, but she couldn't wait to get back to California. In Los Angeles her life had expanded in ways that it never had here. Perhaps she had been too introverted, too much a loner. Or perhaps there was something about the sunshine out there—it helped things to grow, even if it did have to swim through all that pollution to find its way through.

Love was like that. All the emotional pollution it had to battle— but miraculously, sometimes it still made it through.

I miss you so much, little sister. I wish we hadn't lost all those years. I wish I could hold you, right here and now. If you could have talked to me more, would that have helped? Would you be standing here now, alive and laughing, with tropical fish in a can and caterpillars in your pockets?

Brushing her eyes, she turned to go, her boot heels sinking into snow. Across the white hillocks and stones of the cemetery, a tall figure stood beside her car. She began to walk toward it, squinting through the snow, wiping moisture from her eyes.

"Dan?"

One hand was scrunched into the pocket of a white-and-blue ski jacket. The other held a small bouquet of limp marigolds. His hair was wet from fallen snow, as if he had been standing, watching her, for a long time.

"I, uh, brought these from the house in Malibu. I wanted to say goodbye to Mary."

"How did you get here?" She didn't see a car. But an overnight case was at his feet.

"Taxi. When I saw you, I let him go. I hoped you might give me a ride to my hotel."

"Of course."

He looked toward the grave. His eyes were rimmed with a telltale blue; he hadn't been sleeping. "Will you come with me, Nikki?"

She nodded.

He hefted the strap of the overnight to his shoulder, and she walked beside him, then waited a few steps behind as he stood silently by the too-fresh mound. The edges of the blanket of turf were still visible; they wouldn't blend into the lawn until spring. *Dear God, let it hurt less then. Please.*

"I'm sorry for the way I acted that night," Dan said, turning. "I didn't mean to frighten you or hurt you. I was exhausted, at the end of my rope. And I was outraged that you could believe I'd hurt Mary. But that's no excuse."

She was silent.

"Nikki, let's talk. We never really had time. There's a bench over there."

She nodded, then followed him, sitting a short distance away and shoving her gloved hands into her pockets for warmth.

"This seems right, somehow," he said. "Here, I mean. I want Mary to know I've told you everything." He glanced awkwardly away. "I guess that sounds weird."

"No . . . I've been talking to her myself."

He shook his head wearily. "Where to begin . . ."

"Begin with the photograph. How did it happen, Dan?"

"The photograph." He laughed softly, bitterly. "I never dreamed . . . Well, Rorrman had invited Mary out on the *Haokah* when we were all out here in L.A. last April. Mary was nervous. Rorrman had been exerting pressure on her to turn over the formula to him. He wasn't just anxious by then, but threatening."

"And she still accepted an invitation from him, to go out on a boat?"

"She thought it was a party with other people. Safety in numbers. And she hoped to convince Rorrman to leave her alone until she got Immu-Phor right."

"But it wasn't a party."

"No. Just the four of us—me and Mary, Rorrman and Kitty. The whole day turned into a mess. I went along, supposedly, as a date— really just to be there in case there was trouble. But Kitty Rorrman kept coming on to me. She tried to get me off somewhere without Mary. She'd say things like, 'Come with me, Danny Boy. I'll show you the captain's quarters.' Or, 'Let's invade the galley and see what goodies we can find.' Mary and I figured she was trying to separate us so her uncle could get Mary alone. We decided to play it cozy between us—inseparable. And when Mary caught that fish,

I hugged her. I tried to make it clear we were together in every way."

He caught Nicole's expression. "I swear, I didn't lie to you about thinking it was her first catch. Maybe she faked her excitement, I don't know. I congratulated her, I hugged her. That was it."

"And she got nowhere with Rorrman about holding off on revealing the formula?"

"No. She ended up going to Sister Paula, telling her about her fears, and the pressure. Paula had her own suspicions by then. She stood by her."

So Jack had been right about that. "The formidable Sister Paula was one of the good guys."

"In her own way. She saw the money Immu-Phor could bring into the hospital, and she wanted it badly. But she also agreed with Mary's ethics regarding the drug. So she was on her back constantly, pushing her to perfect it, yet at the same time protecting the formula from falling into the wrong hands before it was ready."

A light rain began, easing out the snow. Nicole shivered.

"What about Kitty Rorrman? You were with her at Harriet's party. You sounded intimate on the phone. . . ."

"After Mary died, Kitty moved in on me again. She's not very subtle, and from the questions she was asking, I knew she was working for her uncle, hoping to find out if Mary had left a copy of her notes —or even the formula itself—with me. I thought if I stayed close to Kitty, I'd be a step ahead of Rorrman all the way."

"Which brings up the blue notebook. If Mary trusted you, why did she give it to me?"

"She thought it would be safer with you. Since Rorrman knew she and I were close, she was afraid they'd search my house. In fact, they have. There were signs when I got back from my trip. Cans of film put back in the wrong order, files out of place."

"She didn't think they'd search my house?"

"Not at first. But a couple of weeks ago, she told me she wasn't so sure anymore. Then you came out here, and you didn't mention it. I didn't know what the hell had happened to it."

"Why didn't you just tell me about all this, Dan? We'd have saved so much time, so much . . ." *Agony.*

"I know. I'm sorry, Nikki. But Mary made me promise not to involve you unless it became absolutely necessary. 'She's always taken care of me,' she said. 'This time I have to be the strong one.' When Mary died, it hit me hard. I felt I had to keep that promise. It was the least I could do."

"Even so, you haven't been honest with me."

"Honest?" He gave her an irritated look. "Nikki, you weren't honest with me. When you came out here, you said it was for a vacation. I asked you if Mary had left you anything for me. You said no. I believed you—and I didn't have time to worry about it. I was too busy working the infamous Miss Kitty, trying to find out whether Rorrman was responsible for Mary's death."

"What about your contract with Rorrman? For the Century industrial film?"

"He offered it to me last spring, after that day on the *Haokah*. Mary and I decided he was trying to get to her through me. It seemed like a good idea to take it and use the inside track to do an exposé instead of an ad."

"And the check from Kitty?"

"I told you the other night, I never intended to cash it. I took it to throw her off the scent."

"So you were working Kitty . . . who in turn was working you."

His cheeks flamed. "I'm not proud of it. But, yes."

Another man with two hats. Not to mention a woman or two. Was anyone as they seemed these days?

"Were you sleeping with her?" she asked. She had to know.

"Kitty Rorrman?" Dan looked disgusted. "Please."

No. Of course not. He never gave pieces away.

"You know, Dan, I used to feel that being with you was like hanging out with a rock—or a redwood tree. I realize now that that's exactly what I wanted back then. A rock is steady, dependable, doesn't change much from day to day. And it's not too emotional."

His gray eyes were less than amused. "Are you saying we were perfect for each other?"

"For a while, yes. The minute I let my walls down, you threw up yours. And the minute you let yours down . . ."

"I have to admit, I've been thinking about that. My two closest female friends in the past two years have been you and Mary. And neither one of you was really accessible. Maybe I thought if we kept everything light, I'd never have to make any decisions. Never have to *do* anything. Loving entails responsibility, Nikki. Once you declare love, you have to live it."

"I guess you do."

They sat silently for a time. Finally he stood. "I have to say good-bye to Mary."

She walked with him, and he linked his arm through hers to protect her from slipping on patches of ice, the way he used to do. They stood that way, together, above Mary's grave. Nicole closed her eyes.

I have so far to go, little sister. So many years to live without you. How will I ever make it?

She looked up. The evening star had appeared, bright on the horizon.

"I've always been fascinated by stars," she said, removing her arm and drawing her velvet hood close. Hugging herself for warmth. "We make such a big deal of them, write poems about them, sing songs. Yet all we're really seeing is their light. It's taken millions of years to reach us, and by the time it's arrived, the stars themselves are often already burned out."

Dan gave her a patient look, one she remembered. "Somehow I feel a message coming on."

"Well, I've been thinking. I was up there in some kind of mental space, loving you all those eons ago, sending down all that light. And now that it's finally reached you—Dan, I think I may have burned out."

He regarded her pensively, then began to grin. "You were always so good at making metaphors. Okay, I accept the challenge. But how about this for your star theory? Maybe the star is dead, but its light is still real. And the light may have taken a while to get here, but that doesn't mean it can't shine just as bright."

She cast him an irritated look. "What are you saying, Dan Rossi?"

"What do you think?"

"I think you're still too scared to say what you mean."

"Look who's talking."

"Yeah, well, someday . . ."

"What?"

She shook her head. "We've got to learn to speak English to each other."

Giving a shrug, he smiled. "We'll see."

He handed her a portion of the marigolds. She took them and held them to her nose, inhaling their heart-wrenching scent. Then she and Dan placed them on the grave and said a final, silent prayer together—united, for the moment at least, in their common love for Mary Clare.